Tessa Scott is a lover of [obscured] happily-ever-afters. She l[obscured] Connecticut surrounded by lots of trees, wildlife and a menagerie of pets. A copywriter by day, she enjoys that magical moment when the characters she creates come to life and help take the story in new and exciting directions.

USA TODAY and *Wall Street Journal* bestselling author **Janice Lynn** has a Master's in nursing from Vanderbilt University and works as a nurse practitioner in a family practice. She lives in the southern United States with her Prince Charming, their children, their Maltese named Halo and a lot of unnamed dust bunnies that have moved in after she started her writing career. Readers can visit Janice via her website at www.janicelynn.com.

Also by Tessa Scott

Healing the Baby Surgeon's Heart

Also by Janice Lynn

Heart Doctor's Summer Reunion
Breaking the Nurse's No-Dating Rule
Risking It All with the Paramedic
Flirting with the Florida Heart Doctor

Discover more at millsandboon.co.uk.

A DATE WITH HER RIVAL

TESSA SCOTT

FALLING FOR HIS NASHVILLE NURSE

JANICE LYNN

MILLS & BOON

All rights reserved including the right of reproduction in whole or in part in any form. This edition is published by arrangement with Harlequin Enterprises ULC.

This is a work of fiction. Names, characters, places, locations and incidents are purely fictional and bear no relationship to any real life individuals, living or dead, or to any actual places, business establishments, locations, events or incidents. Any resemblance is entirely coincidental.

Without limiting the author's and publisher's exclusive rights, any unauthorised use of this publication to train generative artificial intelligence (AI) technologies is expressly prohibited. HarperCollins also exercise their rights under Article 4(3) of the Digital Single Market Directive 2019/790 and expressly reserve this publication from the text and data mining exception.

® and TM are trademarks owned and used by the trademark owner and/or its licensee. Trademarks marked with ® are registered with the United Kingdom Patent Office and/or the Office for Harmonisation in the Internal Market and in other countries.

First published in Great Britain 2025
by Mills & Boon, an imprint of HarperCollins*Publishers* Ltd,
1 London Bridge Street, London, SE1 9GF

www.harpercollins.co.uk

HarperCollins*Publishers* Macken House, 39/40 Mayor Street Upper, Dublin 1, D01 C9W8, Ireland

A Date with Her Rival © 2025 Tessa Scott

Falling for His Nashville Nurse © 2025 Janice Lynn

ISBN: 978-0-263-32515-7

08/25

This book contains FSC™ certified paper and other controlled sources to ensure responsible forest management.

For more information visit www.harpercollins.co.uk/green.

Printed and Bound in the UK using 100% Renewable Electricity at CPI Group (UK) Ltd, Croydon, CR0 4YY

A DATE WITH HER RIVAL

TESSA SCOTT

MILLS & BOON

In memory of Piper, my sweet, beautiful boy who was with me for twenty-eight years and is now galloping through meadows beyond the Rainbow Bridge. Until we meet again.

CHAPTER ONE

Maya Evans stared wide-eyed at her dad, hoping that she had misheard him. "You didn't just say you hired another vet."

He gingerly raised his thick, gray eyebrows, as though bracing for further objections. "*Temporarily*," he emphasized. "Just long enough for you to get fully back on your feet."

Maya looked down at her sturdy work boots, which were planted firmly on the dirt-trodden ground. She looked back up at her father as if to say, *I'm good, but thanks for checking!*

He let out a long sigh, followed by a begrudging smile. "You're more stubborn than a mule. Even Betty looks like a cream puff next to you," he said, referring to a recent patient who was, in fact, a mule. The comparison slightly amused Maya, and she felt the corners of her lips curve upward. But then, reality set in and the smile melted away.

The last time her dad had brought another vet on board their practice, it had ended in heartbreak. Not only for herself, but also for her eight-year-old son, Jeremy. What had started as a professional relationship with Dr. Max Shepard had turned into a romantic one, and when Max decided to relocate to Texas for a prestigious veterinary college teaching position, both she and Jeremy, who had come to see him as a surrogate father, were devastated.

Of course, her father was hiring a temporary vet, not a potential romantic interest for her. For all she knew, the doctor was female. *But that's not the point.* He should have consulted her first. Yes, he had started Northern Vermont Equine Associates back when she was still in diapers and had built it from the ground up, but now he was semiretired, with full retirement expected in the very near future. Which meant the brunt of the burgeoning practice fell on her increasingly weary shoulders. So shouldn't she have an active say in any hiring decisions, temporary or otherwise?

"I like to work alone, Dad," she said quietly.

"I know you do, Maya," he said with empathy in his eyes that indicated he knew this wasn't just about her streak of independence. "But your arm is still in a cast, and given that you wince every time you turn, I'm going to assume those cracked ribs still have some healing left as well." He paused. "Am I right?"

As if on cue, her left side pinched as she drew in a deep breath. "I can still do my job."

"It's your job that got you injured in the first place—remember?"

Maya pursed her lips in silent acknowledgement. It was her fault, and hers alone, that Roofus the giant Clydesdale had kicked her like an errant tumbleweed when she'd been treating his hoof abscess several weeks ago. He had *seemed* to be fully under the effects of a mild sedation, still standing as needed for the procedure, his lower lip drooping and eyelids half closed.

But one clamp of the hoof pincers to find the sensitive area hiding the abscess, and Roofus had rustled up enough lingering adrenaline to promptly send Maya flying across the matted floor of the clinic. She shuddered at the recollection of ending up in a heap several feet away, struggling to breathe as immense pain had gripped her side and shot through her left forearm.

Shake it off. A few deep breaths, and Maya was back in the present, searing pain replaced with residual discomfort at the still-sensitive sites of her injuries.

"Dad, you know this is just part of being an equine vet. How many times over the years did you end up bruised and battered from a particularly difficult client?"

"Are you talking the horses, or their pain-in-the-butt owners?" he asked with a grin.

Maya shook her head and reluctantly chuckled. If anyone knew the highs and lows of life as a horse veterinarian, it was her dad. She couldn't remember a time when he hadn't been tending to whinnying, four-legged patients for a living, but arthritis in both of his hands had made it increasingly difficult to perform even the most basic of equine care.

"Look, Maya. At some point, we're going to need to bring another vet on board. We're at capacity right now with our current clients, and it seems like every week we're getting calls for potential new ones. I've had to ask Maria to put them on a waiting list," he said, referring to their part-time business manager.

Maya's eyes flashed with surprise and concern. "Seriously?"

"Yes. I haven't said anything to you, because I know you don't like to turn down anyone needing help for their horse. And I did instruct Maria to give them the names of other vets in the area. But we're no longer a two-person team. More like one and one-eighth person team, given the limited hours I can put in. And by the end of the year, I plan to be fully retired." He pushed out a smile. "Not that I don't love Vermont winters, but I don't think my creaky, old hips can take another season of wading through two feet of snow to get to a patient out in the field."

Maya's face softened with understanding. "I know. And believe me, I don't want you to have to deal with another tough winter. You should instead be on the beach someplace warm, sipping on margaritas and working on a tan."

Her father grinned. "Actually, I plan to be in my mountain chalet right here in Maplewood, sipping on hot cocoa in front of a roaring fire. The only difference is I won't be heading out at midnight in a snowstorm to help deliver a foal."

Maya smiled, even though the mere thought of frigid January temperatures triggered a brief shiver under her lightweight fall jacket. "That's where I come in."

His face relaxed, as though relieved to see that Maya was slowly coming around to the idea of temporary help. "I realize it will take some time to find a vet that you're comfortable with bringing on board permanently, but in the meantime, we have someone to help pick up the slack for two months. That's all this is. Think of it as buying some time while you start searching for someone who *you* want to bring on board full-time. After all, the practice will be fully yours soon enough."

Maya's eyes scanned the panoramic scenery as she and her dad stood outside the main barn. Mid-September in Vermont was a feast for the eyes, with the rolling mountains in the background awash with the brilliant red, orange and golden swatches of autumn. But in only a few months, the colorful leaves would be dropping from the trees, signaling the arrival of winter—and the official passing of the torch with her dad's inevitable retirement.

It wasn't that she didn't realize the practice was too busy to handle all on her own. That was a no-brainer. But working in tandem with another vet meant gelling with them on multiple levels. It wasn't enough that they came fully equipped with an expert veterinary skill set. Did they also share her compassion and love for horses? Which would seem like a given but—in the same vein as medical doctors devoid of a bedside manner—wasn't always the case. Would they respect that she had two main priorities at this point in her life—her young son and the horses in her care—and everything else came third?

She could go on and on in her thoughts…but the bottom line was she *did* need an extra set of hands. Which meant she had to accept the current game plan, like it or not.

Maya turned to her father. "So, what can you tell me about this temporary hire?" Just saying the word *temporary* made her feel at least a *little* better, given that it implied she had some control over future events.

"Well, I fully vetted him." He paused for effect. "No pun intended. I think you'll like him."

Him. So it was a male vet, not too surprising given there was a fifty-fifty chance of that being the case.

"And he's Australian."

Maya did a double take. "Australian? And he's here in Vermont?" Though she couldn't picture a more perfect place to live than in the quintessential New England town of Maplewood, with its vibrant four seasons and yesteryear charm… she also couldn't imagine it registered on any map found in the pocket of a global traveler.

"He said he prefers to not stay in any one place too long, so he picks up veterinary gigs wherever the wind takes him."

Maya had to force her gaping mouth to close. Only then could she reply, her voice rising with each word. "Wherever the wind takes him?"

"I think that's how he described it." Her father shifted his weight from one leg to the other, as though realizing he was quickly losing ground with his dubious daughter. "Think of it as…I don't know…like a traveling nurse. Only in this case, he's a traveling horse vet."

Maya narrowed her eyes. "That sounds *very* fishy to me. You sure he's not a fugitive pretending to be a vet?"

Her father chuckled. "I'm sure. His credentials all checked out, and I even had him weigh in on a few cases while he was here. I have to say, I was quite impressed."

Maya's disbelief was snowballing. "When did all of this happen?"

"This morning. I thought you'd be here, but you had that emergency colic case in Cantonville. He recently finished a gig in California, and was looking for something on the East Coast. We had a phone interview a few days ago that went really well, so he flew in for an in-person interview. I had planned to loop you in sooner, but I know how busy you've been and everything happened so fast." He paused, eyes probing hers as though trying to land on what to say next. "He, uh, reminded me a bit of Crocodile Dundee."

Maya scrunched her lips together. If her dad thought he was sweetening the pot with this comparison, he was way off the mark. "There were no Australian vets applying for the job who could double for Chris Hemsworth?"

Her father looked perplexed. "Who?"

She smiled and shook her head. "Never mind." There were already so many red flags popping up at every turn that all she could do was accept the situation and take solace in the fact that it was a short-term solution. "When does he start?"

"Should be any day. He's looking for a place to rent while he's here, and once that's taken care of, he'll be reporting for duty."

"Can't wait," Maya deadpanned.

Her dad smiled warily. "Try not to bite off his head."

Maya pointed to herself with mock indignation. "Me?"

It was early dusk when Maya returned to the main barn. She pulled her phone out of her back jeans pocket and called Clara, the trusty caregiver who looked after Jeremy while she was at work. "I'll be home in about twenty minutes," she said, smiling as she received a comforting update about her son. He was playing with their dog, Rusty, after finishing his school homework.

She was about to ask Clara to pass the phone to Jeremy, then thought better of it. He was having fun with Rusty, just as a young boy should. There was no need to pull him away from that.

Maya's smile wavered as she thought about how much he'd already been through in his short lifetime. At the tender age of three, he had lost his father, George. Even now, the thought of her late husband pried open the floodgate to bittersweet memories. A fellow horse vet in the family practice, George had died tragically in a car accident on the way to an emergency call.

It hadn't been easy picking up the pieces after his death, but Maya had been determined to stay strong for both of them. And then, just over two years ago, Max came onto the scene... slowly working his way into both her heart and Jeremy's.

Maya winced. She knew how that story ended, too, and wasn't about to go there again in her thoughts.

"Maya?"

Carla's voice brought her back to the present.

"I'm sorry," Maya said into the phone. "Did you say something?"

"I just wasn't sure if there was something else you needed to tell me."

"Oh—no, I don't think so." Her smile slowly returned. "I'll see you guys in a little bit."

Maya ended the call, acknowledging to herself once again how lucky she was to have found Carla. In her mid-fifties and exuding natural warmth and nurturing, Carla lived in a cozy apartment above the garage on Maya's ten-acre property. It was a mutually beneficial arrangement, with Carla enjoying rent-free housing in exchange for keeping a watchful eye on Jeremy while Maya was at work.

And that could pretty much be any time, and often with little notice. The life of a horse vet promised many things, but working a nine-to-five job was not one of them. At least not with a smaller practice that provided twenty-four seven emergency service for its clients spread out over a fifty-mile radius.

After doling out grain and filling water buckets for the five horses currently receiving on-site care, Maya sighed wearily at the realization that there were no hay bales available in the barn aisle. Jenna, the local horse-loving teen who worked part-time after school at the clinic, normally pulled a few bales down from the loft before heading out for the night. Maya nodded to herself and murmured, "Oh, that's right," as she vaguely recalled Maria mentioning that Jenna had called in sick.

Placing the hand of her cast-free arm on the ladder, she looked up at the twelve wooden rungs that ascended vertically into the dark loft opening. It was a simple enough task to make the climb and throw down a couple of bales—at least it was with two good arms and pain-free ribs. Still, she could do this. She *had* to do this.

Here goes nothing. She drew in a deep breath for good measure. Grabbing onto the closest ladder rung with her right hand, she began the climb, carefully balancing with her left hand as well. There was a strange pulling sensation in her left forearm as she closed her hand around the ladder rungs, but that was to be expected. Though her radius was close to fully healed, the muscles surrounding it were atrophied from limited use.

A few more steps up the ladder and she was in the loft area, surrounded by rows of hay bales stacked six deep. She removed the metal hay pull that hung on the wall, yanked down three bales with her good arm, then dragged them to the loft opening and pushed them through.

Each landed with a muffled thud, followed by anxious whinnying that rumbled through the barn.

"Hang on, guys," she called out as she started her descent down the ladder. "Dinner's coming!"

This is easier than I expected, she thought as she lowered herself from one rung to the next, her right hand singularly grasping the side rail to steady herself. "Proof that I do *not* need another vet getting in my way," she said aloud, the defiant declaration sailing from her lips only moments before her foot slipped out from under her.

Grabbing the nearest rung with both hands, she yelped as pain shot through her left arm. Logic told her to hang on anyway, but in the split second that she had to commit to a course of action, logic was replaced with panic.

Flying backward, she squeezed her eyes shut and braced for impact. Except...instead of slamming onto the ground, she was pulled out of thin air by...*something*.

A guardian angel? She had read about such unseen interventions in moments of peril. But as she opened her eyes and peered downward, the lightly tanned, muscular arms wrapped around her waist looked anything but ghostlike. The arms remained in place for several moments—long enough for her to become fully aware of the body they were attached to. She couldn't *see* the body yet, but she could feel its warmth and strength bolstering her up from behind.

"You good?" a male voice asked with an Australian accent so deep and sexy that it made her male Vermont counterparts sound like Pee-wee Herman.

Maya swallowed hard and winced, then slowly turned around, nearly shuddering as her eyes fell upon the man who had just spared her from more broken bones. With greenish-blue eyes, a chiseled jawline and dark blond hair that skimmed his shoulders, his vibe was definitely more Chris Hemsworth than Crocodile Dundee—and with smoldering good looks that were uniquely his own.

"Sorry," he said as he let go of her waist, a subtly mischievous grin on his face. "I didn't mean to get in your way."

Maya grimaced sheepishly. "Oh...you heard that..."

His grin widened. "No worries. It's the kind of thing I would've said myself, to be honest." He held out his hand. "Cal Parker."

"Maya Evans," she replied, shaking his hand while simultaneously trying to steady herself. Whether from the adrenaline rush that accompanied her fall, or the shock of landing in the arms of a handsome stranger, she was feeling more than a little disoriented. "You must be the vet that my dad hired this morning."

He nodded. "That would be me."

"I wasn't expecting you for a few more days, but glad you showed up early." Maya cocked her head in the direction of her cast-covered arm. "Another broken bone, and I'd be out of the game for good."

"Glad I remembered how to catch," Cal said, seeming to stop just short of a wink. "It can be hard enough doing this job with full mobility. I can only imagine what it's like with an arm that's out of commission."

"Well, hopefully not for much longer. My cast comes off in a few weeks."

"I like the color," Cal said as he glanced at the turquoise moldable wrap covering the hard cast.

Thanks, it matches your eyes.

Luckily, Maya only *thought* this reply—but even that was disturbing to her.

Cal nodded to her midsection. "And the ribs?"

"Guess my father really filled you in," Maya said, nearly squirming inside as his intense gaze worked its way back up from her waist. *Gulp.*

"He just told me about the accident you had, that's all. But sounds like you're healing up nicely."

Maya was tempted to say more, if for no other reason than to hear Cal reply in his sexy accent. Heck, he could recite the alphabet right now, and she'd be hanging on every letter.

Get a grip on yourself, girl!

Maya's shoulders twinged slightly, jolted by her inner admonishment. But it was the wake-up call that she needed.

"Are you still looking for a place to stay?" she asked, doing her best to get back to all business.

"I already found one this afternoon—a cabin at the base of Hickory Mountain. The owner lives in New York and uses it during ski season, but he's traveling overseas until late January." He paused to smile, revealing a slight dimple in his left cheek. "So I guess it's home for me for the next couple of months."

Maya forced a smile of her own, in part to keep her mouth from blurting out a less-than-friendly question. After all, asking Cal whether he couldn't commit to a permanent job because he was on the lam from the law *probably* wasn't the best way to get their working relationship off the ground.

"That's a beautiful area," she finally said. "And the skiing come winter is great. Do you ski?"

"On water," Cal said with a slight grin. "Although I'm always up for a new challenge."

"Hmm. I'm sure you are."

Cal's eyes widened at her pointed barb, but it had slipped out of her mouth before she had a chance to clamp down on her cynical thoughts. But could he blame her? After all, it was hard—make that *impossible*—not to picture him eagerly chasing down a new two-legged filly each time he breezed into a new gig. Although, with his rugged good looks and oh-so-smooth bonhomie, most of the fillies no doubt willingly galloped his way, no chase needed. But there was always an exception to the rule, and Maya was determined to be the one woman who would *not* succumb to his charms. *Nope. Not me.*

"Did you come by to tell my dad that you found a place? He's only here until noon most days, so he's back home for the night."

"I came to check on Baxter, actually."

Maya raised an eyebrow. "Oh…?"

"Not sure if your dad mentioned this to you, but when I came by for the interview this morning, he asked me to weigh in on some of the tough cases you're working on."

Maya bristled. It already felt like Cal was encroaching on her territory, especially after she was so used to working alone. Yes, she needed help…but did it have to be this sudden? Realizing she was possibly being…*oh, just a tad bit*…unreasonable, Maya did her best to drop down her guard a notch.

Cal intensified his gaze on her and squinted, as though sizing up her apprehension. It was a by-product of working around horses, Maya thought to herself. One couldn't help but learn to read the slightest shifts in body language, just like equines did. And Cal was reading her now.

"I probably should have given you a heads-up that I was coming by," he said.

Maya quietly caught her breath. "That's okay." She held up her left arm. "It's good that you did—remember?"

There was an earnestness in Cal's eyes that made her dial down her distrust of the situation. *Give him a chance*, she inwardly insisted, before nodding toward a stall at the front of the barn. "Let's go see Baxter."

For someone used to casually rolling into new situations without so much as the blink of an eye…*both* of Cal's eyes were now uncharacteristically working overtime. How could they not, when the most beautiful woman he'd ever seen was smack-dab in front of him?

As he followed her to the stall, Maya briefly looked back and narrowed her eyes at him as if to say *Are you looking at my butt?*

Heck, yeah, he silently acknowledged. But the gentleman in him was not about to give away as much. Instead, he did his best I'm just moseying on along impression, looking to the left and then the right, and stopping himself just short of breaking out into nonchalant whistling. No need to be *too* obvious in covering his tracks.

Maya turned to face forward again, but not before Cal caught a glimpse of a slight smile on her beguiling face. Or maybe it was a grimace, and he only imagined that the curve of her lips faced upward instead of down.

Either way, once he was out of her eyesight, *his* eyes wasted no time picking up where they had left off. Maya was petite, about five foot two, he reckoned, but she had enough lean curves to fill out her tight jeans in all the right places. Her dark ash-brown hair tumbled down her back, bouncing with every determined step.

In fact, he couldn't recall ever seeing someone of her diminutive size covering ground at such a rapid pace. He quickened his own step to keep up, prompting several horses to stick their heads out over the stall gates as he whizzed by, side-eying him as if to say, *No trotting in the barn.*

Maya entered Baxter's stall and held the gate open for Cal.

"Hi, sweetie," she said to Baxter, a compact, dark bay Morgan, as she scratched him under the chin and nuzzled him affectionately. Cal watched, mesmerized, wishing he could instantly grow a tail and pointed ears so he could receive some of Maya's nuzzles as well.

When she turned to him, her light gray eyes latching onto

his, he patted Baxter on the withers. Anything to avoid looking like a fool with a too-obvious stare back.

"So, as I imagine my dad must have told you, Baxter's been here for just over a week with pastern dermatitis that refuses to heal."

Given that Maya seemed more than a little leery of his presence, Cal knew he had to find a way to pass muster with her. Forget about a flirty smile, which he could tell would be about as warmly received on her end as a *Titanic*-sized iceberg. Rather, he needed to prove his equine veterinary chops—and fast.

Right…pastern dermatitis, he repeated inwardly as a quick refresher.

He knew that the oozing, crusty skin condition, also known by no fewer than a half dozen other names, such as mud fever and dew poisoning, had a variety of causes, including bacteria, fungus or excessive moisture in the back pastern area just above the hoof. It typically cleared up quickly with topical treatment, but every once in a while, there was a stubborn case that defied the norm.

"We've tried everything," Maya said. "Antibiotic and steroid creams, zinc oxide cream, a silver antibacterial sock…"

Cal pulled a small jar out of his jacket pocket—the reason for his unannounced visit in the first place. "Triple Strength Healing Clay, found in every horse barn and veterinary clinic in Australia. Works wonders for pastern dermatitis. I can't tell you *why* it does when all these expensive pharmaceutical solutions fail…but sometimes it's the old farmers' remedies that work best."

Maya glanced at the jar, looking less than sold on its merits. "We've already tried a clay drying paste that helped for a couple of days, before the area started oozing again."

Cal flashed a half-smile. "Ahh…but was it clay from Lake Mungo in New South Wales?"

She stared at him unblinkingly. "No."

Well, she didn't inherit her dad's warmth, that's for sure, Cal thought ruefully as he handed her the jar. "Give this a try." He waited for her to reply, then decided to take matters into his own hands. Removing disposable gloves from his jacket pocket, he snapped them on and bent down, lifting Baxter's infected leg. "I'll put some on him now."

Maya opened the jar and bent down so that it was within Cal's reach. As her lightly perfumed hair swung in front of her shoulder, he forced himself to double down on his concentration. Otherwise, he could end up slathering clay on the wrong leg altogether.

And that wouldn't make me look too competent, now would it?

"All set," he said a few moments later, straightening up and patting Baxter on the neck. "Now, all this clay has to do is work its magic overnight."

As Maya raised a less-than-convinced eyebrow, Cal's own eyebrows knitted together. Damn, she was a tough sell, staring him down like he was nothing more than a snake oil salesman.

If this is what I have to look forward to, these two months are going to feel like an eternity.

Cal kept his woeful thoughts to himself, flipping to a need-to-know question. "So what time should I be here tomorrow? Six a.m.?"

Maya balked slightly. "Um, not if you want to greet me before I have my morning coffee. And trust me, you don't."

Thinking he saw the hint of a smile on Maya's face, Cal readily laughed before realizing he must have imagined amusement on her behalf. Perhaps she needed another cup of that coffee. And *he* could use a strong swig of whiskey right about now, anything to dull his growing impression of a potentially stern taskmaster. Or maybe this was simply Maya's way of making clear who was in charge.

Okay, you're the boss. Can we move forward now?

"During the school year, I usually get here by eight a.m., after my son gets on the school bus," Maya continued. "So, why don't we shoot for that starting time."

The fact that Maya had a child caught Cal by surprise, although he couldn't be sure why. Instinctively, he glanced down at her left hand, noting that there was no wedding ring. Not that this meant anything. Plenty of large-animal vets preferred to have unadorned hands, given that they all too often ended up covered in slop of one kind or another.

"How old is your son?" Cal asked, genuinely curious.

It *seemed* like a harmless enough question, which was why Maya's suddenly stiffened, guarded body language caught him by surprise.

"He's eight," she replied, after several awkward moments of silence.

Cal smiled and nodded. He knew better than to dig further. Perhaps she had an extreme take on the "keep it professional" motto, a thought that left him more than a tad disappointed. He preferred a casual work environment…a laugh here, a joke there, some chatter about weekend plans…

He sighed inwardly, but adapting to new situations was his forte. It had to be, given that he preferred never staying in one place for too long. So he'd make the best of it, and at least the scenery would be enjoyable. He cleared his throat, only too aware that the colorful Vermont countryside was not the only thing that would be catching his eye for the next couple of months. Although with that frosty attitude…

Cal twisted his mouth to the side. Forget about autumn. Winter had already arrived.

* * *

Twenty minutes later, Cal entered the chalet-style cabin that would be his home for the next couple of months. Dropping his truck keys on the kitchen counter, he scanned his surroundings, nodding his head in approval of the rustic vibe.

The silence surrounding him was pierced by a chuckle as an image of Maya slid into his thoughts. She was quite the little spitfire, that was for sure. Then again, someone of her small stature had to radiate confidence and strength in order to work around horses. They could read these sorts of things. A two-hundred-pound brute of a man emanating fear in their presence? They'd steamroller over him like he was a mere pebble in their path. A one-hundred-pound wisp of a woman who mentally stood her ground? It could turn a snorting, bucking stallion into a docile puppy dog.

All of which begged the question…was he going to be the stallion in this situation?

Don't even go there, mate, he told himself, though he was admittedly intrigued by the prospect. Still, he came here to do a job, and that's what he needed to focus on. Especially since the two-month contract would be over before it had barely begun. But wasn't that his specialty? *Swoop in…and swoop right back out.*

He shook his head, grateful that his interviews had been with Maya's father, Gus, rather than Maya herself. Otherwise, he probably wouldn't have gotten past a coast-to-coast hello via cell phone. She seemed wary of him, and it wasn't a stretch to think that his history of bouncing from one job to the next might have set off her spidey senses. Especially when her own professional background seemed so closely tied to family and the small town of Maplewood.

Cal recalled how Gus had spoken about Maya with so much pride during their interviews, expressing his concern for her well-being as she took on increasingly more responsibilities within the family vet practice. He wondered what it must be like to be part of a tight-knit family, to know they always had your back and you had theirs.

But his brain simply couldn't go there. Then again, how could it? Despite having traveled the world and holding his own in several languages, *family* was one word that held no meaning for him, even in his native English. Not when his mother, a drug-addicted teenager, had disappeared from his life shortly after his birth in Queensland, Australia. But that was still a longer presence than his father, whom he'd never known. And then bouncing around from one foster home to another...

Stop.

Cal's forceful, one-word directive was enough to shake off his chokehold of thoughts. At least for now. But his mind was such that it couldn't be rudderless for long. It had to latch on to something, and as that *something* became an image of Maya, he wondered what her story was. She'd been through a lot—he could see it in her eyes. A reminder that heartache and disappointment spared no one, regardless of the strength of family ties. Perhaps that's why she had her guard up. And though his attraction to her was immediate, he needed to be careful.

Because there was no way he'd want to be another reason for sadness in those soulful light gray eyes.

CHAPTER TWO

THE NEXT MORNING at precisely 8:03 a.m., Maya entered the clinic barn and headed toward Baxter's stall. She was a few feet shy of the gate when Cal popped his head over, prompting her to jump backward.

"Sorry—I didn't mean to scare you," he said.

As sunrays peeked in from the barn windows, illuminating Cal's blue-green eyes, Maya felt her knees tremble. And it wasn't due to her startled hop a few seconds earlier.

"That's okay. I'm used to being the first one here in the morning, and you caught me by surprise—that's all." She cleared her throat, hoping it would also clear her head. "How's he doing?"

Cal flashed a half grin as he held the gate open. "Come see for yourself."

"Wow!" Maya exclaimed moments later as she examined Baxter's pastern area. "I can't believe how much the dermatitis cleared up overnight."

"Lake Mungo scores again," Cal said, prompting a grin from Maya.

She stood up from her kneeling position, not realizing how close she had been squatting next to Cal. Standing just inches away from him now, feeling nearly dwarfed by his six-foot-two, rugged body, Maya felt like the stall walls were closing in on her. How else to explain that she could barely catch her breath?

As Cal's magnetic gaze locked on to hers, she felt like a horse whose fight-or-flight switch had just been triggered. And flight it would be.

Wincing at a jab of pain as she grabbed the stall gate latch with her left arm, Maya nearly stumbled out into the barn aisle, then took a deep breath to calm herself. If she was going to adhere to her "keep it professional" motto, then that also meant not acting like a skittish colt in his presence.

Cal entered the aisle and closed the gate behind him. His eyes were slightly squinted as he cast them in her direction, and something told her it wasn't due to the burgeoning sunlight filtering through the barn.

No, he was sizing her up, trying to discern why she had just acted the way she did. Maya knew there were all sorts of things he could ask or say in this moment—things that would only add to her self-induced uncomfortableness—but to his credit, he merely smiled.

"Well, whatever's next on the agenda, I'll follow your lead," he said.

Maya felt the tightness in her chest begin to recede. "I figured we could go on calls together for the next few days while you get the lay of the land, then after that, we'll divide and conquer. Although, there'll be occasions when we'll need to pair up."

He nodded. "Sounds like a plan."

"Great. Let's check in on our patients here, and then it's off to our first appointment." She paused long enough allow a subdued smile to escape. "I think you'll like where we'll be heading."

Fifteen minutes later, Cal turned to Maya from the passenger seat of her large, fully stocked, capped pickup truck. "Are you going to keep me in suspense?" he asked.

It took several moments for the meaning behind his question to sink in. "Oh—that's right. I said you'd like where we're headed. It's a place called Happy Hooves Horse Rescue."

"A rescue. I like it already," Cal said with a quick but definitive nod.

"I've known Cathy—the owner—since I was a kid. My dad did a lot of pro bono work for the rescue, and it's a tradition I'm more than happy to continue." She turned to Cal, nearly flinching at the way his intense gaze was focused on her with seeming admiration.

"That's great. There are far too many horses in this world that are discarded without a second thought." He paused, clenching his jaw. "That's one of the reasons I left my last gig."

Maya raised an eyebrow. "Oh?"

"I was working at a racetrack in Southern California. Never really gave a huge amount of thought to the horse racing biz, but seeing how so many of the owners cared only about money, and not the welfare of the horses…it was hard to take."

Maya nodded. Cal's concern for the horses had just bumped him up about, oh, one hundred-plus pegs in her eyes.

"Believe me, I know what you mean. In fact, several of the horses at the rescue are young Thoroughbreds that didn't make the cut on the racetrack, and were being shipped to…" Maya stopped, unable to say the word.

As Cal shook his head, eyes blazing, it was clear that she didn't need to.

"Anyway, there are lots of happy endings at Happy Hooves," she said, needing to hear something more positive to focus on, even if it came from her own mouth.

"Happy endings at Happy Hooves. Now that's the kind of happy-happy that I like."

They shared a brief laugh, a much-needed respite from the shared angst over the plight of unwanted equines. Not since George had Maya felt a connection to another vet who seemed to care as deeply as she did about such issues. Even Max, as highly competent as he'd been in veterinary medicine, seemed capable of shutting off the empathy gene whenever it had suited him.

She couldn't shut off that endless well of compassion even if she tried...and something told her the same could be said of Cal.

Ten minutes later, Maya pulled the truck onto the long gravel driveway that wound its way up to the rescue's main buildings.

A tall, slender woman waved from the porch of a white farmhouse, then headed out to meet them.

Dressed in tight jeans, worn cowboy boots and a black T-shirt with white letters that read Horses, Yay!... People, Neigh!, Cathy left no second-guessing as to her priorities in life. Her tanned, weathered face proudly hid none of her sixty-eight years, and the long salt-and-pepper braid that fell halfway down her back only added to her horsewoman mystique.

"Cathy, I'd like you to meet Cal. He's going to be helping out for a bit while my dad starts to transition to retirement."

"Nice to meet you," Cal said as he shook Cathy's hand.

"Same here," Cathy said, eyes squinting as she homed in on him.

Taking a step back, Cathy used her hand as a visor to shield her gaze from the sun, then looked Cal up and down as though she was ready to bid on him at an auction. Little did Maya know that this wasn't so far from the truth.

Cathy stepped slightly to the side, as though sizing up Cal's broad-shouldered physique from another angle.

Maya dropped her head to conceal a muffled snicker. What

was next? Opening Cal's mouth and giving his teeth a once-over? Grabbing his leg and flexing it sideways to test his joints? It certainly looked that way.

"Say, how would you like to help out with the horses?" Cathy asked Cal in her no-nonsense, clipped voice. That's how Maya knew Cathy was addressing a human. If she had been talking to one of her horses, her voice would have been much softer.

Cal bent his head to the side, shifting his weight from one leg to the next.

He looked over at Maya, a "what the heck" appeal beaming from his widened eyes. She thought to reassure him with a supportive nod, except that she wasn't quite sure what Cathy was up to, either.

"That's, um, why we're here today—right?" Cal asked as he turned back to Cathy. "To examine and vaccinate some new arrivals?"

Cathy smiled, the creases around her brown eyes deepening. "I'm talking about helping out in another way. We're holding a Hunks for Horses fundraiser in a couple of weeks, and you'd be perfect."

Cal cleared his throat. "Perfect for what?"

"Bringing in the dough."

This time, Maya didn't bother to hide her chuckle. *Damn, this is getting good...*

"Bringing in the..." Cal stopped short of fully repeating Cathy's explanation.

"You just have to strut your stuff on stage, and some lucky gal will be paired up with you for a date," Cathy said matter-of-factly.

Cal ran his fingers through his dark blond hair. "Well, I'm not sure that I've ever been auctioned off on a date before."

He turned to Maya, his face softening into a grin. "But if it can help the horses, then I'm game."

"Glad to hear it," Cathy said, pulling her phone out of her back pocket. She stepped back and focused the camera on Cal. "Can you turn your body to the side a bit, and give me some bicep?"

Maya did a double take. She'd heard that Cathy had been briefly married years ago, but since she'd known her, the only males that had caught Cathy's attention were all gelded and trotting on four legs. So to see her size up Cal now like a slab of beefcake was *quite* unexpected. Then again...Maya found it hard to believe that any woman—no matter how dormant her hormones—could be oblivious to Cal's rugged Aussie charms.

Did I just think that?

Maya tried to steer her thoughts in another direction, but her built-in GPS seemed to be set on Cal's muscular arms. She watched with *way* too much enjoyment as Cal posed this way and that, all based on Cathy's eager directives. *Could this get any more surreal?* Maya wondered.

Finally, Cathy appeared to be done, and Maya squelched her impulse to shout out, *Are you sure you don't want another pose?*

"Thanks," Cathy said to Cal. "My niece takes care of social media updates for the rescue, so I'll be sure to have her plaster your picture everywhere."

Cal was beginning to look uncomfortable again. "I'm not the only bloke signed up for the fundraiser—right?"

"No, but you're the only one everyone will be salivating over," Cathy said, prompting yet another surprised head swirl from Maya. "Trust me. I've got Lonnie, the local sheriff who also plays Santa every year—no costume needed. Let's see, there's also my handyman, Ed. Super nice guy, but has the face of a meerkat. And the body, too, for that matter. And then there's Mike—"

Cal held up his hand and laughed. "That's okay—I think I've heard enough."

Cathy launched into a grin. "Great. Then let's get down to business and go have a look at the new residents."

As Maya and Cal followed Cathy to the nearest paddock, Cal slowed his pace, prompting Maya to do the same.

"You could have warned me that I was walking into a trap," he said, his voice low and eyes flashing with a mix of disbelief and amusement.

"I would've thought this sort of thing was right up your alley," Maya whispered back tersely.

As Cal did a double take, she felt slightly guilty for her harsh reply. *Slightly.*

"I honestly had no idea she was going to ask you to participate in the fundraiser," she quickly added, a half-hearted attempt to neutralize some of the salt she'd thrown into the wound. Which was true. And another truth, one that she was more than happy to keep to herself? There was no way she'd be throwing her name into a hat—or most likely in this case, a stable bucket—and risk the possibility that she'd be the one chosen for a night out on the town with Cal. Not when her top priority was maintaining a strictly professional relationship with him. That's what was clearly best for her...and more importantly, best for Jeremy.

For a split second, she wondered if she was putting the cart before the horse. Why all the inner protests about keeping things professional, when in fact Cal had so far been the perfect gentleman, with not a single inappropriate comment or innuendo tossed her way? Except...if eyes could talk, *his* eyes would be saying *Fancy having some fun on the side while I'm here?* Maybe she was reading a little too much into his stolen glances in her direction, or the physically electrifying vibe that she felt reverberate between them whenever he was near, but there was nothing wrong with being proactive.

Glad we got that resolved, Maya thought triumphantly as she trod onward with determination in her step. Sensing Cal's gaze upon her, she glanced at him sideways, feeling an instant ripple in her resolve. Everything about him was a smorgasbord for the eyes, but this was one buffet she needed to steer clear of.

Maya grimaced. It was never easy turning down dessert, but with a little…okay, a *lot*…of willpower, she could do it.

Cathy led her and Cal into a smaller barn where three new rescues were being temporarily quarantined. It was always a good idea to separate newcomers for at least a few weeks, just to be sure they weren't carrying any contagious diseases that could be transmitted to the rest of the herd.

After Cathy gave a run-through of their backgrounds—an American quarter horse surrendered by his owner due to financial hardship, a Standardbred retired from the racetrack due to a career-ending leg injury and a former Amish-cart-pulling Belgian Draught removed from an auction and spared a potentially life-ending fate—Maya and Cal got down to business.

Working in tandem as they performed thorough physical exams, Maya was almost surprised to find how easy it was to collaborate with Cal. He worked like she did—evaluating physical and behavioral issues based on solid medical guidance, but also through gut instinct. With horses, that instinct often spoke volumes.

All three horses were underweight and in need of a good hoof trim, but once Cathy confirmed the farrier was scheduled for later in the week, and a game plan was agreed upon to safely build up their weight, both Maya and Cal felt it was safe to administer the core vaccines for rabies, tetanus, the mosquito-borne viruses of eastern and western equine encephalitis, and West Nile virus. With mosquito activity at its highest in the fall, Maya felt relieved to know they'd now be protected from these potentially fatal illnesses.

As the trio left the barn and walked back out toward the main buildings, Cal suddenly halted.

"Who's that?" he asked as he nodded toward a caramel-colored horse with a long cream mane in one of several large, fenced pastures. The horse stood by itself, away from a small herd that was contently grazing, its head hanging dejectedly downward.

"That's Molly," Cathy replied. "She's a BLM mustang rounded up two years ago in Nevada. Not sure if you're familiar with the Bureau of Land Management program where they try to place wild horses in homes, but she was bouncing from one adopter to another, and on her way to auction when I intervened and brought her here. I knew what her fate would be if I didn't."

Maya felt a cloud of sadness descend upon her, and as she briefly locked eyes with Cal, she could see that he shared her deep concern with the fate of unwanted horses.

"Do you know why her adopters gave her up?" Cal asked.

"She's withdrawn to the point that she won't assimilate with the herd—never mind bond with a human being. Can't say that I blame her, after she was separated from her family and taken away from the only home she'd ever known."

Cal nodded slightly, his gaze still fixed intently on the mare. "Mind if I go meet her?" he asked, turning back to Cathy, then locking eyes with Maya.

In that moment, there was a knowing exchange between them, a feeling of *we're cut from the same cloth*. She was an American and he an Australian...she'd never left her small-town roots and he apparently couldn't be tied down to any one corner of the globe…yet together they shared a deep empathy and love for horses that transcended words.

"Sure," Cathy said, turning to Maya as Cal strode off toward the pasture. "*Where* did you find that perfect specimen of a man?"

Maya gasped, partly for effect, and partly out of genuine shock that her normally reserved client and friend had just uttered something that seemed miles out of character.

"What?" Cathy retorted with mock defense as she shrugged her shoulders. "I might not have much use for men these days, but that doesn't mean I can't appreciate a good-looking guy who knows a thing or two about horses."

Both women shared a laugh, then looked out onto the field as Cal approached Molly. The mare pricked up her ears, then lifted her head in Cal's direction.

"Well, that's a first," Cathy said in a quiet voice. "Normally, Molly runs off as soon as you approach her."

Maya held her breath as Cal inched his way toward Molly. He had the mare's rapt attention, but Maya wasn't sure how. *Something* was preventing Molly's fight-or-flight instinct to kick in. Was it the energy that Cal emanated, a concept that was pure woo-woo to the average person, but not to someone like herself, who understood how horses could pick up on a person's heartbeat from four feet away? And that was just the beginning of their heightened perceptions.

Maya watched intently as Molly took a step toward Cal. Even from a distance, she could see that the mare was responding to some invisible cue. Whether it was Cal's body language and his energy, or a sixth sense that both human and horse were tapping into, Maya couldn't be sure. But she was mesmerized by what she was witnessing firsthand.

"Amazing," Cathy said in a low voice, her eyes glued to

the unexpected scene before her. "Is he a horse vet, or a horse whisperer?"

"It certainly looks like both," Maya said quietly. Which was good news for the horses, but bad news for her. Curtailing her attraction to a man that was based solely on his irresistible looks? That was doable. But when this same man had depth and integrity, and a shared love for and connection to horses...*that* attraction wasn't so easy to outright dismiss. But she'd have to...and she would.

Cal looked up from his deliberate stare at the ground, then cast his eyes—his *soft* eyes—on Molly. If someone was to ask him what the heck "soft eyes" were, he wasn't sure he could adequately explain. It wasn't so much a physical stance as it was a mental and emotional one. It was as if his eyes were verbally saying, *Don't be scared. I won't hurt you.*

When he had first spotted Molly, it was like seeing a ghost. Everything about the mare—from her cream-colored mane and sorrel coat, to her timid and fearful demeanor—reminded him of Flaxxie, the first horse he'd ever bonded with as a young teen. His eyes flickered for a moment before he willed their softness to return, an involuntary response to painful memories dotted amongst happier ones.

It was always a mixed bag of emotions when he looked back on the years that he'd been placed in the care of Thomas and Mabel Crawford, a couple in their late sixties who ran a large horse ranch in the outback. It was the first—and last—time he'd ever felt he was part of a family who cared about him. And it was also here where he quickly developed an affinity for horses that transcended any bond he had ever known.

Flaxxie's mother had tragically died during her birth, and the young filly had struggled to bond with other mares in the herd, increasingly acting out as they continued to ostracize her. As a fifteen-year-old who'd already experienced a lifetime of disappointment, Cal had found a kindred spirit in Flaxxie. He'd intrinsically understood her angst, the desire to be part of a family, the defiant "Fine, I don't need anyone" attitude in the absence of anyone stepping up to the plate.

So *he* had stepped up, helping to build her confidence on the way to full acceptance within the herd—and with no formal training on his part. But then again, none was needed. He was simply a natural around horses. It was as if he could look into their eyes and see their very soul, sensing their fears or contentment…just as they understood *him* on the deepest level. It was daily equine therapy—before he ever knew that such a healing mode officially existed.

Its effect on him was so powerful that it had spurred his desire to become an equine veterinarian, a lofty goal that he knew would normally be out of reach for someone like himself, without a penny to rub between two fingers. But he had wanted it too much to be deterred. And so he doubled down on his secondary school studies and tagged along on farm visits with the local vet every chance he had. His perseverance had paid off in the form of a full scholarship to a veterinary college in Victoria. That was one of the happy memories from his time at the ranch.

As Molly snorted, bringing him partially back to the present, Cal wondered if she sensed the darker recollections that tagged along with the happier ones.

Don't go there.

Cal closed his eyes and breathed in deeply, searching for a zen moment to melt away everything but the *now*. Only by being fully present would he be able to connect to Molly. When he opened his eyes again, she tossed her head and pawed at the ground, then took a step closer. She was tentatively in his space now, and it would be easy enough to reach over and gently stroke her face.

But he needed her permission first. Another half step. She was so close now that he could feel her warm breath on his bare forearm. He stood motionless, as though he had all the time in the world. In this moment, everything and everyone else was blocked out. It was just him and Molly...and a silent dance of trust and vulnerability between them.

Several minutes passed, and then Cal spoke quietly. "I'll be back, Molly," he said. Her dark brown eyes seemed to register understanding.

As he approached Maya and Cathy outside of the fence gate a short time later, he couldn't help but notice how they were both viewing him through disbelieving eyes.

"I thought for sure she was going to let you touch her," Maya said, her long brown ponytail bobbing with every animated word.

"I almost did," Cal said. "But one too-soon move now, and it would be very hard to ever gain her trust." He turned to address Cathy. "I'm not sure if you'd be okay with this, but I'd love to work with Molly during my free time, see if I can bring her out of her shell a bit more."

"'Okay with this'?" Cathy repeated incredulously. "I'd be thrilled! You just established more of a connection with her in five minutes than I've been able to do in almost five months."

Cal smiled. "Great. I really think I can make some significant progress with her. She *wants* to trust—I can just feel it."

"Just be sure she doesn't kick you before the fundraiser," Maya noted with a mischievous twinkle in her eye. "You don't want to be strutting your stuff on stage with a bum knee."

"Good point!" Cathy chimed in as Cal let out a good-natured chuckle.

"Glad you both have my well-being in mind," he said with a wry grin.

After a tour of the rescue, Cal and Maya bid goodbye to Cathy and the horses, then headed for the truck.

Cal felt relieved that the first day of his stint with Equine Associates was rolling out on such a positive note. Any initial qualms he'd had about working with Maya had quickly been nixed. She wasn't the know-it-all, micromanager type that he had worried she might be, questioning his every diagnosis or treatment suggestion. Rather, she seemed to approach horse care much like he did—with an inquisitive mind, a keen eye and a sensitivity to their emotional as well as their physical makeup.

"Mind if I drive?" Cal asked as Maya opened the driver's side door. She was about to hop in, but paused. "No pulling any wheelies."

He laughed. "Promise I won't."

Once they were on the main road, Maya turned to him. "I still can't believe the way you were able to connect with Molly like that. Cathy said she's barely able to get near her—and she's no slouch around horses, obviously. Is it something you were taught, or does it come naturally?"

No one had ever asked him this before, and though Cal knew the answer, it was slow to depart his lips. "Comes naturally, I guess."

"Well, Molly really seemed to gravitate toward you, and it was pretty amazing to watch."

"She reminded me of one of the first horses I ever worked with."

"As a vet?"

"No, it was at a horse ranch in the outback. I was a teenager at the time."

"What was her name?" Maya asked, her voice upbeat.

Perhaps she was expecting some joyful recollections, Cal thought, but nothing could be further from the truth.

His throat clamped shut, rendering any answer impossible. Why did he even bring this up? He'd never mentioned Flaxxie to another person before, in part because of the painful memories that reignited in even a passing reference, but also because they could never understand. But Maya could. She shared his deep compassion for horses, and she wouldn't look at him like he had two heads if he told her things that still haunted him to this day.

Still...he couldn't finish what he started. At least not now. He wasn't ready to be this vulnerable in front of Maya, who he was just getting to know, and maybe he never would.

Stalling for time, Cal stared straight ahead at the road, but he could still feel Maya's eyes upon him as she waited for an answer.

He pressed down slightly on the gas pedal, as though accelerating the truck would drive him out of the dark place where his thoughts had landed. But he was still there, the determined young man in his final year of veterinary school who had lost so much seemingly overnight. When Thomas and Mabel had passed away within months of each other just before his graduation, the ranch that he had called home...and the horses he had deeply cared about...were passed on to their two biological sons, who wanted nothing to do with any of it.

Even now, years later, he could feel the sharp sting of anger, and the dull pang of helplessness, that had defined his last days in Australia as he tried desperately to ensure that the horses would be cared for. If only he could have bought the ranch himself, but it had been a financial impossibility. He'd done everything in his power—of which he had little at the time—to track down Flaxxie, but he never learned of her fate. His anguish at the time had been debilitating enough to vow to leave the country with his newly acquired degree in hand, a decision he had never regretted.

"Are you okay?" Maya asked, her voice tentative, as though she'd picked up on his sudden shift in demeanor.

Cal forced a smile, scrambling to think of something to say that would instantly lighten the mood. "I'm fine. I was just wondering about what I should wear for my fundraiser debut. I don't know… I'm thinking maybe a pair of backless chaps, minus the jeans?"

He held his breath, hoping that Maya would somehow not notice that he'd evaded her question.

She noticed, he thought as he briefly met her puzzled eyes. But to her credit, she didn't push the matter, and instead let out a throaty chuckle.

"I can't believe you just said that."

Neither could he, considering she was technically his boss, and he had no idea how she'd react to the comment. It was one of those speak first, think later moments…and luckily, it hadn't backfired on him.

It was dusk by the time they pulled into the clinic after their last appointment for the day.

"Looks like my dad's here," Maya said as she glanced at his SUV parked next to the office. "Let's go say hi and let him know I didn't fire you yet."

Cal chuckled. She was kidding, after all…*right*? Still, he breathed a little easier when she turned back to him with a smirk on her face.

"It's the man of the hour!" Gus boomed good-naturedly as they entered the office. "How did your first day on the job go?"

Maya glanced at Cal, her face tired yet beaming. "It went great. Cal here is quite the horse whisperer."

Gus smiled and nodded his approval. "Is that so. Well, can't say that I'm surprised."

Suddenly, the office door opened and a young boy boisterously entered. "Hey, Mom," he said as he headed toward Maya. Cal noticed a flicker of tense surprise on her face, and how she immediately turned back to her dad.

"Oh—I should have mentioned this already," Gus explained, "but Jeremy asked if he could come by with me to visit with the horses." He looked at his grandson. "Everyone A-OK?"

The boy smiled. "Yup. They're eating their hay and farting up a storm."

"Jeremy!" Maya admonished, though she chimed in with a chuckle as Cal burst out laughing.

Gus looked over at Cal. "Jeremy here is a budding horse vet."

Cal smiled. "Runs in the family, I'd say."

His smile faded as he saw a flash of pain on Maya's face. Was it triggered by his comment? He couldn't imagine why. Unless she didn't want her son to become a horse veterinarian...and that certainly didn't make any sense.

"Jeremy, this is Cal," Gus said. "He's going to be working with your mom for the next couple of months."

"Nice to meet you, Jeremy," Cal said, feeling Maya's stern eyes upon him like laser beams set on high as he approached the young boy.

Jeremy looked up at him inquisitively. "You talk funny."

"That's called an accent," Maya said with a hint of amusement in her voice.

"Oh—sorry," Jeremy replied sheepishly. "Where are you from?"

"I'm from Australia," Cal said as he looked down on the freckle-faced boy. "But I've lived pretty much all over the world."

"Wow, that's cool," Jeremy said, prompting low-key laughter from Gus and Maya.

As Cal straightened up, his eye caught a row of framed photos on the side wall. Jeremy followed his gaze, then walked over and pointed to one of the pictures.

"That's me helping my mom examine Crackers."

Cal approached his side and studied the photo of Maya resting the front hoof of what appeared to be a Shetland pony on her bent knee, pointing something out to a younger Jeremy as she did.

"Hmm. Hoof bruise?" Cal asked.

"Stone stuck in the frog. I helped pick it out."

"Way to go!" Cal said, genuinely impressed that he was honing future veterinary skills at such a young age.

Another photo caught his attention, this one of a younger Gus standing proudly with one arm around the shoulder of a school-age Maya, a large vet bag dangling from his other arm. The top of Maya's head barely reached Gus's chest, but even so, her smiling face exuded the same determination and grit that he saw in her now.

Cal's lips silently curved upward as he focused in on a small vet bag in her grip. It was even embroidered with fancy cursive writing that read Maya's Vet Kit. He wondered if it had been a Christmas or birthday gift. *No Barbie dolls for you, right?*

"That's me and my dad," Jeremy said, pointing to another photo. In it, Maya stood with her arm around the waist of an outdoorsy-looking man, who held a toddler-aged Jeremy up against his chest with one arm. Given that he wore a Northern Vermont Equine Associates T-shirt like Maya did in the photo, he must have been a fellow vet, Cal reasoned.

If they were divorced, was he still in the picture? He certainly didn't look like the type to run out on his family. Cal frowned at his thoughts. As if he could tell *anything* about the man by merely glancing at a single celluloid moment from the past.

Feeling eyes upon him, he turned to find Maya watching him intently, and as a quiet stillness descended over the room, he wondered where all the oxygen had gone.

Glancing at his watch without actually reading the numbers, he declared, "Well, I think I'll go check up on our patients in the barn before dark."

Closing the office door behind him as he stepped outside, Cal looked up at the purplish-orange sky, drawing in a deep breath. It had been quite the day. And working with Maya could only mean one thing…it was going to be quite the two months.

CHAPTER THREE

Maya gripped the steering wheel of her personal SUV as she drove from her house to the clinic. It was Saturday morning—technically a day off—but that never stopped her from swinging by the main barn for a quick check on onsite patients.

All around her, the colorful brilliance of a Vermont autumn was in high gear. Quite simply, she didn't believe there could possibly be a more beautiful place—or time of year—on the planet, and the seasonal influx of leaf-peeping tourists seemed to second this notion.

Yet, despite the scenes of splendor that whizzed by the side windows, Maya was feeling distracted and tense. An image of Cal flashed in her mind, as if to say, *Am I the reason you can't focus right now?* Maya twisted her mouth to the side, refusing to inwardly reply. *As if I don't know the answer to that question...*

Cal's first week on the job had officially wrapped up yesterday, and Maya couldn't imagine a more competent colleague. He didn't just know his way around horses...he knew a way into their souls. And that, in her experience, was an incredible gift.

Still, there was no shortage of caution lights flickering around him. He jumped from one job to the next, and in just a couple of months, he'd be departing this current one as well.

He seemed to be running from *something*, that was for sure. From boredom? Adult responsibilities? A jilted ex-lover?

Maya snorted at this last improbable possibility. Or maybe it wasn't so improbable, given that she of the "I can't be bothered to look" missive had in fact been looking. A lot.

Not that this was Cal's fault, of course. He couldn't help the fact that he was quite literally a Hunk for Horses. That had been apparent from the moment they had first met. But his deep caring and compassion for equines—something that had exposed a vulnerability behind his *very* solid exterior? That had come as more of a surprise.

And now, as Maya replayed in her mind all the instances when she'd treated him dismissively since they had first met, she was feeling pangs of regret. He'd been nothing but friendly toward her and her dad and Jeremy. Maybe it was time to cut him some slack.

As she pulled into the clinic's long driveway, Maya vowed to make amends when the time and circumstances were right. She wouldn't address her behavior to Cal directly, but perhaps she could offer a goodwill gesture of some sort when the opportunity arose.

Yes, I can do that...

Maya's thoughts were cut short as she spotted Cal's dark blue truck in one of the parking spots by the main barn.

Forehead creased as questions swirled in her mind, Maya quickly exited her truck and headed for the barn entrance.

"Morning!" Cal exclaimed as he walked out from the barn into the sunlit morning. "I thought I heard a car pull up."

"It's Saturday," Maya said as she viewed him quizzically. "Your day off."

Cal flashed a one-sided grin. "Yours too—isn't it?"

Maya wasn't sure how to respond to that observation. "I'm

part owner of the practice. I never have a day off," she finally said, only half kidding.

"Well, that's no fun." There was a twinkle in Cal's eye that was *fun* personified.

Maya pretended to herself that she hadn't noticed this.

"I came by to check on Razzle," Cal explained, referring to the American paint horse gelding that was being rehabbed for a torn suspensory ligament in his hind leg.

He came by on his day off to check on one of the horses! Maya held her breath as she let that thought sink in.

"I came by to check on him, too. How's he doing?"

"He seems fine. Must have tweaked something yesterday, but whatever it was, it's gone now. Mark said he saw no new signs of lameness this morning."

Maya breathed a sigh of relief. "That's great news."

She knew that Mark, a fourth-year veterinary student who worked on weekends as a vet tech at the clinic, would have caught anything that was amiss. Still, she remembered her own days as a final-year student on the brink of becoming a bona fide veterinarian. You could never have too many highly trained eyes weighing in on cases while trying to rack up actual field experience.

"Anything you'd like me to do while I'm here?" Cal asked.

"No, but thanks for asking. Go enjoy your day off."

Cal smiled and nodded, seeming to hesitate slightly before turning to head to his truck.

Maya watched as he started to walk away, then allowed impulse to take over. "Have you ever had pancakes and maple syrup before?" she quickly blurted out, before she had a chance to change her mind about following through with her goodwill gesture.

Cal turned and looked at her quizzically, as though wondering if this was a trick question. "Sure."

"No—I mean *real* maple syrup."

"If you mean something other than artificial syrup with fake maple coloring and a lot of fine print that says Bad for Your Health…then the answer is no."

Maya snickered. "Come on," she said, nodding toward her SUV.

Cal looked equal parts confused and intrigued. "Where are we going?"

"Marie's Breakfast Nook in downtown Maplewood. It has the best melt-in-your-mouth pancakes and *pure* Vermont maple syrup."

"Maplewood has a downtown?" he asked cheekily.

"Ha! Yes, but no one would mistake it for a metropolis, I can tell you that."

Cal grinned. "All the better."

The breakfast café was bustling with local regulars and tourists when Maya and Cal entered after a short drive over. With wooden furniture, gingham place settings and the scintillating aroma of freshly baked muffins and cinnamon rolls, the café was a feast for the senses.

"There's a spot," Maya said as she pointed to a booth tucked away in the far-left corner that had just been vacated by another couple. "Let's grab it fast!"

They were barely seated before a young waitress whizzed by, then paused and backtracked.

"Coffee?" she asked in a chirpy voice as she cleared the plates with one hand and deftly cleaned the tabletop with a damp cloth pulled from her apron pocket.

"Sure," Maya replied.

"Please," Cal said with a friendly nod.

"How many cups today will that be?" Cal asked with a grin once the waitress departed.

"Maybe my third—but who's counting?"

Cal chuckled as he scanned the laminated one-page menu. "Pumpkin pancakes," he said with curiosity as he perused the menu.

"Oh—you've got to try those," Maya said enthusiastically. "They are *delicious*."

As Maya scanned her own menu, she suddenly became aware of a deafening silence. Just moments earlier, she could barely hear herself think above the din of overlapping conversations around them...and now this?

She peered up at Cal, who also seemed keenly aware that something was amiss. "Did it just suddenly get quiet in here?" he asked in a near whisper.

Maya discreetly nodded, then scanned the room. Given that they were quite literally in their own little corner, she didn't think they could possibly have drawn the attention of others. But either she was being totally paranoid...or every patron was in fact looking their way. Actually, that wasn't quite accurate. Every *female* customer was pointedly staring in their direction.

"Do I have something on my face?" she whispered to Cal as she leaned in closer for some privacy. At least what little they had under the circumstances.

Cal's eyes darted around him. "Just the same look of surprise that I have." Suddenly, his lightly tanned face turned ghostly white. "Oh, no. No, no, no..."

"What?" Maya exclaimed in a hoarse whisper, her heart now racing. She grabbed his forearm, then pulled her hand back as though she had touched a burning stove.

"Sorry," she said of her grab-now-think-later reaction, though in that split second of feeling the warmth of his skin on the palm of her hand, her true feeling could best be summed up as: *Sorry, NOT sorry!*

Cal glanced down to where she'd touched his arm, his eyes lingering there several moments before looking back up at her.

Locked into a mutual gaze, she felt the magnetic pull of attraction dance between them. Only when she forced herself to avert her eyes away—*we're just colleagues, after all*—did Cal nod to a tent-shaped advertising display that was propped up in the middle of the table. She stared at it for several moments, then slapped her hand over her mouth to muzzle her laughter.

"Not funny," Cal said in a low growl, though there was no mistaking the reluctant smirk on his face.

Maya picked up the display and discreetly read the print aloud. "'Don't miss our Hunks for Horses fundraiser on September 20 at the Maplewood Grange. Throw your name into the bucket for the chance to win a date with one of these dreamy, horse-loving hunks! Tickets are fifty dollars each—no limit to the number of purchases. All proceeds will benefit the Happy Hooves Horse Rescue.'"

Cal squeezed his eyes shut. "I'm afraid to look around, but they're probably on every table—am I right?"

"Ah…yup," Maya confirmed. "And right now, every woman in here is looking at you and licking her lips."

Maya knew that Cal assumed she was exaggerating in order to needle him further…except that she wasn't. Not that she could blame all the rapt gazes in his direction.

Cal sunk further into his chair. "I think I want to disappear."

"Oh, come now. It's for the horses—just keep remembering that." Maya paused, shaking her head in astonishment. "Although, I have to say—I've always thought of Cathy as a salt-of-the-earth horsewoman with little patience for the business end of things. But turns out she definitely has a bit of a shrewd marketer in her!" Maya held up the display. "I mean—look at this!"

Cal sighed, cupping the side of his head with his hand. "Believe me, I can't unsee it if I tried."

Maya chuckled as she continued to study the advert. To

say that Cal's photo was the most prominently displayed was an understatement. His bicep-baring pose was encased in a large circle that was front and center, with smaller circles surrounding him that contained pictures of the other men. The only thing missing was a string of blinking neon lights around his photo. Maya had no doubt that if such an adornment had been an option, Cathy would have personally slapped it on every display.

"Looks like you'll be the main course at Hunks for Horses," she teased.

"Poor Ed," Cal said as he allowed himself a quick glimpse of the photos. "He really *does* look like a meerkat."

Maya laughed, then gave a brief shrug of her shoulders. "That's okay. Meerkats are cute."

Cal's focus swiftly reverted back to Maya. "Does that mean you'll be rooting for a date with him instead of me at the fundraiser?"

Cal's brash question, coupled with an even brasher smile, left Maya sitting on the hot seat. Whether it was actually the seat that was hot, or herself, didn't matter. She needed to redirect the conversation—and fast.

"Here you go," the waitress said as she appeared at the table with a coffeepot in hand. Maya was used to caffeine coming to the rescue, but not quite like it did in this instance.

"Cheers," she said as she raised her mug to Cal's.

He toasted her back, either oblivious to her deliberate segue, or gallant enough to pretend otherwise.

"So, what do you think so far of Maplewood?" she asked, further cementing a change of subject.

"I can see why you like living here. You've got mountains, four beautiful seasons and so far the people seem very friendly. Maybe not as much as the horses—but close."

Maya sputtered on a sip of coffee. "Oh, that's too funny.

Well, we New Englanders do have a reputation of being a bit, shall we say, reserved with our friendliness. But I tend to think of it as kind of like the difference between dogs and cats."

Cal raised an amused eyebrow. "I *think* I know where you're going with this, but humor me anyway."

"Dogs like everyone, but cats—you have to earn their like. That's how it is with a lot of New Englanders. Or so they say…"

Cal leaned back in his chair, a devilish smile on his face. "So have I earned your like yet?"

This time, Maya choked on her coffee. Was he really going to go there? Still, as she caught a mischievous twinkle in his eye, it was clear he was keeping it lighthearted, so she decided to do the same. "I don't *dis*like you, so that's a start."

"Meow."

Maya laughed again. He certainly had a way of removing any *dis* from *dislike*.

"So, have you lived here your whole life?"

Maya nodded. "I have, except during my college years in upstate New York. It's beautiful up there, too, but this has always been home to me."

"What about siblings? Any brothers or sisters?"

"I'm an only child, believe it or not." Seeing the look of surprise on Cal's face, she added, "My parents wanted to have more kids, but it wasn't in the cards. I guess that's another reason why I've stayed in the area. When my mom passed away several years ago, it was incredibly hard on my dad—as I'm sure you can imagine. Jeremy and myself are all he has left."

In the crosshairs of Cal's intense gaze, Maya felt like he was sizing her up…and very much liking how the pieces fit together. "Your dad's lucky to have a daughter like you."

Maya smiled, both appreciative of the compliment and slightly uncomfortable being under a prolonged spotlight.

Time to flip the conversation around.

"So what about you? You said it yourself last night—that you've lived all over the world. Do you have a favorite place?"

"I haven't been *everywhere*, mind you," Cal said, looking upward as though conducting a quick inventory of previous residences.

"Yet," Maya replied with a wry grin.

"Let's see... Switzerland was pretty amazing."

"That doesn't surprise me," Maya said, instantly conjuring up images of alpine meadows strewn with wildflowers. "But do they have pure maple syrup made from local trees?"

Cal chuckled. "Not sure about that, to be honest. I only know about the watches and cheese."

Maya smirked. "What about Australia? Do you ever miss it? I imagine you must still have family there."

Cal's smile faded faster than Maya could say the words *wrong question* in her mind. But *why* was it wrong? It seemed like an innocuous-enough inquiry. Unless, of course, he in fact was harboring some dark secret from his past. She certainly hoped that wasn't the case.

"Are you ready to order?" the waitress asked as she suddenly appeared at the table.

Saved by the pancakes, Maya thought as Cal wasted no time relaying his order of pancakes, hash browns and orange juice to the waitress. He probably would have ordered fried rubber if it meant a chance to change the subject—or so it seemed.

When the conversation resumed a short time later, Maya made sure to skirt any potentially triggering subject matter.

So, nothing about my past or his. Maybe talk about the weather?

"I do love the cool autumn air," Cal said, unknowingly on cue.

Maya managed a half smile. "Remember that when 'cool' transitions to 'frigid.'"

Cal appeared nonplussed. "I had a four-month gig in Alaska at the height of winter a few years ago, so I'm prepared."

Maya struggled to maintain a smile in the midst of Cal's revelation. It should have been something that made her chuckle, but instead, she was filled with unease. Why did he feel the need to hop from one job—and hence, one place—to another? Was it truly a matter of benign wanderlust, or was there more to it than that?

She pushed her concerns aside for the sake of a peaceful outing.

"Can I get you anything else?" the waitress asked once they had finished their meals, approaching their table with a check in hand.

"We're all set, thanks," Maya said, opening her purse to grab her bank card.

"I've got this," Cal said as he reached for his wallet.

Maya held out her hand in the waitress's direction. "No, let me—"

"Actually," the waitress interjected. "The bill's been paid."

Maya and Cal exchanged surprised glances.

"By who?" Maya asked.

The waitress sported a conspiratorial grin as she pointed at a table toward the center of the café. Maya's eyes widened as a trio of young, attractive women waved in their direction. As one stood up, tossing her long honey-blond hair off her shoulders before making her way over, Maya felt her throat clamp shut.

"Uh-oh…" Cal said quietly under his breath. "Is it too late to hide under the table?"

Given that the woman was clearly a looker, Maya was secretly pleased by Cal's less-than-enthused observation.

Like a heat-seeking missile, Cal's admirer quickened her

step as she closed in on the table, her eyes laser-focused on the prize. The only thing missing was a big red bow on Cal's head.

"Hi there," she said to him, conveniently ignoring Maya as though she were merely an added condiment at the table. "I'm Susie."

Cal smiled, quickly glancing at Maya before shaking the slender, manicured hand before him. "Cal. Nice to meet you."

Susie's fake eyelashes fluttered like writhing centipedes around her widened eyes. "Oh, wow! Are you Australian? It doesn't say that in your write-up."

Cal looked about as comfortable as if he were sitting on a pincushion—minus the cushion. "I guess they were trying to keep the focus on the horses," he said with the slightest hint of impatience in his voice. But given that it was paired with a polite smile, his borderline annoyance seemed to sail over Susie's well-coiffed head.

"Oh, you're too funny," Susie said, reaching over to brush her hand over his forearm.

Maya's eyeballs popped out so hard that she half expected to hear them bounce off the tabletop.

Unfortunately, Susie wasn't quite finished. "Well, I came over here to let you know my friends and I are in town from New Jersey for another week—just in time to attend the fundraiser. In fact, we've already bought our tickets."

"That's great," Cal said with restrained enthusiasm. "Happy Hooves Horse Rescue will put the donations to good use."

Susie bent down to whisper in his ear. "I bought five tickets—which means five chances that I'll win a date with you."

Having honed her hearing to be almost on par with that of horses, Maya caught every overly inflected word.

Suddenly, Susie turned to her with narrowed raccoon eyes. In that moment, all Maya could think was how much she loved raccoons—as she did all critters—and that Susie should apologize to them for species misappropriation.

But before Maya had a chance to even silently react, Susie turned her attention back to Cal. "Um, you're single—right?"

Maya watched as Cal's Adam's apple rose and fell like a weighted ball in his throat. "I am," he replied…tersely? Sheepishly? Perhaps another adverb? Maya struggled to read into the tone of his response, but then quickly caught herself.

It doesn't matter… He's a temporary colleague who joined me for breakfast—end of story!

Which meant Susie could flirt all she wanted with Cal… and vice versa.

Not surprisingly, Susie seemed pleased with Cal's relationship status. "I just wanted to be sure the rescue isn't setting up a date with someone's husband, you know?" She play-slapped Cal's arm, then tossed her hair back over shoulder. "I'm silly like that."

Maya half rolled her eyes, straightening them out just in time to catch Cal's amused look in her direction.

Ten minutes later, Maya and Cal headed down the sidewalk to Maya's SUV.

"Are you sure you don't want be my fundraiser date and save me from that barracuda?" he asked.

"I don't know…she seems like your type," Maya deadpanned.

"*Pfftt!* Yeah…*no*."

Maya chuckled, perhaps enjoying his heated denial a little too much. "Your date will be the luck of the draw—remember? That's how these things work. Cathy will dip her hand into the bucket and pull out a name. It might be Susie, given that she's stacked the odds, or it might not."

"Hopefully not," Cal said between slightly clenched teeth.

"Besides, it's never a good thing for colleagues to cross that line."

Cal glanced at her sideways as they continued walking in sync. "What line are we talking about?"

Maya wasn't buying his feigned ignorance. "You know what I mean."

"We just had breakfast together. What's the harm in dinner—especially one that's for a good cause like Happy Hooves?" He paused just long enough for a subdued grin to cross his lips. "Or is it only meals with Vermont maple syrup that are allowed?"

Maya cast him an "okay, wise guy" look. "Just trust me on this." There was *so* much more she could say on the matter... but she also knew it was best to steer clear from anything too personal. Not that Cal, he of the "can't talk about my homeland" mantra, should have a problem with that, she thought pointedly.

Cal sighed inwardly as they turned a corner and continued walking toward the side street where Maya's SUV was parked. It wasn't that he didn't understand the obvious, which was that his fundraiser date would be determined by an anonymous piece of paper pulled out of a bucket. But boy, Maya had *really* jumped on the opportunity to squelch any possibility of them ever straying from a strictly-colleagues stance. Still, he wasn't about to let the matter drop altogether, if for no other reason than she looked so cute when she was annoyed.

"Well," he began as nonchalantly as possible, "since I have to pick the restaurant for my fundraiser date, can you at least suggest a few good ones in the area?" Silence. Followed by more silence. Cal cocked his head to the side in Maya's direction. "That wasn't a trick question, by the way."

She looked up at him. "I'm just trying to think of a place. There are a couple of nicer restaurants that come to mind, but one closed a year ago, and the other is under new ownership, so I can't vouch for how good it is now."

Cal sighed for effect. "Geez, you're not making this easy.

Don't worry—I'm not asking you out," he said, wondering if he sounded as unconvincing on this declaration as he felt. "Just looking for some restaurant recommendations. I mean, where did you go on your last date? I'm assuming not McDonald's."

Maya shot him a perturbed glance. "I haven't been on a date in a while. By choice," she added curtly. "I don't have time for that sort of thing right now."

Something about the sharpness behind Maya's reply told Cal that time wasn't the only thing holding her back from stepping out with a male companion. Still, he'd already witnessed enough to know that between a grueling clinic schedule and raising Jeremy as a single parent, she was doing her best to keep a number of plates spinning in the air. If anyone deserved a night to be wined and dined in an upscale venue, no work beeper or chore list in sight, it was Maya. And the fact that he'd be able to spend more one-on-one time with her without a pitchfork or a muddy pasture in sight? Well, that was just a bonus. Correction—a *huge* bonus.

All of which meant…if she wasn't going to agree to such a night out on the town willingly, then he'd need to find a more underhanded way to make it happen. But how?

Your date will be the luck of the draw—remember?

As Maya's earlier forceful reminder popped back into his thoughts, Cal nodded to himself and smiled.

"What's so funny?" she asked as she side-eyed him suspiciously.

He shrugged, his smile widening even more. "Nothing. Nothing at all."

Maya was glad that Cal had dropped the subject of dating on the drive back to the clinic. She still couldn't figure out whether he genuinely wanted to go on a date with her, fundraiser or otherwise, or if he'd been rattling her cage just to provoke a reaction. *I guess I gave him one*, she thought, wishing she could have more of a poker face—and attitude.

Truth was, his flirtatious manner left her feeling both elated and cautious. Elated because it indicated that her attraction to him was not one-sided. And cautious because she knew she had to maintain a strictly professional relationship. And while she trusted herself to do the right thing, that didn't mean it would be easy.

As she pulled into the clinic parking area, Maya was surprised to see her dad and Jeremy lingering outside the barn.

"It's my two favorite guys," she said as she headed over, with Cal close behind. "Is everything okay?"

"Everything's fine," Gus said with a smile. He turned to his grandson. "Jeremy here called me this morning to say he was bored and wanted to come see the horses."

"Jeremy!" Maya exclaimed with mock indignation, hand on her hip. "I asked if you wanted to come to the barn with me this morning, and you said no."

"I was still watching cartoons," he said matter-of-factly, eliciting all-around laughter.

"Say," Gus began, "I'm thinking of taking a ride to Carlisle Orchard to do some apple picking. Would you two like to join us?"

Maya couldn't help but notice how Jeremy looked at Cal, and not her, with almost visibly bated breath as he awaited an answer.

Cal seemed to realize this as well, glancing at Maya before replying to Gus. "Actually, I called Cathy earlier this morning to see if I could come by to work with Molly, so I'll be heading over there soon. But apple picking sounds fun. Maybe another time?"

Jeremy's face instantly lit up. "Can I go with you?" he asked eagerly, looking to Cal and then Maya.

"Honey, I'm sure Cal needs to focus one-on-one with Molly," Maya explained, doing her best to downplay her apprehension.

As Cal looked in her direction, she sensed he disagreed with her assumption, but was hesitant to step into a parental quagmire.

Maya's shoulders dropped. Was she making the right call for Jeremy? That's what mattered most in this moment. He had met Molly on more than one occasion, and each time had been clearly drawn to the timid mustang. Her fear-based, skittish behavior made her too unpredictable for Maya to allow Jeremy to ever have closer proximity than that afforded by a sturdy fence between them, but it hadn't dampened his fascination with her.

"You don't want me to go?" Jeremy asked Cal directly.

"It's fine with me," Cal said carefully. "But if your mum's not comfortable with the idea…"

"I'm sure Jeremy knows to give Cal space while he's working with Molly," Gus offered, turning to his grandson and adding, "Right?"

Jeremy nodded. "I won't get close—I'll just watch." He turned to Maya. "Please?"

Maya bit her bottom lip, feeling three sets of eyes staring at her intently.

Perhaps she needed to rethink her stance. Yes, she was trying to protect Jeremy from a repeat of what had happened with Max. But he was older now. And surely he knew that Cal was strictly her colleague, not also her boyfriend, as was the case with Max.

Plus, there was no possibility that this was going to change. Right?

I said, right?

Maya swallowed hard. Of course that was right. It wouldn't

be long before Cal was on to his next chapter in life. Or, maybe it was more like his next few pages. To complete a chapter, you had to actually commit to something. And that didn't seem to be part of his playbook.

"Mom?" Jeremy asked, snapping Maya out of her thoughts. "Can I go?"

Maya bunched her lips together as she looked at her son. He wanted this so badly, and it wasn't fair to deny him the opportunity to see a real horse whisperer in action.

Let go of the other stuff, she told herself.

"You can come, too," Cal said, sounding as though he hoped she would.

"I have a Maplewood Community Events Committee volunteer meeting at noon, so I won't be able to go. I can't miss planning for the October Harvest Fair, now can I?" She paused to grin, but also to push through her fears. "But you can go, Jeremy. Just make sure you listen to Cal. He's going to need some space and quiet to work with Molly, but you'll learn a lot just from watching him. I know I did the other day."

As Maya locked eyes with Cal, she could almost physically feel his appreciation—not to mention surprise—at her comment.

"Well, looks like I'll be picking apples by myself," Gus said with a one-sided grin.

"Do you want to come with us?" Cal asked.

"Appreciate the offer, but I'm craving a good McIntosh apple. Plus, if I know Cathy, she'll stick a pitchfork in my hand and put me to work instead."

Cal laughed, as did Maya. But as Cal and Jeremy drove off a short time later, she turned to her dad with angst in her eyes.

He hugged her shoulders from the side. "Relax, Maya. This will be good for Jeremy." When she didn't immediately respond, he hugged her even tighter. "I know what you're thinking."

"Do you?" she snapped, before shaking her head. "I'm sorry."

"Don't be. I understand. You don't want Jeremy getting too attached to Cal, but he's older now and I think he's looking at this as a chance to learn more about natural horsemanship. That's all."

Maya looked up at her dad and smiled. His eyes, both kind and wise, instantly helped blunt the edge of her worries.

"Besides," he added, "it'll be good for Jeremy to be around a strong male figure, someone he can aspire to."

Maya was about to point out that emulating someone who seemed incapable of putting down roots *anywhere* was probably not the best role model. But she knew what her dad meant. Jeremy loved horses, and had already talked about following in the family footsteps toward a career in equine medicine. If George were still here, he'd be that perfect male role model.

We'll skip over Max. But George wasn't here. And Cal *was*.

"You okay?" Gus asked, pulling Maya back to the present.

Maya looked up at him and smiled. "Yes," she replied, hoping she wouldn't live to regret her answer.

CHAPTER FOUR

Cal was a few minutes into the drive to Happy Hooves Horse Rescue when he glanced over at Jeremy, and it suddenly hit him: This was the first time as an adult that he could recall spending one-on-one time with someone who *wasn't* an adult.

He let that thought sink in, realizing how crazy it sounded—even to himself. It wasn't that he didn't like kids. Quite the opposite, actually. But the opportunity to spend some quality time with a child or even a young teen had never really presented itself. And the reason was quite simple. One had to have family in order to play the role of uncle or older cousin or brother.

He thought of previous romantic relationships, several of which he'd considered serious at the time...albeit serious by his "let's enjoy each other's company exclusively...while I'm here" standards. A couple of those women had young children, but even so, he hadn't been fully enough entwined in their lives to merit one-on-one outings.

Glancing to the side at Jeremy, he wondered what it would be like if he'd gotten a different start in life. Would he be settled down somewhere with a family of his own? He'd still be a horse vet—that was nonnegotiable. But would he be looking over to the passenger seat now at his own son or daughter? Would they share his love of horses, and perhaps be joining him for a horse sanctuary visit—just like Jeremy was now? Would their mother be like Maya—

Whoa!

Cal suddenly hit the brakes, as though trying to dodge a thought that was both disconcerting and unexpected. He'd never before even entertained the idea of having a family of his own, and yet suddenly, the notion had seeped into his psyche. *Could it be because—*

Cal cut off his own question, but not before an image of Maya flashed in his mind, perhaps providing an answer regardless.

"Sorry about that," he said, turning to Jeremy to make sure everything was okay.

"Was something in the road?"

"Yeah...it was, um, a squirrel, I think. But it ran off in time."

Even though the squirrel was fictional, Cal couldn't in good conscience suggest anything less than a safe getaway.

"Good," Jeremy said, looking back with eyes that were nearly translucent gray. *Just like Maya's.* Seeing those eyes made Cal feel as though Maya's essence was somehow in the truck with them. He found himself wishing that she was there in person, and swallowed hard as this revelation reverberated through him.

Pulling into the Happy Hooves parking area fifteen minutes later, Cal was grateful for the chance to hyperfocus on Molly. At the very least, it would keep his thoughts from wandering into off-limits territory.

"I see you brought a helper along," Cathy said as the trio convened in the aisle of the main barn. With a wink, she reached over and tousled Jeremy's hair. At least she didn't slap him on the rump like a prized yearling, Cal thought.

"He wants to learn the way of the force," Cal replied with a wink of his own.

"Lucky you," Cathy said to Jeremy. "You're learning from an equine Jedi Master."

Jeremy looked up at Cal and smiled. "Is Molly outside?" he asked, turning back to Cathy.

"She's in a smaller pasture today by herself. She finally made an attempt to approach the herd the other day, and Moxie and Storm bullied her away."

Cal's smile flattened out. He knew it was just normal horse behavior, an alpha mare and gelding asserting their top of the pecking order. Still, he wished Molly's first attempt at assimilation had gone smoother.

Looking down at Jeremy, he said, "Why don't you head out and say hi to Molly. But don't go inside the pasture," he added, having been given his marching orders on that subject by Maya earlier as he'd been getting ready to leave. "I'll be out in just a minute."

As Jeremy eagerly headed off, Cal turned to Cathy. "Say, Cathy, I wanted to ask you something."

She raised an eyebrow. "No, you can't back out of the Hunks for Horses fundraiser. Ticket sales are soaring, and we've had more than a few inquiries asking if you're actually just an AI-generated image created to boost sales."

Cal chuckled and shook his head. "So that's what the world's coming to. Nice."

Cathy grinned. "You have to understand—all the townsfolk know the other men who are being raffled off. They've never seen you before, and let's just say your picture's got some people champing at the bit."

Cal smirked at the horse analogy, but his amusement was short-lived as Cathy expounded further.

"In fact, there's one gal who's called here a few times offering a nice chunk of change if I rig the winner in her favor."

"Don't tell me her name is Susie."

Cathy cocked her head to the side. "As a matter fact, it is. Do you know her?"

"I ran into her at…" Cal paused, deciding the less that was said, the better. "Never mind. Let's just say she's the persistent type."

"I did get that," Cathy replied, her amused eyes reading his uncomfortable body language. Damn, it was hard to hide something from a horse person, he thought.

"Anyway—what were you going to ask me?"

Cal took a deep breath. *C'mon, buckaroo. You had this all worked out in your head just a few hours ago—remember? You can do this.*

He cleared his throat. "I was wondering if you'd be able to, uh…"

"Spit it out, boy!"

Cal jumped slightly in place, half expecting Cathy to pull a crop out from behind her back. It was now or never. "Okay, if I donate five hundred dollars to the rescue, would you make it so that Maya is the one who's drawn as my date?"

Cathy appeared momentarily frozen as Cal's question sank in. "Well, I'll be damned. You're trying to bribe me."

Cal's eyes bulged. "No—no, it's not like that! I was planning to donate the five hundred dollars regardless. But I just thought… I mean, it would be nice to take Maya out for a night on the town, that's all. I can see how hard she works, and after her injuries and all…"

Okay, I'll be quiet now, Cal thought as he pondered how far he'd plunged in Cathy's eyes.

She studied him closely for several moments. "You could just ask her out on a date, you know."

Cal sighed, his shoulders dropping. "Actually, I can't. Maya's made it clear that she has no interest in dating anyone, especially a colleague. Or maybe it's just me."

Cathy looked Cal up and down in a way that made him momentarily question whether he remembered to put on clothes. "Nah—it's not you."

"That's good," he replied, not sure what else he could say in the moment.

Cathy bunched her lips together and nodded. "I guess I shouldn't be surprised. She got burned badly by another vet in the practice."

"Oh...?" Cal knew it was none of his business, but the one-word comment still slipped out.

Cathy paused. "I probably shouldn't say anymore, since it's not my story to tell."

Cal pursed his lips together as he silently sucked in a breath. Of course. It *wasn't* any of his business, really. Well...maybe a *little*, given that whatever had happened with the other vet seemed to have deterred her from dating anyone—especially a colleague.

But as Jeremy raced back into the barn, a look of near terror in his eyes, that thought would have to wait.

"Something's wrong with Molly," he said breathlessly. "She's walking weird, and her head is like...it's stuck sideways."

The words hit Cal like a nail-spiked thunderbolt. This was not good. Not good at all.

He froze for all of a second, then ran out of the barn, with Cathy and Jeremy initially on his heels, until he quickly accelerated well beyond them.

"Whoa, girl," he said as he reached Molly, grabbing her halter to help steady her. To his gut-wrenching dismay, Jeremy hadn't been exaggerating. Molly looked at him through fearful eyes…but the fear was different this time. It was as if she knew that something was wrong with her body. He winced at her head tilt, so uncomfortable to even view, and he felt her muscle under his hand as he brushed it across her neck.

"I need a lead rope!" he called back, not taking his eyes off Molly as he did.

"Here!" Jeremy exclaimed a minute later, handing a rope to Cal. "Cathy called my mom."

"Good," Cal said as calmly as possible, hoping to stem any further fear or alarm on behalf of Jeremy. He'd intended for Cathy to enter the pasture with a rope and not Jeremy, but it was too late to change that now. "Why don't you go in front of me, just to be safe."

He snapped the hook onto Molly's halter, waiting for Jeremy to clear the area before slowly walking backward, gently coaxing Molly to follow. Her gait was both hesitant and shaky, like a drunk sailor trying to find his way back to the ship. Whatever was going on with Molly was neurological—of that, he was certain.

Still focusing his highly trained eyes on even the slightest movements or behavior that could provide diagnostic clues, Cal ran the possible scenarios through his mind. Mosquito-borne illnesses and rabies were the most obvious culprits, but he couldn't imagine Molly hadn't been vaccinated in the spring, as was typical. He'd confirm this with Cathy, but in the meantime, he wondered if Molly could have a head injury, although in the absence of other horses nearby, that seemed unlikely. Unless she'd been kicked earlier when she was out with the herd—another question he'd need to run by Cathy.

All of which left equine protozoal myeloencephalitis—or EPM, as it was most commonly known—high on the list of possibilities. Cal drew in a deep breath. At least EPM was not an absolute death sentence, unlike rabies and 90 percent of

EEE cases. A parasitic disease most commonly transmitted when a horse came into contact with opossum feces, EPM was survivable when caught early and treated aggressively. But even then, some horses were left with permanent neurological damage. And worse…no, *infinitely* more worse…some horses still perished despite medical intervention.

Let's not go there yet, Cal silently acknowledged, his lips pulled in tight.

"Maya's on her way," Cathy said as she slowly jogged toward him. At ten feet out, she gasped and bent down to grab her knees, her face ghostly pale as she breathed laboriously.

"Are you okay?" Cal asked, his head swiveling back and forth between Molly and Cathy.

She nodded, still bent over. "Just not used to moving this quick anymore, I guess."

"Try and take it easy," he said, knowing well that the current situation made that next to impossible. He waited a moment for Cathy to slowly straighten up, then said, "I'm bringing Molly into the barn. She has her own stall—right?"

"Yes, but there's an empty double box stall that might make it easier to work around her."

"Good—let's bring her in there."

"Is she going to be okay?" Jeremy asked as he approached Cal while he and Cathy slowly walked Molly to the barn. Cal was about to tell him to back away, then stopped. "Just stay on this side of me," he said gently, gesturing to his left side, as his right side faced Molly. She was in too compromised of a state to dangerously act out at this point, but as Cal saw the fear and concern in Jeremy's eyes, he momentarily held his breath. The last thing he wanted to do was make a promise he couldn't keep.

"We're going to do everything we can to help her," he said,

doubling down on reassurance in his voice. The statement was true—it was the outcome that was still up for grabs.

Cal had nearly completed a thorough physical exam of Molly when Cathy called out from her surveillance spot at the barn entrance. "Maya's here!"

Cal felt a surge of relief flow through him. It wasn't just from knowing there would now be two veterinary experts weighing in on Molly's condition. It was a recognition that Maya's presence *did* something to him. He wasn't sure exactly what, but only knew that he felt an unusual sense of *everything is going to be okay* when she was near.

"I got here as soon as I could," she said as she entered the stall, voice calm but eyes registering deep concern.

As Jeremy ran to her and threw his arms around her waist in a tight hug, Cal watched as she winced in pain from her still-tender ribs. "It's okay, honey," she said soothingly. "We're going to do everything we can for Molly."

Her eyes immediately locked on to Cal's. "Cathy gave me a rundown of Molly's symptoms on the drive over. What are you thinking? EPM?"

He nodded. "I assume she was vaccinated for triple E, West Nile and rabies—right?"

"Yes, in late May," Maya said quietly as she continued to closely examine Molly. She turned to Cathy. "How was she this morning?"

"Perfectly fine." Cathy's voice was laden with disbelief. "Whatever this is, it came on suddenly."

Maya took a deep breath, matching the tightness that Cal felt in his own chest. "That does make me question whether she had some kind of head injury."

Cal nodded, turning to Cathy. "You mentioned she was bullied by the other horses before you put her in a separate pasture. Is it possible she was kicked in the head or fell?"

Cathy shook her head. "I watched the whole interaction. It looked like Moxie got a nip in on Molly's rump when she turned to run off, but that's it. I immediately put her in her own turnout after that."

Maya glanced at Cal, her face strained. He knew there was a twofold reason for her angst. Concern for Molly, of course, but also for Jeremy, who was now bearing witness to a horse in neurological distress. He looked over as the young boy stood silently by, only the brief wringing of his hands indicating the true depth of his worry for the stricken mare. Should they ask him to wait outside? Cal pondered the thought for a quick moment, until recalling how he, too, had insisted on being present as a boy whenever the vet came around for a sick horse.

Cal let go of the breath that he'd been holding, reminding himself that as both a vet and a mother, Maya clearly knew what she was doing. If she felt Jeremy should be somewhere else right now, she'd have said as much.

Instead, he watched as she reached over and squeezed Jeremy's balled-up hand, looking into his eyes and holding on until his fingers relaxed. "You okay? You can wait in the truck while we—"

"No," Jeremy forcibly interjected, his eyes pleading with her. "I want to stay. *Please*."

Maya nodded, her tightened lips working overtime to push out a smile.

She turned to Cal, her eyes fraught with emotion, but her voice all business. "Let's draw some blood for serological testing, and do a spinal tap."

Cathy, who had been standing several feet away, her face grim with concern, broke her silence. "Can you detect EPM in the blood and spinal fluid?"

"Not the actual parasite, but antibodies from exposure," Cal explained. "If the exposure is very recent, there might not be any antibodies yet. If that's the case, we can retest in a week or two."

He gripped Molly's halter and steadied her with a firm hand on the outer right side of her neck as Maya rubbed an alcohol swab on the left side of the neck that faced them. She inserted the needle deftly into a vein, her turquoise cast in full view as she girded her left hand just above Molly's shoulder, then pulled back on the plunger. Crimson-red blood instantly pooled into the chamber.

The next fluid withdrawal would not be as easy. Spinal fluid could be collected from the cervical neck area or the back lumbar region of a horse, with the former method requiring general anesthesia and the latter standing sedation only. Opting for the less risky procedure—especially in the context of a stall versus a hospital setting—Maya administered an IV injection of detomidine hydrochloride, followed by a localized injection of lidocaine hydrochloride to numb the withdrawal area.

Once the sedative had taken hold, Cal shaved and cleaned a triangular patch between the L6 and S1 vertebrae, then palpated the juncture between the bones. As he slowly inserted an 18-gauge, six-inch-long needle into the spinal canal, Molly arched her back, a normal reaction to pressure that could still be felt despite adequate sedation.

The fluid withdrawal now complete, he handed the vial to Maya, her look of relief matching his own.

"Nicely done," she said, her eyes meeting his and conveying that the compliment was more than one vet admiring the skills of another. Perhaps she sensed his emotional involvement in Molly's plight, a shared desire to save the mare no matter what it took, but also a keen awareness of how Molly's fate would impact Jeremy. He'd worked with many other equine vets over the years, got along perfectly fine with most of them—a few know-it-alls being the exception—but never did he feel a deeper connection with a colleague like he felt now with Maya.

She carefully placed the vial in the carrying case next to the blood sample, then turned to Cathy, who'd been viewing the procedure from the far end of the stall. "I'll get this sent off to the lab ASAP."

"Do we wait for results before starting any medication?" Cathy asked.

"With suspected EPM, we typically start treating right away. Especially when the symptoms are this pronounced. The thing with testing is that it's not one hundred percent conclusive—even with the gold standard of testing both blood and spinal fluid, rather than just the blood."

Maya turned to Cal. "Do you agree?"

"Absolutely." Looking into Maya's soulful eyes, she could say that the moon was made of green cheese and he'd wholeheartedly agree. But take the mesmerizing effects of her presence out of the equation, and her treatment assessment was still entirely spot-on.

"This is ponazuril paste," Maya said, handing several tubes to Cathy. "Each tube contains seven days of treatment, but we'll start her on a triple loading dose today."

"How long will she be on this for?" Cathy asked.

"The normal course is twenty-eight days. It does cross the blood-brain barrier to directly target the parasite, but doesn't completely eradicate it. But what it doesn't get, Molly's immune system should be able to kick in and finish off."

"Hopefully," Cathy said quietly, reaching over to stroke Molly's flaxen mane. "The fact that she's even let me touch her right now is hard to believe."

Cal, too, had made a mental note of Molly's sudden transformation from skittish to subdued. Was it a side effect of her neurological impairment? He couldn't be sure. Or maybe she knew they were trying to help her. It wouldn't be the first time he'd witnessed an untrusting, hard-to-control horse turn docile when its life depended on human intervention.

"We'll also give her an injection of Banamine today, and I'll leave some Banamine paste with you to continue treating for seven days," Maya said, a syringe of the medication already in hand. A quick swab of Molly's neck, and it was administered within seconds.

"Do you have vitamin E on hand?" Cal asked.

Cathy nodded. "I do."

"You'll want to start her on a high dose of ten thousand IU per day."

Cathy raised her eyebrows. "Wow—that *is* high."

"I know," Cal conceded, "but it can help counteract some of the oxidative stress that EPM can cause."

"Well," Cathy began, lips curved upward into a wry smile. "Far be it for me to question advice from a Hunk for Horses."

Maya spit out a laugh at Cathy's tension-breaking comment. Cal chuckled as well, but his brief laughter ended as he spotted Jeremy out of the corner of his eye. Maya turned to Jeremy as well, as though sensing Cal's concern.

"You doing okay?" he asked as walked over to the far end of the stall and kneeled down next to him.

Jeremy nodded solemnly. "She's really sick, isn't she?"

Cal knew he needed to strike a balance between truthfulness and hope. But as he looked into Jeremy's distressed eyes, he felt compelled to let the pendulum swing more toward hope. "Yes, but your mom and I are doing everything to help her get better. And Cathy, too."

Out in the parking area, Cal approached Maya as she was straightening out supplies in the back of her work truck. "Need help with anything?"

She turned to him and smiled. "I'm good, thanks."

The sun caught golden highlights in her hair that he hadn't noticed before. He stared at her, both realizing he shouldn't be so obvious—and also not caring. Well, he *did* care…but not enough to look away. With her delicate features and petite, lithe body, she could easily be mistaken for a ballerina. Albeit…a ballerina in jeans, mud boots and a ponytail with a couple of wood shavings tacked on to the ends.

Cal held in a snicker at the thought, though he couldn't completely put the brakes on a smile.

Maya viewed him from slightly narrowed eyes. "What's so funny?"

"Nothing," he lied, knowing she would probably welcome the comparison to a ballerina like he would to a…well, the same. *I never did look good in tights...*

But Maya, however, in a dainty tutu? She'd knock that look out of the park. Even so, he'd take her natural, outdoorsy appearance over something so frilly and contrived any day of the week—hair shavings and all.

"Are we going home now?" Jeremy asked as he walked over, cutting into Cal's very enjoyable thoughts.

"I'm going to drop the sample vials off at FedEx on the way, and then we'll head back home," Maya replied as she shut the truck doors and turned to him. "And how about we make it a pizza night? I'll put an order in for delivery, extra cheese and mushrooms—your favorite. How's that sound?"

Jeremy looked up at her, his eyes widened. "Can Cal come over, too?"

Maya visibly stiffened at the question, but Cal couldn't blame her. He was feeling bunged up by the unexpected inquiry as well. Her eyes darted over to him, and they certainly weren't saying, *I'd love for you to join us.* More like, *I'd love if you could get me out of this predicament right now.* And so he did.

"I actually have plans tonight. But thanks." He forced a smile. "And enjoy the dinner. You can never go wrong when pizza's on the menu."

Seeing the near relief in Maya's eyes was hard to take, but Cal reminded himself there was a reason for her reaction. Her immediate nuclear family consisted of herself and Jeremy, and it was a tight-knit, treasured cocoon that had no room for an outsider like him.

Is that what I am? An outsider?

Cal's breath caught in his throat. Why was he even asking himself this? It wasn't a question he'd ever posed to himself before. And if he had, the answer would have been, *Yes, I am, thank you very much*. No shame. No regrets. No thought that it ever could be…or should be…anything different. The harsh reality clashed with what he felt had been a growing closeness as they worked in tandem earlier on Molly. Did he just imagine a deeper connection?

"Cal?"

Cal snapped back to attention as Maya's voice penetrated his runaway train of thought. "Sorry—did you say something?"

"Just that I'm on emergency call tonight, so I'll be looking in on Molly if things take a turn for the worse. But the fact that we got her started on ponazuril as soon as her symptoms were spotted… I feel reasonably confident that we caught things just in time."

Cal smiled and nodded. If he had displayed his true feelings, the smile would be curved downward…or flatlined, at the very least. Not that he didn't want to share Maya's optimism. But he'd seen enough of "things are looking good" scenarios that had boomeranged over the course of a night, to know that when it came to equine medicine, things could change on a dime. Still, he'd do his best to stay positive.

"Well, I guess I'll be heading out." It was hard to conjure

up a smile after everything that had happened earlier at Happy Hooves, but for Jeremy's sake, he managed to flash one his way. "Thanks for helping out today. You did good. Especially alerting us to the fact that something was off with Molly."

Maya peered down proudly at her son, then back to Cal. As she locked eyes with him, he wondered what she was thinking. It had to be *something*, because instead of looking away, she held his gaze. In fact...if he didn't know any better, it almost seemed as though she was having second thoughts about including him for dinner. *Almost.*

Then again, he reasoned, it had been a long, stressful day, and his powers of perception were probably not fully up to par.

Climbing into his truck, he waved out the window at Maya and Jeremy, then headed down the long, pebble-strewn driveway.

Maya watched as Cal's truck rambled past her and continued down the driveway. Moments later, it turned right onto the main road, then disappeared from view. She continued to stare straight ahead, trying to steady her roller-coaster thoughts. If she could will his truck backward like a reverse tractor beam, would she do so? That she was even posing this question to herself was just one step short of shocking.

You don't do casual. You know *this. Don't cross professional boundaries, and you and Jeremy will avoid getting attached.*

She turned to look at Jeremy, his solemn face grabbing her hard in the gut. She couldn't assume it had anything to do with Cal driving off...could she?

Perhaps he was lamenting Molly's situation. They were all feeling it. A beautiful mare, on the cusp of coming out of her shell, who was now facing a potentially deadly condition.

"Come on," she said to Jeremy as she squeezed his shoulder. "Jenna's coming by to feed everyone tonight, but how about we stop by the clinic and check in on the gang before heading home."

Jeremy looked up at her and nodded, the hint of a smile on his face. It wasn't much, but she'd take it. Because there was one other reason she could be smiling right now…and she just sent him away to eat a lonely dinner by himself.

CHAPTER FIVE

MAYA GRIPPED THE steering wheel of her truck as it hit a shallow pothole on a poorly lit back road in the town of Porterville. Twenty minutes earlier, she'd been roused from a relatively sound sleep after receiving a page from the Equine Associates after-hours answering service. It wasn't about Molly, who was now three days into her treatment, but rather a horse who had become cast in its stall. The most typical way that a horse became cast was when it rolled on the ground and up against a stall wall, rendering it unable to get back up on its feet.

As prey animals, horses panicked when they found themselves in such a vulnerable state, and Maya had seen more than her share of the self-inflicted injuries—sometimes grave—that resulted from a horse trying to kick its way free.

Which was why she was now wide awake and relieved that her GPS indicated she was one minute out from her destination. Turning onto a narrow dirt driveway, Maya drove up to a small parking area, her focused and alert eyes popping open to maximum width.

It can't be... she thought as she spotted what looked like Cal's truck directly in front of her headlights. Realizing how common dark blue trucks were in the area, Maya shook her head at the silliness of jumping to such an improbable conclusion.

Cal on the mind much?

Swinging the door open to her own truck, she quickly hopped out and gasped as she face-planted into something very solid.

"Whoa!" a familiar voice said as two strong hands reached out to steady her by the shoulders.

Her face now removed from Cal's chest, Maya looked up, eyes wider than the nearly full moon that hovered overhead. "Cal! What are you doing here?"

He greeted her with a smile and a minimal reply. "Helping you."

Maya shook her head in confusion. Something—no, *lots* of things—were not adding up. "How'd you know there's an emergency? The answering service has our schedule—that's why they called me tonight, not you."

"I asked them to notify me as well on your nights."

Maya's confusion was growing. "Wait...what?"

"Maya, your arm's still in a cast, and I'm going to hedge my bets that your ribs aren't fully healed yet, either. If you're going to pull up a kicking, one-thousand-pound horse, you're going to need my help."

He looked down at her cast-covered arm, and it was only then that Maya realized he was still holding on to her. There was no danger of her falling at this point, so she knew she should pull away. Except...*let's just stay here a little bit longer.*

As Cal locked eyes with her, he seemed equally unwilling to let go. "I mean, how in the world were you planning to do this on your own?" he asked softly.

She knew he had a point, but couldn't fully shelve her stubbornness. "If I couldn't do it with the owners' help, I was going to call the volunteer fire department."

He stared hard at her for several moments, and she couldn't tell if he was annoyed by her answer, or impressed. Maybe it was a little of both. Slowly, he broke into a smile. "I'm the only volunteer you'll need tonight."

Reminding herself that time was of the essence in any emergency, she took a step back and gently slipped out of his embrace. "I'm not sure what to say. Other than thank-you."

He grinned. "No need to thank me. Now, let's go save a horse."

Twenty minutes later, the grateful owners of Buttercup, a palomino mare, effusively thanked Maya and Cal as they all headed out of the barn. Cal wrapped up the rope that he and Maya had tied to Buttercup's lower legs in order to flip her over and away from the stall wall, enabling her to rise up on her own.

Walking to their vehicles, Maya thanked Cal again. He'd been right—how *would* she have been able to pull Buttercup up on her own? It was a reminder that even though she truly believed the human brain was the strongest muscle when interacting with horses, it certainly didn't hurt to have some brute strength on hand in physically challenging situations like this.

Arriving at their trucks, Maya paused as her pager vibrated against her hip. She pulled it off her belt and read the text.

"A colic case in Dearbon." She looked up at Cal, who had halted beside her. "This is so weird how emergencies seem to happen all at once. We'll go weeks without a single call, and then there'll be several in one night."

Cal looked up at the night sky. "No full moon, but I know what you mean. I've seen the same thing happen at other practices."

Standing oh-so-close to Cal, Maya could do little more in this moment than stare into his eyes. Because, well...why not? There might not be a full moon, but there was enough of a crescent glow to capture their unique hue. His gaze latched on to hers, and she felt something shoot through the entirety of her body. Electricity? Moonbeams? A combination of both?

With an eye squeeze and a headshake, she forcibly extracted herself from the almost hypnotic pull that Cal...or his eyes, or the moment itself...had on her.

An emergency was unfolding, and she needed to leave *now*.

Maya pulled her truck keys out of her jacket pocket. "Well, thanks again for your help. I'll see you in the morning."

Cal seemed almost amused by her announcement. He raised his eyebrows, lips twisted to one side as he flashed her a look that said, *Really?*

"Sorry—you can't get rid of me that easy."

Maya's heart skipped a beat, until it fully registered that he was strictly talking about emergency visits.

She shook her head. "No—I'm on call tonight, not you. Go home and get some rest."

"I'm already here, and there's no way I'm going back to bed when there's a horse who needs my help." With a twinkle in his eye, he nodded to Maya's cast-covered arm. "And perhaps a veterinarian who does, too."

Maya opened her mouth to protest, but nothing came out. Which both frustrated and surprised her. How could she say no to Cal's help, when they made such a good team?

It was nearly 4:00 a.m. when Maya and Cal walked back to their trucks in the Shady Acres Farm parking lot.

Zeus, an off-the-track Thoroughbred, was resting comfortably in his stall after an acute colic episode that had required pumping mineral oil into his stomach through a tube that had been inserted into his nose and snaked down into his gut.

"Another happy ending," Maya said, her voice sounding as fatigued as the rest of her. She opened the back of her truck and began loading equipment back into its place.

"My favorite kind," Cal said as he stood next to her. "Here, let me." He picked up a large metal pail with tubing and a hefty jug of mineral oil, and placed them back in their spots under a shelf on the right.

"I can lift that, you know," Maya said, not sure whether to be more annoyed or appreciative of his gallant gesture.

Cal casually shrugged, his reply equally nonchalant. "I know you can."

A simple observation, and yet one that prompted Maya to recall all the times that Max had taken the opposite stance, standing back and watching her struggle to lift something heavy. "You don't need special treatment," he'd say. Which had been true. *And yet...*

The recollections quickly shifted the scales in favor of appreciation for Cal's kindness.

Five minutes later, everything was packed up, and Maya closed the back of the truck. She turned to Cal, slightly unnerved to find that he'd been staring at her.

Say something, she chided herself—anything to override the awkwardness she felt.

She opted for a truthful observation. "At this point, I'm tired, but still wide-awake, if you know what I mean."

"I do." Cal cocked his head to the side, continuing to watch Maya intently. "You know, we're not far from my cabin. How about if I make us some breakfast? I don't have any maple syrup, but I've got coffee and..."

Oh boy, oh boy, oh boy, oh boy...

Maya's gulp nearly caught in her parched throat.

"Breakfast bars?" he continued in a questioning tone.

Another hard swallow. "What about them?"

"I have some," Cal said, a one-sided grin forming. "Blueberry strudel, I think. And coffee. Which I already said, but I'm repeating because I know it's your thing."

It was. But still, she couldn't answer.

Even under his jacket, Maya could see Cal's chest—his *fantastic* chest, which she imagined must be rippling with muscles—heave with...something. Anticipation? Exasperation?

Just keep heaving, she thought, before forcing herself to pry her eyes away.

Cal let out a slight sigh. "Look, I know what you said about colleagues not crossing the line. But this isn't a date. It's more like two tired vets who worked together all night to save some horses, just kicking back with a cup of coffee to reenergize and get ready for another day's work." He glanced at his watch. "It might still be dark now, but not for long."

Nope, thought Maya. *I can't do this. And I'm just going to tell it to him straight.*

She held her breath for a moment, then gave her answer. "Okay."

Cal grinned, his eyes wide with surprise.

I know how you feel, Maya wanted to say, wondering how the *no* in her brain had turned into a *yes* when it had exited her mouth.

"Follow me," Cal said as he nodded toward his truck.

As Maya watched Cal walk to his truck with an unassuming swagger...replaying all the ways he'd helped her tonight despite no obligation to do so...she wondered no more why *no* had been flipped on its head.

Colleagues just kicking back with coffee to reenergize for another day's work. I can't believe she bought that line.

Cal stopped short of letting out a *whoop whoop!* as he waited for Maya to pull her truck up behind his. She flashed her headlights, and he pulled out onto the main road.

Fifteen minutes later, he held the front door open to his cabin and waited for Maya to enter. As she passed by him, just inches away, he half closed his eyes as an enticing scent traveled with her like a portable floral breeze. How could anyone smell literally as fresh as a daisy after a full night of physically grueling work?

You can ponder that later. Because right now, his only concern was not screwing up the opportunity to get to know Maya better.

"Wow, this place is great," she said as she admired the cabin's rustic charm.

"Isn't it?" Cal agreed. "I guess for the rich guy who owns it, this is the equivalent of a tiny house that he visits once or twice a year. But for me, there's lots of space and a great loft upstairs. Plus, the deck." He nodded to the front of the cabin before rummaging through the cabinets for coffee and breakfast bars.

"I have a deck on my house, too. Well, more like a wraparound porch. But I can't imagine not having a spot like that to sit outside and just take in the peacefulness of nature."

Cal turned on the coffee maker and waited several seconds for the first percolating gurgle before turning back to Maya. "Glad you feel that way, because I thought we could have coffee out on the deck and watch the sun come up."

She stared at him, her expression momentarily frozen.

"Or…not," Cal said slowly.

Maya gave a quick shake of the head, as though tossing off her cautious hesitation. "No, that's fine."

Seated on the deck a short time later, Maya looked out to the purplish-black sky that hovered over the distant mountaintops.

"I'm sure you've seen your share of beautiful sunrises, given that you've lived all over the world," she said reflectively.

"I have. But the sunsets here have been pretty awesome. And sharing them with someone makes them that much more amazing."

Maya swung her head in his direction, a look on her face that said, *Did you just say that?*

He did, and it was a surprise to him, too. Not that he didn't actually feel this way, especially when—no, make that *only* when—this *someone* was Maya. But he had to be careful about oversharing his attraction to her. At least for the time being, given that he couldn't be sure where he fell in her eyes on the romantic spectrum of *not a chance in hell* on one end, and *I'm open to the possibility* on the other.

"Does Jeremy know when you leave during the night for an emergency?" A genuine question, but also the chance to redirect the conversation.

"It depends. I don't like to wake him on a school night, since he needs his sleep. But I might if I think there's a chance I'll still be gone when he gets up. I do text Carla, though. She lives in an apartment above my garage, and looks after Jeremy when I'm at work." Maya paused to take a sip of coffee, looking out wistfully as streaks of lighter violet emerged seemingly out of nowhere in the sky. "Pretty soon, he won't need anyone watching over him so closely. It's hard to believe how quickly he's growing up."

Cal smiled. He could almost viscerally feel Maya's love for her son. It was the way that it should be, even if his own experience was devoid of any such maternal bond.

"He's a great kid, and a natural around horses."

Maya seemed pleased by the observation. "Between my genes and his father's, I don't think he has a choice." She paused, as though wondering whether to say more. "You probably know from the picture in the office that he was a horse vet, too. He died when Jeremy was three years old."

Cal thought back to how he had assumed that Maya and her former husband were divorced. The tragic reality was so much more devastating, and he winced at the thought of what she must have gone through. "I'm so sorry, Maya."

She acknowledged his sympathy with a pained but appreciative smile. "I always tell myself that he died doing what he loved. He was heading out during the night to an emergency call and was hit by a drunk driver." Maya paused for several moments. "It was my night for emergencies, and he insisted on going instead."

"I'm sure he'd make that same decision all over again," he said quietly. He didn't know the man, but he *did* know—or was at least getting to know—Maya, and there was no way she wasn't harboring some undeserved guilt about how things had played out on that fateful night.

"You're probably right." Maya bent forward to pick up a breakfast bar off the plate, then took a bite. "Not bad," she said, an obvious attempt to segue into a less emotionally charged conversation topic.

Cal figured she'd have said the same if it tasted like cardboard—anything to change the subject. He readily played along, scooping up a breakfast bar and taking a good-sized bite. "Better than if I baked them myself, I can tell you that."

Maya laughed, and Cal felt his shoulders loosen up with relief. It was good to see her finally relax.

"Look," he said, pointing to the first golden rays that were peeking through the treetops to the east. "The sun's just starting to rise."

"Beautiful," Maya said softly. "The start of another day."

Cal lifted his mug of coffee and raised it in a toast. "To an even-keel, emergency-free day."

Maya grinned as she lightly clanged her mug against his. "I'll sip to that."

Their eyes met, and his gaze dropped to her lips. If he leaned in now and kissed those sweet, lovely lips…would she meet him halfway? A *quarter* of the way? Would she throw up a hand and stop him in his tracks?

Time stood still as more potential scenarios raced through his mind. She'd kiss him back hard. No—it would be a soft kiss…soft and lingering.

Wait. She had made it clear that she didn't want to cross that line, so maybe she'd kick him in the…

Bzzzzzzzzzzzz

Maya's vibrating pager pierced the silence, prompting both of them to jerk up straight in their chairs. For a split second, Cal wanted to thank the pager for putting the brakes on his dizzying overanalysis of a kiss. *What ever happened to simply seizing the moment?* But then, reality set in. If the pager was buzzing, then an emergency was heating up somewhere.

Maya pulled the pager from her belt clip, pausing to meet Cal's eyes. It was a momentary hesitation, but enough to convey to him that she knew where his thoughts had been heading. As in right smack onto her lips. Had her thoughts been going in the same direction? Cal couldn't tell, but right now, they needed to focus on other things.

"It's Molly," Maya said, looking up from the pager message, gray eyes clouded with concern.

Cal lurched from the chair. "Let's go."

He held out his hand to help Maya to her feet, but she was already standing. A moment of hesitation, then she reached out and clasped his hand. The touch lasted for only a second… actually three—yes, he was counting—but he'd take it in lieu of a kiss. To him, it was a sign of growing trust, and right now, that trumped everything.

CHAPTER SIX

"I'M SORRY. I know it's early," Cathy said as Maya and Cal exited the truck in the Happy Hooves parking area. Her eyes were both anxious and fatigued, and Maya wondered if she'd been making around-the-clock checks on Molly.

"That's okay," Maya said. "It's been a busy night for emergencies, so we were already up."

"What's going on?" Cal asked, a calmness in his voice that Maya knew masked his concern.

"She's having what looks like a seizure."

Maya didn't like the sound of that, and judging from the look on Cal's face, neither did he. "I'll get some phenobarbital," he said, heading to the truck.

"When did it start?" Maya asked.

"I'm not sure. Tonight was the first night that I didn't sleep out in the barn since this started. I mean, she seemed to be responding to the medication, so I thought we were out of the danger zone."

Hearing the distress in Cathy's voice, Maya reached over and gently squeezed her arm. "It's okay. You were right to think that."

Cathy drew in a deep breath as she allowed Maya's reassurance to sink in.

"But when I woke up at five thirty," she continued, "the first thing I did was head out to check on her. She was down in the stall, her whole body was just like…quivering. I called right away."

"I'm glad you did."

"In all my years, I've never seen a horse have a seizure before and it's…" Cathy's voice cracked before it dropped off altogether.

"I know," Maya said softly. "It's hard to witness, but just know that Molly is most likely completely unaware of what her body is doing, and isn't in any pain."

"It doesn't look that way," Cathy said, her voice slightly choked. "But I know they say the same when people have seizures. Do you know why this is happening?"

"EPM targets the spinal cord and brain, and that can lead to seizures."

"Even after the start of medication?"

This question wasn't so easy to answer. Maya had treated her share of EPM cases over the years, and when caught early like it had been with Molly, the disease typically didn't progress to seizures. But there were so many mitigating factors that played into the disease—into *any* disease—that Maya knew she could only make an educated guess at best.

"Ready?" Cal asked as he headed toward them, an injectable syringe in one hand and a carrying case with emergency supplies in the other.

Maya hadn't yet answered Cathy's question, but it would have to wait. The trio quickly headed to the barn, with Cal entering first into the stall. Molly was lying flat on her side, eyes closed and her entire body twitching wildly. He knelt down beside her, with Maya quickly dropping to her knees next to him.

Cathy was right, Maya thought. It was hard to see a horse in the throes of a seizure, even as an experienced vet. She briefly held her breath as Cal placed a hand on the mare's shoulder, sweeping upward to palpate the jugular vein in her neck. Maya watched closely as he injected the needle, pulling back on the plunger for the telltale sign of blood that he was in the vein, then administering the medication.

Almost instantly, the full-body twitching began to subside. Only when it stopped altogether did Maya feel it was safe to breathe.

Cal turned to her, relief in his eyes as he locked on to her gaze. But Molly wasn't out of the woods yet. In higher doses, phenobarbital was an effective sedative strong enough to function as anesthesia, but that wasn't its purpose today. They needed for Molly to fully come around and get back on her feet. Only then would Maya feel that Molly still had a fighting chance, and judging from Cal's furrowed brow, she knew he felt the same.

A minute passed, and then another. As Molly finally blinked open her eyes, Maya grabbed Cal's forearm in a mix of relief and excitement, then quickly let go.

Hands off the hunky vet, she reminded herself.

But the look in Cal's eyes as she released her grip—the same longing gaze that she had seen during their almost-kiss at his cabin—made it clear that the directive was hers alone. In fact, she half expected him to say *Hands* on *the vet, please?*

As Molly began to stir, Maya decided to shelve that thought for another time.

"That's it, girl," Cal said soothingly as Molly lifted her head.

It pained Maya to see how her head was still tilted to the right, a stark reminder of how EPM could wreak havoc on a horse's body through a myriad of neurological impairments. Hopefully, this symptom—along with the others—would improve as the treatment took hold. But Maya wasn't kidding herself. She knew Molly had a long road ahead of her. And right now, it wasn't clear if this was a journey she could even make. All it would take was another seizure and...

Maya bit down on her bottom lip to derail her worrisome thoughts. She looked up at Cal and immediately felt better. Where there was angst in her eyes, there was reassurance in his. *We'll help Molly get through this together.* And for the first time in years, she felt it wasn't such a bad thing having another vet by her side to help tackle a tough case.

"Oh, thank god!" Cathy exclaimed from just outside the stall as Molly kicked her forelegs out in front of her, then heaved herself up into a full stand.

"I second that!" Maya replied, exchanging a relieved glance with Cal.

He blew out a puff of air, then shook his head with a smile that widened from ear to ear. "I don't know about you, but I think I just held my breath for two minutes straight."

"Same here," Maya said, relief in her voice.

"I'm going to get some more shavings, make things nice and comfy for her," Cathy said.

Alone with Cal, Maya fought the urge to hug him over their shared relief that Molly was still hanging on. As she looked up at him, he reached over and brushed a lock of hair away from her eyes. "That was a close one," he said quietly, surprise registering on his face as Maya briefly clasped his hand before letting go.

Still, with Cal just inches away, she closed her eyes, leaning into the moment...both wishing that it was...and glad that it wasn't...more. A conflicting wish, true, but she had her guarded heart to thank for that.

A loud snort from Molly snapped Maya out of her dreamy state, her shared moment with Cal paused as together they turned to the mare and grappled with the latest setback. The lab test results that she'd received the night before confirmed

EPM. But if that was true, why wasn't Molly responding quicker to the treatment?

"I wonder if the issue is that coming from out West, she hasn't had the same exposure to the parasite," Cal said, as if reading her thoughts.

"Yes," Maya replied, quickly realizing that he was onto something. "In fact, not long ago I read up on a study that showed most horses in New England have been exposed to Sarcocystis neurona. Most never develop EPM symptoms, but they have a heightened immunity to the disease if they're ever exposed to it again. Molly most likely had zero immunity built up, so she's been hit that much harder."

"We may just need to give things more time," Cal said. "Let's stay the course, and hopefully things will start to turn around."

Outside the barn entrance, Cathy approached with a bag of shavings, which she promptly dropped to the ground before lobbing a teasing question at Cal.

"So are you ready for the Hunks for Horses fundraiser next weekend?" she asked, followed by a wink in Maya's direction.

"Is it that soon?" Cal replied beleagueredly, though he grinned just the same.

Maya let out a faint chuckle, which she quickly squelched as the image of Susie and her long, fluttering eyelashes flashed in her mind. No doubt she'd be just one of many overeager bidders at the event, all hankering to win a date with Cal. Which meant *someone* would soon be cozying up to dinner with him…but it wouldn't be Maya. She'd made sure of that right off the bat, buying a half dozen tickets from Cathy the day after Cal had been roped into participating—and insisting her name not be entered into the drawing.

"Afraid you might get paired with Santa Claus or the meerkat?" Cathy had asked at the time.

"No," Maya had said with a wry smirk. "Just want to steer clear of any complications in my life."

Cathy had raised a knowing eyebrow at the time, and as far as Maya was concerned, no further explanation was needed. Still…it didn't hurt to remind both present parties of her "leave me out of this" intentions.

"You put my tickets aside so they won't be added to the draw—right?"

"Of course," Cathy said, eyes wide and a smile so stilted that it looked like it had been propped open with invisible toothpicks as stilts.

"You're not going to be entered into the draw?" Cal asked, his elbow shooting out into Cathy's side. She hopped with a yelp, then resumed her wooden smile.

Maya narrowed her eyes at him. "Why are you nudging Cathy?"

Cal lifted his bent arm and stared at his elbow. "I did? Huh. It must've been a knee-jerk reaction."

"You mean an elbow-jerk," Cathy nervously corrected him.

Cal greeted her observation with a plastered smile. "Right."

Eyes further tapered to near slits, Maya looked at Cathy, then back to Cal. "You two are acting weird."

"Me?" they asked in unison.

"Yes, you. *Both* of you." Her sigh turned into a smile. "Well, call us if you need anything, Cathy."

"I will."

Maya looked at Cal, waiting for him to join her on the walk back to their ride. "You coming?"

"Actually, I'll meet you at the truck."

Maya's hackles were now raised to the point that they nearly lifted her off the ground. "Okayyyyy…"

"I need to talk to Cathy about what I should wear for the fundraiser," Cal further explained. Or so he apparently thought.

Maya twisted her mouth to the side, a *Yeah, right!* expression doing the talking for her.

"Seriously!" Cal exclaimed. "And I want it to be a surprise for you, too. Even though you're not actively participating in the name draw." He turned to Cathy. "I'm thinking maybe there might be some kind of sexy male vet costume like those female nurse ones, but I have other ideas, too."

"Fine," Maya said, shrugging her shoulders. "Just make sure it's something Susie will like."

She capped her observation off with a teasing-slash-bratty smile, and headed for the truck.

"That can't be the same Susie…"

Cal didn't let Cathy finish the question. "I have to make this quick," he said, one eye on Maya's truck across the way. "You never did answer me about calling Maya's name out in the drawing."

"How could I? Jeremy came running into the barn about Molly."

"I know." Cal softened his voice. He normally wasn't this relentless about…*anything*…but there was so much riding on Cathy's answer.

"What I didn't have a chance to tell you is what Maya just mentioned herself. She doesn't want to be entered in the draw."

Cal sighed, his shoulders slumping under the weight of defeat.

Cathy looked up, twisting her jaw as she silently pondered. "Although…"

Boom. Cal stood up straight, renewed with hope before he even knew what Cathy was about to propose.

"Oh, this is good," she said, shaking her head with a devious chuckle.

"Tell me!"

"Remember how I told you my niece takes care of social media for the rescue?"

Cal nodded, wondering where she could possibly be going with this.

"Well—and how do I say this nicely about my sister's daughter—she's a screwup."

Cal nearly choked on his amusement. "*What?*"

"Oh, you know how the younger generation is these days. Eyes glued twenty-four seven to their phones, unable to follow directions that a pet rat could master in two seconds. I know Maya's heard me gripe about how many times Charlene's messed things up, or forgot to post something that she promised to take care of. I put up with it because I can only afford to pay her peanuts, and so far, she's not made an issue of it."

Cal grinned. "That's what family's for."

Cathy half rolled her eyes. "I suppose."

"This is pretty funny...but I'm still not sure what this has to do with explaining to Maya how her name ended up being called at the drawing."

Cathy grinned. "I'm getting to that. All I have to do is tell her that Charlene was in charge of tickets, and that I told her to put Maya's aside and *not* add them to the bucket. In fact, I probably won't have to say any more than that, because she'll instantly assume Charlene messed that task up, too."

A smile slowly worked its way from ear to ear. "Cathy, you are brilliant."

"Stop flirting with me," Cathy pretend-growled, though her eyes added a one-word caveat: *Not*.

CHAPTER SEVEN

CAL STARED INTO the full-length bathroom mirror, then shook his head. That a rustic cabin would even have such a vanity contraption was one thing. But to be actually *using* it was another. And yet, here he was...turning his head from side to side to evaluate the angle of an Australian cowboy hat that rested on his head, and rolling his shirt sleeves up, then down, then up again.

Dude!

He stepped away from the mirror, irritated with himself, yet also on the verge of a chuckle. Had it really come to this? Preening in front of a mirror like a puffed-up peacock in the Aussie version of a Stetson, hoping to impress the girl? And not just *any* girl, mind you, but the one who'd been consuming his thoughts day and night. He hadn't *intended* for this to be the case, but the more time he spent around Maya, witnessing firsthand her fierce devotion to both her son and the horses in her care, it was impossible not to see that she was as beautiful on the inside as she was on the outside.

And now, he was a mere hour away from strutting across the stage at the Maplewood Grange, doing his best to feign surprise as Cathy called out Maya's name. And then what? Would Maya be glad for the "mistake" of having her name entered in the draw and landing a date with him? Furious instead? Cal sighed, realizing there was no point in overanalyzing the potential outcome. He'd find out soon enough.

Turning to leave the bathroom, he stopped and pivoted around to face the mirror once more. Tipping his hat, he murmured, "You got this, cowboy."

Then he rolled his eyes at himself and headed out the door.

Thirty minutes later, Cal peeked out from behind the thick stage curtains where he and the other fundraiser "horse hunks" had been milling about while waiting for the start of the draw. It was a full house, for sure, but there was only one audience member whose presence mattered to him.

Turning briefly back, Cal winced as the town sheriff lifted his plaid shirt out of his pants and patted a hairy stomach before rearranging the shirttails and tucking everything back in.

I didn't need to see that, he thought, before turning back to the mission at hand. Maya. He had to find where she was sitting. Not only to confirm she was here—even though she had promised when they had parted ways at the barn last night that she wouldn't miss the chance to witness his "Hunk for Horses debut," but also because just seeing her would put his mind at ease. And his body at…well, that was a thought that could wait for their date.

Suddenly, a hand shot up in the air. It was attached to a forearm stacked high in bejeweled bracelets that nearly blinded him as they reflected the harsh fluorescent lights above.

"Cal!" exclaimed an unfortunately all-too-familiar voice. "I see you!"

Cal lurched his head back and pulled the curtain panels shut with white-knuckle ferocity. How in the world had Susie recognized his one eyeball sticking out of the tiny opening?

A tap on the back of his shoulder nearly sent him flying out of his cowboy boots.

"Whoa! Jumpy much?" Cathy asked, one eyebrow raised in amusement as he whirled around to face her.

He held his breath, then allowed a smirk to form. "Not usually, but I am tonight."

"I can see that." She leaned in with a conspiratorial whisper. "Relax. Everything's going according to plan."

"But I don't see Maya out there."

"Don't worry—she's here. She offered to help set up refreshments, so she might be in the kitchen. I'll make sure she takes a seat in time for the big surprise."

Glancing at her watch, Cathy looked up and clapped her hands twice. "Okay, guys. It's showtime! Remember, this is all to benefit the horses. So if you need to flex a muscle or two for the women…" Cathy paused, surveying the less-than-strapping participants who circled around her. "Or, um, flex your wonderful personalities, then go for it."

"*You* can show some muscle," she quipped out of the side of her mouth to Cal. He grinned, though there was only one woman he wanted to impress. And something told him Maya preferred the not-so-showboaty type.

I hope Cal shows some muscle, Maya thought as she took her seat toward the back of the room. Reminding herself that *someone* was going to end up on a date with him, and it wasn't going to be her, Maya did an about-face. *Okay, keep everything buttoned and zipped, please.* After all, there was no need to tempt herself with what she couldn't have.

Feeling slightly embittered over her earlier decision to sit out the actual draw, Maya reminded herself why it had to be this way.

He's leaving in less than two months. You already like him way more than is good for you. You think *you can have a fling and not get attached, but girl...you know that's not true.*

"Blah, blah, blah, blah, blah."

"I'm sorry—did you say something?" asked a woman seated next to Maya.

Maya's cheeks grew hot at the realization that she'd been talking gibberish out loud. "Oh—hi, Mrs. King. I was, uh, reciting my grocery list to myself." She forced a smile. "Helps me remember things."

"I do the same," Mrs. King said with a chuckle. Dressed in a sharp navy-blue skirt suit, low-heeled shoes and with graying hair that was freshly curled and teased out into a lacquered helmet, the town seamstress—and fellow Maplewood Community Events Committee member—was at her usual regal best.

"Glad to see you here," Maya said, though substituting *surprised* for *glad* would probably be more accurate. "I can tell you firsthand that Happy Hooves Horse Rescue does some very important work."

"Well, I'm not much of a horse person, but I do try to support local charities."

Maya smiled. "Me too."

Mrs. King leaned in, her voice dropping down an octave. "Although, I have to say, when I got the flyer in the mail last week—that really sealed the deal for me."

Maya raised an eyebrow. "Oh?"

"Did you get a look at that horse vet who's in the draw?"

Maya's eyes bulged as the older woman licked her top lip and whispered, "Yummy."

The prim and proper Mrs. King...reduced to an overzealous admirer salivating on behalf of a Hunk for Horses. Maya let that sink in, concluding that she'd now officially seen it all.

"The flyer didn't mention what horse vet practice he works at. It's not yours—is it?"

Her jaw still partially ajar, Maya was relieved as Cathy took the stage to resounding applause that would've drowned out any potential answer. Maya pointed to the stage and clapped, nearly getting whacked in the head by a sturdy pocketbook as Mrs. King lifted her arms to join in the revelry.

One by one, Cathy introduced the Hunks…*er…participants*…drawing one name out of the bucket each time before moving on to the next.

When Susie's name was called, pairing her with Ed the Meerkat, Maya choked on a snicker. At least she was out of the running for Cal's draw, Maya thought, though poor Ed had no idea what he was in for. Judging from his ear-to-ear smile, however, he was more than game for whatever those monstrous eyelashes were bringing his way.

"And last but certainly not least," Cathy said into the handheld microphone after working her way through six back-to-back draws, "please give a hand for Cal Parker, our final Hunk for Horses participant tonight. Cal, do you have anything to say to this very eager audience?"

Cal lowered his head toward the microphone, dipping his hat as Maya swallowed hard. If ever there was a melding of gentlemanly manners with vibes that were sexy as…yeah, *that* word that rhymed with *muck*…then this was it.

"Just that I'm looking forward to my date with whoever is about to be picked from the bucket. And it means a lot to me knowing that the horses at Happy Hooves are benefiting from this very special event." He turned to Cathy. "Thanks for all you do."

Cathy's look of surprise was quickly followed up with a smile, and as she gestured with her free hand to Cal for the rapt audience, it took a moment for Maya to realize that her jaw was once again hovering just above the ground. But how else could she react when all around her, the normally staid townswomen—this was quaint, turn-back-the-clock Maplewood, after all—were practically climbing over each other to get to the ultimate prize?

Half expecting panties to start flying onto the stage, Maya could only hope that Mrs. King wasn't about to hike up her skirt and yank down a girdle.

Please...

But Maya's silent plea wasn't just about sparing herself a sight that would be hard to unsee. It was also an appeal to the universe.

Please don't let Cal like his chosen date too *much.*

Yes, it was a small and petty plea, Maya silently acknowledged, but she felt compelled to think it just the same.

"And the winner of a date with Cal is…"

Maya squeezed her eyes shut and dug her nails into her palm—anything to soften the blow.

"…Maya Evans!"

Maya opened her eyes, wondering why everyone was staring at her. For a second, she thought Cathy had called her name, but of course, that wasn't possible. Was there another Maya in the room? Maybe? Possibly?

"You lucky dog," Mrs. King whispered loudly in her ear as she leaned over.

Only then was Maya hit with reality. As Cal stared at her from the stage, a sexy, one-sided grin on his face, she revised that thought. A *smoldering, smoking-hot* reality. And a kind and compassionate one—qualities that might not be game changers for some women, but for her, they only added to Cal's attractiveness.

"Come on up here," Cathy said, waving Maya forward.

Maya nervously did as instructed, hoping her wobbly legs would survive the brief journey. Once the applause died down and Cathy announced that refreshments were about to served, Maya turned to the coconspirators.

"Can I have a word with both of you—privately, please?"

"Of course," Cathy said, exchanging a quick, wide-eyed glance with Cal. "But if this is about your name being called... you can thank Charlene for that. I told her you didn't want to be entered into the draw, and looks like she screwed up again."

Maya wasn't buying it for a second—especially after their strange behavior at the barn the other day. Now, it was all starting to make sense.

"Guys, I'm not dumb," she said, not sure whether to feel angry, annoyed...or maybe just a teensy-weensy bit thrilled that her earlier directive had been ignored.

"No...no you're not," Cal readily agreed, gazing into her eyes and dialing up the teensy-weensy by, oh, about a thousand notches.

Maya tried to stand her ground, not the easiest task when her roller-coaster feelings made her legs feel like spaghetti.

"Look, it's not the worst thing in the world—the two of us having dinner at a nice restaurant—is it?" Cal asked. "That's all this is."

Cathy tiptoed backward. "I think I just heard someone call my name. I'll catch up to you both later."

As she scurried off, Maya turned back to Cal. Their eyes once again met, but this time, they both slowly broke into a smile.

"That Charlene," Cal said with a feigned nonchalant shrug.

Maya grinned. "Yeah. That Charlene."

Okay, I think she's warming up to the idea, Cal thought as he gave silent thanks for the fact that she hadn't kicked in his kneecaps. In fact...if he didn't know any better, it *almost* looked like Maya wanted this dinner date as much as he did. And he wanted it a whole lot.

"So, I was looking online at restaurants the other night,

and I came across one that's at the top of Mount Chester. Real cozy, with a couple of fireplaces in the dining room, and everything is cooked fresh from scratch."

Maya cocked her head to the side and flashed a half smirk. "Hmm. You went through a lot of trouble finding the perfect restaurant, considering you had no idea whose name would be called."

Cal knew she was one step short of calling his bluff, but he was more than happy to play along. "You know, that's just how I am. I'm a do-your-homework kind of guy."

"Huh. I didn't know that about you."

"Well, we'll have to use this dinner to get to know each other better."

As Maya's eyes widened, Cal cleared his throat and quickly added, "I mean, by talking. As colleagues. Nothing like good conversation to go with dinner."

Maya nodded, her deer-in-the-headlights visage slowly dropping away. "I agree."

I have my work cut out for me, Cal thought as he held on to the hope that the dinner would be the first course of Maya seeing him as more than a fellow vet.

And then what?

Even he couldn't answer that question. But the fact that he was asking it? That alone was nothing short of groundbreaking.

Maya entered her living room, dropping first her purse on the couch, and then herself. The fundraiser had wrapped up an hour ago, and after some friendly mingling with various townsfolk, she'd decided to make a quick getaway.

Everything seemed to be happening so fast, and she needed some time alone to think. Her cats Willow and Sam were quickly on her lap, and she laughed softly as they pawed at each other while competing for her attention. The rigid cast on her left arm made it more difficult to pet them both simultaneously, but she managed to improvise by bending her left elbow back as far as she could.

"I can't wait to get this thing off," she said, as much to herself as to the cats. She closed her eyes, silently acknowledging that her date night with Cal was another thing she couldn't wait for…but this realization was fraught with mixed feelings. The more she got attached to him, the harder it was going to be when he left Maplewood—and her life—for good. And the clock was already ticking on that end point.

A short time later, she quietly entered Jeremy's room, watching his blissfully peaceful face as he slept, illuminated by moonlight that shone through the side window.

Her smile wavered as she recalled standing in this very spot two years ago, slipping into the room to kiss Jeremy good night, only to be greeted by his tearful face. Even now, as she recalled the questions he had asked, there was a sharp tightness in her chest.

Why did Max leave? Did I do something wrong?

Maya drew in a breath with such force that she feared the sound might wake her son. A few seconds passed, and relief set in as he continued to sleep.

She hated Max for breaking his heart. No—hate was too harmful of an emotion to hold onto. *I severely dislike what he did*, she revised in her thoughts. But still…some hate remained, only it was directed at herself, which somehow seemed more acceptable.

The truth was, Max had never made promises that he didn't keep. As their relationship evolved from strictly professional to also a romantic one, it had *seemed* like they were a family, just the three of them…but it was all an illusion. The word *forever* had never left his lips, so why had she assumed that's where things were headed?

She only knew one thing for certain at this point, which was that sometimes, the adage that "actions speak louder than words" was a load of bullcrap. Max had fully integrated himself into her and Jeremy's life like a husband and father, minus the official titles. And then, he was gone.

She couldn't—no, she *wouldn't*—make that mistake again.

The truth was, she could take care of herself. She'd had enough disappointment in recent years to know that if she were knocked down again, she'd manage to pick herself back up. Sure, she might get to the point of hanging a do-not-disturb sign off her heart, but she'd survive.

But Jeremy was still too young and vulnerable to have the rug pulled out from under him again. Instinctively, Maya turned her gaze toward the dresser against the far side wall. In an almost mystical fashion, as if to say, *Look here*, a moonbeam had settled upon a framed picture of George holding a two-year-old Jeremy. George was smiling ear to ear, the proud father that he was, and Jeremy's eyes were half closed as he giggled during the shot.

Maya remembered taking that photo as though it were yesterday. It had always pained her to read how children didn't start forming memories until three years old—the exact age when Jeremy had lost his dad. Still, every once in a while, Jeremy would recall a specific moment with George, and she was grateful that he had those few but precious recollections.

But his memories with Max? There were many…

Maya shuddered as she tore herself away from her thoughts. It had been a long day, and certainly an eventful night. She leaned over and kissed Jeremy on the forehead, just soft enough to silently wish him a good night's sleep, but not enough to wake him.

It's just dinner with Cal...it doesn't mean anything, she said in her thoughts over and over again as she quietly closed Jeremy's bedroom door, then headed to the bathroom to wash up before bed. Staring through weary eyes at her reflection in the bathroom mirror, Maya knew one thing for sure. She was never good at lying—and that included to herself.

Sitting at the kitchen table after heading back from the fundraiser, Cal closed his laptop and breathed a sigh of relief. His reservation at White Peaks Restaurant was still booked for Saturday night. Not that he had any reason to think otherwise, but there was so much riding on this date that he needed to be sure.

There was so much riding on this date?

Even though the conclusion originated in his own brain, Cal still felt surprised by its implications. Was this actually going to be a date...as in a *date* date? Would Maya even allow as much?

He closed his eyes, picturing a small, intimate table by the fireplace, the flames casting a warm, sensual glow over Maya's exquisite face, her petite hand entwined in his...their lips about to touch...

Aruuuuu rooo rooo roo!

Cal popped an eye open. *Really? A coyote just destroyed my fantasy?*

He twisted his mouth to the side as several other coyotes joined the chorus. Was this the Vermont version of serenading a romantic interest? If so, he might as well make the most of it. With that, he closed his eyes again, picking up where he'd left off and brushing his lips against Maya's, pulling her in closer and feeling her petite body press against his...

"Hoo boy!" he exclaimed out loud, standing up abruptly from the chair. He tugged at the top of his shirt, feeling hot under the collar...and under the rest of his clothes, for that matter.

Sliding open the deck door, he took a pocket of chilled air into his lungs. Not exactly a cold shower, but it would do. "Woo!"

His exclamation started up another round of coyote howls, and pent-up angst gave way to laughter.

Stepping fully out onto the deck, Cal stared up at the starry sky, not allowing himself to dodge the second half of his earlier declaration.

A lot is riding on the date.

What did he mean by that? It was pretty bad when one had to question one's own statement...*but here we are.* He certainly had been on dates in the past with women he'd met during temporary vet gigs at one place or another, and it was never something he had felt the need to analyze ahead of time. Or during or after, for that matter.

But something was different with Maya. Was it because she'd made it clear that she had no intention of crossing the line from colleagues to something more?

He let that thought simmer for a moment, then realized it went beyond this. In the past, he knew that if he struck up a relationship with someone, it was bound to end once he moved on to the next gig. And he was okay with that. No—more like he *preferred* that scenario. But he wasn't feeling those "here today, gone tomorrow" vibes right now.

You'll feel that way when it's time to leave. That's just who you are.

Words that in some warped way would have comforted him in the past. But now, they felt oddly out of sync.

CHAPTER EIGHT

JAW JUTTED FORWARD and lips curled around her teeth, Maya stared into the bathroom mirror as she applied rose-colored lipstick. Smacking her lips, she admired the results for all of two seconds, her smile quickly turning into a frown.

She wiped the color off with a tissue, then glided her go-to clear, fruit-flavored lip gloss in its place, instantly satisfied with the swap.

Hey—at least I changed out of my jeans and stable boots, she thought as she looked down at her formfitting burgundy cocktail dress.

As she entered the kitchen a short time later, Carla looked up from the stove, where she was tending to a sizzling stir-fry.

"I shouldn't be too late," Maya said, leaving out the unspoken addendum of *unless Cal kisses me, in which case, I won't be in a rush to come home.*

She nearly shuddered at her own thoughts.

Don't go there. Don't go there. Don't go there.

Carla smiled at her—almost a little too knowingly, Maya surmised.

"That's fine. Jeremy and I have a fun night planned. After dinner, we're going to watch the latest Marvel movie, and I've got some popcorn and cocoa lined up for when the munchies strike."

Maya smiled. "That sounds great." She paused, looking out

into the living room that opened from the kitchen. "Speaking of my little guy…where is he?"

"He's out playing with Rusty."

As if on cue, the front door at the far end of the living room flew open, and Jeremy and Rusty bounded inside.

"Look at you!" Maya said affectionately as Jeremy breathlessly made his way over, dirt caked on his cheek. Maya cocked her head to the side as she spotted a matching dirt patch on Rusty's nose. "Did you guys get in a mud-wrestling match?"

"We were running and I tripped, and Rusty was trying to nudge me up from the ground."

Maya petted the loyal golden retriever, who was now by her side. "What a good boy," she said affectionately. Rusty looked up at her with wide amber eyes, tongue hanging out in a rapid pant.

"Are you leaving for your date with Cal?" Jeremy asked matter-of-factly.

Maya's hand froze in midstroke of Rusty's silky fur. She swallowed down a gulp, and then another one. "It's not… I'm not…" Now *she* was the one sporting wide eyes with a nervous pant. "It's a fundraiser thing for Happy Hooves, that's all. Cal wanted to help the horses like Molly by being a participant, and my name was called in the draw. Just a…a weird coincidence."

Maya glanced over at Carla, who quickly diverted her gaze back to the stir-fry, a widening smirk on her face.

Great. Even Carla suspects something's up.

Jeremy shrugged, then looked down at Rusty. "Come on, I'll feed you now."

As the two trotted off, indifferent to the date-or-no-date debate, Maya laughed and shook her head. Spotting headlights closing in on the picture window facing the driveway, Maya caught her breath. Cal had arrived, and there was no turning back now. And what troubled her even more? She didn't *want* to turn back. *Uh-uh. Nope.*

"Enjoy your non-date," Carla said with a barely suppressed grin as Maya headed out the door.

"*Carla...*" Maya tried to sound ominous, but her pretend warning only made Carla's grin widen.

Cal pulled Maya's chair out at the restaurant and waited for her to be seated before pushing the chair back in. At least that was the plan, but his hands grabbed onto air as she scooted it back to the table herself. *We've got to work on this roll-out-the-red-carpet thing,* he surmised with a tinge of amusement, recalling how she similarly had hopped into his truck earlier in the evening before he'd had a chance to open the door for her.

When drinks arrived at the table ten minutes later, Cal raised his glass of beer. "To Happy Hooves."

Maya repeated the toast with a clink of her wineglass.

"So am I allowed to tell you that you look beautiful tonight?"

Maya blushed while simultaneously looking pleased by the compliment. "Thank you." She held up her cast. "I was worried about a color clash, but what the heck. Burgundy and turquoise are the new orange and black."

Her smile prompted a small crinkle on the side of her left eye that Cal found endearing. *No*—sexily *endearing*, he silently revised.

After the waiter came by to take their order, Cal took in his surroundings. It was hard to look away from Maya, but as her eyes scanned the dining room, he decided to do the same.

"This place is amazing," he said, nodding appreciatively at the warmly lit string lights, two roaring fireplaces, aromatic pumpkin candles and autumn-themed pine wreaths scattered about. "Have you been here before?"

"A few times."

Maya's reply was terser than Cal expected, and though he was curious to know more, he decided not to pry. He didn't have to.

"The last time I was here was with Max." Running her finger over the rim of her wineglass, Maya paused, as though debating whether to say more. "He was a vet at Northern Vermont Equine Associates, and we ended up in a relationship that lasted nearly two years. Another horse vet. I guess you could say I have a type."

Okay, now we're getting somewhere. He waited for her to elaborate, but was met with silence.

"So...did he leave the practice because the relationship ended?" he gently nudged.

"More like the other way around. I thought things were serious with us—enough so that I'd be a part of any major life decisions. Instead, he announced out of the blue one day that he'd been offered a position at a practice out in Texas. It was affiliated with a major university, so he'd have a prestigious teaching role as well. I mean, I did understand the allure of the position."

"Did he ask if you wanted to join him?"

"No, but in his defense, he already knew the answer. My home is here—and my work. Not that I couldn't leave my current practice for another. People change jobs all the time." She paused to flash a wry grin. "Not that I need to tell someone like *you* that."

"Ouch." Cal felt the pinch of that pointed poke...and liked it. He'd take a woman who spoke her mind any day over one who played "guess what I'm thinking" games as a side hobby.

"Anyway, point being, my dad built the practice from the ground up, and I couldn't imagine tossing it all aside to go chase after someone else's dream. *My* dream is here, the town

I grew up in, where I'm raising my son and I still have family, and clients that I love. I know this probably sounds way too provincial for some people, and I get it. But this is what makes me happy."

Cal nodded, his eyes still focused intently on Maya. Everything that she had just said made sense. She was happy here. She loved her job and was surrounded by family. But... was it just him who felt there was something missing from this equation? *Such as...oh, I don't know...a partner? Someone to share it with.*

Maya stared back at him with widening eyes. "What?" To *his* widened eyes, she added, "You look like you want to say something."

"Only that I can understand why you wouldn't want to leave here."

Maya silently assessed him, as though not entirely buying that he *could* understand her priorities.

"The worst part of Max's leaving was how it affected Jeremy," she said pensively.

Cal took a deep breath and leaned back in his chair. He obviously didn't know Max, not that he could possibly learn anything additional about the man that would raise him up from the depths of Loserville. But the fact that his actions hurt Jeremy? Yeah...that was an unforgivable offense.

"In some ways, it was harder on him losing Max than his own father," Maya continued, "but only because he was so young when George died. I always wonder what would have happened if I hadn't let him take my place for the emergency call. Would Jeremy still have both parents? Or..."

He knew what she was thinking, even though it remained unsaid: Would Jeremy have lost her to a drunk driver instead?

"But, I'll never know because he *did* take my place."

Cal could almost viscerally feel the undeserved guilt over

his death that he knew she'd been carrying around for years. "That's what good husbands do," he said quietly.

Maya seemed surprised by his comment. Maybe she didn't think he was capable of knowing what made a decent husband. *Fair enough.*

"When you showed up at the barn for Buttercup's emergency, it reminded me of George." Maya silently gasped, then gave a quick headshake. "I'm sorry—that didn't come out quite right."

"It's okay. I know what you're trying to say." *Kind of, sort of...*

"I'm glad, because you're two very different people in other ways."

In mid-lift of his beer glass, Cal paused, then decided to take a sip so as not to appear too taken aback. Still...*what did she mean by that?*

"You mean because I'm Australian?" he asked, unable to fully let go of the comment.

Maya seemed caught off guard by the question. "No, more like George loved his home and his family. He didn't have your adventurous spirit. That's all I meant."

"Oh." Cal was unsure how to feel about this observation, but he understood how she'd naturally arrived there. After all, how could he come across as anything but the antithesis of a dedicated family man, given that he'd never been able to stick around long enough for a permanent job or a place to put down roots?

Tearing away from his thoughts, Cal once again looked into Maya's eyes. She held his gaze, and he felt an unspoken understanding pass between them. He wondered if she was thinking what he was...and hoped this wasn't the case. Or was it best that she did? Because the last thing he'd ever want to do was hurt her, and right now, in his sea of thoughts, there was one that kept bobbing to the surface.

I am so not the kind of man that she wants or needs.

He was grateful when their meals arrived a short time later. Truth be told, his appetite had taken a hit as the conversation had veered toward conclusions—or one in particular—that left a bitter taste in his mouth. But at least with a plate of clam linguini in front of him, he could keep his mouth occupied with something other than his foot.

"So," Maya began, throwing a wrench, or more like a fork, in his plans to stay mum. "You did say this dinner was a chance to get to **know** each other better. I've had my turn on the confessional—now it's yours."

"I said that?"

A one-sided grin. "You did."

Cal squelched a grimace as his words came back to bite him in the butt. *Again.*

Still, he managed to actually sound almost gregarious in his reply. "There's nothing to say. My life has been boring."

Maya nearly spit out a sip of wine. "Says the guy who's lived all over the world and probably has a gal stashed away at every port."

Now it was Cal's turn to choke on his drink. "Uh…no, that's definitely not the case."

Maya playfully cocked her head to the side. "At every train station?"

Cal chuckled, partly out of amusement and partly to avoid having to explain his life choices. How could he *not* come across as an untethered stallion, galloping from one field or tundra to another, no mare deemed special enough to rein him in?

He inwardly rolled his eyes at himself. *Hey, you're a horse guy—what else are you going to use for an analogy? Cars?*

But Maya wasn't finished. "Come on. I thought we were going to be real with each other tonight. Not to mention that I spent three hundred dollars on Hunks for Horses tickets—including the one responsible for us being here right now." She paused, adding mischievously, "You know—because *Charlene* accidentally added it to the bucket."

"Okay, you're right," Cal finally acquiesced with a chuckle. "What do you want to know?"

Maya shrugged her slender shoulders, in more of a flirty than indifferent manner. "What makes Cal tick?"

A simple question, and yet Cal was stumped. In part because no one had ever asked him this before. And certainly not someone who'd captured his full attention like Maya had.

Should he cherry-pick what to tell her, given that there were far more sour than sweet cherries in his background? He pondered the question for a moment. He rarely shared much of his past with others. No—that wasn't quite accurate. He *never* did, and that included with women he'd dated in the past.

Not that some of them hadn't probed him to learn more. But what was the point of sharing such personal details with them? Better that they knew him as the life of the party, rather than a killjoy whose past could suck all the happiness out of a room.

But with Maya, something was different. She had a grounded, drama-free air about her that made him feel safe to open up. *Feel safe to open up?* Cal bristled at the thought. Now was not the time to psychoanalyze why he'd been a closed book with other people in his life, and now with Maya, he was ready to turn the page. Or at least skim through a foreword that touched upon his past.

The drug-addicted mother who had abandoned him at birth. The father he had never known. The string of foster homes where genuine love and care had been in short, if any, supply. And the one exception to all of this—his time on the horse ranch with Thomas and Mabel and a life-altering bond with a timid mustang named Flaxxie that had started out hopeful, but ultimately led to heartache.

When he finished, Maya stared at him in stunned silence. "Cal, that's just..." She paused, clearly still grappling with his unexpected revelations. "I had no idea."

"Not many people do," Cal said, a slight fib given it implied that at least a *few* other people were privy to his past. But that was a few more than the actual reality.

"I'm trying to think of what my life would be like if I hadn't had family like I do...and my brain simply can't go there. I can't imagine what it must be like not to feel that someone's looking out for you, no matter what." She paused, her face pained.

There was no way Cal was going to let *his* life circumstances bring Maya down. Which meant he needed to put a positive spin on things...and fast.

"You have nothing to be sorry for. In some ways, it's been my superpower."

Maya blinked hard with surprise. "What do you mean?"

"Don't get me wrong—I'm sure it's great to have the support system of a solid family, but not having that has its benefits, too. The decisions I make—the jobs I take, the places I live—are based on where I think I can make the biggest difference. I don't have to confer with anyone else before making a move. I can just do it."

Maya started to open her mouth as if to speak, then stopped.

Cal cocked his head slightly to the side. "Go ahead—you were going to say something."

"You're right. I was going to say that sounds lonely, but then I realized I was projecting my own feelings about things onto you. Like I said—you have an adventurous spirit. So why be tied down by anything...or anyone. Right?"

Coming from anyone else, this observation would have sounded like a thinly veiled insult. But Cal knew that Maya was genuinely trying to understand what motivated him in life. He'd avoided sharing such personal revelations over the years and now he knew why. No one would've had the capacity—or desire—to truly empathize with his past actions and decisions like Maya was demonstrating now.

"And I would imagine the situation with Molly has brought up a lot of painful memories for you," Maya said quietly.

Cal pursed his lips and nodded. "There's been a few times that I actually caught myself thinking that Molly is Flaxxie, which I know sounds crazy."

"It doesn't," Maya said gently. "You didn't have the happy ending that you should have had with Flaxxie, and it's going to mean that much more when Molly pulls through."

Cal wondered if Maya truly believed that Molly was on the road to a certain recovery, or if she was piling on the hope for all of their sakes—but especially his.

"So, what was it about coming here that drew you in?" Maya asked after a span of silence ensured. "And I mean to Vermont, and Northern Vermont Equine Associates."

"Well, I'd never been to New England before, and there were actually a few opportunities that I was looking into. But then I talked to your dad, and that really sealed the deal for me."

A slight smile formed on Maya's lips. "How so?"

"He talked about you, and how you were trying to almost single-handedly keep the practice running, despite having a broken arm and cracked ribs. I almost couldn't believe what I was hearing, to be honest. It's hard enough doing this job with no broken bones, never mind *with*."

Maya grinned. "No argument there."

"Plus, just hearing the worry and concern in his voice when

he talked about you. That's the kind of dad that everyone should have, and I felt I could really help out in this situation."

Maya met his eyes and held his gaze. He felt a tingling warmth travel the length of his body, and it wasn't from the pepper sauce on his green bean salad.

"I'm glad my dad didn't listen to me when I told him not to hire you."

Cal did a double take. Or maybe it was triple. "Seriously?"

Maya briefly chuckled at his reaction. "Don't take it personally. I hadn't met you yet, and let's just say I was a little apprehensive about having a new colleague encroach on my territory."

Cal raised an amused eyebrow. "Sounds like you've been picking up some alpha mare behaviors."

"Ha! You might be right about that."

Walking out to the parking lot forty minutes later after a shared dessert of maple-infused cheesecake, cognac-spiked coffee and more easy conversation borne out of their natural rapport, Cal stopped short of his truck and turned to Maya.

"So apparently there's a lookout tower at the very top of this mountain that's open twenty-four seven. It's a short drive from here. I thought maybe we could do some stargazing after this? It has a glass elevator, so you don't have to worry about climbing stairs in those four-inch heels."

Maya smiled nervously. "Three-inch heels," she said after a long pause. Though something told Cal her delayed answer had little to do with footwear aesthetics.

Maya let Cal's question float in the air as she tried to get her bearings. She'd been enjoying this night with Cal so much that she almost forgot a few hard truths behind it. Beginning with the fact that Monday morning, at exactly 8:00 a.m., she and Cal would be showing up at the clinic together, ready to start another day as colleagues.

Repeat after me. AS COLLEAGUES.

And what happened when colleagues became romantically involved? She grimaced at her own question. *Nothing good, I can tell you that.*

Still, despite her small inner voice that was seemingly being filtered through a megaphone, she felt compelled to dig into this some more.

What was the worst that could happen if—just this once—she approached things like Cal? Which meant fully realizing from the get-go that the situation between them was temporary. No hand-wringing about what would happen when he left, which was inevitable. No getting attached. Simply living in the moment, and when the moment ended, so did all the feelings.

Could she even do this? It was such a departure from who she was at her core. But maybe that's why she *needed* to switch things up, to get out of her comfort zone and peel back a layer of the protective shell that surrounded her.

And then…an image of Jeremy flashed in her mind. Because none of this was just about her. Far from it. Nor did she have to question whose needs mattered most—hers or her son's. Hands down, she had to do what was best for him. Case unequivocally closed.

She looked back at Cal, a pang in her side as she mentally prepared to shoot down his invitation. "I think I should call it a night. I told Jeremy I wouldn't be out late and…" Her voice trailed off.

Cal rolled his lips together as though trying to smile, but not quite getting there. "Of course. I understand."

Maya wondered if he actually did grasp her inner dilemma, but either way, he seemed to respect her decision. And she really couldn't ask for more than that.

As they resumed walking farther out into the parking lot, Cal looked up at the sky and pointed to a long purple nebula intertwined with streaks of light and stars.

"Wow—look at that."

Maya glanced upward. "The Milky Way. Amazing."

"Who needs an observation tower, I guess."

"Right?" Maya wondered if her one-word reply sounded as awkward as it felt.

Dropping her gaze from the sky, she looked back at Cal, trying to stay fully in the moment. But the moment was inextricably tied to the past. *Cal's* past. He had revealed things to her that she never would have imagined. Things that happened to him in his youth that could have turned him into a hard and bitter adult. He had neither of these qualities...but only because he'd chosen a path of self-reliance and spurned attachments of any kind. Could she blame him?

Staring into his eyes, she voiced the answer in her mind. *No.* A realization that only further cemented the need to avoid any attachment herself. And kissing him was not going to further that agenda. Not with the off-the-charts desire that was coursing through her body.

Change the subject. Look back up at the sky. Remove your lips from the scene—STAT!

Of course, Cal couldn't hear any of the hurried directives playing out in her mind. A good thing, given that he was apparently on course to kiss her lips, and nothing was holding him back.

He pulled her close, running his fingers through the back of her hair, pressing his hard, muscular chest against hers, kissing her lips slowly at first, and then more hungrily. She met his rhythm, then took it up a notch. He responded to her eagerness by pulling her closer, if that was even possible.

Her body went limp, and she began to teeter on heels with

legs that were far more used to stable boots. Sensing her unsteadiness, Cal picked up the slack...or more precisely, picked up *her*. Feet dangling several inches off the ground, their lips continued their dance, pulling away, brushing close, reengaging, again and again.

When Maya's feet touched the ground in what seemed like an eternity later, she could only manage to utter one word. "Wow."

Cal slowly grinned. "I second that."

"Ouch!" She leaned forward and grabbed her side as a sharp pain took hold.

"What's wrong? Are you okay?"

She drew in a deep breath. "Yes—strange. It's like I had a delayed reaction to my ribs being squeezed." Seeing the concern on his face, she quickly added, "Don't worry—I'm fine." A tentative pause, and then a smile. "It was worth a few seconds of fleeting rib pain."

As Cal's face softened, she wondered if it was a good idea to be indirectly encouraging more of the same. The uncrossable line had been crossed, and it was potentially a quick, straight path to go from a single kiss to so much more. But that didn't mean it was a journey she should take.

Looking back up at Cal, Maya saw anything but caution in Cal's eyes. *But he's not the one who's in danger of having his heart broken.* So she'd have to be the one to drive what happens next.

"Well, I most certainly got my money's worth with this... outing...tonight," she said softly, the word *date* unable to launch from her lips. Not after everything that had just played out in her mind.

Cal dipped his head slightly to the side, studying her through slightly squinted eyes as he sized up her words.

She should have known he'd be perceptive enough to pick up on what other men would've missed.

"Glad you enjoyed yourself," he said, reaching over to open the passenger door. "And at least this time, I can help you into the truck."

Maya smiled, but as he took her hand to boost her up into the raised seat, she looked away.

Don't let him see your eyes, she told herself. Because if it were true that eyes were windows to the soul, then he'd see how much she wished that circumstances could be otherwise.

CHAPTER NINE

THE ANXIOUS CALL from Cathy came late in the afternoon, not long after Maya and Cal had returned from a shared visit to a large horse farm several towns over for routine exams. What had initially seemed like a promising start to a near-certain recovery for Molly had begun to whittle away with day-by-day setbacks, and now with another seizure, she had taken a sharp turn for the worse.

Maya called over to Jeremy, who'd been dropped off earlier after school by Gus so he could accompany them for a recheck on Molly. But that was before she'd received the grave news.

"Jeremy, I think it's best that you stay here. Maria can watch you until Grandpa can pick you up. It doesn't sound good for Molly, and we might have to make a very difficult decision."

"I still want to see her," he said, his eyes glossy as he struggled to hold back tears.

Feeling another set of eyes upon her, Maya looked over at Cal. He was watching them both intently, and as his gaze locked on to hers, she knew he disagreed with the decision she'd just made.

I'm the parent, she wanted to say. But perhaps that was the crux of the problem. She was trying to protect Jeremy in the event that Molly would have to be euthanized. Even when it was done in the horse's best interest, when there were no other options and it was a means to end suffering, it was still a heart-wrenching task. This was true even for a very senior horse who had lived out a full and comfortable life up until the point when their body began to give out. But for a young horse in her prime like Molly? *You'll get used to it*, she'd been told in vet school. That was fifteen years ago…and there were still times that she'd hold in her tears just long enough to complete the end-of-life procedure, waiting until she was back in her truck before allowing the dam to break.

Maya turned back to Jeremy, weighing the pros and cons of allowing him to accompany her and Cal—and weighing them fast, knowing the clock was ticking. If they did have to put Molly down, he'd have a chance to say goodbye. That didn't mean he had to witness her final moments—they could figure all that out once they assessed the situation.

She reached over and squeezed his arm. "Okay, why don't you get in the truck, and Cal and I will join you in a second."

"I hope I'm doing the right thing," Maya said quietly as Cal came up to her side.

"I think you are. I know how difficult this is, but closure is just as important for kids as it is for us adults."

"I just keep hoping we'll discover something that we missed earlier…something that could turn things around."

"Me too. And we don't know yet that nothing can be done." He nodded to the truck. "Let's go see if we can pull off a miracle."

As Maya entered Molly's stall after a white-knuckle drive to the rescue, she knew that a miracle was probably not going to happen.

"I think that last seizure took everything she had," Cathy said quietly, her voice choking up as they all peered down at Molly, who was lying on her side, only the faintest rise in her chest indicating that she was still alive.

As Cal placed a comforting hand on Maya's shoulder, she

briefly closed her eyes and placed her hand on top of it. So many times in the course of her career, she'd had to make the most difficult decisions and be privy to the most heartbreaking scenes alone. But as their hands touched, she felt buoyed by Cal's strength—not just his physicality, but his emotional depth as well. Everyone in that stall right now was hurting badly over what had to be done, and he was right there in the thick of it with them.

"Is there anything else we can do?" Cathy asked, her face gaunt and pale.

"We've tried all the medications," Cal said, "She's just not responding to them in a way that most horses would."

Maya knew that there was always a subset of horses with EPM that continued to go downhill after commencing treatment. That Molly would be one of them was a fate too cruel for words.

"I don't want her to suffer anymore," Cathy said, no longer able to hold back tears.

Maya nodded, the professional in her putting a stoic face forward, the mother and horse lover in her inwardly struggling to maintain her composure.

She walked over to Jeremy and gently grasped both of his small hands. "Jeremy..."

She swallowed several times, struggling to say the words.

"You have to put Molly down," he said solemnly, saying them for her.

"Yes. We don't want her to suffer anymore. Do you want to say goodbye to her?"

As he wiped tears from his eyes, Maya felt like she'd been pummeled in the gut by a pair of unseen fists.

She held his hand as they walked over to Molly, then let go as he dropped to his knees beside her head.

"I love you, Molly," he said, leaning over and stroking her mane. "I'm so sorry this happened to you."

The sight was almost more than Maya could bear. She turned to Cal, his eyes as pained as hers as he watched the scene play out.

An eerie silence filled the stall, pierced at intervals by Jeremy's muffled sobs. Maya gently clasped his shoulders and turned him toward her.

"Honey, you don't have to stay for this. You said goodbye to Molly, and I know she heard you. You can wait in the truck—"

"I want to stay."

Maya nodded, the lump in her throat now the size of a hard plum. "Okay, why don't you go over and stand with Cathy."

As he joined Cathy against the left-facing stall wall, she wrapped her arm tightly around his side.

Cal was already placing the catheter in Molly's jugular vein when Maya turned her attention back to the mare. She pulled her vet bag over and took out a vial of detomidine, a sedative typically administered to calm a horse before the fatal dose of pentobarbital.

"Just in case," she said in a low voice between them. Though Molly was already fully subdued, the last thing she wanted was for her to suddenly begin to stir and then fight the effects of the pentobarbital. Not only did she not want this to define Molly's last moments, but she'd do anything to spare Jeremy from witnessing such a distressing sight.

Cal nodded in agreement, leaning back to give Maya room to inject the sedative into the catheter. She waited several moments, then prepared to administer a bolus of pentobarbital. Drawing 300 milligrams into the syringe, she momentarily closed her eyes, drawing on her dwindling reserves of willpower in order to carry out what needed to be done.

"Wait."

Maya's eyes sprung open with Cal's one-word directive. She followed his line of vision to where Jeremy stood, wiping his eyes with his sleeve as Cathy pulled him in even tighter.

"Cal…" she said quietly, her own heart aching beyond words. For Molly, for her son…

But she couldn't let Molly suffer any longer. Taking a deep breath, she positioned the needle to insert into the catheter. One push of the plunger, and Molly's suffering would end. This young, beautiful mare who had already been through so much in her short lifetime.

Maya stared at the plunger as time stood still. She could hear Jeremy's faint sniffles, like a stab in the heart. Had she made the right decision by letting him stay through the procedure?

Her hand, normally so steady in the direst of medical circumstances, shook slightly as she gripped the syringe.

You have no choice.

Doubling down to focus through tear-filled eyes, Maya placed her thumb against the plunger as she readied to expel its contents.

"I said wait!" Cal exclaimed.

This time, there was a flash of anger in Maya's eyes as she glared up at Cal. Why was he making this infinitely more difficult than it already was? He knew as well as she did that they had no choice but to carry out this devastating but necessary decision.

"There might be another way."

Maya didn't understand. "To euthanize her?"

"To save her."

As Cathy let out an audible gasp, Maya's breath caught in her throat. She glanced back at Jeremy, wondering why Cal would give her son false hope like this. *He should know better.*

"We know the medication was doing its job killing the parasite," Cal said, taking a step closer.

"And sometimes that's not enough." Maya's voice nearly cracked as she tried to hold everything together. "I've seen this before in severe EPM cases. It's the neurological damage that's left behind—that's what does these horses in."

She stroked Molly's flaxen mane, her unmoving yet still-pristine body making this moment feel all the more unfathomable. None of it made sense—not on a philosophical level, the age-old question of why life was sometimes so cruel. But it made sense from a veterinary medicine standpoint, as much as she wished it hadn't.

"I know," Cal said, his voice subdued yet strong at the same time. He kneeled down beside Molly and rested his hand on her neck, scanning the length of her with a sadness in his eyes. "But what if we could address the neurological issues?"

"We can't," Maya replied, more sharply than she intended. "I mean, we already tried that."

"With the usual drugs—yes. But what about something experimental? We've got nothing to lose at this point."

"Cal—we're out of time. We don't have months or years to wait for a drug to be developed that could change anything." She stared hard into his eyes. He *had* to know this. Why in the world was he tossing out crazy ideas?

"I know. But a drug already exists. Before my last gig in California, I worked for a few months at a large practice in Ohio. One of the vets also worked in research at a local agricultural university. They developed a drug—dorfamin—that repaired neurological damage in clinical trials."

Maya's heart skipped a beat. "For horses?"

"For cows. They were trying to find a cure for mad cow disease."

Maya's shoulders dropped. It wasn't the answer she hoped to hear, but Cal clearly didn't share her skepticism.

"I read through all the white papers and clinical data. It's legit, Maya. I won't go into the details—there's no time—but the mechanism of how the drug worked to reverse neurological damage in cows would theoretically be the same for horses."

"Is this drug available locally?"

"No," Cal said, his eyes darting to the side, as though he was searching for a viable solution. "It's still experimental and not on the market. That's why I didn't even think of it earlier." He pulled his phone out of the front pocket of his jeans and scrolled through the screen. "I still have Joe's number." He looked up, meeting Maya's eyes, then glanced over at Jeremy. Turning back to Maya, he said, "Let me go call him now."

She nodded, almost too numb by the sudden turn of events to react further.

"What's going on?" Cathy asked as Cal exited the stall to talk privately in the barn aisle.

Maya pulled her off to the side and quietly filled her in. Cathy's mouth was still agape as Cal reentered the stall.

"Okay," he said, pausing to take a deep breath.

It took great restraint for Maya not to shout, *What did you find out?*

"The drug still isn't on the market yet, but the patent was bought by a pharmaceutical company for further development."

"So it's not available?" Cathy asked, echoing Maya's silent conclusion.

"Joe said he has an in with the drugmaker and can get us enough medication for a full course of treatment. But it will cost five thousand dollars. He said there's no way around that, now that they officially own the patent."

Cathy shook her head with disgust. "Typical pharmaceutical

company price gouging. Bastards." She shook her head again, then looked back up at Maya and Cal. "I don't have that kind of money. Between stocking up on enough hay for winter, and paying a contractor to put a new roof on the second barn, all the fundraiser money has already been spent. And even if I ran another fundraiser just for this, I wouldn't be able to raise the full amount in time."

She looked down at Molly's seemingly lifeless body, her breath so slow and shallow that it escaped limited human perception. "I'm not a vet obviously, but she would need to be treated, like...*now*."

"I have the money," Cal said, as Maya jerked her head up. There was a collective gasp as Maya and Cathy reacted to Cal's shocking announcement.

"Cal! You can't..." Maya's voice dropped off.

"Can't what?" he asked with quiet forcefulness. "Spend my money on what I want? *This* is what I want."

"Wait." Maya's head was beyond spinning as she tried to piece together the logistics of making a potential miracle happen. "Even if you pay for it, I don't see how we'd get it in time."

"It's an hour's plane ride to Ohio."

Maya's mouth dropped open. Whatever the word was for *crazy times ten*...that's where this situation had landed. She drew in a deep breath, knowing she needed to stay calm and collected—not the easiest of feats under the circumstances.

"The airport is an hour away. And I'm not trying to be a Negative Nelly here, but the chances of there being a direct flight to Ohio today are pretty slim." She looked down at Molly, not wanting to lose sight of what truly was at stake. Her life. The chance for survival, which, only several minutes ago, was nonexistent. Maybe it was still too much to hope for...

"There's a small local airport twenty minutes from here," Cal said, cutting into her thoughts. "I know because I looked into it when I decided to take this job. I have a pilot's license, and they rent out single-engine planes."

It took a moment for Maya to reply as she tried to wrap her head around yet another *where did this come from?* revelation.

"Is there something else I should know about you?" she asked, dumbfounded. "Are you also a secret intelligence agent in your spare time?"

Cal revealed the hint of a smile, which, given the gravity of the situation, was the most that anyone could muster in the moment. "Joe said there's a landing strip in one of the fields at the university. They use it to fly in agricultural supplies. He'll meet us there with the medication. If we leave now, we can be back here in a few hours." He paused. "There's just one thing."

"What?" Maya asked.

"Given that I'm here on a work visa, it's possible there'll be some red tape to cut through before they allow me to rent a plane. I mean…maybe not, but I don't want to take any chances. If one of you comes with me, it could help move things along."

"I'll go," Cathy offered. She turned to Maya. "That way, you can keep an eye on Molly. I wouldn't know what to do if things take a turn for the worse."

Maya wasn't sure how things could possibly get more critical for Molly, but she understood where Cathy was coming from. Still, without the medication, all hope was lost—so securing it needed to be the top priority now.

"Thanks, Cathy. But I think I should go—only because I can show my practice credentials and that might give us an edge if there's an issue." She paused, directing her gaze at Cathy and then Cal. "Hopefully, there's a horse lover or two working at the airport today."

Cal pulled his lips together in a tight smile as he nodded.

"What about Molly?" Cathy asked, her voice shaky with a mix of worry and optimistic excitement.

Maya pulled her phone out of her jacket pocket, scrolled to her father's number and waited several rings for the call to be answered.

"Hey, Maya—"

"Dad, how soon can you get to Happy Hooves?" she hurriedly interjected.

"I can leave now." There was a several-second pause before he asked, "Is everything okay?"

"Yes...sort of. It's kind of a long story, but Cathy will fill you in when you get here. Jeremy's here, too."

A quick thank-you and goodbye, and then Maya turned to Cathy. "My dad will know what to do once you give him the background of what's going on. We don't want to oversedate Molly, so once it starts to wear off, he'll need to monitor her and keep her safe until we get back."

Jeremy...

In the midst of one new development bubbling up after another, Maya's attention had unintentionally been diverted from her son. A pang of guilt gripped her as she hurried over to him and wrapped him in a tight hug. "Grandpa's going to be here soon."

"Can you and Cal save Molly?"

Another grab at her gut, this one provoked by the possibility that she was only prolonging an inevitable sad ending.

"We're going to try. But Jeremy, Molly is very, very sick, and the drug we're going to get might not be enough to turn things around. But Cal thinks there's a possibility it could work, so we want to give her that chance."

He nodded, understanding emanating from his light gray eyes. Maybe he was more attuned to the oftentimes fast-shifting realities of life than she gave him credit for.

"I love you," she said, leaning in and kissing him on the forehead. His hair smelled fruity, and she smiled at the realization that he had been using her shampoo again, rather than his own ocean-breeze soap-and-shampoo combo, made especially for kids. Not that she could blame him. Who didn't want to smell like fresh strawberries?

"I love you, too."

She stood up and turned to Cal. "Ready?"

He nodded, opening the stall gate to leave, then abruptly turning around. As he went to kneel by Molly, running his hand across her side, Maya joined him.

"She looks so beautiful and peaceful," she said quietly. "It's hard to believe…"

As Cal reached over and placed his hand over hers, Maya's breath caught in her throat. She felt his strength run through her. Strength of conviction. Strength of hope. And just plain… *strength*. That of the physical kind, a solid warmth that enveloped her entire hand. And suddenly, in this make-or-break moment with Molly's life hanging in the balance and so much on the line…she felt she could handle whatever the outcome would be. They'd celebrate a miracle together—her hope against hope—or they'd lean on each other to get through the heartbreak.

As a thought entered her head that she might be expecting more from Cal than he could give, she pushed it away. *Not now.* And when that thought returned, as it inevitably would? She'd deal with it then.

Cal radioed into Vermont's North Central Airport, advising the control tower that headwinds had put him fifteen minutes ahead of schedule.

Just over three hours had passed since he and Maya had left—or more like raced—from Happy Hooves Horse Rescue, and it had been the fastest, and yet longest, three hours of his life.

So far, everything had gone according to plan—a miracle in itself given that the plan had been whipped up last minute, or more precisely, last second. With Maya by his side, they had breezed through the plane rental logistics, careening down the grassy landing strip at the University of Ohio one hour and eighteen minutes later.

Joe and several of his medical research team were waiting for them, and after a quick exchange and instructions, Cal and Maya were once again looking over the clouds.

He turned to her now, greeted by her long, dark ash-brown hair as she faced the side window. Silence had filled the cockpit for most of the departing flight, and now that they were three-quarters of the way back, he was itching the break the impasse.

"You're being very quiet."

She turned to him and forced a smile. "I'm just enjoying the scenery."

He raised an eyebrow. "You mean the cloud cover?" Which was more or less his way of saying, *Um...no, you're not.*

He waited for her to reply, and then waited some more. "I know you're worried that I'm giving Jeremy false hope."

Maya turned to him again, and this time her eyes flashed with emotion. Whether it was anger or worry, he couldn't tell. Maybe it was a bit of both. "*Are* you giving him false hope?" she asked, her voice quiet yet sharp at the same time.

Cal closed his eyes for a moment, wondering how to answer her question. Not because he was trying to sugarcoat reality, but because there was no way he could definitively answer that question. No one could.

"I can't say for certain that this drug will save Molly. When it comes to medicine, nothing is foolproof, whether it's experimental or a staple that's been around for fifty years. But I wouldn't have suggested this treatment if I didn't think it could possibly work."

He quietly sighed, knowing that his answer, though truthful, didn't directly address Maya's question. If only he could express the depths of his own emotions right now, he thought. But it was a chasm so deep that he wouldn't even know where to start.

"I saw you look at Jeremy right before I was about to administer the pentobarbital. Would you have suggested this experimental option if he hadn't been there?"

Cal took in a deep breath. "I don't know." He turned to her again, searching her eyes. "To be honest, I'm not sure if trying this other drug would've even occurred to me. Like I said, it's not on the market and it wasn't developed specifically for horses. But then I saw Jeremy crying...and it took me back to being that boy myself. I knew what he was feeling in that moment, thinking that Molly wasn't going to make it. The same, most horrible feeling that I had when Flaxxie disappeared and I wasn't able to find her. I know not all kids get attached to animals like I did, but I see that same quality in Jeremy. And I was thinking in that moment, I would do anything—*anything*—to save Molly's life, and to spare him that pain." He paused, his eyes boring into hers. "And to spare *you* that pain as his mother. And that's when this other drug suddenly popped into my head."

She held his gaze for several moments, then pursed her lips and nodded slightly. "Jeremy's a lot like me in how he naturally bonds to animals. I was the same way as a kid. I think I had more animal friends than human ones. Something tells me you might have been the same."

"For sure."

"I'm still like that, actually. It's easy to trust animals, to know their love is pure and unconditional. It's not always that way with people." Maya paused, as though briefly reliving some of the disappointments that had fueled this conclusion, then looked back at Cal. "But I'd say you're about as close to a horse in my eyes as a human can get."

Cal's breath caught in his throat, but as Maya slowly began to smile, he felt the mood lighten. "I don't think I've ever been paid a higher compliment," he said with a grin. And he meant it.

Still, he could see the effort behind Maya's smile, the anxiousness that hadn't left her eyes. He reached over and clasped her small hand. It tensed up in a ball underneath his grasp, then slowly relaxed.

"It's going to be okay, Maya," he said quietly, ignoring the small inner voice that warned him not to make promises he couldn't keep.

"I don't know the ins and outs of this treatment like you do, but I do know it might not work."

Cal felt his insides plummet, as though the plane had just taken a nosedive. But it was staying the course, and only his fears of future regret were heading into a death spiral.

"But the fact that you're going out on a limb like this to try it," Maya continued. "Spending your personal money and flying a plane yourself to pick it up... I just want you to know that I'm grateful for what you're doing. Maybe this *will* save Molly's life." She paused, her eyes locked intently on his. "And I know you did this for Jeremy's sake, too. That means a lot to me."

Cal wondered if Maya could see him visibly breathe a sigh of relief. Truth was, he had no qualms about putting a dent in his bank account to pay for the medicine. Many of his temporary gigs had included housing arrangements, which meant he'd been able to squirrel away most of his paychecks, and had a nice little nest egg to show for it. It was just money. And if it could buy Molly a second chance—something that he never had with Flaxxie, as much he'd wished had been the case so many times in the years since—then he'd happily spend every dime he had left.

He still had no way to know whether the drug would perform a late-stage miracle for Molly. But he *did* know that Maya was now on his side. Maybe she had been all along, but her protective instincts as a mother made her take pause at everything that had so quickly transpired. He couldn't blame her. If he were a father, he'd react the same way.

If I was a father...

Cal clenched his jaw as this thought reverberated in his head. He of all people should know that sometimes biological parents fell short—if they showed up at all—and those who stepped into the role could make all the difference in the life of a child.

And though he realized now might not be the best time to question his life choices, his brain took things one step further as he envisioned himself teaching Jeremy the ways of natural horsemanship with a fully healed Molly... Maya watching the three of them while leaning her arms over a fence, the biggest smile on her face...

Cal squeezed his eyes shut just long enough to bring himself back to the present. He turned to Maya, and this time, she was already facing him. As their eyes locked, her lips curved upward just enough to form the kind of smile that said *We're in this together.*

And suddenly, he no longer wondered why he'd been questioning his life choices.

CHAPTER TEN

CAL'S TRUCK HAD barely come to a stop before Maya threw open the passenger door and bolted out. She had already talked to her dad on the drive back from the airport, confirming that Molly was still hanging on. But she had suffered another seizure, and time was running out.

"Hurry!" she yelled back to Cal, despite knowing well that he didn't need to be prodded.

As she entered Molly's stall, her dad looked up, his expression grave. He glanced at Jeremy, still in the same spot against the stall wall with Cathy by his side, then back to Maya. She knew her dad didn't want to say anything too dire in front of Jeremy, but perhaps it was too late to pretend that this was no less than a life-or-death gamble.

Cathy's arm was wrapped tightly around Jeremy, and Maya managed an anxious smile in her direction to show her appreciation for looking after him in her absence.

"She's stable," Gus said in hushed tones as he ran a stethoscope over Molly's ribs, "or as stable as she can be, given her condition. I wasn't sure she was going to survive another seizure."

"Did you give more sedative?"

He nodded. "Forty-five minutes ago."

Maya bent down next to Molly and stroked her mane. She could almost feel the precarious dip in her life force, but *some-*

thing was still there. It was as if Molly knew they were trying to help her, and was clinging to life just long enough for them to return with the dorfamin.

Out of the corner of her eye, Maya could see that Cal had entered the stall and was setting up a portable IV infusion stand. "Four bags at a flow rate of eight hundred milligrams per hour," he said.

Gus looked up as he silently did the math in his head. "So roughly five hours."

"I'll stay with her tonight," Cal said as he came over and stooped down to hook the IV line up to her catheter.

"You don't think I'm actually going to leave—do you?" Maya asked incredulously.

Cal met her eyes and gave a quick nod, his smile unmistakable.

"Can I stay?" Jeremy called out, a question Maya knew she should've expected. But even so, she hadn't had a chance to fully think through her answer yet. It seemed unfair to send him home now, when he knew it was possible that Molly could pull through if the dorfamin worked. Still...just the sheer physical exhaustion of trying to stay awake all night was a lot for an eight-year-old boy.

"How about you stay in the house with me and get some sleep, and your mom and Cal can text us if anything happens?" Cathy asked, looking over at Maya with widened eyes as if to say, *I hope it's okay that I suggested this.*

"That's a great idea," Maya said, sharing a quick glance with Cal. His smile and nod indicated that he was on board with the plan as well.

"I don't want to miss anything," Jeremy said, his voice worried.

"I promise I'll let you guys know if you need to come out here."

"How about if I set the alarm for five hours from now, when the treatment ends?" Cathy suggested. "We'll come back out then, unless we hear from you before that."

"Perfect," Maya replied, walking over to kiss and hug Jeremy. "Get some sleep, honey. We'll take good care of Molly." Moments later, Cal was at her side, lowering himself onto one knee as he squeezed Jeremy's shoulder. "Molly knows you're rooting for her," he said quietly. "Get some rest like your mom said, and we'll see you in a bit."

Maya felt a stirring in her stomach as she watched Cal's genuine exchange with her son. Her emotions already heightened, she found it hard not to wish that their growing bond didn't have *temporary* stamped all over it.

Just like the deepening bond that you feel with Cal, too...

"How about if I bring out some blankets and a pot of coffee before I put on my pj's?" Cathy asked. "That way, you can settle your tushes into something more comfy if you get tired."

Maya smiled, grateful for the chance to redirect her thoughts. "Thanks, Cathy. That would be great."

She waited for Cathy and Jeremy to exit the stall, then turned back to her dad. His eyes were focused downward on Molly, but even so, she could see the dark circles beneath them.

"Dad, why don't you go home and get some sleep. Sitting in a cold stall like this all night is only going to aggravate your arthritis."

Gus looked up at her, his shoulders heaving as he loudly sighed. "Did I mention that it sucks to get old?"

His reply drew laughter from both Maya and Cal, a brief respite from the unavoidable tension and heavy emotions that hung over all of them.

"I think I may have heard you say that once or twice before," Maya replied with a wry grin, reaching over to hug him and kiss him on the cheek.

Gus started to stand up, almost instantly staggering in mid-rise. Maya hopped to her feet and helped him straighten up, ignoring the tug on her ribs.

He thanked her, then looked over at Cal. "Well, I know Molly is in the best possible hands with the two of you. But you have to promise you'll call me if you need a third set of hands at any point." He held them up, and Maya discreetly winced at their gnarled knuckles and swollen finger joints. "They might have seen better days, but they're not fully out of commission yet."

"I promise."

Twenty minutes later, Maya scooched back from her kneeled position by Molly and turned to Cal, who was squatted down beside her. "If I don't stand up soon for a minute, I think my legs are going to start cramping."

He looked at her with a flash of concern. "I got this. Why don't you get up and walk around a bit. I'll join you in a few."

"Are you sure?"

He nodded to her, then again in the direction of the IV bag that hung from the infusion stand. "It looks like about a quarter of the bag has emptied, and no adverse reaction so far."

He stroked Molly's neck. Her eyes were half closed, her breathing slow and shallow. But she was still with them. Maya held her breath for a moment, as though exhaling too loudly might startle the mare. An entirely preposterous notion, she realized, but the stakes were so high, she'd do anything to stave off an anything-but-joyous outcome.

"Joe said the dorfamin would have an almost sedative-like effect while it's being administered, so as long as she stays subdued like this, we can hold off on any additional sedation."

Maya nodded. "Let's hope we can avoid that," she said, knowing well that adding sedation into *any* equation was bound to hike up the risk factor.

Spotting the blankets that Cathy had left earlier piled neatly up against the front stall wall, Maya headed over and eased her tired body down onto a floral-print comforter. A pot of coffee with two mugs rested on an overturned crate, but she resisted the urge to pour some for herself. Though physically spent, she was still mentally wired from the nonstop roller coaster of events that had defined the day. But once her adrenaline surge subsided, *then* it would be caffeine—and lots of it—to the rescue.

Pulling another blanket over her legs and waist to buffer against the nighttime chill, Maya leaned back against the wall as she watched Cal in action. Or inaction, given that he was immobile as he guarded over Molly while the treatment commenced. Either way, she could watch him for hours, touched by his unwavering dedication to his patients.

After some time had passed, she roused herself up and headed over to him.

"Hey," she said quietly. He'd been studying the dwindling level of dorfamin in the flowing IV bag, but quickly turned to her and smiled. "Hay is for horses."

She snickered, grateful for the tension-busting retort.

"So, what are you thinking?"

"We're about to start on the second bag, with two more to go." He looked down at Molly, and Maya did the same, making a mental note to recheck her vitals before the next IV bag was started. She was lying peacefully on her side...but that could be interpreted so many ways. And with an experimental drug, it was hard to know what was considered to be a "normal" presentation.

"This isn't based on anything other than my gut right now," Cal continued, "but I'm feeling optimistic."

Maya drew in a breath and held it several seconds before

letting it out. "I trust your instincts. Your gut assessment is as good as gold in my book."

Cal looked both surprised and pleased by her comment.

Maya readied her stethoscope and knelt down by Molly's head, then looked back up at Cal. "Once you swap in the new bag, why don't you go sit down for a while and have some coffee. I can take over monitoring things."

"To be honest, I think as long as she's stable once we start the new bag, we can both sit back for a bit and let it work its magic."

A few minutes later, Cal examined the IV line with the new bag in place, nodding to confirm that everything was flowing smoothly.

"Shall we?" he asked with a half smile as he turned to Maya, gesturing toward the blankets.

Her heart skipped a beat as they walked over to the wall, and was downright pounding as he sat down on the floral comforter, then held up a corner of the top blanket so that she could slip underneath it and sidle up next to him.

Maya held her breath as she felt the heat of Cal's body seep into her own. He put his arm around her shoulders and pulled her in even closer. "You warm?"

She smiled and nodded. "Yes."

"Good."

Moments ticked by in silence. She'd been alone with Cal before. But not *alone* alone like they were now. Though a dim light from a ceiling fixture shone directly over Molly, the outskirts of the stall were darkened with shadows. Another few minutes of silence, then she discreetly turned to look at him, only to find that he was already staring at her.

"You know," he said, his voice a low whisper. "I've had some amazing, exhilarating experiences in my career as a vet, and there have been times when I would think to myself, 'I'll never forget this moment.' But right here, right now…waiting for a miracle to happen with you by my side…this moment tops them all."

Maya closed her eyes. If ever there was a moment that she too wanted to last forever…this was it. But could she tell him that? Seconds ticked by. Yes…yes, she could.

She opened her eyes and looked into his. "I feel the same way."

Even in the shadows, she could see a smile form on his face, but it was short-lived since he had other ideas for his lips—and hers.

His kiss quite literally took her breath away, but she'd gladly trade oxygen for the chance to be this close to Cal, to feel his lips brush against hers, his strong body keeping her warmer than a thousand comforters ever could.

Maya awoke with a start, her face buried deep into something solid and warm. Only when she pulled her head away did she realize that the *something* was a fleece-covered nook between Cal's shoulder and chest. And then suddenly, everything came flooding back to her. Molly. An experimental treatment. *Oh— and Cal, cuddled underneath a blanket with me.*

Shaking herself fully awake, she looked up at him with widened eyes. "I can't believe I fell asleep."

He peered down at her with a half grin solidly in place. "That's okay. It's been a long night."

Maya jerked herself forward to get a better look at Molly, then blinked her eyes hard to make sure she wasn't imagining things. "Oh my god, she's sitting up!"

Cal's one-sided grin expanded into a full-on smile. "It happened about a half hour ago—just after you fell asleep, actually."

No longer lying flat out on her side, Molly had her four legs tucked beneath her belly, her head and shoulders fully raised off the ground.

Maya gasped. "Her head tilt is gone."

"I still can't believe it myself," Cal said quietly. Suddenly, his eyes widened. "Should we text Cathy to come out here with Jeremy?"

"Good idea," Maya said, pulling her phone out of her pocket. "They'll be out shortly," she said moments later. "I did tell Cathy they'll need to be very quiet when they enter the stall, so they don't startle her."

"Okay, good. From what I can see from here, there's less than a quarter of the last bag left to go. I think maybe we should sit tight, just to make sure the rest of it gets into her. Then we'll slowly approach her, remove the catheter and do an assessment."

Maya nodded in agreement. The good news was that Molly was awake and alert…but that also was the cautious news, given that she could decide to fully stand up at a moment's notice, potentially yanking out the IV catheter.

Several minutes later, the stall door creaked open. Cathy maneuvered Jeremy in front of her so that he could enter first. Maya put her finger to her lips and gently braced his shoulder with her other hand to halt him. He froze, then opened his eyes and mouth wide in shocked surprise as he spotted Molly's upright stance. The smile that emerged on his face, so pure and genuine and all-encompassing, grabbed Maya in the gut in the very best way. As Cal turned and witnessed the scene, he stood up beside them, his own smile bursting wide.

Suddenly, Molly nickered and pushed her front legs out from beneath her belly. Maya grabbed Cal's arm and gasped. He squeezed her hand and slowly moved up into a half-squatting position, ready to launch forward should Molly do the same.

In a flurry of shavings and snorts, Molly stood up, with

Maya and Cal at her side before she had time to fully shake off the shavings that stuck to her hair.

"Let's keep her steady," Maya said, her eye on the nearly empty IV bag.

Cal gripped Molly's halter, talking to her in a low but still-affectionate voice. "Look at you, Molly. You are amazing..."

Drip...drip...drip...

Maya watched as the last drops of dorfamin emptied out of the bag and traveled down the IV line. A few more seconds, and then she removed the catheter from Molly's neck.

Too overcome with joy to utter a single word, Maya locked eyes with Cal, hoping he could read what she was thinking. But even her thoughts were tongue-tied.

We did it! No—you did it! Molly did it! Make that—we all did it!

Cal grinned, an expression she'd seen on his face many times before, but never with such intensity.

Maya turned back to Jeremy. Cathy's arm was stretched across his chest, as though ready to hold him back, should he try to run over to Molly too soon.

"You guys can come over. Just walk slowly," Maya said softly.

As Jeremy nimbly approached, Cathy waited back, as though giving him the opportunity to have a moment alone with Molly.

He reached up and petted her nose, then turned to Maya and threw his arms around her waist. Before she could fully react, he turned to Cal and did the same, but in this instance, there was no letting go.

"Thank you, Cal! You saved Molly..." Tears streamed down his face as he looked up at Cal. "You saved her!"

Maya rubbed her eyes with the sleeve of her jacket. In veterinary medicine, as in the human kind, one had to put personal emotions on hold. At least, that had been the adage drummed into her from her earliest days in veterinary college. *You won't be able to survive the sheer number of disappointments otherwise*, she'd been told time and again.

But that wasn't going to happen today. Her emotions were too raw…and yes, too personal.

As Cal looked over at her, still locked in an embrace with Jeremy, she caught her breath at the expression on his face. He wasn't just hugging Jeremy back in a perfunctory manner. No—there was real emotion there, and it seemed to go beyond feeling glad that his horse-saving actions had made someone ecstatically happy.

He almost looked…fatherly.

Maya briefly closed her eyes, warning herself not to go there. And where exactly was *there*? It was any colorful scenario she was conjuring up in her mind that glossed over the black-and-white truth: Cal was strictly a colleague, and a temporary one at that. Which meant any perceived affection toward her or her son—regardless of how genuine—was equally transitory, and it would be a grave mistake to ever think otherwise.

Except…the "black-and-white truth" had morphed into something grayer. Her deepening connection with Cal was making it nearly impossible to continue seeing him as a temporary colleague only. Or, for that matter, a temporary colleague with whom she shared a real but going-nowhere attraction. *We're past that point.* The question was…did he feel the same?

CHAPTER ELEVEN

MAYA PULLED INTO the parking lot of the practice barn and clinic, ready to start another day with a spring in her step. Nearly a week had passed since Molly's nothing-short-of-miraculous turnaround, and the happy ending seemed to have buoyed the spirits of everyone involved in her recovery.

Not that she didn't have reason to still hold on to a snippet of caution. Just due to their sheer strength and size, horses were often thought to be hearty and resilient in the face of illness, but that was far from the truth. Even the slightest dietary changes could set off a deadly case of colic, and up until fairly recently, a leg break—so treatable in other animals—almost inevitably led to euthanasia.

But spotting Cal's truck as she hopped out of her own, Maya was back in Happyville again. Entering the barn, she ran through the day's tasks in her head. A hoof laminitis case at 9:00 a.m. A blood draw for a metabolic blood panel at 10:30 a.m....a hindgut ulcer consult at noon...

It was quiet as she walked down the aisle while ruminating on her to-do list—emphasis on *was*. Suddenly, the washroom door flew open, and in a flash of brawny flesh, a shirtless Cal came charging out. He skidded to a halt as he came chest-to-face with Maya.

"Oh," he said, wide-eyed.

"Oh," she replied, wider-eyed.

All together now: "*Oh!*"

He looked down at where his shirt should be, saying, "I was syringing Fern with dewormer paste, and she spit it back out on me."

"Well, at least you don't have to worry about carrying around a tapeworm."

Maya squinted her eyes shut. *Did I actually say that?* There was something about seeing Cal with no shirt and...*gulp*...all muscle that put her brain, and other body parts, in a tizzy.

Cal laughed heartily. "Not my first thought when she spit on me, I'll say that. But can't argue with the logic."

As he took a step toward her, she tripped a step back. But it was a *teensy-weensy* step, because apparently even her feet knew a good thing when they saw one.

"Someone's going to see us," Maya said breathlessly as he pulled her close and nuzzled her neck.

"Only Fern," he whispered as the feisty thoroughbred stuck her head over the stall gate.

A half dozen other horses followed suit, but Maya paid little heed. It was the first time she was ever glad that horses couldn't talk.

"We can't cross that line again—remember?" she said almost dreamily, doing very little to actually halt said crossing.

"You mean this line?" he asked softly as he play-bit her bottom lip.

Uh huh...

He pulled the bottom of her shirt out of her jeans, and she did little to stop him. Correction—she did *nothing* to upend the pleasurable sensations that were welling up inside her. His hands caressed her back, sending shivers down the length of her body. As they moved to the front, she caught her breath, startled by the sound of her own gasp.

Or was something else tugging at her ears?

She pulled back slightly. "Wait—is that a car I hear?"

Cal froze as well, turning an ear toward the open barn entrance. "Is a client scheduled to come by?"

"No. Hold on a sec." She scurried over just in time to see her dad exiting his SUV and looking toward the barn. "Oh no—it's my dad!"

Maya took a deep breath, reminding herself that she was not a little girl anymore, and if she wanted to canoodle with her hunky colleague in the barn aisle...*then that's my prerogative!*

Still, a bare-chested Cal would be hard to explain.

"Hurry—put your shirt on!" she whisper-shouted.

"I can't! It's soaking in the sink."

Maya grabbed her head with both hands to think, accidentally clunking herself with her cast in the process. "All right. Look—all we have to do is tell the truth."

Cal balked. "That we were making out?"

"No! That you had to take your shirt off because of Fern." She grabbed his arm and pulled him forward. "Let's go. We need to cut this off at the quick!"

Her directive, both serious and intentionally humorous at the same time, prompted a nervous chuckle from Cal.

Nearly stumbling out together into the morning sun, Maya greeted her dad with a chirpy "Hi!" that sounded one note higher than Alvin the Chipmunk.

Cal's not-so-discreet nudge at her side alerted her to the fact that her shirt was askew, one half tucked into her jeans and the other half flailing about. Clearing her throat, she pulled the tucked half out, hoping it would be less obvious than pushing everything back in. Judging by the quizzical expression on her dad's face, it wasn't.

He looked at Maya, then at Cal, then at Maya, then at Cal.

That's quite the head swivel, Maya thought as she tried to pull back on a teeth-baring grimace.

"*Callll?*" her dad began, eyes narrowed while drawing out the name as though it had twelve letters instead of three.

Cal cleared his throat. "Yes, Mr. Evans?"

"I've told you before to call me Gus—remember?"

"Yes, Mr. Gus—" Cal immediately shook his head. "—I mean, yes, Gus?"

"Is there a reason why you're not wearing a shirt in fifty-degree weather?"

"Fern spit dewormer paste on him," Maya hurriedly interjected.

"What she said," Cal added, pointing to Maya in case it wasn't clear who *she* was.

Gus studied him further, mouth twisted to the side and eyes in a tight squint. "Huh. Well, I do have some clean shirts in the office if you want to borrow one." He held his lanky arms out in front of himself and inspected them closely, then homed in on Cal's brawny physique. "Although, you might have to take a scalpel to the sleeves if your arms are going to fit through them."

Maya bowed her head in a muffled snicker.

She turned to Cal, whose reddened cheeks told her he'd be sweating under his shirt if he was actually wearing one. Instead, he nervously shifted his weight from one foot to the other. "Thanks. But I have a change of clothes in my truck. Kind of a necessity with this job."

Gus slowly eased into a smile, signaling to Maya that she could breathe again. "It is, isn't it."

Suddenly, the door to the office across the way opened and Jeremy strode out, a red lollipop from a bowl on Maria's desk in hand.

"Jeremy!" Maya exclaimed. "What are you doing here? Why aren't you at school?"

"I was about to get to that," Gus said. "There was a water pipe break at the school, and the students were sent home."

She turned to her son. "Why didn't you ask the school to call me?"

"I asked them to call Grandpa to come get me because I knew you were working."

Maya's tense shoulders eased up a bit. "Oh, okay, that makes sense."

"I know Carla could look after him today," Gus began, "but I figured he'd be bored at home all day, so he's going to tag along with me on some errands."

"Thanks, Dad." She turned back to Jeremy. "Although, my day is mostly standard appointments, so you can come with me if you'd rather do that."

He looked over at Cal. "Can I go with you, instead?"

Maya started to open her mouth, but wasn't sure what should come out. She hadn't seen this question coming…but perhaps she should have.

"That's fine with me," Cal said, turning to Maya with slight apprehension in his eyes. "But only if it's okay with your mom."

In a way, she couldn't blame her son for wanting to spend the day with Cal. Heck—she'd do the same, if it weren't for the fact that they were splitting up appointments today.

She could imagine Jeremy's thought process on the matter. *Do I spend the day with my—*yawn!*—predictable mom, or with Cal, the Indiana Jones of the horse world?*

"Are you sure?" she asked Cal, wondering if he could sense how difficult it was for her to navigate Jeremy's growing attachment to him. "I know you have a couple of surgical procedures scheduled."

"I'm excising a skin growth and stitching up a gash. Nothing too complicated." Cal turned to Jeremy with a wink and a grin. "And we can probably squeeze in a visit to see Molly. How does that sound?"

Jeremy let out a loud gasp. "Awesome!"

Maya felt her lips curve into a smile. Few things could bring her as much joy as seeing her son's unfiltered happiness. But her smile wavered as another truth set in. The stronger that Jeremy's bond with Cal grew, the harder it was going to be for him when Cal inevitably moved on.

And harder for you, too.

Maya pushed the obviousness from her thoughts. Maybe she would need to reevaluate how much one-on-one time Jeremy should have with Cal, but right now, she was not going to spoil his excitement.

Loading her truck for the day after Cal had set off for his own set of appointments with Jeremy, Maya turned to pick up a portable X-ray machine and nearly jumped to find her dad quietly standing just inches away. "You scared me!"

"Sorry."

She cocked her head to the side, reading the concern on his face almost too easily. "Is there something you want to say?" she asked, figuring it was best to just get things out in the open.

"Not really," he replied unconvincingly.

She silently coaxed him with raised eyebrows.

"Maya, you're a grown woman, and what goes on in your personal life is your own business. The only thing that matters to me is that you're happy. And Jeremy, too, of course. The two of you mean the world to me."

Maya heard his "not my business" words, but his troubled eyes told another story.

"But…" she prodded.

He opened his mouth as if to speak, then stopped and shook his head. "Nothing."

"No—tell me, Dad."

"I had a call yesterday from a vet clinic in England, of all places. They were checking references for Cal. Seems like he's already started searching for his next job."

The revelation pulled all the oxygen out of Maya's lungs, and it took several moments to recover her breath. She steadied herself with the reminder that nothing her dad had just said should have come as a surprise. Cal wasn't doing something devious behind her back. He was merely making plans to ensure that he stayed employed *somewhere*—as well he should.

"Well, that's understandable—right?" she quickly countered. "The contract that you had him sign was for two months. I'm sure he's just trying to line something up now, so he won't have a long gap of unemployment when his time here is done."

"You're right. Which is why I wasn't going to say anything. But—and maybe I'm just imagining things—it seems like you and Cal have grown closer recently, and it's obvious that Jeremy thinks the world of him, too." He paused, a "should I say more?" look on his face. "I just don't want to see you guys get hurt like you did when Max left."

"This is different," Maya said, though she knew well that her dad had a valid point. "I was in a long-term relationship with Max."

Gus pursed his lips together and nodded, then reached over and gently squeezed Maya's shoulder. "You're right. I'm just being a silly, overprotective dad who needs to mind his own business. In fact, I can hear your mom looking down on us right now and saying, 'Goddamn it, Gus, leave poor Maya alone. Let her live her life.'"

Maya snickered, though she knew her mom *would* be saying those exacts words if she were here. But at the same time… she'd probably also find an unobtrusive way to share her concerns as well.

"I appreciate you looking out for me, Dad, I really do. But I'll be okay, and so will Jeremy. I'll make sure of that."

He smiled. "I know you will."

As Maya watched his SUV head down the driveway and onto the main road a short time later, she wondered why his words of reassurance only made her feel worse.

Was she making sure that she and Jeremy would be okay? Her actions, both in the barn earlier with Cal, and then allowing Jeremy to tag along with him for the day, seemed to suggest otherwise. And though she had outwardly tried to casually shrug off her dad's revelation about Cal's job inquiry, inwardly she was still reeling.

Maybe she *was* getting too caught up in a fantasy notion of what she and Jeremy meant to Cal. And the one thing about fantasies? They eventually all came to an end.

Unless…was it possible he had applied for the job early on, before their growing closeness?

Maya took a deep breath, then continued loading her truck. She couldn't definitively answer that question—at least not yet.

Cal pulled his truck into the long driveway leading to Maya's house, coming to a stop in front of the large, wraparound porch. He was surprised to see her truck parked in front as well, given that it was 4:45 p.m., and she had mentioned her last appointment was at 5:00 p.m.

"Thanks, Cal," Jeremy said, opening the passenger door. "I can't wait to tell my mom that we saw Molly."

Cal smiled, a feeling of *all is right in the world* coursing through his veins.

Hokey, much? he wanted to ask himself. Except that the feeling was too genuine…and too full of goodness…for him to want to tear it down.

"I thought you'd still be on rounds," he said to Maya as she came out to greet them from the top of the porch steps. She dodged to the side as Jeremy rushed past. "Rusty inside?" he asked, already through the front door before she fully had a chance to answer.

"Slow down!" she exclaimed affectionately before turning back to Cal. "My last appointment had to reschedule. Ten sheath cleanings at Mountain Acres Farm. Can't say I'm disappointed."

Cal was surprised that Maya put that image into his head of her slathering cream over ten horse penises, but perhaps he was letting his powers of visualization get the best of him. Still, he shuddered slightly before scanning her property. With trees at the height of autumn colors, rolling fields still prefrost green and a backdrop of mist-covered mountains, it was hard not to be moved by nature at its most glorious.

"It's beautiful out here," he observed. "I didn't see much when I picked you up for the fundraiser because it was dark. But you have a lot more land than I realized."

"Ten acres," Maya confirmed as she stepped down off the porch.

Cal stretched his neck to get a better look at a large structure off in the distance. "Is that a barn back there?"

Maya nodded. "Twenty stalls, believe it or not. Plus three fenced pastures."

"And no horses of your own?"

"Kind of doesn't add up—right?" Maya acknowledged, scrunching her lips together for emphasis. "Horse vet with a barn and pastures...and no horses."

"Well, not like you have a ton of free time to care for them if you did, I suppose."

"Free time? What's that?" Maya flashed a wry grin, but it was quickly followed by a sigh of resignation. "Truth is, I'd always planned to get horses when I moved here. But this place was a bit of a fixer-upper—especially the barn and fencing. George and I..." She paused momentarily, as though wondering whether it was appropriate to bring her late husband into the conversation. "We talked about starting a sanctuary for unwanted horses. We knew how Cathy had to turn some away because she had no room. But...we weren't even here half a year before he died, so all those plans came to a halt." She paused again, pulling her lips in tight before forcing the hint of a smile. "Anyway, someday I'll get to the repairs."

"What kind of repairs are we talking about?" Cal asked, ready to throw a workbag full of tools over his shoulder. Not that he actually had one—yet.

"Well, the barn has a leaky roof, and the electricity's not working. Some of the stall gates need to be replaced, too."

"Are there at least a couple working stalls?"

"There are, but there are some major breaks in the fencing that would need to be repaired before I could house any horses here. To be honest, with enough time and money, it's all doable stuff that could be fixed in a probably a week or two. I had planned to hire someone, but then Max came into my life and insisted he'd help me get everything up to speed..." She paused, her train of thought hitting a roadblock. "Well, let's just say that never happened. And between his leaving the practice, and my dad having to cut back his hours, I've had to put this on the back burner." There was a faraway look in her eyes as she viewed the bucolic surroundings. "But someday," she quietly added.

The front door opened and Jeremy emerged with a full backpack hanging off one shoulder.

"Where do you think you're going?" Maya asked.

"Mark's for dinner. I told you yesterday—it's his birthday."

As if on cue, a car slowly rambled up the driveway. Maya

looked at Cal, her brow furrowed, then turned to wave to Mark's parents as the vehicle came to a stop in front of her.

"Hold on!" she exclaimed, halting Jeremy midstride to the car. "What time are you coming home?"

"I'm staying over—I told you that, too."

Maya shook her head in bewilderment. "There's been so much going on, I forgot all about it. Well, have fun—and be careful!"

Cal waited for the car to disappear from view, then turned back to Maya. Was he going to take advantage of this sudden development? *Heck, yeah!*

"Well, looks like it's just the two of us. How does dinner sound?"

"It sounds good," Maya replied a little too quickly. "I'm reheating lasagna from the other night. What about you?"

"I'm cooking some burgers on the grill on my deck. Care to join me?"

"I can't," Maya replied a little too quickly. "I'm a vegetarian—not sure if I ever mentioned that to you. So, veggie burgers only."

Oh, you aren't going to push me off that easily... "Not a problem. We'll pick some up on the way."

If ever there was a make-or-break moment, this had to be it, Maya thought. Her decision now could reverberate for a long time to come…unless, of course, Cal simply just wanted to cook her a veggie burger. Although judging by the hungry look in his eyes, there's was potentially more on the menu than dinner.

Still…as long as she made a pledge with herself to simply enjoy the present moment and rein in her emotions…then there was no harm in throwing a little caution to the wind. *Right?*

"Okay," she said, pushing her doubts back and a smile forth.

Twenty minutes later, they entered Cal's cabin, grocery bags in hand. "It's chilly in here," Cal said. "I'll start a fire."

Crackling orange flames added a warm glow to the already-cozy living room as he headed back over to the adjoining kitchen.

Maya pulled out a stool to sit at the counter, but paused as Cal looked at her quizzically and said, "Something's different…"

She grinned and held up her left arm. "I was wondering how long it would take you to notice."

His eyes widened. "You got your cast off!"

"This afternoon—finally!"

"How does your arm feel?"

"A little weird, to be honest. I'm used to having the weight of the cast, but I'm sure that will quickly pass."

As Cal closed the space between them and gently touched her arm, she held her breath. His blue-green eyes locked on to hers, and all her inner protests, the can't do this, shouldn't do this, will live to regret it proclamations, slowly melted away.

"Does this make it feel better?" he asked, lifting her arm, his eyes still locked on to hers, and then kissing the inside of her wrist.

Maya silently gasped and closed her eyes, her knees nearly buckling as desire flooded through her. As Cal's lips moved to her neck and then her lips, she grabbed on to his shoulders to steady herself, then clasped his neck as he suddenly picked her up and quite literally swept her off her feet.

Time stood still as he carried her into the bedroom. A large fur blanket was draped over the queen-size bed, and as he laid her down on top of it, he softly added, "Don't worry, it's faux fur. I checked."

Damn, this man really knows me…

And it wasn't just knowing how her mind worked. With

every sensuous kiss, every scintillating touch, he blissfully brought her to places that she never could have imagined. It was as if they'd been lovers forever.

And yet...as they basked in the afterglow of their lovemaking, Maya couldn't help but think how *forever* was the one thing she'd never truly have with Cal.

"Are you sorry we crossed the line?" he asked with a slightly mischievous grin, kissing her on the forehead as he stroked her arm.

Maya smiled and gently shook her head. But the answer in her thoughts?

In this moment, no, but tomorrow, which will be one day closer to you leaving for good...maybe.

CHAPTER TWELVE

"There's no easy way to say this...but I have cancer."

Sitting across from Cathy, Cal felt his insides plunge. As Maya gasped and grabbed his knee, he placed his hand over hers and held it tight. Earlier that day, Cathy had called to ask that they stop by together, and though she cryptically left out a reason for her request, never in a million years did Cal expect such a devastating announcement.

"Cathy—" Maya began, seemingly too shocked to say anything more.

"I know. You thought I was an invincible Wonder Woman, right? I thought so, too—minus the big boobs and curves."

Though Cathy smiled wryly at her attempt to diffuse the gravity of her announcement with humor, Maya's face remained stricken. She glanced at Cal, whose face was equally grave.

"Truth is, I haven't been feeling well for a while. Couldn't really put my finger on it, just an overall sense of fatigue, sometimes breathlessness. But given that I'm pushing seventy, I kept writing it off as old... I mean, as less-than-young age. My doctor ran some tests, and turns out I have Hodgkin's lymphoma. The good news is we caught it fairly early. But I'm still looking at several rounds of chemotherapy, possibly followed by radiation treatment.

"And if I *were* younger, I'd figure I'll beat this and then come back stronger than ever. I'm still going to do everything I can to kick this cancer to the curb, but I can't kid myself. It's been getting harder to do all the physical work of taking care of the horses, and even if I hired help—which I really can't afford—the upkeep of a place this size is more than I'm going to be able to handle. My sister Karen has offered to let me stay with her while I'm going through the treatments, and then once I'm on the other side of that, I can look for my own place, something smaller and more manageable."

"Cathy, I'm so sorry," Maya said, her voice quivering.

Cathy leaned over and grabbed both of Maya's hands. "No crying now. You hear me? I'm going to get through this. And what's going to help me do that is knowing that my horses are going to good homes."

Maya glanced at Cal, and he knew what she was thinking. *Where exactly are these homes?* The reason that rescues like Happy Hooves existed in the first place was because it was so hard to find caring and qualified people willing to take on the time and expense of caring for a horse.

"Have you thought of selling the rescue to someone who'd take it over?" Maya asked. "And by that, I mean someone who'd continue your mission of rescuing horses, or at least caring for the ones you have now."

"Believe me, I thought about that, and I put out some feelers to some local real estate agents. But it's a tough sell. I mean, let's face it—running a rescue is a lot of work, and the money to keep it going is always an issue. If it weren't for the generosity of you and your dad over the years with all the pro-bono vet care, Happy Hooves would probably have fallen under a long time ago."

Maya hung her head downward, and Cal could almost feel the despair emanating off her. As he squeezed her hand, she turned to him with a sadness in her eyes that felt like a knife in his own heart.

"Are you okay?" he asked on the drive back to her house, his question piercing a long stretch of silence.

"Not really. Cathy has always been such a strong person and a tremendous advocate for horses that I never thought this day would come. And in case you're wondering, don't think my mind didn't jump to the barn and fields on my property. But running a rescue is a lot of work, and I don't think I can realistically take that on by myself on top of my job and Jeremy…not to mention that part of my property would need a major upgrade first."

"I wasn't wondering that," Cal said quietly. "I already know how much you're carrying on your shoulders." He paused, glancing at her sideways. "Your *tiny* shoulders, I should add."

"They're still big enough to have helped pull Buttercup up off the ground."

Cal could see the effort behind her slight smile. "True that."

Maya's smile faded as she looked out the passenger window. "You know, when I was a little girl, tagging along with my dad on client visits… I remember going to Happy Hooves and thinking that someday, I'd have my own horse rescue."

"Maybe you will, when the time is right."

She glossed over his suggestion. "I guess all we can do right now is get the word out to clients about the horses being up for adoption."

He reached over and brushed away a loose lock of hair that obscured the side view of her face. She turned to him abruptly, eyes momentarily surprised, then clasped his hand and brought it up to her lips.

The soft kiss on his knuckles still hit him hard…because it was so much more than a kiss. It was a confirmation that she knew she could lean on him. He'd do anything to be there for her, to be the rock that had long been missing in her life.

And what happens to that rock when you up and leave in a month?

Cal ignored his own question.

The sun was just starting to set when they arrived back at Maya's place. He pulled the truck up in front of the house, leaving the engine idling as he turned to her.

"Thanks for picking me up," she said, her troubled eyes saying more than her words.

"Of course."

Another span of silence. "Well, I'll see you in the morning."

Maya hopped off the passenger seat before Cal could reply, but instead of closing the truck door behind her, she froze with her back facing him.

Seconds ticked by, and he wondered whether to ask if she was okay. Just as his mouth started forming the words, she swiftly turned around.

"Do you want to come in for dinner? I'm just heating up a casserole that Carla prepared earlier, but she's a much better cook than me, and it's way more food than Jeremy and I can finish alone."

Cal greeted the invitation with a slightly agape mouth and widened eyes. On the one hand, it was simply an on-the-spot dinner invitation. But on the other, it had to have come with a heaping serving of trust on Maya's behalf. He knew how closely she guarded her homelife with Jeremy.

"I'd love to," he replied.

Cal followed Maya into the living room, surprising Jeremy as he did. He'd been tussling on the carpeted floor with a large golden retriever, who froze and barked at Cal's presence.

"It's okay, Rusty," Maya said. Her reassurance was all the

dog needed to snap out of attention and resume playing with Jeremy.

"Cal's joining us for dinner tonight," Maya said.

Jeremy greeted the news with a huge smile and a thumbs-up.

Cal looked around the living room and adjoining kitchen, impressed with what he saw. He was no Martha Stewart, but if he had to put a label on the decor, he guessed it would be "modern country."

"I don't have any beer," Maya called over as she pulled two wineglasses out of a cabinet. "But would you like a glass of wine?"

"Sure." He felt something rub up against his leg, then leaned over to pet an orange tiger cat.

"Wow," Maya said as she looked over. "Willow almost never comes out when company is here. She must know you're an animal lover."

Cal grinned. "Win over the cats, and everything else is a piece of cake."

Maya laughed. "There's definitely some truth to that." She headed over and handed him a glass of merlot. "It won't take long to heat up the casserole."

"I'm in no rush," he said, which was the understatement of the year. They hadn't even sat down to eat yet, but just being in her home, with Jeremy playing with his dog, Maya sipping wine while readying dinner, a cat—now two—circling him affectionately... If was as if the term *domestic bliss* had suddenly sprung to life and pulled him into the center of it.

It was the quintessential family home life he didn't know he needed. Or...did he in fact already know? Not having something and not wanting it were two different things. He'd had a taste of this sense of belonging with Thomas and Mabel at the ranch, albeit with a bitter ending that had soured him on ever pursuing a lasting attachment again.

Yet, slowly but surely, this previously wrought iron resolve was beginning to crumble. He could feel it in every fiber of his being, in every pang of *I don't want this to end* that grabbed at him each time he thought about leaving Maya.

But it *had* to be this way...or did it? Just because running away had always worked for him in the past, did that mean there was no other option now? What if he wanted more? A life with Maya and Jeremy? The *what-ifs* continued to circle his mind with no answer in sight, perhaps because he'd never asked them before.

It was dark as Cal and Maya retreated to the porch to finish their glasses of wine.

"I can't remember the last time I had a delicious, home-cooked meal like that," Cal said as he seated himself on a cushioned wicker bench.

Maya sat down beside him. "You mean a home-heated-up meal," she replied with a wry smile. "But it *was* cooked from scratch earlier in the day, courtesy of Carla."

He chuckled, his easy laughter tapering off as a deeper revelation crept into his thoughts. Sitting at the dinner table earlier with Maya and Jeremy...talking and laughing and just being themselves...he couldn't think of a better way to end the day. No—that wasn't quite right. He couldn't think of a better way to end *every* day.

The distinction caught Cal hard in the gut, and he turned to Maya with what he realized too late had to be a deer-in-the-headlights look on his face.

"What's wrong?" she asked, forehead creased and eyebrows raised.

"Nothing." He silently caught his breath in an effort to hide his angst, adding in a forced smile to boot. "Nothing at all."

Which, of course, wasn't exactly true. Because in about a month from now, he'd be packing up his bags on the way to his next gig. That was the contract he'd signed—happily and willingly—at the start of his temporary employment with Northern Vermont Equine Associates. The sort of contract he insisted on, no matter where the wind had taken him.

Which was all fine and dandy, except for the fact that the wind had last deposited him *here*...right smack in the midst of a woman he could truly fall for.

Could truly fall for? As in it hadn't happened yet? Who in the world was he kidding? He wouldn't have been questioning his gig-hopping ways just a short time ago if Maya was like all the other colleagues—female or otherwise—whom he'd easily moved on from in the past with little more than the flick of a departing handwave.

Yes, this was all new to him. Yes, it was scary. But perhaps he could take a few baby steps before attempting to jump feet-first into a life of happiness that had always seemed out of his reach, but was closer now than ever before.

He cleared his throat, readying for that first tiny step. "We'll have to do this again. How about if I cook dinner for you and Jeremy at my place tomorrow night? You can bring Rusty and the cats. We'll make it a family affair."

He expected Maya to laugh at his comment, but instead, she stared at the ground, looking one step short of stricken.

"Did I say something wrong?" he gingerly asked.

It took her a moment to reply. "Cal—I know I'm the one who asked you to stay for dinner, but I'm not sure that I thought things through enough. After learning about Cathy's situation...it felt good having you by my side, like I wasn't facing such horrible news alone. I guess I wanted to continue that feeling once we got back here. But relying on you like this... that's just going to make it harder when you leave."

"Maya..." He wanted to say more, but knew he'd only be digging a deeper hole for himself. It wasn't as though he could counteract any points that she had just made. And there were more points to come.

"You have to understand—I'm not like you. The whole 'I'll land wherever the wind takes me' thing—that's just not me."

Cal's eyes widened. He didn't remember using that phrase in front of her before. But maybe it was written on his persona.

"I don't get attached to many people," she continued. "It's just the way I am—maybe it's in part a protection thing. But when I do…it's not…"

"It's not what?" he asked, nudging her after a lapse of silence ensued.

"It's not a temporary feeling that I can just shrug off when the person is no longer in my life." She paused, searching his eyes. "Do you understand what I mean?"

He nodded, unable to say more.

"And the fact that you're able to leave one job—or one continent, for that matter—at a moment's notice while heading to another, tells me you're not like this."

"Maya—"

"Please, let me finish. I can't imagine you haven't met women along the way who you've become involved with."

Cal clenched his jaw. There was involved, and then there was *involved*. A distinction that was clear in his mind, but it would only make matters worse if he tried to explain this to Maya.

"And it's not just about me. Jeremy has gotten close to you, too. And yes, he's older now than when he was with the whole Max fiasco—and I'm not trying to imply that we're in any sort of relationship like I was with Max, because we're not."

Cal wondered if Maya knew how skillful she was with a dagger. She wasn't *intentionally* skewering him, of course. But her words pierced him sharply just the same.

"But it will still be very hard on Jeremy when you leave.

And even more so if he thinks there's a chance that you'll stay. I told him when you were hired that it was just for a couple of months. But I don't think he's looking at it that way right now." She paused. "You know how kids are—they live in the present."

Cal couldn't recall ever being at a total loss for words as he was now. But what could he possibly say? It wasn't a stretch to put himself in Maya's shoes and realize that as a mother, and as a woman who'd already experienced her share of romantic heartbreak, everything she'd said made sense. She was protecting herself and her son.

Think about that. You want to protect her...but she needs protection from you.

"Maya, it's not like I have one foot out the door—"

"Really?" she asked pointedly. "Because my dad mentioned he was recently contacted as a reference for a job in England."

Cal froze. *She knows.* He had applied for a four-month gig in the Cotswolds to cover an upcoming maternity leave only days after arriving in Vermont. With this new role scheduled to start a couple weeks after his current contract ended, it had seemed like perfect timing. Emphasis on *seemed*. But that was before his growing feelings for Maya. When he'd received an email the night before confirming that he was moving forward in the hiring process, the normally happy news had actually filled him with a sense of dread.

But even if he tried to explain this to Maya, she wouldn't believe him. Besides, what would he say? *Yeah, I hate to have to leave, but I'm going to do it anyway.* Because that was always the bottom line with him, wasn't it?

Except...the line was beginning to shift. And yet, as he looked into Maya's eyes, he felt too paralyzed to do anything about it. He knew what he was feeling...for Maya, for the life they could have together...but perhaps it was too big of a leap.

He thought he could start with baby steps, but with Maya laying it all out on the line like this, he couldn't even stick out a toe. Whether it was due to fear of failure, or just plain fear, it almost didn't matter at this point.

As if sensing his inner turmoil, Maya took a deep breath, her voice now softened. "I didn't mean to end this night on such a sour note—especially after such a difficult day. I just wanted us to be clear on a few things for the remainder of your time here."

He nodded. "I appreciate your honesty."

Which he did. The question was…could he be honest with himself?

CHAPTER THIRTEEN

MAYA WATCHED AS her dad drove up the clinic driveway with Jeremy in tow. Two days had passed since she and Cal had received Cathy's devastating news, and between this and Cal's imminent departure, she was having a hard time finding reasons to smile.

But seeing Jeremy's excitement as he bounded out of the SUV temporarily put her angst on hold. Her dad had promised to take him to see Molly after school, and it was clear that the visit had been a positive one.

"How's she doing?" Maya asked, smiling for the first time all day.

"I got to pet her!" Jeremy exclaimed, which prompted her smile to widen even more.

"That's great, honey."

"I'm going to get a lollipop," he said.

"Just one—cavities, remember?"

He rolled his eyes, then nodded before heading to the office.

Maya turned to her dad as he came up beside her. "Don't worry. Cathy didn't say anything about the cancer or closing the rescue in front of Jeremy."

She breathed a sigh of relief. "I know we can't keep the truth from him forever, but I want it to be done the right way. It's a lot for someone his age to take in, and I want to sit down with him and explain everything."

Her dad nodded. "I agree."

"I know the first thing he's going to ask is what will happen to Molly."

"Did you talk to Cathy yet about adopting her?"

"Not yet," Maya said with a sigh. "She started chemo yesterday and I don't want to throw too much at her right now. I'm also not going to say anything to Jeremy about the adoption until I've ironed out all the details. If we take in Molly, we should adopt a second horse as a companion. There's no way I can completely overhaul the barn and fencing right now, so I need to figure out the minimum that needs to be done to get things up to speed. For two horses, it shouldn't be too bad."

"I'm sure Cal would be willing to help."

Maya didn't disagree with her dad's assessment, but the bigger question was whether having Cal around her home, helping out more like a partner than a fellow vet, would be too misleading for Jeremy. *Or for me.*

But before she could share such concerns with her dad, she turned to the sound of Cal's truck heading up the driveway.

As he slid out of the driver's seat moments later, Australian cowboy hat in place, dark blond hair scraping his shoulders and sturdy cowboy boots firmly on the ground, Maya's heart fluttered.

Don't do that, she reprimanded it. And still, it fluttered again.

Jeremy had just exited the office with a lollipop in hand, and spotting Cal, immediately ran over to him. "Hey, Cal—guess who I saw today?"

"Let's see…was it someone with two legs or four?"

"Four!" Jeremy exclaimed, game to play along.

"Tail or no tail?"

"Tail!"

"Black, white, red or brown?"

"Brown—but really light brown."

Cal's grin widened. "I'm going to take a wild guess here and say Molly."

Jeremy lifted his small hand in a high five, which Cal quickly but gently slapped.

Maya exchanged a curious glance with her dad. "Since when does Jeremy high-five people?"

"Apparently since he's met Cal," her dad replied with a light chuckle.

"Grandpa said that come spring, Molly should be strong enough to start building up her muscles again. I want to learn how to lunge her and stuff. Do you think you'll be able to show me?"

Cal had been straightening out supplies in the back of his truck, but slowed to a halt as he fielded Jeremy's question. He briefly turned to Maya, then looked away as if he knew she was holding her breath for his answer. Which, in fact, she was.

"I think it might be a little too soon to start her on a lunge line," Cal said, swinging the truck doors shut and turning to give Jeremy his full attention.

"I don't mean now. But can you show me in the spring?"

"I, um…" Cal's stammered nonreply was like a jackhammer to Maya's heart.

This was the scenario she'd been dreading, and now it was playing out in real time before her.

"Jeremy, honey," Maya said as she slowly approached, "Cal's probably not going to be here in the spring."

Of course, she knew that *probably* was actually *definitely*, but she couldn't quite bring herself to unleash the harsh reality full force upon her son.

The shock on Jeremy's face, first aimed at her until he whipped his head in Cal's direction, knocked the wind out of her.

"Where are you going?" he asked, his voice rising.

"I'm not sure yet. Probably England." Cal paused, momentarily locking eyes with Maya before turning back to Jeremy.

"The job here was just for a couple of months, to help your mom while she was healing from the horse kick."

Jeremy turned to Maya, eyes darting to her dad and then back to her. "But don't you still need another vet now that Grandpa's retiring?"

Maya flinched as she felt her father's hand on her shoulder from behind, her head quite literally buzzing as high-pressured blood whooshed through her ears.

"Jeremy, Cal's a traveling vet." She had no idea if he ever ascribed to this label himself—but she also didn't care. Right now, her only priority was to soften the blow of Cal's near-future departure. "That's why he's lived all over the world. He's done a great job helping us out here, but it was always the plan that he'd move on after a couple of months."

Jeremy nodded solemnly.

"I know plenty of great horsemanship instructors," Maya continued, doing her best to add an optimistic inflection to her voice, "and we'll find someone who can work with you and Molly in the spring. How does that sound?"

Lips pressed into a thin line, Jeremy half nodded as he kicked an imaginary stone on the ground.

She turned to her dad, not sure whether to be more upset with him for hiring Cal in the first place, or with herself for allowing him to whittle his way into her and Jeremy's lives. But it was futile to point fingers, she realized. All she could do now was fix the situation before it got worse—and fix it fast.

"Can we talk for a minute?" she asked her dad as she nodded toward the office.

He answered *yes* with his eyes, and together they headed off.

Cal leaned against the back of his truck, wondering what the heck had just happened. Or at least wondered for all of two seconds.

Do you really need to ask?

He closed his eyes, fully realizing that Maya's fears had just unfolded in front of her. Jeremy was looking to him to be someone that he wasn't. A role model. A father figure. His mother's significant other.

But in reality, he was just the "traveling horse vet" who was temporarily filling in until a permanent replacement was found. *Right?*

But if that were true, then why was he feeling so utterly miserable right now? With Maya and her dad holed up in the office, and Jeremy having wandered off to the barn, there was no one around to answer his question.

It's only you, mate.

But wasn't that the story of his life? A story that his actions perpetuated. But recognizing a pattern, and abandoning it for a better alternative, were two different things. *I am who I am.* A defiant declaration that had brought him solace so many times in the past. But not so much right now.

He checked his watch: Two more late-afternoon appointments were about to get underway. He wondered whether to seek out Maya and let her know that he was leaving, but decided to quietly depart. The notion of leaving—regardless of the context—was simply too much of a weighted issue to touch right now.

It was near dusk when he arrived back at the clinic. Spotting Maya's truck in the parking area, he felt the knot in his stomach—first tied when Jeremy had asked about helping with Molly in the spring—flip over itself in a manner that would make a gymnast proud.

Maybe she already forgot about this morning—a thought that he knew should be filed under Wishful Thinking.

"I thought that was you," Maya said as she emerged from the barn, wiping a spot of dirt from her forehead with her sleeve. No confrontation. He was feeling better already. And then, the three most dreaded words known to man.

"Can we talk?"

His smile froze in mid-curve, then slowly deflated. "Sure."

Maya scanned their surroundings, then pointed to a small picnic table to the right of the office.

Cal brushed fallen leaves off the top of the red-stained wooden table as he sat down on the attached bench, more to distract himself from the dread of what was possibly coming than to ensure a clutter-free surface.

Maya sat across from him, her soulful gray eyes looking into his own before casting downward. She took a deep breath and then another, as if gearing up to deliver some news that she knew would not be well received. Finally, she looked back up at him.

"I talked with my dad, and we're going to pay you for the rest of the contract that you signed, but after you finish out this week, we…I mean I…would like you to leave."

She squeezed her eyes shut, as if trying to soften the blow, but whether it was for her sake or his, Cal couldn't tell.

Stunned into silence, he could do little more than stare at Maya in disbelief. He knew she was upset about his exchange with Jeremy earlier that day…but upset enough to show him the door, and with a swift kick in the butt on the way out? *That* he hadn't seen coming.

"Like I said," Maya continued, "you'll be paid in full. My dad and I are both in agreement on this, so no worries there."

"It's not about the money, Maya. I just don't understand—"

"Yes, you do," Maya interjected, eyes determined yet pained at the same time. Her harshness further tightened the knot in his stomach, and added a new obstruction into this throat.

"Jeremy's become attached to you in a way that I hoped wouldn't happen. And I know you're probably thinking you just have a month left on your contract, so why not finish it out. But that would be a month more of him seeing you as someone you're not."

Cal jerked his head back, as though dodging the knife behind her words. But unfortunately, he didn't move fast enough.

"Seeing me as someone I'm not?" Heat rose from his cheeks, searing his brain in the process. Was she implying that he had somehow deceived them as to his true nature? "I've never pretended to be someone other than who I am."

It seemed like such an obvious statement to make. But then again, he knew there were plenty of people in the world who *did* put a false self forward, so perhaps the distinction needed to be made.

"I know, Cal," she conceded, her voice softening. "None of this is anything that you've done wrong. Or deliberately. I want you to know that. But Jeremy sees you as someone in his life—in *our* lives—who's going to continue to be a part of that, and it's just not true. It never was. All I'm doing is trying to lessen the hurt for him." Her eyes, now glossy and vulnerable, met his. "And for me."

"What are you going to do without an extra set of hands?" he asked. It was a filler question as he stalled for time. He needed to process everything, but the gears in his brain were shocked into stupor.

"We've already posted a job ad, this time for a permanent position. That was the plan all along after my dad hired you to fill in temporarily. We just moved up the timetable a bit."

Cal nodded. There were so many questions swirling in his mind, but only one that he gave voice to. "Have you told Jeremy yet?"

"No, but I plan to talk to him tonight. After what happened today, it's not like any of this will be coming out of left field. But I know he's going to have a hard time accepting things."

"I'm so sorry, Maya." She stiffened as his voice choked up. "It was never my intention to swoop in and turn things upside down for the two of you like this. I care too much to…"

Care too much to what? Maya waited for Cal to say more, but was instead greeted with eyes that were filled with regret. It's not how she wanted his time here to end. *She* cared too much to have him hurt this way.

"It's all going to be okay," she said quietly, gently squeezing his hand as it rested on the table. "Children are more resilient than we sometimes give them credit for. He'll get through this."

"And you?"

Ugh, why did he have to ask this?

From the get-go, Maya's number one concern had been to protect Jeremy. After all, she was an adult who could handle heartbreak, or so she had convinced herself. But clearly she had miscalculated, because right now, her heart was shattered into a million pieces. And she wasn't sure it would ever be whole again.

Her mind raced back to all the opportunities Cal had to say what she so desperately wanted to hear. *I don't want to leave. I want to stay here forever with you. I don't want to run anymore.* But in the end, all he could say was goodbye.

"I'll be okay," she finally said, hoping she only imagined that her voice had just cracked in front of him. And the pained look on Cal's face? Perhaps she was only imagining that, too.

Later that night, Cal felt around on the bed for his phone in the dark, then pressed the side button to illuminate the screen and check the time. It was 2:00 a.m. Three hours of lying awake… and counting.

Jumping from one gig to the next, to one corner of the world and one new set of temporary colleagues and acquaintances... *this* was his jam. And always had been.

But something was different now. It was as if he'd previously sailed through his adult life tossing aside attachments before they even had a chance to form, and now something... or more like *someone*...had stuck. And stuck big.

He stared up the ceiling, fully recognizing that his life was now at a crossroads. He could continue on his usual trajectory, making decisions based solely on his wants and needs. The only problem was...something had shifted inside of him, rendering it impossible to continue thinking of himself as a lone beacon in the night.

It was him, Maya and Jeremy.

But *feeling* something, and living the reality, were two different things. And separating the two? That was one thing known as courage.

CHAPTER FOURTEEN

"I PRINTED OUT some résumés and cover letters that came over," Maria said, handing several sheets of paper to Maya.

Maya grimaced as she leafed through the sparse printouts. "That's it?"

"I know. But we did just post the job. And it's not like there's a ton of available horse vets circulating around."

"Two female candidates and two male." She handed several sheets back to Maria. "No men—I should have mentioned this before we posted the job."

"Maya!" Maria exclaimed incredulously. "You can't do that. It's discrimination."

Maya was just joking…kind of, sort of…but it was worth keeping the ruse going just to see Maria's eye-bulging reaction. "I'm making hiring decisions based on what I know will and won't work. That's not discriminatory."

Maria took off her reading glasses and set them on the desk with an exasperated sigh that was quickly followed with an empathetic smile. "Look, I know what you went through in the aftermath of Max leaving, and your dad filled me in yesterday on your concerns with Cal and Jeremy's attachment to him."

There was something in Maria's kind eyes and tone of voice that told Maya she knew the attachment issue was not Jeremy's alone.

"But you could be missing out on the perfect candidate by

outright dismissing all men." She glanced at a sheet of paper, then held it up. "This one, for example, is highly qualified and he's married, so you don't have to worry about him being anything but a professional colleague."

Maya knitted her eyebrows together. "He says that on his résumé?"

"No—in his cover letter. Here, I'll read it to you." Donning her reading glasses once more, she began: "'Dear Sir or Madam…'" She paused to look up at Maya. "I guess you're a madam."

Maya grinned. "I've been called worse."

Maria chuckled, then resumed reading. "'As a board-certified equine veterinarian who has devoted my life to the care and welfare of horses, I read the job posting at Northern Vermont Equine Associates with great interest. Maplewood looks like a wonderful small town for my wife and I to settle down in and raise our family. I believe being a horse vet is more than a career—it's a way of life, and one that my family is fully on board with. I feel confident that I can provide compassionate, expert veterinary care for your equine clients, and I look forward to the chance to share my qualifications with you in person. Sincerely, Jackson Smith.'"

"Hmm."

"Hmm? Does that mean you'll follow up with him?"

Maya knew it was ridiculous to even toy with the idea of automatically disqualifying male vets. After all, what did that say about *her* if she was concerned about becoming romantically involved with another colleague? Did she not have the ability to keep her personal and professional lives separate?

Of course I can do that, she silently acknowledged. The problem was, she hadn't. But that was on her…and there was no reason why she couldn't learn from her mistakes. She thought she had after the Max fiasco, but then Cal came into her life and snuck into her heart…

Maya squeezed her eyes shut, as if doing so could catapult Cal from her thoughts and feelings. But he was still too much a part of both.

As if she needed a reminder of this—which she didn't—the office door opened and Cal stepped inside. He did a double take upon seeing Maya, which she returned in full.

"I need to check on some supplies for reorder," Maria said unconvincingly as she rose from her desk. "I'll be back in a few." She smiled a little too knowingly in both their directions before heading out of the office.

Cal waited for the door to close behind her, then turned to Maya. "I just came by to sign an amended contract." He glanced at the résumés in her hand, then looked back up at her, his expressionless face giving away little. "How's the job search going?"

Maya wished it wasn't so easy for him to ask about his replacement, as though his leaving was simply business as usual. But wasn't that his MO to begin with?

"Only four candidates so far, but it's still early," Maya replied, doing her best not to look too deeply into his eyes. A good thing to practice, given that soon Cal—and his dreamy eyes—would be firmly planted on another continent.

"Anyone good?"

She debated whether to give him the full rundown. Two candidates just out of veterinary college, but both referring to the position in their cover letters as a "first step" in their careers, which hardly boded well for longevity. Still, that didn't entirely rule them out. And two more established candidates, one who felt the need to disclose his marital status in his cover letter— perhaps to paint himself as family friendly and with small-town values—and the other who was "looking for a change after being micromanaged for too many years." *Oomph.*

She opted for a quick and truthful summary. "There are a couple of promising prospects."

Cal's smile was tight, his voice pleasant enough yet more terse than usual. "Glad to hear it."

"What about you? Are things moving ahead with the job in England?"

He nodded. "I've had a couple of Zoom calls, and the next step is an in-person interview."

An in-person interview. In England…three thousand miles away…an insurmountable ocean and unnavigable circumstances between them.

The energy required for Maya to maintain a smile through these thoughts was enough to propel her through a twenty-mile marathon. *And I'm not even a runner.* Still, she did her best to appear happy for him. "That's great. Well, good luck with that."

"Maya…"

She waited for him to say more. When he didn't, she realized that maybe it was just as well. After all, what could he possibly say at this point? *Sorry that I broke your heart. Take care and have a nice life!*

"I said goodbye to Jeremy earlier," Cal finally said after a prolonged silence.

Maya gave the slightest nod. "He told me." She wouldn't share the part about Jeremy crying to her as he did. "Well, good luck with everything," she said, her voice cracking slightly before she could finish the forced sentiment. She looked at the office door, hoping he'd take the hint. He did.

And so, moments later, he silently walked out of the door—and her life—for good.

CHAPTER FIFTEEN

MAYA STOOD OUTSIDE the clinic office and cupped her hands over her eyes to shield them from the midday sun. In the distance, she could see the tiny white speck of a passenger jet as it made its way across the sky.

Was Cal possibly on board, heading to his next adventure? It was Wednesday—five days since his official last day at the practice. They hadn't spoken since their awkward parting of ways in Maria's office, so she could only assume he was en route to England—or already there.

Inside the office once again, she sat in Maria's chair behind the desk, nervously tapping the butt of a pen on a desk pad. She didn't have much experience interviewing job candidates, but that wasn't the only reason she was struggling to focus. Images of Cal incessantly flooded her mind. Would she ever get over him? It simply didn't seem possible.

A knock on the slightly ajar door pulled her from her thoughts. "Come on in," she said in as friendly a voice as she could muster up.

The candidate did as instructed, entering the room and taking a seat across from Maya.

Ping!

The pen dropped out of her hand and bounced off her open laptop. "Cal! What are you doing here?"

A grin slowly spread across his face. "Nice to see you, too."

She had so many questions that it was impossible to get even one off the ground. "I'm about to interview someone for the vet position any second now."

"I know."

"How do you…?" Her question was cut short, in part because her gaping mouth refused to cooperate. *No…it can't be.*

Cal leaned forward and extended his hand. "Jackson Smith. Nice to meet you."

"Hold on a minute." She leaned forward and held her head in her hands, as if worried that it might topple off due to shock. Then she picked up the résumé and cover letter, flapping it in the air. "Are you saying this has been *you* all along?"

Cal's already expansive grin further widened to the point that Maya wondered if the corner of his lips would soon meet at the back of his head. "Yup."

She glanced at the cover letter, her hands trembling. "So all of this is one big lie?"

Cal teetered his head from side to side. "Ehhh…not exactly."

"Well, your name isn't Jackson Smith—let's start with that."

"Jackson's my middle name."

"And Smith?"

"Okay, that one's a fib. But it's generic enough that I figured I probably have an ancestor or two by that name, if you go back far enough."

Maya's heart was now racing so hard that she was convinced her chest must be visibly pulsating. "And you're married and want to raise a family in Maplewood." *Let's see how he talks his way out of* this *concoction*, she thought pointedly.

Cal stared at her. And stared some more. "Not a lie." He paused, "At least I hope not."

If Maya's head could swivel 360 degrees, it'd be twirling like a top. But since it had to conform to the laws of physics, she continued to look straight at him, her eyes deeply perplexed. "Cal... I am so confused right now. Can you please tell me what the heck is going on?"

"Maya, I wrote that cover letter imagining what I hope I can say about myself...about *us*...in the very near future."

Maya wanted to say, *Of course, now I understand!* Except that she didn't. Because it *almost* sounded like he was implying that she was the wife, and together with Jeremy, the three of them were the family. But that couldn't be what he meant...*could it*?

"I've been doing a lot of thinking this past week. *A lot.* And I've come to realize that in so many ways, my life has been a cliché."

Between her widened eyes and über-raised eyebrows, Maya looked like she'd been zapped by a cattle prod. "A cliché?" she repeated tepidly.

"The young boy tossed around from one foster home to another, never feeling like he was truly loved. So he spends his adult life reenacting that very same pattern, never sticking around one place too long to form real relationships. That is, until he meets an amazing woman who makes him see everything in a whole new light."

It took several moments for a slightly stunned Maya to form a reply. "Have you been binge-watching *Dr. Phil* or something?"

Cal chuckled. "I know—I kind of scared myself with the way I've been self-analyzing things. But that's what love will make you do."

Oh boy...

Maya felt like she could melt into the chair, but that wasn't going to happen. Not when Cal had already walked around the desk and pulled her up into his arms. "I love you, Maya Evans. And I want to spend my life with you and Jeremy."

"I love you, too," Maya said, her voice as stunned as the rest of her. Could this actually be happening? It seemed too good…too unbelievable…to be true, but reality came crashing back in the best way possible as Cal pulled her into a passionate kiss.

"I do have a question," she said once they finally came up for air. "Why didn't you just say from the get-go that you wanted to stay, rather than send a résumé pretending to be someone else?"

"I could have," he conceded. "But wasn't this surprise more fun?" As Maya laughed, he added, "Plus, I was working on a few things behind the scenes, and I wanted to make sure everything was in place before the big reveal."

Maya's stomach butterflies began to dance again. "What big reveal?"

Cal's grin returned full force. "Let's take a drive to your place."

Fifteen minutes later, Cal pulled his truck into Maya's driveway.

"Who are all these people at my place?" she asked, eyes scanning a small crowd spread out in front of the porch.

"Friends who are here to help."

Maya's confusion was growing exponentially. "I don't think I have this many friends," she said frankly. Truth was, she had never been a social butterfly, flitting from one superficial friendship to the next, but more like a reserved caterpillar who clung tightly to several long-held, cherished friendships. And yet, she estimated the group mingling just in front of the open porch to be at least fifteen individuals.

"Cal, *what* is going on?"

"Come on," he said with a grin as he nodded toward the group. "Let's go find out."

As they walked hand in hand, familiar faces began to come into view. Some were clients, others were their spouses whom she'd met on occasion during vet calls.

Cal gestured to the group. "Maya, I'd like you to meet the *new* Happy Hooves Horse Rescue operations team."

"I'm not sure I understand what's going on here."

"Well—and don't get upset with Maria for this—but I talked her into sharing the Equine Associates mailing list with me. Last week, I sent out an email asking for volunteers to help get the barn and fencing in working order. Everyone's here to help make your dream…" He reached over and squeezed her hand, then called to Jeremy, who'd been standing in front of a smiling Gus, his hands clasping both of his grandson's shoulders. Jeremy quickly trotted over, his cheeks nearly bursting with an outsize smile. "To make *our* dream, as a family, for a horse sanctuary come true."

"I don't believe this," Maya murmured in sheer awe. "Is this really happening?"

Clapping and cheers ensued as Cal leaned over and kissed her on the cheek. "It most definitely is." He leaned in further to whisper in her ear: "I'm keeping it G-rated for the all-ages audience, but get those soft, beautiful lips ready for when we're alone later."

I've now officially died and gone to heaven. Though Cal's strong arm around her side, propping her happy-shaky body upward, confirmed that she was still very much amongst the living.

Cal pointed to a burly man with a thick beard, who stood across the way. "We have an electrician…"

"Hi, I'm Rick."

"He's with me," Georgette, a longtime client who raised miniature horses, said with a laugh.

"And a roofer," Cal continued.

"I'm Mike, Janice's son. And I brought along a couple of my roofing buddies. This is Craig and Dave."

Maya hoped everyone could see the immense gratitude in

her eyes as she nodded in their direction with an unbridled smile, because at the moment, words escaped her.

"We also have a special guest of honor today," Cal said as he pointed to Cathy. Standing next to her sister, she waved to Maya. "Once I kick the crap out of this cancer, I'll be back here to visit everyone. And I can't wait."

That's it. I can't hold it together anymore. As Maya began to cry, Cal pulled her in even closer. She looked up at him, only to find that his own glossy eyes were just barely holding back tears. "It takes a village," he said quietly.

"True," she said softly. "But there wouldn't be this village if it weren't for one incredibly special man who made it happen. I love you."

He smiled. "I love you, too." Defying his G-rated promise, he kissed her on the lips, a long, lingering smooch that prompted another wave of applause from the crowd.

"Come on," he said to Jeremy as he tousled his hair. "Let's go pick out the perfect stall for Molly."

Holding onto Jeremy's hand, he reached out and grasped Maya's hand as well.

And with that, the trio headed to the barn. Together…like the family they were always meant to be.

* * * * *

If you enjoyed this story,
check out this other great read from
Tessa Scott
Healing the Baby Surgeon's Heart
Available now!

FALLING FOR HIS NASHVILLE NURSE

JANICE LYNN

MILLS & BOON

To Janie B Green for her never-ending kindness
to everyone who was fortunate enough
to cross her path. Love you forever.

CHAPTER ONE

NEWLY GRADUATED NURSE practitioner and busy single mom Everleigh Bennett did not have time to be reminded that she wasn't completely numb to the opposite sex, after all.

Time or not, Dr. Wryn Cooper discombobulated her hormones. It didn't help matters that her new coworker seemed as nice as he was gorgeous. His smile should come with a voltage warning.

Stepping up to the nurses' workstation counter where she stood, working on a chart, he flashed a megawatt smile. Butterflies took flight in Everleigh's belly. Indigestion, she corrected. Those weren't butterflies. She was simply battling a nervous stomach over starting her dream career. That rumbling in her stomach was just a tsunami of nerves.

"How's your morning going?"

What would he say if she told him that her morning had been great until he'd turned her brain to mush? Her brain and the rest of her, too. Ugh. Once upon a time, before Bryan had crushed her heart, she'd have called Wryn *meltworthy*. Now, she preferred the hormonally dead existence she'd been in for the past five years over the excited all-over tingles.

"It's fine." She waved her hand dismissively, getting a waft of hand sanitizer that she hoped masked the light spice scent she'd picked up on the first time they'd met. Had that really just been two weeks ago? Must be because she'd had a week with Human Resources and was now starting her second week of clinic. She avoided making eye contact. If she did, his dimples would dig deeper, the corners of his eyes would crinkle and her knees would wobble.

"You look as if something has you stumped." He leaned against the countertop partition in the corner of the clinic's L-shaped walkway that separated where the nurses sat. A couple of triage stations, patient restrooms, and reception and checkout staff lined the short end of the L. The longer end of the hallway had sixteen examination rooms. A double-doored partition at the end of the L led to provider and support staff offices, storage areas, a kitchen breakroom, employee restrooms and a conference room. "Tell me how I can help."

By disappearing. By not being so nice. By not waking up her slumbering insides. Everleigh swallowed. Um, yeah. Her mind was mush. She needed to get a grip.

"I'm good. Living the dream." She really was. Being a nurse practitioner, working for the internal medicine department of the prestigious Nashville clinic fresh out of school, had been a goal for so long that Everleigh had to pinch herself to prove that she was awake. Being able to better provide for Hayes and to have more quality time with him was worth the crazy hours, sacrifices and lack of sleep of the past few years. She'd burned the candle at both ends for so long she wasn't sure she knew how not to, but she looked forward to figuring out how to relax and enjoy more time with her son.

"Living the dream, eh?" Wryn chuckled. "I like you, Everleigh. You remind me to be grateful to be here."

Why was her heart racing that he'd just said he liked her? This was not high school. His comment had been innocent.

Even if it hadn't been, she wasn't interested in a relationship. Not with him or anyone other than with her son and her mother.

"Are you not grateful to be here?" She glanced Wryn's way. Big mistake. Her gaze connected with his. Just as it had done on the day they'd met and every time since, her heartbeat stalled. With his unusual combination of coal-black hair and smiling blue eyes, he was undeniably striking. How could eyes smile? His did, full-on, radiating-joy smiling, which was why his comment seemed out of place with the happy-go-lucky man he presented as.

Looking thoughtful, he nodded. "I'm grateful. For the job and for sunshiny new coworkers."

Everleigh snorted. "I hope you don't mean me. *Sunshiny* I am not."

She was sunshiny around Hayes, though. How could she not be when he was such a bright light? Being a single mom wasn't easy but would be much simpler now that she wasn't juggling school on top of working full-time as an emergency room nurse. She'd had to maintain her work hours to keep their bills paid and to keep her health insurance. She'd learned long ago how devastating not having health insurance could be on one's finances.

Wryn's dark brow arched. "You look sunshiny to me."

Everleigh fought sighing. "Don't let the hair fool you."

Although the long strands were clipped up, her golden hair had caused her to be the brunt of so many dumb-blonde jokes over her lifetime that she'd considered more than once dying it to a darker shade just to be taken seriously. Most of the people she met underestimated her intelligence and expected her to have a bubbly personality. She had too many responsibilities to bubble. Always had. With her mom's fickle diabetes, she couldn't recall a time when she hadn't had to adult. Usually, she just brushed off blond assumptions about herself, but she clung to Wryn's, telling herself he wasn't nearly as nice as he seemed.

"I can see why you might think that." His words came out a slow drawl. "But I wasn't referring to your hair. I meant how you bounce through the hallways as if you're living your best life."

Heat burned her cheeks.

"Oh." Not that she believed she bounced. She wasn't a bouncer. Realists didn't bounce. However, she'd decided long ago that she could face life with a good attitude or with a bad one, but either way she was presented with the same set of circumstances. How she viewed those circumstances was what she had control over. Life wasn't perfect, but there was so much good. She had Hayes, had finished nurse-practitioner school and had started her job at the prestigious Nashville Medical Clinic. Things were finally on the upswing. She could breathe without worrying about what paper she hadn't written or what test she hadn't studied for. Despite Bryan's lingering insults floating through her mind on occasion, she'd graduated with honors and could now reap the rewards. Maybe she had been bouncing because after a long period of barely keeping her head above water, she really was living her best life.

"Dr. Cooper, room four is ready." Wryn's nurse came around to sit at her workstation, having finished triaging the patient. "I'll have the chart open and ready for you in a jiffy."

Still smiling, Wryn shifted his gaze to the nurse he'd apparently worked with from when he'd started at the clinic a few years prior. "Thanks, Eva."

He lingered another moment, his eyes so blue they made her think of the sky on the clearest day, then with another heart-fluttering—er, acid-inducing—smile, he headed to room four. Everleigh hadn't consciously realized her gaze followed him down the hallway until Eva cleared her throat. Face on fire, Everleigh glanced toward the nurse. From where she sat at the computer, Eva gave a knowing look, like, *Oh yeah, girl, we get you*, but didn't say a word, which Everleigh greatly appreciated. Did the nurse think she was one of Dr. Cooper's many admirers? She wasn't. Much.

Refocusing on work, Everleigh saw a few more patients and was back at the counter, trying to figure out where to log the date of her previous patient's abnormal mammogram results. She sensed Wryn coming down the hallway prior to seeing him. That he stopped at the nurses' workstation didn't surprise her. It's what the providers did, charting on their laptops while standing there prior to popping in to see their next patient. She just wished he wouldn't.

"That scowl is deep for someone living her best life." His tone was teasing as he reminded of her earlier claim.

Ignoring him was impossible. And rude, which she liked to think she never was. So without meeting his intense blues, she said, "Even sunshiny days can have puffy white cloud moments."

"True." Grinning, he gestured toward her screen. "Tell me and maybe I can point you in the right direction."

He was right. She'd accepted help earlier from Dr. Woods. So why did having Wryn show her something feel different? Maybe because her tongue was stuck to the roof of her mouth. Heart flutters, caught breath, mushed brain, stuck tongue—the man sure did funny things to her insides.

"Liz can help me when she finishes triaging my next patient," Everleigh managed, swallowing in attempt to moisten her mouth. In her early forties, Liz was a curvy brunette with a snarky sense of humor that often made Everleigh laugh.

Wryn shrugged. "Or I could help you now so you'll be ready to jump in with your next patient when Liz finishes."

He was right. Everleigh was making a big deal out of something that wasn't.

She turned her laptop to where he could more readily see the screen. "I know where to record health maintenance." She tapped the keys to pull down the menu. "My patient had an abnormal mammogram screening, then a follow-up coned-down diagnostic mammogram and an ultrasound. I'm searching for a way to document those additional tests but only see where to record the screening test. I want to be specific on what she had done."

Wryn glanced up from the computer monitor screen. "Liz can do that for you. Eva records this information before I go in the room."

Everleigh was still adjusting to the transition from nurse to provider role. She was so used to doing those types of things in her nursing role at the emergency room that she just automatically did them. Although she'd transferred from another department, Liz was a fairly new hire as well, and Everleigh didn't want to bother her any more than she had to, especially if it was something she could easily do herself.

"Liz usually records my patients' health maintenance items, but this particular patient failed to mention to Liz that she'd had the tests as they were done through her gynecologist's office rather than us as her primary care," she said in defense of her nurse. "She's seen at a clinic off West End."

"Happens a lot where patients tell us things they've forgotten to mention during triage. Here's where you can add notes to your health maintenance section." Leaning close, he placed his finger on her keypad and guided the arrow on the screen to the tab. He smelled amazing, like fresh air with a subtle hint of spice. It was all Everleigh could do to keep from moving in for a closer sniff. *Hello*, she did not sniff coworkers. She'd not ever wanted to sniff anyone. Not even Bryan. Or if she had, that desire was so long gone that she'd forgotten.

There was a party pooper thought and why she rarely let thoughts of her ex into her head. Everything about Bryan had been negative. Well, almost everything. Without him, she wouldn't have Hayes. At some point he must have done something right for her to have fallen for him. They'd married because of Hayes, but she often wondered why he'd bothered since he'd left when Hayes was only a few months old. Sadly, she'd mostly felt relieved.

"If you click here, then on this tab," Wryn demonstrated as he talked, bringing her attention back to Mr. Smells So Good, "this drop-down menu will appear. Click the Additional Information tab."

"Ah, that makes sense." She put his instructions to memory. "Thanks."

He should have straightened, should have moved out of her workspace, instead he turned toward her and smiled. "You're welcome."

Good grief, even up close he was perfection. Every. Single. Pore.

Everleigh gulped, and even though it put her at an awkward angle at her computer, she stepped back. Seeming to realize that he was in her personal space and no longer had a reason to be so close, Wryn straightened and looked a little disconcerted himself. "Anytime."

With that, he headed toward his next patient's room.

What was it about him that got to her so? That made her all breathy and like she couldn't think? She'd been around good-looking men before. Granted, Wryn topped the list, but Bryan had been no slouch when it came to looks. His slouching had been as a life partner and father. There, Bryan excelled.

And served as the perfect reminder of why she'd been so comfortably numb.

Dr. Wryn Cooper moved his stethoscope diaphragm to the right second intercostal space to listen for aortic valve abnormalities on the seventy-two-year-old African American gentleman sitting on the examination table. Thankfully, he didn't hear any murmurs or other issues. He finished listening to the patient's heart sounds, then auscultated his breath sounds. Unfortunately, Mr. Peterson's lungs weren't nearly as good as his cardiac exam had been.

Wryn finished listening over the right lung's lower lobe. "Have you had shortness of breath?"

"Some, Doc. Mainly it's just with activity, though." Mr. Peterson went on to elaborate. "It doesn't bother me too much. I take breaks as I need to. Things take longer, but I get them done."

No doubt. Wryn got the impression the mechanic had always worked hard, and the success of his garage gave testament to that.

"I'm ordering a chest X-ray. I think you have right lower lobe pneumonia."

The man's face contorted with surprise. "Is that why I've been so tired?"

"Probably." He explained how fluid and mucus could fill the alveoli, causing poor oxygen exchange in the air sacks and how that led to shortness of breath and fatigue. "The radiology department is on the bottom floor. My nurse will give instructions on going there and what to do afterwards. I expect the radiologist to have at least a verbal report to me before the end of the day."

Wryn spoke with the patient a few more moments prior to giving verbal orders to Eva then moved on to his next patient. The busy afternoon passed quickly, and when the call came regarding Mr. Peterson's X-ray results, the images did show right lung lower lobe pneumonia.

Wryn called him, explained the findings and the treatment plan, for which Wryn had already called in the prescriptions. He finished going through messages, logged out of his computer and left his office to go meet friends. Only, as he made his way down the back hallway, his gaze did what it had done continuously for the past couple of weeks. It shifted to the right as he reached Everleigh Bennett's shared office. He hadn't meant to pause, but alone in the small room, Everleigh sat at her desk, rubbing her temples. She hadn't noticed him, and he took the moment to study her. Her big brown eyes were locked on her computer screen. A few strands of her golden hair had worked loose from her ponytail. Her full pink lips pursed from her intense concentration.

Everleigh had intrigued him from the first when the human resources director introduced them. Wryn wasn't used to his heart jumping into tachycardia, but around Everleigh, it raced as if competing for the Indy 500's pole position.

Everleigh glanced up, spotting him in her doorway. Surprise lit on her face. "Dr. Cooper?"

"It's Wryn," he reminded, not liking the formality of his professional name when it was just the two of them. "Headache?"

Her hand dropped from where she'd been massaging her temple. "Just trying to figure out my best course of action on a patient's abnormal labs."

"Want a second opinion?" He expected her to say no.

Why was she so reluctant to accept his help? Providers consulted with each other even after practicing for many years. He still did at times, especially with some of the clinic's specialists.

"I—" She started to prove his suspicion correct by saying no, he could see it on her face, but then, looking embarrassed, she nodded. "Sure. That would be great."

His smile radiated through him, starting in the pit of his stomach and shooting outward. He sat across from her desk and waited for specifics. Sitting meant not getting too close as he'd done earlier. The last thing he wanted was to make her uncomfortable. Yes, he'd been close, but he'd been helping her so wasn't doing anything out of line, not beyond behaving like an awkward teen who was in the presence of the stunning homecoming queen.

"On Monday, I saw a fifty-four-year-old Caucasian female. Rita is new to the clinic and hasn't had a primary care provider in a few years. Fatigue was her chief concern. I ordered all the usual health maintenance–type things to get her up-to-date for her age. She appeared jaundiced so I wasn't surprised when her liver enzymes and bilirubin came back elevated." She told him the numbers. "Because of the jaundice, I got a hepatitis panel, too."

"Good thinking."

"Thanks. It was negative so not the cause of her jaundice, though." Her cheeks flushed. "Her vitamin B twelve levels were elevated, while her red blood cell count and folate were low," she continued, oblivious or just ignoring how he studied her face. "Her iron and ferritin counts came back extremely elevated."

When she told him the readings, he whistled. "Any personal or family history of hemochromatosis?"

Everleigh shook her head. "There's no history of any

iron disorders that she is aware of. She denies supplements of any type and lives in a newer home on city water where the water supply shouldn't be an issue. I do have genetic markers for hemochromatosis and methylenetetrahydrofolate reductase on my list of items to check, along with an ultrasound of her liver."

"Good plan," he praised. "Does she drink alcohol?"

"Two to three glasses of red wine a day."

He'd guess it to be more than that. Studies showed how much a person reported drinking was usually much lower than their actual alcohol consumption. "With her labs, she needs to quit."

Everleigh took a deep breath. "I called her earlier to discuss her results, to make recommendations, including suggesting she stop alcohol, and asked her to come by the lab to have more blood drawn for the additional tests. Those orders were what I was studying when you came in, doing online research to make sure I wasn't overlooking anything obvious that I should order."

"So, you have the hemochromatosis and MTHFR markers. What else?"

"Rita's ferritin and iron were so extreme that a repeat check is warranted." Her shoulders lifted, as did her chin, almost as if she expected him to contradict her.

Instead, he nodded. "Agreed. What else?"

"I was considering pancreatic enzymes—amylase and lipase. Probably a carcinoembryonic antigen and cancer antigen-nineteen-nine, too, although she didn't report any family history of cancer."

"Not a bad idea since her numbers were so elevated. You may get a false-positive due to how out of range her liver labs are, but getting a baseline may prove useful. What else?" he prompted. Seeing her brain at work to figure out her patient's diagnosis was an enlightening mix of confidence and need for reassurance that she was making the right decisions. She had heart and cared about her patient. He liked that.

"A gamma-glutamyl transferase test to further evaluate her liver disease."

"Okay." His gaze met hers, and he couldn't help but smile. He did that a lot around her. She just made his lips curve upward. "You've got a great start. I'm impressed. You've covered all the blood tests I'd order to follow up on those initial results. So why the temple rub?"

She gave a self-deprecating laugh. "I'm the new girl and straight out of school. I don't want to miss something."

"You're always welcome to run anything by me for a second opinion." He hoped she would. It would provide opportunity to interact, which he seemed to crave. "Dr. Woods and Dr. Evans are great resources, too. Any feedback you get will be meant to help you learn."

Everleigh leaned back in her chair. "Everyone tells me I'll learn more in the first six months of working than I did while in school."

"There's some truth to that." He was glad to see that she'd relaxed a little. "For whatever it's worth, the only thing I'd add to what you're doing is that I'd put in a hepatology consult referral to get the ball rolling on the appointment being scheduled. Regardless of the additional test results, your patient needs specialty care."

Everleigh's cheeks pinkened. "I planned on doing that, and a hematology consult to assess the low red blood cell count, elevated vitamin B twelve, high iron and ferritin, too."

"Perfect." Smiling, he nodded his approval. "Rita's an interesting case. Keep me posted on the results."

"Okay." She stared at where he sat across from her, probably wondering why he was still there. He was wondering that himself. He had places to be.

"A few of us play pickleball at the facility just down the street. Would you like to join us?" His question surprised him but shouldn't have. Everleigh fascinated him.

Her eyes widened. "I don't have a membership."

"The complex allows members to bring a guest. You can be mine." He willed her to say yes.

She shook her head. "I'll have to pass. Thanks for the invitation, though."

That's when it hit him that she already had plans. His stomach knotted. Of course she already had plans.

"Are you not a pickleball fan?" What he really wanted to know was who she was spending her evening with. Not that it was any of his business. He'd heard through the grapevine that she wasn't married, but that didn't mean she was single.

She shrugged. "I've never played."

"I'll be happy to teach you." There he went offering to spend time with her again.

She crinkled her nose. "Pickleball?"

"Don't knock it until you've tried it. It's fun and a great way to burn off energy." Maybe the exercise would get blood pumping to his brain so he could think more clearly.

"Fair enough," she conceded. After a moment's hesitation, she added, "Maybe some other time."

So if in a relationship, it must not be anything of consequence. Why did that make him happy? He was not in the market for a relationship. He dated, but never anything long-term. Not since Kara, and that had never been intended to get serious. Not by either of them, but fate had dealt them a different story.

"I'm going to hold you to that, Everleigh." Because not

even thoughts of Kara were enough to dim his attraction to Everleigh, which was disconcerting. Thoughts of Kara usually triggered a guilty tailspin as mistakes made during his late teens dragged him into darkness.

For the first time in a long time, Wryn longed to step into the sunshine.

For all his inability to stay away from Everleigh, he knew better.

Sunshine exposed things better kept in the dark.

CHAPTER TWO

"How's your elevated-iron patient's labs?"

Jumping when Wryn came into the employee break room, Everleigh managed not to spill coffee from the mug she held. Barely. How could he look so great first thing in the morning? He'd opted for navy scrubs that had his name embroidered on the left breast. That name, and the man it belonged to, played through her mind much too often.

"Not great." Steadying her cup, she grimaced at recall of the labs she'd reviewed that morning. The previous day, her patient had had labs drawn, and the results had been waiting for Everleigh's review when she'd arrived. "The CA-nineteen-nine and carcinoembryonic antigen were elevated." She'd hoped those results would be within normal ranges to decrease the likelihood of cancer being the cause of her patient's abnormalities. "But, like you mentioned, that may be from her liver being so stressed."

"Hopefully so." A blue-and-gold hockey team mug in hand, he walked to where she stood near the coffeepot.

"Her hemochromatosis genetic tests were negative." Meeting Wryn's gaze, Everleigh fought gulping. He was way hotter than her coffee had ever been, and that was so not what she should be thinking.

Wryn's brow arched. "The negative hemochromatosis

markers are surprising. Her liver disease must be driving her iron levels upward, then. How were her other labs?"

Everleigh took a sip of her coffee then answered, "Her MTHFR was positive, so that explains the low folate level."

"You've started her on a methylated folate supplement?"

"I sent a script to her pharmacy and advised that she could pick up an over-the-counter version if her insurance didn't cover the tablets," Everleigh assured him. "Her appointment with hematology is next week, and her hepatology appointment is the following week."

"She's a fascinating case," he mused.

Darn that smile and how it sent her heart racing. Maybe it was the coffee. Maybe she'd accidentally grabbed a high-octane espresso. "The negative hemochromatosis threw me in what I was thinking might be triggering a lot of her issues."

He picked up the coffeepot and poured his cup mostly full. "Did Dr. Evans make recommendations when reviewing your chart?"

Everleigh shook her head. "Nothing so far. Hopefully, that's a good sign that he doesn't think I'm missing something major."

"Based on our conversations, you've covered your bases." He put back the coffeepot. "I need to cut down on this stuff."

It was something she heard her mother say time and again. Everleigh automatically smiled. "You probably should."

She wasn't positive she would have survived graduate school without coffee but had cut back herself. With not having such long days or sitting up studying after having already finished a twelve-plus-hour shift, she'd not required as many perk-me-up infusions. Noting that Wryn didn't add anything to his mug, she gestured toward it. "You take your coffee black?"

The corner of his mouth lifted. "Is there any other way?"

She tilted her cup just enough so he could see the tan liquid.

He chuckled. "Looks like you like a little coffee with your cream and sugar."

"I've only added milk," she countered.

His brow arched. "No sugar or cream?"

She shook her head. With her mother's diabetes, Everleigh avoided adding sugar, and milk had been more affordable than cream. She'd grown accustomed to the taste and now preferred it.

"Adding milk cools my coffee to where I can start drinking sooner. So there is that," she said in mock defense, taking a big sip of the warm liquid to prove her point.

He didn't look convinced that was justification for what he deemed as her ruining her drink.

"Whereas yours will be too hot for several minutes still," she continued, smiling.

Eyes crinkling at the corners, he took a big drink.

Knowing how hot the recently made coffee was, Everleigh's mouth dropped. "Did you seriously just scald your mouth to prove me wrong?"

"Nope." He laughed. "Being right isn't that necessary." He took another drink, then twinkling eyes smiling, he added, "Don't tell, and I'll let you in on my secret."

There went her lungs forgetting how to exchange oxygen again. Fighting the urge to suck in a deep breath, she eyed him as she waited for him to continue.

Leaning back against the countertop, he took another drink. "I topped off what was already in my cup."

"You had cold coffee in your cup?" Her heart pounded as if she'd drunk the entire pot by herself. What was it about Wryn that made her insides so jittery?

"Not intentionally." His grin was almost too much. "What was there had grown cold while sitting on my desk."

"Oh, uh, okay." What was wrong with her that she was smiling back at him and sounding like she had no brain? Wryn Cooper messed with her head big-time. "I should get back to my patients. Fortunately, my schedule is fairly full today. Enjoy your coffee."

Two weeks later, Everleigh smiled at her patient, reminding the woman to be sure to schedule her lab recheck appointment. Following the woman out of the exam room and, not having another patient prior to her lunch break, she planned to go to her office. She'd check messages prior to joining the pharmaceutical-sponsored lunch in the clinic's conference room. Still feeling as if she had so much to learn about the different medications and their uses, Everleigh enjoyed the educational lunches. Plus, the group lunches gave her opportunity to get to know her colleagues better without cutting into family time with Hayes.

There were eight physicians and ten midlevel providers in the clinic's internal medicine department. With most on four-day work schedules, there were usually a dozen or so at the luncheons. Inevitably, Wryn sat next to her or directly across from her. Today he was beside her. Every so often, she could smell the fresh outdoorsy scent that she'd forever associate with him. That had to be her imagination playing tricks, though, because she couldn't really smell him over the catered lunch that included several Italian dishes and garlic rolls.

The pretty pharmaceutical representative smiled and hawked her product, telling all about the latest and greatest of the heart failure medication. Everleigh tried to pay close attention, but Wryn being right next to her was a big distraction.

"Are you taking notes?" he whispered, leaning in close.

Cheeks heating, Everleigh fought inhaling deeply. "With my fork, you mean?" she whispered back, waving the utensil.

"You looked intense. I thought you might be making mental notes." His tone teased, and she knew he was just making conversation. He did that a lot. So much so that she was starting to think she'd miss it if he stopped. What was she thinking? She'd known him for under a month. She would not miss his conversation if it stopped. Her life would be simpler if he did just that.

"I'm trying to learn as much as I can." She gave him a pointed look. "You should be doing the same."

His eyes twinkled. "It's a clean drug, so not a lot to remember on this one. No renal or liver adjustments. No medication contraindications. Expensive, but has a decent co-pay card that can be used for patients with commercial insurance. No lab monitoring required."

"Got it." She doubted she'd forget anything about the medication since he'd been the one to tell her. "The company should hire you because that's a lot easier for me to remember than all these computer slides."

"I'd miss patient care," he said. "On trying to remember everything, don't be afraid to look up things. We all do."

"I'd be more afraid of not looking up things," she admitted.

He nodded his approval. "Learn dangerous medication combinations. The rest you'll pick up with time and experience. Fortunately, our electronic medical record system alerts us when we attempt to prescribe something to someone we shouldn't."

Everleigh had been grateful for that feature numerous times already, mainly when she kept trying to prescribe a sulfa-based antibiotic to patients who took a certain angiotensin receptor-blocker blood pressure medication. You'd think she'd have that one put to memory by now.

The representative said something directly to Wryn, returning his focus to the meeting. Unfortunately, Everleigh's attention lingered on him. Ugh. What was wrong with her? She'd never been so gaga over Bryan's smile.

With Bryan, she'd been young and easy prey for his frequently vocalized belief that she was lucky he gave her the time of day. He'd been good-looking and charming when he wanted to be and had broken her heart time and again with his verbal abuse. How many times had he told her how stupid she was? How worthless? Swallowing, Everleigh blocked memories before they took hold. Over the past five years, she'd blocked a lot of memories concerning her ex and wished she could block more. Such as the one where he'd walked out on her and Hayes after barely a year of marriage. She didn't want to block that one. It served as a reminder that nothing was forever. She knew that. Hadn't her dad done the same, leaving his eight-year-old daughter to fend for his ill wife when he'd abandoned them?

Everleigh blew out a breath then forced a smile when Wryn's gaze cut to her. No wonder she'd not missed dating. She'd not even thought of her lack of companionship until meeting Wryn. Now he grinned and…could one ache from loneliness? And what did that even mean? She wasn't lonely. She had her mother and Hayes. Yet, staring into Wryn's eyes made her very aware that something might be missing.

Swallowing, she turned and tuned back into the representative. The educational portion of their lunch meeting ended. Several lingered, chitchatting with the pharmaceutical rep and among themselves. Wanting to avoid more conversation with Wryn and to get to her messages so she could get out of the office sooner that evening, Everleigh thanked the woman for lunch, excused herself and then pushed back from the table. Her heart kicked up when Wryn did the same and walked out of the conference room at her side.

"How's your patient?" he asked. "The one with the elevated iron and liver tests?"

Did he really want to know, or was he making small talk? He did that a lot, which left her flustered. Because the look in his eyes was more than just professional coworker interest, and her crazy body lit up around him like a Fourth of July celebration. She didn't have time for such nonsense.

Yes, you do. Now that you've earned your doctorate in nursing, you have more free time than you've ever had. Just look at what a great few weekends you've spent with Hayes.

Where had that voice come from? No matter. It was wrong. Any extra time she had would be spent with her son, making up for the long hours she'd worked for all of his short life. Not by choice but by necessity to keep their family afloat. She'd been determined to provide him with a better life. Perhaps she owed Bryan for leaving, as his doing so had made her even more determined to be successful in her academic pursuits.

"She's improving."

"That's great," Wryn praised. "What did you do?"

"It's what she did." At his look, Everleigh clarified, "She stopped drinking alcohol."

He continued to walk down the hall at her side. "With her liver disease, every sip was like dumping fuel on a fire. I imagine she is feeling better."

Everleigh nodded. "Unless everything stems from the alcohol, we've not gotten to the root problem. But that she's feeling better is a start, and hopefully the specialists will figure out the rest."

"Good job."

Everleigh glanced toward him. Her breath caught at his smile as their eyes met. Wowsers! He was hot. She had to stop thinking that. She was not the type of woman to categorize a man by his looks. She wasn't. Yet, with Wryn... categorizing him that way was easy but unfair because he was intelligent, kind and charming and had the best smile and...and she'd obviously suffered some type of mental lapse. One that had released a surge of hormones that she'd assumed were gone but had obviously been awaiting the opportunity to burst free. Hadn't she just been thinking of Bryan? Why wasn't that providing protection from Wryn's effect on her? Why wasn't she able to shake free from whatever chemistry burned between them? Was she destined to keep making the same mistakes? She needed walls between them, because her life was going too well to risk a repeat of the past.

"Thanks for letting me run my care plan by you." She chose her words carefully. She did appreciate his kindness, but she needed a little less friendliness. Not because of him but because she didn't want to be aware of him as a man, and until she wasn't—which was likely never because he was very manly—well, they needed well-established boundaries. "If I haven't said it before, I'm grateful for how helpful a colleague you are. You're a great coworker."

"You're welcome." His smile wavered, then as they reached her office, he gave a soft chuckle. "I'm trying to decide if that was a true compliment or if you just purposely coworker-zoned me."

Everleigh's breath caught. He didn't miss a thing. "My compliment was sincere."

Studying her, he arched his brow. "Does that mean you weren't coworker-zoning me?"

"I'm not sure I know exactly what that means," she semi-fibbed. *Semi*, because with anyone else she'd make certain assumptions about what it meant. With Wryn, was he implying he didn't want to be coworker-zoned? Don't be a dunce, Everleigh. You know he's interested. You've seen the way he looks at you, the way he smiles at you and seeks out your company.

"If it isn't obvious what I'm asking, then you've not been paying attention, which gives me my answer as I never want to make you feel uncomfortable." He gave a half smile then shrugged. "Coworkers it is, then. Well, coworkers and friends."

Too late. Everything about him made her feel uncomfortable because Dr. Wryn Cooper shoved her outside her comfort level.

Coworkers and friends? That worked. She hadn't had a lot of time for friends over the past five years, either, and Wryn was a genuinely likable person. Yeah, that made sense, she assured herself. He had been helpful and kind and was a well-respected colleague. Of course they'd be friends and coworkers.

But that was all they'd be.

"Good morning, Everleigh. I see you're still drinking that polluted pale stuff."

Automatically smiling at the man who'd entered the break room just as she'd done every time their paths crossed since their friends-and-coworkers talk the previous week, Everleigh lifted her mug toward Wryn then took a sip. "No reason to mess with a good thing."

He laughed. "If you say so. Big plans for the weekend?"

Only if he considered spending every precious moment

with Hayes and her mother, because they were the only plans she had. She loved that her schedule was so free. She'd give Hayes options on ways to spend their Saturday and let him pick. On Sunday, they'd accompany her mother to the church she'd gone to all her life. Everleigh had barely attended the past few years with school and work, but her mother had brought Hayes every time the doors were open, and it was where his preschool was. She'd miss him being there when he started kindergarten that fall.

"Nothing too exciting by most standards," she admitted. "Just spending time with family. You?"

"Not spending time with family," he answered immediately, filling his cup with coffee before turning back toward her.

"You sound as if you're glad of that."

He shrugged. "I don't have family in Nashville, so spending time with family isn't a viable option, nor is it a big deal."

"If you say so," she tossed back. To Everleigh, family was everything. Her mother, her son—she couldn't imagine not living near them. Of course, some might look down upon the fact that she lived with her mother, but as Everleigh had paid most of the rent for years and had needed the help with Hayes, it's how their little family had survived. Plus, Everleigh liked being close with her mother.

"Not all families are created equal."

"True," she conceded, realizing that outside of work, she really didn't know much about him. As his friend, she should, right? "Did you purposely move away from yours?"

"Purposely?" He shook his head. "I never said family was my reason for moving away from Missouri."

Missouri, she noted. That's where he was from.

"What would you say were the reasons?" she pressed, curious.

"School," he supplied without hesitation. "I got a scholarship to Vanderbilt for undergrad and stayed for medical school. I interned in Rome, Georgia, then Columbia, South Carolina but made my way back to Tennessee after finishing residency."

"Why Nashville?"

His face contorted for such a brief second that she wondered if she'd imagined it. Whatever, his smile returned as he said, "I like Nashville. You?"

"I suppose so. It's all I've ever known. I grew up just outside the city limits, went to school here and work here."

His brow lifted. "A homegrown girl."

"I am."

"Nothing wrong with that. The city has a lot to offer."

"That it does." She glanced at her watch. "Oh, Liz will have my first patient in a room soon. Enjoy that icky black stuff you drink."

"I'll do that," he affirmed, his laughter warming her insides in ways it shouldn't. It was just laughter, but she couldn't help but smile back. "See you in a few."

Because they bumped into each other multiple times every day. With their work schedules overlapping, they always would.

Her eyes met his, and ignoring the quickening sensation in her belly, her smile widened.

She was just smiling so big because they were coworkers who were having a friendly conversation because they were also friends. She'd be doing the same if she'd had a similar conversation with Eva or Liz.

Hands shaking, Everleigh went to her office and placed her coffee mug on her desk.

The same as with Eva and Liz. Right.

CHAPTER THREE

IN A PERFECT WORLD, Everleigh would have taken off a few weeks over the summer to spend with Hayes prior to his starting school that fall. There were bills to be paid. Taking off hadn't been an option. Working four ten-hour days wasn't so bad, though. The ten-hour days were more like twelve depending upon how much preplanning for the following day she did. Fortunately, she could sign into the EMR system after she put Hayes to bed. On the days she worked, Hayes enjoyed preschool and time with his grammy.

Vivien hadn't come to the park with Everleigh and Hayes. She'd had plans to meet a friend for a late breakfast prior to starting her waitressing shift. Everleigh hoped to soon have them financially at the point where her mother could quit the waitressing job she'd worked Everleigh's entire life. The diner's crew were great, more like family than coworkers, but her mother worked too hard with too little to show for it.

"Can we have s'mores with our picnic?" His brown eyes in full puppy mode, Hayes bounced along next to her as they walked toward the park's playground. It wasn't the closest playground to where they lived, but as it was much nicer, it was worth the extra fifteen minutes' drive. A light breeze ruffled Hayes's blond curls and broke the warm summer day's heat.

"S'mores?" Everleigh smiled at her whole world. "We

would need a fire pit to melt the marshmallows." Not that she'd packed marshmallows or s'more-making supplies. "But after our picnic, maybe the ice cream truck will run." To help keep her mother from straying from her low-carb diet, they didn't keep sweets in the house. Everleigh didn't mind and the lack thereof was all Hayes had ever known. Everleigh wanted him to grow up with good dietary habits but wasn't opposed to the occasional treat.

"I like ice cream." Hayes grinned, completely melting Everleigh's heart. "I'm glad I picked the park by my school."

"It was a great choice." Very few good things had come out of Everleigh's relationship with Bryan, but Hayes more than made up for all the bad she'd endured. Hayes was the best of everything, and there was nothing she wouldn't do to protect him. Unable to stop herself, she reached for his hand, and he happily clasped his tiny fingers within hers. Bryan was the one who had lost out by leaving, just as her father had lost out. Being a parent was such a blessing.

"I hope the ice cream truck has the blue kind," he continued, excited and having completely forgotten about s'mores. "It's the best."

Blue was Hayes's favorite color. Anything blue must be way better than any other shade, no matter what they were referring to. Smiling, Everleigh placed her bag near a base, then pushed Hayes on the swings. Next, she swung next to him as they pretended they were airplanes and talked about the places they'd go.

"The moon!" Hayes exclaimed.

"The moon?" Everleigh enthused. "That's a great place to go."

"Where are you going?" he asked as they swung back and forth.

"If you're going to the moon, then that's where I'm going, too," she assured him.

He glanced her way and grinned.

They swung for a while longer, but soon Hayes joined about twenty other children on the playground. Soon, they were all running and hiding in the various nooks of the playground's slides and elevated walkways. Everleigh sat on a bench at the edge of the padded play yard, watching with the same awe and pride she felt at most times when looking at her son. Keeping a check on him, she pulled out her phone and, from habit, opened the smartphone app that let her see her mother's glucose level. Although programmed to notify Everleigh if her mother's numbers jumped outside the preset range, after numerous occasions of scary hypoglycemic episodes prior to their getting the continuous glucose monitor, Everleigh couldn't keep herself from checking. The monitoring system had been a game changer. It wasn't cheap, but it was worth every penny. Her mother's high-deductible insurance plan didn't cover the device but had helped keep them from losing everything during her hospital stays, so the hefty monthly premiums were worth it.

After about thirty minutes, a pink-faced Hayes ran to her. "Did you know Kevin and Timmy from my school are here? I'm thirsty."

"That's awesome." She handed him his blue drink bottle they'd filled with ice water prior to leaving home. "You have thirty more minutes, then we'll have our lunch."

"Okay." He started to take off to rejoin his friends when something beyond her caught his eye. Something that must have been amazing because his entire face lit up. "Can I go see the dog, Mama?"

Everleigh turned. The fenced dog park that was just behind her had been empty when they'd arrived, but now a medium-size black-and-white mixed-breed dog was leaping to catch a Frisbee its owner had just thrown. Its very gorgeous and familiar owner. What was Wryn doing at the park?

Coworker and friend, that's all, she reminded herself. Heaven help her, because that was the zone she needed to keep him safely tucked in. Doing that seemed more and more impossible each time she saw him. His easy smile as he praised the dog, the ripple of arm muscles as he tossed the Frisbee, the sunshine casting a glisten to his skin and dark hair. Everleigh gulped.

Hayes ran straight toward the gate.

"Hayes!" Why hadn't he waited on her response prior to taking off? He knew better. Yes, she could see him, and he wasn't going that far. It was where he was going, to whom he was going, that had her heart pounding. She hadn't been prepared to come face-to-face with Wryn outside of work.

Grabbing her backpack, cooler bag and their drinks, Everleigh took off after Hayes, arriving inside the dog park just in time to hear him say "I like your dog."

Hayes liked every animal but especially dogs. They'd never had one. With school and work and trying to be a good mom and daughter, Everleigh hadn't added Dog Mom to her list of titles or household expenses. Maybe she'd take on that responsibility soon now that she was finished with school and had completed boards.

"Yeah? Brady's a great dog." Wryn took the Frisbee from the fortyish-pound dog and gave him a good scratching along his neck. "Aren't you, boy?"

The dog gave an affirmative woof then licked Wryn's hand.

"Can I pet him?" Hayes's eyes added *pretty please* to the end without him saying the words out loud.

Wryn glanced at Everleigh long enough for their eyes to meet. Surprise at seeing her shone there, then he returned his attention to Hayes. "Sure, if you get permission from your...aunt?"

"Mother," she corrected, wondering at Wryn's odd expression. Did he feel as discombobulated as Everleigh that they'd bumped into each other outside the office?

"Can I, Mama? Please." Hayes gaze was full of assurance that his world would end if she said no.

Everleigh glanced at the dog with his tongue hanging from his mouth with a bit of drool dangling from it. Although looking as if he could barely hold himself still, he patiently waited for Wryn to give his approval for him to love on Hayes.

"Okay." It wasn't as if she could say no when Hayes was so eager to pet the dog, and the dog appeared just as eager to reciprocate. What explanation could she have given? No, he couldn't pet the dog because she worked with his owner who had been nothing but kind and helpful? "You can pet the dog, and then we need to go back to the playground and leave Dr. Cooper and his dog alone."

Wryn's gaze narrowed at her in question, but Hayes was excitedly trying to decide how best to approach Brady, soon capturing Wryn's full attention. "Just hold still and let him come to you," he told her son then nodded at the dog, who wasted no time in greeting Hayes with a sloppy doggy kiss.

"Oh!" Hayes exclaimed, protecting his face. "He's licking me."

"It's his way of saying hello."

Hayes giggled as the dog continued to show his affection. "His tongue is wet."

"Yep. Brady, stop with the face-licking."

The dog looked up at Wryn, gave a woof and, to Everleigh's surprise, stopped licking Hayes. Seeming to be waiting for guidance on what was permissible, the dog continued to stare at his owner.

Kneeling, Wryn pet him. "Brady won't hurt you. He loves to be petted, especially here." Wryn scratched the dog's neck. "Don't you, boy?"

Moving close to where Wryn knelt, Hayes pet Brady, talking to him then giggling more when Brady bounced around, obviously wanting to play.

Why did seeing Wryn next to her son do funny things to Everleigh? Like make her hand go to her temple because her head felt as if it were spinning? And make her want to grab Hayes and leave as quickly as her feet would carry them? Maybe because her son was looking at Wryn as if he was right up there with Brady on being the greatest thing ever.

Wryn offered the disk to Hayes. "Brady wants you to throw the Frisbee to him."

To Everleigh's knowledge, Hayes had never held a Frisbee. Not unless they'd had one at his preschool, but she doubted it with the way he looked at the plastic toy. He took the disk and awkwardly flung it. The toy landed a few feet away and rolled farther than it had soared. Brady's gaze went from the disk to Hayes to Wryn as if he didn't understand what had just happened.

"I didn't throw it very far."

Everleigh's heart ached at the disappointment in Hayes's voice. "You've never thrown a Frisbee." She placed her hand on his shoulder, wanting to reassure him. "No worries, though. You'll get the hang of it with practice."

"Not bad for a first time." Making eye contact with Hayes then with the dog, Wryn pointed at where the disk lay a few yards away. "Fetch it, boy."

If dogs could shrug, that's what Brady did prior to retrieving the toy and bringing it to him. He took the Frisbee, gave Brady an appreciative pat then handed the flying toy back to Hayes.

"Give it another go. Hold it like this." Wryn demonstrated the hand motion. "Then flick your wrist outward."

Hayes positioned the disk in his much smaller hand, readjusting a few times until he was in decent imitation. He mimicked the movement Wryn had done but let go too late. Had Wryn not reacted quickly, catching the Frisbee, the disk would have smacked him in the face.

"I'm sorry." Hayes grimaced, glancing from Everleigh to Wryn. "I didn't mean to do that." His face burned a bright red. "I think you should throw the Frisbee so Brady can play. I'm not very good."

That her son was stepping back when he'd been so gung ho to go to Brady squeezed Everleigh's heart. He'd jumped right in with the other children but was self-doubting with Wryn and Brady. Was it because he'd never spent any significant amount of time around a man? With Bryan leaving when he'd just been a baby and there being no consistent males in their lives other than Joseph at the diner where her mother worked, Hayes's usual confidence seemed nonexistent.

"Try again. You can do this," she heard herself say, even though she wanted nothing more than to leave.

"You just need practice, and Brady will have a new play buddy," Wryn added, perhaps sensing the gravity of the moment. Or maybe he was just being the kind human being he usually was. "Brady doesn't mind, do you, boy?" The dog woofed in answer, making Hayes smile and look less uncertain. "See," Wryn assured the boy, "he hopes you'll keep trying so he can play with you."

"I can try." Hayes took the Frisbee that Wryn offered and

stared at it. He glanced at Wryn. "Will you show me again? I want to do a good job so Brady can play."

"Sure thing." Wryn moved to where he could position the Frisbee in Hayes's hand. Brady leaped around them, excited to continue his fetch game. While Everleigh watched with mixed feelings, Wryn walked Hayes through the motion of throwing the Frisbee several times, guiding his hand through the movements. "Okay, this time we're going to go faster, and when your hand reaches here," he positioned Hayes hand at just the right angle, "I want you to let go. Ready?"

Hayes nodded. Wryn guided him. Hayes let go at near the right spot. This time the plastic disk stayed flat. It didn't go far, but Brady retrieved it.

"Yay!" Everleigh cheered, dancing around. "You did it. You did it."

Watching her, Wryn grinned then glanced toward Hayes. "Good job—I don't know your name."

"Hayes William Bennett." Hayes held out his hand for a shake, and Everleigh couldn't resist feeling proud of his good manners. They practiced that a lot.

Wryn took Hayes's hand into his much larger one and gave a hearty shake. "Nice to meet you, Hayes William Bennett, and great job on that throw. I'm Dr. Wryn Cooper. I work with your mom."

Brady brought back the Frisbee. With it clasped in his mouth, the dog looked to and fro between Wryn and Hayes.

"Good job, boy," Wryn praised, taking the toy and handing it to Hayes. With a determined look and Wryn advising him on specifics, he tossed it again, this time without Wryn's hand guiding his throw. The plastic disk sailed a bit farther through the air, and Brady snatched the flying toy before it hit the ground.

Excited, Hayes spun to face them. "Did you see that, Dr. Cooper? He caught it!"

Wryn high-fived her son. "That was a great throw."

"I know." Hayes grinned at Wryn with pride before glancing toward Everleigh. "Did you see it, Mama? Brady caught the Frisbee."

"I did see." Still fighting the mixed emotions of seeing Hayes interact with Wryn, Everleigh high-fived her son, too. "You did great. It went really far, too."

"Not as far as when he threw it, but really far." Obviously proud of himself, he petted Brady's head. "Come on, boy. You want to catch again?"

Hayes gave the Frisbee another fling then laughed as the dog dashed off to catch the disk midair. They repeated the toss-and-catch, Hayes laughing each time.

Seeing the pure joy now shining on his face, Everleigh's gaze met Wryn's. *Thank you for being kind to him*, she mouthed. Between work and now his interactions with Hayes, it seemed she was always thanking Wryn for something.

Maybe that was all that emotion swirling around in her was. Gratitude.

Warm, fuzzy gratitude.

Between coworkers and friends.

Right.

"You're welcome." Wryn would never have guessed he'd run into Everleigh at the park. Nor that she had a son. He'd hoped the mini-me male version of her was just a close relative. Deep down he'd known even before she'd clarified she was the boy's mother. Hayes's hair was a darker blond with a few curls, but his chocolate eyes were Everleigh's made-over.

Stunned, he might have not been able to hide his shock so well if not for Hayes's uncertainty at petting Brady. Whether actual kindness as Everleigh had just thanked him for or just self-preservation to give himself a moment to let the fact that she had a child sink in, he'd welcomed the interaction with Hayes. Which was an anomaly in and of itself.

His heart thundered. Everleigh was a mother. He dated, but not a lot. Always, though, Wryn steered clear of women with kids. Of all people, he had no business being around someone with a kid. Especially one who seemed as awesome as Hayes. Guilt burned through Wryn. He'd been young, but he'd been old enough to know better.

"Whenever you need to leave," Everleigh began, "you'll have to speak up. Hayes is going to want to keep throwing the Frisbee as long as Brady keeps fetching it."

Swallowing back his shame that always burned just beneath the surface, Wryn arched his brow. "Do you want me to need to leave?"

"I didn't know if you had to be somewhere."

"There's nowhere I have to be other than breathing in fresh air with Brady." Then, wondering if she'd said what she had in case he was holding her up, he added, "Unless I'm holding you up."

"I didn't know you'd be here," she unnecessarily assured. Although they'd agreed to be coworkers and friends, he wasn't oblivious to the fact that she had mixed feelings about him. She liked him but never really let her guard down. He'd wanted to date her. That was out of the question now.

"I'm spending the day with Hayes." Her words rushed with nerves. "We were planning to have lunch then ice cream if the ice cream truck comes by."

"I can call Brady if I'm keeping you."

"We'll wait another minute or two. Hayes is getting better with each throw and enjoying himself. He'll be talking about Brady for the rest of the weekend. Longer, probably." Her gaze flickered his way, her eyes big and cautious. "I wasn't expecting to see you."

"I can say the same thing about seeing you here."

She arched her brow. "I don't look like someone who goes to the park with her son?"

"You don't look like someone who has a son," he clarified, then winced at all the ways what he'd said could be taken. He hadn't meant it derogatorily but knew it sounded that way because of his own selfish interest in Everleigh, despite their agreement that they were just coworkers and friends.

"What does that mean, exactly?" She put her hands on her hips. "Is there a look for someone who has a son?"

He shook his head. "I meant what I said as a compliment, but I realize my words didn't come out right. I was just shocked to see you here." He took a breath. "I didn't know you had a child."

Still eyeing him as if she wasn't quite sure what to think about his comment, she shrugged. "You don't know a lot of things about me."

That was true. Although they talked regularly at work, their conversations centered around work or were short conversations where he'd find something to chat with her or tease her about, like how she drank her coffee, pickleball 101 facts and why she needed to learn to play, patients, the weather or lunch, but personal things? Obviously not. "You're right, but not because I haven't wanted to know more, Everleigh."

Which was more than he should admit. She had a kid. A cute kid who was now demonstrating to a few other kids standing on the opposite side of the fence on how to throw the Frisbee. Brady was in dog heaven to have the handful of kids all giving him attention.

Everleigh eyed Wryn. "If I recall, there was something about you being in a coworker zone."

"Coworker and friend zone." He glanced toward where Hayes and Brady were playing a tug-of-war game with the plastic disk before the dog let Hayes win so he could give it another fling. "Why haven't you mentioned Hayes?"

Following his gaze, she frowned. "Why should I have? I don't usually share my personal life with coworkers, especially not where Hayes is concerned."

"You should have told me. I'm not good with kids." Which might be the understatement of the century. How could someone be good with kids when he'd given up rights to his own son? Doing so had been in his son's best interests. Wryn had been so young, so foolish, but that didn't change the fact that he'd failed his own child and would always carry that guilt. It's why he'd never dated someone with a kid. How could he form a relationship with someone else's child when he'd never had one with the son he'd fathered as a teenager?

Surprise lit in Everleigh's eyes. "You would have a difficult time convincing Hayes of that. Me, too, for that matter. I appreciate how patient you were with him."

Wryn shifted his feet. "All I did was show him how to play with my dog."

She smiled. A genuine smile with no hesitancy that sucker-punched him right in the gut. Or maybe the hit had been higher, because it was his chest that bore the impact.

"Sometimes it's the simplest kindness that means the most." Her gaze shifted to watch her son. "Especially with children. In general, they appreciate our time and attention most."

Their time? Wasn't that what he'd not been willing to give to Seth once he'd found out that Kara had given birth? Why hadn't she told him she was pregnant? Instead, she'd only contacted Wryn years later when she'd needed him to sign away his rights so her husband could officially adopt him. She'd admitted to regretting listing Wryn on the birth certificate. Had she not done so, he'd never have known, and Henry could have legally been Seth's father as he'd been in every other way since Seth's birth. A good man with a successful dental practice, Henry loved Seth and was a good father to him. Wryn had been a broke college kid about to start medical school. He'd had nothing to offer Seth except a life of being tugged between two households. Wryn knew firsthand how miserable that life was. He'd done the right thing, but that didn't ease his guilt that he'd not done better by his own flesh and blood.

"Time isn't always enough." No amount could erase the past.

"Perhaps not," Everleigh agreed. "Goodness knows it's been in short supply during most of Hayes's life with my working full-time while going to school. We made it work, though."

Wryn studied her, how her gaze had gone to Hayes and watched the boy laughing as he tossed the disk again. Protectiveness and strong resiliency shone in her eyes.

"Is Hayes's father in the picture?"

Not looking his way, she shook her head. "No."

"Does he know about Hayes?" He had no right to ask but couldn't hold back the question. Not all fathers knew about their kids. Three years had passed before he'd learned about Seth. For a moment he thought she was going to tell him to mind his own business. It wasn't his business. Yet, he needed to know that Everleigh hadn't done to some man what Kara had done.

"Of course Bryan knows about Hayes. We were married." Everleigh's look was a *duh* one, triggering a fresh spasm of guilt in Wryn. At moments like these, he wondered if the past influenced him even more than he thought. "Bryan's not knowing has nothing to do with why he's not in the picture. He chose not to be in Hayes's life. End of story."

"Maybe he had his reasons." Wryn knew his motivation for pressing the issue, but the look Everleigh gave him was one of disbelief that he was.

"I'm sure he did," she scoffed. "And doing right by his wife and son weren't among those reasons, but then, doing right by us wasn't a priority even before he left."

"I'm sorry." Wryn's heart clenched at the pain he heard in her voice. The guy had ripped her heart to pieces. If Wryn needed another reason to stay clear of Everleigh, this would be it.

Taking a deep breath, she shrugged and seemed to let go some of the tension their conversation had caused. "Don't apologize. It's not your fault Bryan was a bad husband and father."

No, but it was his fault that he was what she'd also classify as a bad father. The circumstances were different. He hadn't known about Seth. Not at first. When he had, it hadn't been difficult for Kara to convince him that their son was better off without Wryn being a part of their lives. He'd been young, stupid, overwhelmed with school and trying to work. He'd done what was best for Seth, but a day didn't pass that Wryn didn't question if he'd chosen that path because it had also been what had been easiest for himself at the time. Seth was a teenager himself now, and although he knew he had a biological father somewhere who was open to meeting him, he'd never expressed a desire to meet Wryn. Wryn understood. He didn't deserve to get to know Seth, not after essentially giving him to another man to raise.

"It's good you coworker-and-friend-zoned me." It hadn't felt good at the time. It didn't feel great currently because of the chemistry between them. But her having done so had been a blessing in disguise. "I don't date women with kids."

She opened her mouth to say something, but Hayes ran back over to them, Brady at his side.

"Brady is hungry."

"Is he?" After one last confused look toward Wryn, Everleigh smiled at her son. "What about you? Are you ready for our picnic?"

Hayes looked torn. "I want to share lunch with Brady because he's hungry, too."

Seth was older, bigger-framed, but blinking at the boy and seeing another, Wryn fought back the emotion hitting him. What was wrong with him? He never did this. Not in public. He came to the park regularly to let Brady stretch his legs. On occasion, kids visited with the dog, petting him, and never had Wryn gotten choked up. But now he was, and pretty Everleigh Bennett was there to witness evidence of his darkest moment. Wryn turned toward her, knowing she'd answered Hayes, but not having a clue what she'd said.

Meeting his gaze, concern filled her eyes. "Is everything okay?"

Wryn was saved from answering by a shriek from behind them. He and Everleigh's heads jerked toward the direction the cry had come from near the swings on the other side of the chain link fence.

A boy about the same size as Hayes lay on the ground and wasn't moving.

"Call for an ambulance," he told Everleigh as he took off

out of the dog park and raced toward the motionless kid. Brady would either follow or stay close to Hayes. Whether or not he was good with kids, Wryn was about to interact with another, and this one appeared to be seriously injured.

"I'm Dr. Wryn Cooper," he introduced himself to the two women hovering over the motionless boy on the ground. Kneeling, Wryn placed his fingers on the boy's wrist to check his pulse. A strong, steady beat throbbed there. He let out a relieved breath. The kid was alive. As still as he'd been, Wryn had wondered. Unconscious wasn't good but was way better than what Wryn had feared. "What happened?"

"He was swinging so high. We think he fell," a woman answered, not the one sobbing next to the boy but another who'd joined them and was holding onto the frantic woman.

"Has he moved?" Wryn asked as he felt air movement beneath the boy's nostrils.

The woman shook her head.

"It's important we make sure he doesn't have a neck injury prior to his being moved."

She nodded, as did the distraught woman he assumed was the boy's mother.

Wryn examined the unconscious kid the best he could without any of the tools of his trade. The boy was breathing okay and had a normal heartbeat and pulse, all good signs, but had he injured his neck or hit his head? Something had knocked him unconscious.

"Kevin," the boy's mom wailed. "Why isn't he moving? Why aren't his eyes open?"

Questions Wryn wished he had answers to.

"Is he alive?" the other woman asked almost simultaneously. That one Wryn could answer.

"He's alive." He assessed the kid while being careful not

to move his neck. Another wave of relief hit when Kevin's eyes opened and stared at him, albeit a bit unfocused.

"Kevin? Just lie still and don't try moving. Not yet. I'm Dr. Cooper. You've had an accident falling off the swing."

"Not a accident. Jumped," the boy said, correcting them that he hadn't fallen. Further relief hit that the boy spoke coherently.

"The ambulance is on the way." Everleigh joined them with Brady and Hayes in tow. Hayes looked pale and nervous. Brady must have sensed Hayes's fear as he opted to stay with the boy and nuzzled against him, nudging him with his nose, and instinctively offering comfort. Good dog.

"Thanks." Wryn made eye contact with Everleigh. Concern filled her eyes. Concern and something more that he couldn't quite label.

"I... Yes. What can I do to help?" she asked.

Wryn wasn't sure there was anything she could do, not with the injured kid or regarding his past mistakes, but having her there soothed something raw within him.

Something raw that had refused to be soothed for more than a decade.

Unfortunately, Wryn didn't deserve soothing, and if Everleigh knew the truth about him, she wouldn't want to provide even the slightest balm for his ailment. She'd detest him for leaving his son for another man to raise.

He and Everleigh could be coworkers. They could be acquaintances. Maybe they could be friends. But certainly they could never be more than friends.

CHAPTER FOUR

EVERLEIGH'S HEART ACHED at the scene before her, both for the injured boy and for her son witnessing the injury when she wanted to protect him from the world. She'd wanted to run with Wryn to the injured child but had delayed long enough to make sure Hayes and Brady came with them rather than being left behind. She was not leaving her child inside the dog park unattended.

One hand on Brady, Hayes tugged on her shirt hem with the other. "Mama, is Kevin okay?"

"Dr. Cooper will take good care of your friend," she reassured him, realizing the injured child was one of the kids who attended Hayes's preschool that he'd been playing with earlier. "He's a good doctor." She put her hands on his shoulders, willing him to look at her rather than Kevin. "I'm going to help Dr. Cooper. Stay close where I can see you at all times. Take good care of Brady for Dr. Cooper while we check Kevin."

Hayes's worried gaze going back to the hurt boy, he nodded.

"Thank you, Hayes. You're a great helper." Everleigh kissed the top of his head, thanking God for small blessings, then knelt next to Wryn and Kevin. Seeing a child so similar in size and age to her son, lying so still on the ground, tore at her insides, made her want to wrap Hayes in a hug and not let go. "How can I best help?" she asked, not wanting to be in Wryn's way.

"Kevin had his breath knocked out and is just coming to, aren't you, bud?" At Wryn's question, the kid blinked. "He's being very brave while I check him."

Fear shone in the kid's eyes, and he began crying. "Where's my mommy?"

The two women hovering next to them let loose with a sob.

"I'm right here, honey." One leaned over him. "I'm right here. Just do what the doctor says, baby."

"Just hold still for Dr. Cooper while he checks you," Everleigh said in her gentlest voice, hoping the boy could hear her over his crying. "It's important for you not to move."

"I'm going to be super easy while I check you." Wryn ran through a quick neuro examination. Kevin's pupils were dilated and didn't respond appropriately to the light from Wryn's cell phone. In the middle of the day and being outdoors wasn't a great testing environment, but there still should have been some response. With Kevin having been knocked unconscious, it was pretty much a no-brainer that he had a concussion. He also had a broken arm.

"Right distal radius and ulna." She didn't elaborate. She didn't need to. Wryn nodded, probably having already noted the fractures.

Whether from pain, fear or confusion, Kevin had had enough of lying still and wiggled to try to sit up. Dizziness obviously hit, and his upper body weaved. "Mama."

"I'm here, baby. I'm here."

That's when Kevin vomited. His mother jerked back, but it was too late. Crying, Kevin aspirated, choked, then began trying to clear his throat. Tears streamed down his face.

Everleigh immediately slapped him on the back. Kevin

began coughing and gasping for air, finally breathing normally again.

They kept a close check while waiting for the ambulance. Everleigh focused on Kevin but was mindful of where Hayes was playing with Brady for a minute or two. Dog and boy had returned to stand with the crowd that had gathered around where Kevin lay. Hayes looked calm, but Everleigh recognized that he was upset. How could he not be?

Once the paramedics were on the scene, she stepped back, letting Wryn tell them what had happened while she moved to where Hayes watched the scene unfold with forlorn eyes. His tiny hands had a tight grip on Brady's leash that Everleigh had put back on to the dog prior to rushing to help Wryn, but the dog seemed just as entranced by what was happening as Hayes and had plopped down on the grass. Panting, he returned to all four paws when Everleigh spoke.

"Did you and Brady get tired of playing?" She knelt face-to-face with him and so she could give Brady a don't-you-dare look to keep him from licking her.

Hayes's gaze strayed beyond her to the emergency workers loading Kevin onto a board. "Is he going to die?"

Everleigh's heart ached. "No, honey. He fell and is banged up, but he is going to be okay."

Hayes's lower lip disappeared between his teeth. "His arm broke?"

Brushing a hair away from his cherub face, Everleigh nodded. "It is broken, but it will heal."

Hayes's gaze met hers. "Is his tummy broke, too?"

"His tummy?" she asked confused, then it hit her. "Sometimes if we hit our head too hard it can make our stomach not feel so good. That's all. Kevin's stomach is working just fine, and he's going to be okay." She prayed he was. She didn't want Hayes worrying about the boy, and currently her son looked stressed. No wonder. "Wryn is going to be so glad you took care of Brady while we were taking care of Kevin. You did a good job."

Hayes glanced down at the dog, but if Everleigh thought she was going to distract him from the boy being loaded into the ambulance, she was wrong.

"I think he's going to die, Mama." Hayes's voice broke, a tear running down his sweet face. Everleigh pulled him to her.

"He's not, Hayes. I promise." She tried to never promise things she had no control over, but in her heart, she had to believe Kevin was going to be okay. She definitely had to reassure her son. Her momma's heart was breaking.

After a few moments, Hayes pulled back.

"Hey, kiddo. Thanks for keeping Brady safe," Wryn said, joining them after the ambulance was on its way.

Hayes glanced down at the leash still clutched in his fingers, then, first swiping the back of his hand over his damp eyes, he held it out to Wryn. "He was a good dog."

Wryn's heart tugged at the little boy's expression. No doubt what had happened must have scared him. Everleigh had looked so desperate to distract Hayes from what had happened that Wryn hadn't been able to stay away a moment longer. Poor kid.

A voice whispered that he had no right to try to help anyone with their kid, but Wryn ignored it. Instead, he knelt to Hayes's level. Brady immediately moved to him and licked his cheek. Wryn petted the dog. "Hayes says you were a good boy. Is that right?"

The dog licked him again.

Hayes sniffled. "I fed him."

"You fed Wryn's dog?" This came from Everleigh. "What did you feed him? Did you feed Brady our lunch, Hayes?"

After a few seconds, he nodded. "Brady was really hungry. Don't be mad."

Everleigh's expression instantly eased. "I'm not mad." She gave a slight shrug of her shoulder. "We may be hungry, though. That was our lunch."

"I was hungry, too," Hayes sniffled, "and thought I would eat a snack, but Brady was hungry. I gave him some first, and he wanted it all."

"So you gave it all to him?"

Wiping his hand at his eyes again, Hayes nodded.

"I missed when you did this, which is a bit concerning," Everleigh admitted, staring at her son. "That must have happened super fast."

"It was super fast, Mama. He was very hungry."

"It's okay." She smiled at him. "Sometimes dogs are very hungry and just have to eat something. I bet that's how Brady felt."

"He did." Hayes nodded. As it got to the end of the park's parking area, the ambulance turned on its sirens. Hayes jumped and, leash still in one hand, covered his ears. "Aighh!"

Everleigh inhaled sharply. "It's okay," she said to calm him as soon as the siren faded enough to be readily heard. Hands back at his sides, Hayes didn't look convinced.

"How about we grab lunch? My treat," Wryn offered, surprising himself. What was he doing? He needed to step back from this situation. He didn't belong and never could.

When they met his, Everleigh's eyes were tumultuous. "I... You don't need to do that."

But his offer had caught Hayes's attention. "My belly is starving."

"It's only fair that Brady and I buy lunch since he ate yours."

Looking torn, she glanced back at Hayes.

Hayes sucked back a sniffle. "I'm really hungry."

"We can get pizza or whatever you like," Wryn upped the ante. What was wrong with him? He should be running for the hills, not proposing to spend more time with Everleigh and Hayes. But Hayes's being upset gutted him, and Brady was the best distraction Wryn knew. He'd use Brady to help give the kid better memories about the day, then he'd steer clear of Everleigh and her son.

Hayes gave him a watery-eyed look. "Does Brady like pizza?"

"He loves it," Wryn answered, thinking that if those tears spilled from the kid's eyes that he was a goner.

Hayes's gaze cut to Everleigh. "Can we, Mama?"

Whether Everleigh wanted to or not, she nodded. "Pizza sounds delicious."

"Just a few minutes from here, there's a really great place that allows dogs. We can go there." Wryn told her the name of the pizza place and went to take the leash from Hayes, but the boy clutched it tighter, looking alarmed at letting it go. Wryn exchanged a look with Everleigh. He didn't want to overstep, but seeming to sense his wanting to help, she nodded.

"How about you walk Brady to my car for me?" he offered.

Hayes nodded, gripping the leash. "Does Brady have a car seat?"

"Sort of. He sits in a seat in the car."

"I have a car seat. I'm getting bigger and before long, I won't have to sit in it."

"I bet your mom is in no hurry for you to grow up so fast."

"She's not," Hayes said at the same time as Everleigh said, "I'm not."

They all chuckled, even Hayes, who was looking perkier as he said something to Brady then petted the dog's head.

Thank you, Everleigh mouthed to Wryn.

You're welcome, he mouthed back, wondering at how warm and fuzzy his insides had gone when he shouldn't be spending more time with Everleigh and Hayes. Yet, he couldn't just walk away when he'd seen how forlorn Hayes was.

"I need to get my bag."

"Hayes, hold up while we wait on your mom," he told him. Hayes came back, Brady at his side, and Wryn was hit with nerves on what to say as the kid stared up at him. "I appreciate you keeping an eye on Brady. It was nice to have someone to watch him."

"I could watch him some other time, too." Hope shone in Hayes's eyes. "He likes me."

"That he does." Wryn scratched the dog's neck, thinking he should keep silent. He didn't want to make promises he couldn't keep.

"Is my friend going to die?"

Silence was a failure. Wryn should have kept talking about the dog.

"Hayes, we talked about this," Everleigh reminded, rejoining them with her bag hanging from her shoulder. "Kevin is going to be fine. Right, Wryn?"

"Right." He wasn't going to argue with the look Everleigh was giving him. "How about after pizza I call the hospital to check on Kevin? They may or may not tell me much due to patient privacy, but if not, I'll stop by the hospital."

"Can I go, too?" Hayes piped up with eyes so big that Wryn wondered how Everleigh ever denied the kid anything.

"Hayes! You can't invite yourself to go with Dr. Cooper."

"Sorry," he told his mother, then turned his eyes that were so similar to Everleigh's back toward Wryn. "Can I?"

"How about we get lunch then call about Kevin? He may not be allowed to have visitors for a while."

"I guess that would be okay. I like you, Dr. Cooper."

Wryn swallowed, then, unable to stop himself, he tousled Hayes's hair. The curls were soft beneath his fingertips and had him wondering if all kids had such soft hair. He stopped his train of thought. He'd been down that rabbit hole enough for one day.

Hayes chatted, mostly to Brady, as they made their way to the parking lot. He stayed close, but when he was just enough ahead that Everleigh must have thought he was out of earshot, she said, "I'm sorry. What happened has shaken him."

"Understandable. Even to an adult, seeing something like that can be traumatizing."

"Brady is a great distraction. Kids are resilient, but I worry. I don't want anything to ever hurt him, but he'll balk if I smother him."

"Spoken like a good mother." Which he knew she was. He could see it in how she and Hayes interacted.

"I try," she said. "But I'm not sure one really knows how good a job they did as a parent until their kid is grown and they can see if all those years of worrying produced a good human being."

"Hayes has a kind heart. He's going to be a good human being." Of that Wryn had no doubt. With Everleigh guiding him, how could he not? Would Seth grow up to be a good human being? Henry and Kara seemed to be doing a good job raising him. Although he'd never met him, Wryn had hired an investigator once to be sure the boy was truly happy and well cared for. The man had assured him that Seth was a thriving, happy kid.

"I think he will be, too." She smiled, albeit softly. "Thanks again. I meant what I said about not wanting anything to hurt him. Under normal circumstances I'd never have agreed for him to spend time with you."

Shocked, he stared at her. "You think I'd hurt Hayes?"

She grimaced. "What I think is that I'd rather him not spend time with a stranger who says he doesn't date women with kids."

"I can understand that. I didn't mean to put you in an awkward position when I invited you and Hayes to lunch." Guilt hit. "Actually, that may not be completely true. It's no secret that I want to get to know you better."

"Even knowing I have a kid?"

He shrugged. "It's just lunch."

"I suppose, but nothing with you feels like it's *just* anything."

"Meaning?"

Eyes on where Hayes and Brady were ahead of them, she shrugged. "What happened shook Hayes. I'm glad you were there today."

"There's a first time for everything."

Her gaze flicked his way. "What's that?"

"You being glad that I was around."

"Not wanting you around isn't the problem, Wryn." Her confession was soft and heartfelt. "The problem is quite the opposite."

Wryn swallowed. Had Everleigh really vocalized that she wanted him around? He'd thought there was something in her eyes when they met his. Something powerful that had him wanting to plunge into their chocolate depths.

But he couldn't, shouldn't, want her to do that, not when she had Hayes.

"It's okay, Everleigh. I understand. It really is just lunch." It had to be. "We'll stay in the coworkers and friends zone."

For both their sakes. Hayes's, too.

Then she surprised him by pausing from walking to look him straight in the eyes. Doubt shone in hers. "I think that's for the best, don't you? I mean, I wouldn't want Hayes to ever be hurt by getting close to someone who wasn't going to be in our lives long-term. But we both know there's something going on between us that's more than just being coworkers and friends. And therein lies the problem."

"You're right." Despite how much she fascinated him, she had a kid. That was the biggest red flag there was, where he was concerned. How could he in good faith spend time with a woman with a kid when he didn't spend time with his own child? He gulped back the guilt that hit. "That's a problem, but not if we're in agreement that we are just coworkers and friends."

The disappointment she failed to mask sucker-punched Wryn. Had a part of her wanted him to say something to the contrary? To admit how attracted to her that he was? She had to know. She wasn't blind, and he couldn't stay away from her at work nor, apparently, in his leisure time even when he'd had no idea she'd be at the park.

"We're in agreement." Whatever he'd thought he'd seen in her eyes, her words sounded sincere. Wryn looked away. Otherwise, it would be her seeing disappointment shining in his eyes.

They came to his vehicle. Still trying to figure out what to say, he unlocked the door to let some heat out. "I'll see you in a few minutes at the pizza place."

"Pepperoni is my favorite," Hayes told him. "Does Brady like pepperoni?"

Wryn turned to the boy. "How about that? Pepperoni is his favorite, too. Something else you and Brady have in common."

Happy, Hayes told the dog bye then surprised them all by planting a kiss on top of Brady's head. The dog took it in stride, giving Hayes a sloppy, wet cheek kiss in return, making the boy giggle.

Everleigh did funny things to his inside, so Wryn shouldn't be surprised by how her son's delight in his dog compared to the boy's somberness from earlier would affect Wryn.

Maybe he couldn't be friends with Everleigh and her son.

For the briefest moment he considered canceling the lunch. He couldn't do that, either. Not when he'd invited Hayes and said he'd check on Kevin.

Wryn had a lot of shortcomings, especially when it came to kids, but he did his best to keep his word.

Even when doing so was dangerous to his peace of mind.

Why had Everleigh agreed to lunch? She didn't want to spend time with Wryn, and she sure didn't want Hayes becoming more enthralled with him. Every sentence on their drive there had started with *Dr. Cooper* or *Brady*. He'd been so despondent after Kevin's accident that she'd been grateful for the distraction, though. If only Wryn wasn't such a distraction for her.

Not liking Wryn was impossible when he was such a decent human. He'd been great with Kevin and with Hayes. He'd also known Hayes needed something fun to imprint over the trauma of Kevin's fall. Hayes had never seen anything like the injured boy's injuries. Currently, her giggling son played a video game with Wryn. He wouldn't just remember bad things from the day. Of that she was certain, and it made all her other worries take a back seat.

Apparently, Hayes and Wryn accomplished something good on the game because they looked at each other and high-fived, then went back to playing. Everleigh had stayed at the table with Brady lying at her feet, both watching the guys.

"Can I get you anything else?" their waitress asked, topping off Everleigh's water glass.

She shook her head. "Thanks. We're good."

Wryn and Hayes let loose with some *whoa*s, triggering Everleigh and the waitress to glance their way.

"You are one lucky lady."

"I am," she said, smiling at Hayes. But when she glanced up, the waitress was staring at Wryn. "We're not a couple."

The woman gave her a confused look then shrugged. "A smart woman would do something about that. I've seen him in here on occasion, usually with a group of friends. He almost always picks up the entire tab and is a fabulous tipper. He's a keeper."

Everleigh wasn't a smart woman. A smart woman wouldn't have put herself into this situation where her son was bonding with a man who said he didn't date women with kids. She gave the woman a tight smile then took a sip of water. She wouldn't be doing anything about anything. She didn't want to be a part of a couple. Being a part of a couple had never gone well for her. She sure wouldn't risk it with a coworker. Not that Wryn had offered. Quite the opposite with his comment about not dating women with kids. What was up with that? First, the comment about not being good with kids, and then that. He must have had a bad experience at some point, but he was wrong. He was great with kids. At least, from all she'd witnessed.

Yeah, she wasn't smart. A smart woman would not have let her son spend the afternoon with a man who her impressionable child was growing more and more attached to by the minute. Why was she allowing this to happen? Kevin, she reminded herself. Being with Wryn and Brady was replacing the day's bad memories with good ones. Smart or not, she'd made what she believed the overall right choice, and it was too late for recriminations.

Unable to sit a moment longer, she joined them at the video game. She'd always worked so much that she'd never gotten into video games but was fascinated by the complexity and storylines of some she saw advertised. She recognized the one Wryn and Hayes was playing as one that had been around for many years. Even if she'd not immediately recognized the little men with their colorful overalls and hats, the music was a giveaway.

"How's the game going?" she asked, amused by Hayes's intense focus and that he seemed to instinctively know what to do, even though he'd never played the game.

"Dr. Cooper is really good," Hayes bragged.

"Because I have a great partner," Wryn praised, taking his eyes off the screen long enough to grin at Hayes.

Hayes grinned right back. "We're going to save the princess."

Hayes looked at Wryn with complete adoration. Not good, but not surprising. She sure couldn't fault her son for not being in awe when the man awed her on a daily basis. They'd finish lunch, fill Hayes's day with goodness, then no more Dr. Cooper around Hayes.

"Probably not today." Wryn chuckled. "Saving a princess is hard work and takes more than just a few minutes of playtime at a restaurant."

"Oh." Hayes's face twisted with concentration. "Have you saved the princess?"

"A time or two."

Hayes's face furrowed further. "Does that make you a prince charming? My teacher says Prince Charming saves the princess."

Not looking away from the video game screen, Wryn shook his head. "No one will ever accuse me of being Prince Charming." He glanced toward Hayes.

"Oh." Hayes didn't hide his disappointment, which heightened when the game's music indicated that his character had bitten the dust. "I lost."

"You did a great job getting this far into the game," Everleigh said with enthusiasm. "I wouldn't have gotten nearly so close to rescuing the princess."

"Because you aren't a prince charming, either, Mama."

"Is she the princess we need to rescue?" Wryn's question was teasing, likely meant to lighten the mood, but Everleigh's chin lifted.

"I don't need rescuing," she objected. "I do just fine taking care of myself."

Always had and always would.

Wryn's gaze shifted from the game to her. "Princess Charming who slays her own dragons, eh?"

"Something like that." The game music changed, indicating his character had just lost, too. "Looks as if you won't be slaying any dragons or evil kings today, either."

"Like I said, I'm no Prince Charming."

Unfortunately, Everleigh couldn't quite convince herself that he was telling the truth.

CHAPTER FIVE

As promised, Wryn called the hospital to check on Kevin. The boy had been in the emergency room but was being admitted. An orthopedic surgeon had been called in for another emergency and opted to take Kevin to pin the bones back together in his forearm.

"I need to visit Kevin in the hospital," Hayes announced. "That's what my teacher at church says, that we need to visit the sick."

There was no way Everleigh could argue with her son's logic, so Wryn wasn't surprised when she acquiesced. "You're right. We can visit him and bring him a gift."

Hayes looked pleased. "That will make him feel better."

No doubt seeing Kevin okay would make Hayes feel better, too.

"Can we go now? With Dr. Cooper?"

Wryn didn't have to be a genius to know Everleigh was racking her brain to figure out how to wiggle out of him tagging along. He took mercy on her. "I have Brady. The hospital wouldn't let him visit with Kevin."

"Seeing Brady would make Kevin feel better, though."

"Seeing Brady sure makes me feel better." Wryn smiled. "But I don't make the rules."

Hayes thought a moment, then suggested, "You could

bring Brady home and then go with us to see Kevin. You're a doctor and need to check him to make sure he's okay."

Wryn glanced toward Everleigh.

Her shoulders lifted in a light shrug, then she knelt to talk to her son. "Hayes, Dr. Cooper has things he needs to do this afternoon."

Hayes eyes were intent. "Do you?"

Wryn said the first thing that came to mind. "Brady needs a bath. That's never easy because it's not his favorite thing to do."

"We could help you," Hayes offered. "Then you could go with us to make sure Kevin is okay. I'm a really good helper."

Torn between the kid's imploring and doing the right thing, Wryn's gaze met Everleigh's. Her internal struggle was palpable.

Thinking Hayes needed further distraction must have won out, because rather than give reasons why they couldn't help bathe Brady, she said, "He is a good helper."

Heart racing, Wryn stared at her, then scratched Brady's neck. The only way Everleigh would have said what she did would be that she thought Hayes needed more time around Brady and for Hayes to witness him checking Kevin. "When it comes to bathing this guy, a good helper would be handy."

Hayes grinned, then loved on the dog. "Did you hear that, boy? You're getting a bath."

Wryn hadn't thought through that Hayes helping him bathe Brady meant inviting Everleigh and Hayes to his house. His house wasn't the proverbial bachelor pad, but it wasn't kid-friendly, either. He knew the house was clean. Mrs. Callahan came by weekly. Of course, spoiled by the woman, Brady thought Mrs. Callahan came because of him.

The dog was partially correct. Brady was the main reason he had the cleaner coming weekly.

With Everleigh and Hayes following him, they arrived at his house. Within minutes they were in his kitchen. Brady played tug-of-war with a thick doggie toy rope with Hayes gripping the other end. The boy giggled when his socked feet slid, and the dog pulled him across the tiled floor to the opposite side of the room.

Hoping that Brady would burn enough energy to where he'd be more cooperative for his bath, Wryn gestured for Everleigh to sit on a barstool at the island. "Have a seat."

Everleigh glanced around his kitchen. "This is a beautiful place."

"It's a great investment." He rarely had company, but when he did, he always gave the automatic response. The house was a great investment and also a place he liked coming back to each evening. Although too big for just him, the extra room and great neighborhood would help it sell if he ever decided to move.

"Mama, there's a swimming pool back there." Hayes came running over to Everleigh, sounding in absolute awe that Wryn had his own pool.

"You're welcome to swim sometime," Wryn offered, then wondered if he should have done so when Everleigh's gaze cut to him.

"Did you hear that, Mama?" Hayes bounced around next to her with excitement. "Dr. Cooper wants us to swim with him."

Thinking he must be missing out on the fun, Brady came over, rope in mouth, and bounced at Hayes, trying to get the boy to play with him again.

"That's very nice of Dr. Cooper, but we have the community pool for when you want to swim." Hayes gave her a look as if he thought her nuts if she'd prefer swimming at the packed community pool rather than Wryn's private one. "You enjoy being around the other children there," she reminded him.

"I can play with Brady here," Hayes countered then glanced toward Wryn. "Does Brady like the swimming pool?"

"Brady loves the pool. If I'm in it, so is he, and sometimes," he said and chuckled, "he swims without me."

Hayes's eyes widened. "Brady can swim?"

"Like a fish, er, a dog." Wryn walked to the fridge and opened it. "Do you want something to drink? I don't have a lot of drink choices that might interest a kid. There's almond milk, vitamin water, water and apple juice."

"Apple juice," Hayes said without hesitation, still bouncing.

"A kid after my own heart." Wryn was an apple juice addict. "How about you, Mom?"

Hearing him call her Mom must have struck Everleigh as odd as she looked startled. Apparently to Hayes, too, as he giggled.

"She's not your mom," he pointed out. "She's my mom."

The boy's laughter spread warmth through Wryn. "I was just using the term to reference her, not to imply she was my mom. She's much too young and pretty to be my mother."

Looking taken aback, Hayes's face squished. "She's kinda old, though."

Everleigh's cheeks pinkened then with a smile, she shook her head. "Nothing like a kid to keep one grounded."

"He and I will have to disagree, because you're only *kinda old* to a five-year-old." To Wryn she was just right. In age, he added to his thought. She was just right in age. Nothing more. "What would you like to drink?"

"A vitamin water would be great." She glanced around his kitchen, her gaze skimming over his golden black-flecked granite countertops, black cabinets, and top-of-the-line stainless steel appliances. "This really is a great kitchen, perfectly laid out to cook big meals."

"Not too many big meals cooked here." At her questioning look, he added, "I mainly cook to meal-prep."

"That seems a bit lonely." As soon as the words left her mouth, her cheeks turned bright red. "Sorry. My perspective is that I've never lived alone."

"Never? Not even before your marriage?"

She shook her head. "I've always lived with my mom." She glanced toward Hayes who'd gone back to playing with the dog and didn't seem to be paying attention but probably didn't miss much. "Even during my marriage. After Bryan left, I had Mom and Hayes." She glanced toward Hayes again. "They were all I needed, anyway."

She really had always slain her own dragons, he realized. Admiration for all she'd accomplished filled him.

"You're an amazing woman. They're lucky to have you."

She took a drink of her vitamin water then shook her head. "I'm the lucky one."

"Do you give Brady a bath by putting him in the swimming pool?" Hayes piped up from where he rubbed Brady's fur.

"Not usually, but that would work in a pinch. Speaking of baths, I'll get out our supplies, then we'll bathe Brady."

Wryn headed toward the utility room that had a built-in dog-bathing area.

"Wow, Mama. Dr. Cooper is rich, isn't he?" he heard Hayes say as he left the room. The question made him thankful for his blessings, but not oblivious to what he'd sacrificed along the way. Everleigh would never have made the choices he had. She wouldn't have even considered them.

"He's not poor," Everleigh replied. "He worked hard in medical school and now takes care of sick people."

Wryn had worked hard in medical school. He'd had to keep his scholarships. He still worked hard.

"When I grow up, I want to be a doctor." Hearing the boy say he wanted to do what Wryn had done had that funny flutter inside him kicking into overdrive.

"That sounds like a wonderful thing, so you can help take care of sick people, too," Everleigh told her son. "You can grow up to be anything you want to be."

Hayes giggled. "Even a dog?"

Standing just inside the utility room doorway, Wryn couldn't help but smile at Hayes's question. Such a kid.

"Maybe not that, silly boy."

Wryn could hear her smile, even though he couldn't see her face.

"But I think you'd make a very good doctor, Hayes," she told her son. "Maybe even an animal doctor. You were so good at taking care of Brady today while Wryn and I helped Kevin. I was proud of you for listening so well."

"I was a little scared," Hayes admitted, placing his glass of apple juice on the table.

"It's okay to be a little scared. I was scared, too. A whole lot scared." What happened to Kevin could have been so much worse, but Kevin should recover.

Wryn got out two towels for Brady's bath. He usually just used one to dry the dog but wanted one for Hayes to help, too.

"Maybe we could make Kevin a Get Well Soon card like I do with Grammy for when someone is sick at church," Hayes said from the adjoining room.

"That's a great idea, Hayes. We can definitely do that."

"Do you want to help us make a card for Kevin?" Hayes asked when Wryn came through the open doorway.

"I don't recall ever making a get-well card, so you would have to have help me."

"Do you have markers and paper? Or crayons would work."

"Paper, yes. The markers or crayons?" He shrugged. "I don't think so."

Hayes glanced over at Everleigh and gave her a *Can you believe that?* look.

"What about glitter, Dr. Cooper? We could decorate Kevin's card with glue and glitter."

Wryn shook his head. "No sparkly stuff for me."

"Too bad." This came from Everleigh. "Everyone needs a little sparkle in their lives."

"True, but my sparkly stuff doesn't come sprinkled out of a plastic container."

"Oh?" Her brow arched. "Where does your sparkly stuff come from?"

Good question. One Wryn wasn't sure how to answer. He could give some flip answer but found he didn't want to do that. What he wanted was to not be questioning his life choices so much, but maybe that made sense since Everleigh and Hayes were in his house. How could he not question things when a kid was in his house for the first time ever, and when, if a kid was in his house, it should be different to the one he'd helped bring into the world?

One that he'd given life to but who had never been a part of his life and likely never would be.

"Maybe I should invest in some of those plastic containers."

Sprinkled sparkle would have to do.

Because although he had a great life, he'd avoided sparkle to punish himself for choices made years ago.

Hayes, and even Everleigh to some degree, were soaked by the time they'd finished bathing Brady. Who had known bathing a dog could be fun? It must have been because Hayes had sure smiled and laughed a lot. His happiness translated to Everleigh's happiness. Her son's giggles warmed her heart, especially after the day's events.

Unfortunately, with their wet clothes, they were in no shape to visit Kevin. Hayes's happiness had deflated like a flat tire. Which had led to Everleigh agreeing to visit Kevin with Wryn the following afternoon. Which was probably better anyway as Everleigh had been concerned that Kevin might still be in recovery or groggy during their visit so soon after his surgery. Since her mother had gone straight from church to help fill in at the short-staffed diner, Everleigh had agreed for Wryn to pick her and Hayes up at their apartment. Hayes's *Wryn this* and *Wryn that* from the night before had put Everleigh on further alert and determination that today was it. The last time she'd agree for her and Hayes to spend time with Wryn.

Hayes would look back on the weekend as having been a good one, because even as he'd fallen asleep the night before he'd been singing Wryn and Brady's praises. She'd not vocalized them, but she hadn't been able to keep her own praises from filling her mind. And her own concerns. It couldn't be good that Hayes was so excited when she opened the front door to let in Wryn.

Excited, Hayes flashed a big smile at Wryn. "Do you want to see my room?"

Although nothing fancy, Hayes was proud. He'd gotten a comforter set of his favorite cartoon character for Christmas. The red race car spread covering the plastic blue car bed that she'd bought at a neighbor's garage sale always caught Everleigh's eye first thing when going into the room. Hayes loved that bed.

"Sure," Wryn agreed.

It wouldn't take long. Their rental consisted of three bedrooms and a bathroom. Hayes's bedroom was smaller than Wryn's utility room. Everleigh lifted her shoulders. She'd worked hard to keep this roof over their heads. Very hard. Someday she'd be able to save up enough to put a down payment on something with more space, another bathroom, and a backyard for Hayes to play in and maybe have a dog of his own. She needed to get a bit of a cushion first rather than live paycheck to paycheck, but soon she'd upgrade their living situation.

"This is great." Wryn completely dominated the small room. Everleigh was fairly positive that if he lay on the floor, he'd be able to touch opposite walls. But his smile was genuine, and his compliment seemed to be.

"Did you see my bed?" Hayes hopped up onto the mattress and patted the comforter.

Wryn nodded. "That is one cool bed. I take it you are a fan of race cars?"

"I love them." He started prattling off cartoon race cars. Wryn sent her a look indicating that he was lost.

"They're from his favorite movie," Everleigh clarified.

Hayes pulled out a plastic container that held his cars. "See." He showed Wryn the metal diecast car with its painted-on eyes. He went through naming each one as he showed it to Wryn. "This one is my favorite."

Everleigh's heart squeezed at how Hayes looked at Wryn as he held the red car. Was her son so eager for male companionship that he'd taken up so intently with Wryn in only a day? Why was she letting this happen? She should have said no to going to the hospital with him. She'd said yes for Hayes, but had she done him any favors by doing so?

Wryn took the car and spun the wheels. "I can see why. He's sharp. Seems fast, too."

"He is fast," Hayes confirmed.

Why was Wryn going? She knew why she'd agreed, but what were his reasons? Was he just doing this for Hayes's mental and emotional well-being, too? He'd been so kind at work and the day before that perhaps he truly was just there out of the kindness of his heart. What type of man gave up his Sunday afternoon to visit an injured kid in the hospital?

One completely unlike any she'd ever known.

They stopped by a gift shop to buy a stuffed animal then visited with Kevin. The boy was excited to see Hayes and wanted his friend to sit on the bed next to him so that they could watch a so-funny video on a tablet his mother had brought from home. With his arm cast, Hayes had to help hold the tablet. The boys giggled at something, looked at each other and giggled some more.

"Thank you," Kevin's mother told them then asked if it would be okay if she slipped out to make some phone calls to update family who couldn't be there, that she'd not wanted to give lots of specifics in front of Kevin. Everleigh nodded. To her knowledge they weren't in a rush. At least, she and Hayes weren't.

She glanced toward Wryn who was watching the boys. His face grimaced slightly. Maybe he'd had somewhere to be after all and hadn't planned to stay for however long Kevin's mother took to make her calls. But catching Everleigh watching him, he smiled. Her heart did its usual hiccup.

"Thank you."

He looked confused. "For?"

"Yesterday. Today." As important as it was to prevent Hayes from getting more attached to Wryn, she acknowledged how happy her son had been that Wryn was there. "You saved Hayes from being traumatized by what he witnessed yesterday. All he could talk about last night was you and Brady."

"I'm glad I was able to help."

"There was one other thing he talked about this morning." Everleigh sucked in a deep breath. "He reminded me that we never went for ice cream yesterday. He thought you'd like to go with us. My treat as a thank-you for your help."

"For ice cream?" Clearly shocked, Wryn arched a dark brow.

"Just as a thank-you," she reiterated. "If you're not busy and, um, like ice cream."

His gaze searched hers. "With Hayes thinking I'd enjoy ice cream, how could I refuse?"

When Kevin's mother returned, they said their goodbyes and left the hospital. Ice cream was a hit. Hayes talked a mile a minute, seemingly trying to fill Wryn in on every aspect of his short life. Everleigh watched in awe, adding tidbits here and there to their conversation when called upon to do so. Both would turn to her to ask questions, which she answered. But the reality was that she was content watching their interaction.

Content? Ha. The more time she spent with Wryn, the less the mere word *content* applied. Crazy hormones.

"I don't have a daddy." Hayes's blunt announcement dropped Everleigh's jaw.

"You do have a daddy," she corrected. "He just lives far away."

"He left when I was a baby," Hayes continued to tell Wryn. "But that's okay, because I like you."

Wryn looked completely at a loss but quickly pulled it together. "I like you, too."

Which put a huge smile on Hayes's face.

Not good. Wryn must not have thought so, either, as he finished his ice cream rather quickly and suggested they leave. When he got to their apartment complex, he got out of his vehicle to help Hayes out of the car then told them bye.

Hayes invited him to come inside, but Wryn declined, and for that Everleigh was grateful. They'd done what needed to be done to reassure Hayes so he should have no long-term repercussions from having seen his friend hurt.

Whether or not there were going to be long-term repercussions from his having spent time with Wryn remained to be seen.

For Hayes and Everleigh.

CHAPTER SIX

WRYN HAD MIXED feelings about seeing Everleigh at work the next morning. Excited anticipation seemed to be the norm but also, now, a nervousness that was rooted in having spent time with her and Hayes over the weekend. Unintentional at the park on Saturday, but he couldn't claim that on the previous day. They could have visited Kevin separately, but they'd done right by Hayes. However, spending more time together didn't make sense.

"Dr. Cooper, is everything okay?"

Realizing he'd totally spaced out and needed to get his mind on his patients, Wryn blinked at Eva. The nurse's dark brows were arched, and she stared at him with concern.

"Fine," he said, knowing there was a part of him that would never be fine. Something spending time with Hayes had reiterated. He liked kids. He could tell himself otherwise all he wanted, but had it not been for what happened with Seth, Wryn would have wanted a houseful.

Eva eyed him a moment. "You look as if you don't feel well. Rough weekend?"

The weekend had been the best he'd had in a long time. A very long time. In the past, he'd purposely kept his relationships shallow to prevent getting too close, to prevent increased guilt about Seth by spending time with another kid. Logic said that spending time with Hayes was not cheating on his son, but he couldn't quite convince himself that was the case. So he did what he'd done for more years than he liked to acknowledge and buried the past deep within him and forced a smile. It was amazing what one could hide behind lightheartedness and a smile.

"My weekend was no big deal. Nothing out of the ordinary." He wasn't going to make a big deal of it, and he suspected neither would Everleigh. He'd not been oblivious to the fact she had her own reservations about seeing him outside work. He didn't blame her. "Is my first patient ready?"

"Sadly, no." Eva gave a resigned sigh. "The front desk doesn't have them checked in yet. The computers were down when we first got here this morning. Fortunately, they came back up a short while ago. As soon as they get your first patient registered, I'll get him in a room for you."

Wryn nodded, then wanting to avoid his nurse's curious look and feeling too antsy to stand at the nurses' station, he decided to grab a coffee. When he turned, his gaze locked with Everleigh's.

"Morning." She quickly averted her gaze. Had she also been nervous about seeing him, he wouldn't have been surprised. But that wasn't what he saw in her eyes. He'd seen... hurt.

"Good morning, Everleigh." With the other nurses were around, he didn't say more because he didn't want to draw attention. They'd talk in private later. She must have heard his comment that his weekend was no big deal. What would she say if he told her the truth? That the weekend with her had been such a big deal that he'd barely slept? That having spent time with Hayes and worrying about developing a relationship with her son had haunted him long into the night? Just as Everleigh's expression haunted him as he walked away from Eva's prying eyes.

When he got to the kitchen, he texted Everleigh.

Don't take my response to Eva wrong. I don't share my weekend activities with coworkers.

He hit Send, then got his coffee mug. When his phone dinged, he glanced at the screen.

Hmmm. Yet you did share your weekend activities with a coworker.

Not what I meant, he texted back.

No worries.

What did that mean? *No worries?* No worries because their weekend had been no big deal to her and so she hadn't thought a thing of his comment? No, that couldn't be right. Not with that flicker he'd seen in her eyes before she'd averted them.

Wryn frowned. What was wrong with him? Other than when it came to what had happened with Kara, he'd always been confident, self-assured of what he wanted in life.

I had a good time with you and Hayes this weekend.

There. Now there would be no doubt where his mind was. At least on that matter.

What was wrong with him? He'd spent one weekend with Everleigh, and not even just with her, but with her and her son. It wasn't as if he was close to her, either. He wasn't. And yet…yeah, there was something so different about Everleigh.

Getting his coffee, Wryn headed to his office long enough

to take a few sips, put his half-full mug on his desk then headed to see his first patient. His schedule was packed.

It wasn't until midmorning that his phone dinged with another text from Everleigh.

Same. Thank you again for making what could have truly been a rough weekend into one Hayes will talk about for months.

Warmth spread through Wryn and he smiled. It's one I'll be thinking about for months.

Same, came her response.

Tension eased from Wryn's shoulders. Tension he hadn't really acknowledged because that meant acknowledging just how much he'd enjoyed his weekend with Everleigh and just how nervous he'd been about how she'd respond to him that morning: friendly or standoffish. His comment to Eva probably hadn't helped, but based upon her texts, Everleigh seemed to be okay with that and not to have misunderstood.

Later that morning, he spotted her as he made his way down the exam room hallway. The smile she gave him was brief but real enough that his stride lightened further. Friendly. Nervous, but in a good way.

When he stepped next to where she stood, he asked, "How's your patient doing, Everleigh?"

She gave him a questioning look.

"Your elevated iron and liver function test patient," he clarified. Okay, so he'd been reaching for something to talk to her about, but he was genuinely curious, too.

"Oh." Her gaze widened then she swallowed and used a very professional tone to tell him, "That particular patient won't be back in to see me until later this week."

"Keep me posted."

"Will do." Smiling, then looking self-conscious, she glanced toward her nurse. "Liz, will you fax a copy of room six's labs to her cardiologist, please? She's got a follow-up appointment next week."

"Dr. Cooper, can you sign these home health forms?" Eva handed him a couple of papers at the same time, probably by coincidence. Although, with his nurse, he never knew. She was pretty on top of things.

Trying not to glance Everleigh's way as she charted on the patient she'd just finished seeing, Wryn signed the forms. He handed the completed orders back to Eva. "Got them. Anything else?"

Eva shook her head. "Nothing to sign, but your next patient is ready."

Which was her way of telling him to get on the move. Unable to resist a sneak peek prior to going into the next examination room, Wryn glanced toward where Everleigh charted at the counter. Seeming to sense he was looking her way, she glanced up from her computer screen, met his gaze and smiled. Cheeks pink, she immediately glanced down at the laptop as if she were engrossed in her work.

Marveling at his giddiness over such a simple gesture, Wryn whistled a soft tune as he made his way to see his next patient.

Good or bad, one thing was for sure: life had gotten a lot more interesting since Everleigh arrived.

Would you be available for dinner tonight?

Everleigh stared at her phone and shook her head as if Wryn could somehow magically see her doing so. He was likely still in the clinic somewhere as they'd just finished with their scheduled patients. Wherever he was, it wasn't at the nurses' station where she was charting.

No. I'll have Hayes, she texted back.

He is invited, too.

Everleigh stared at her phone. If ever she was going to spend time with a man, she'd want it to be one who included Hayes. So, she couldn't squelch the pleasure that Wryn invited him. But he'd said he didn't date women with kids, and he'd rushed away the previous evening. She was struggling with her attraction to him, with Hayes's fascination with him. Adding fuel to that fire would just be wrong.

I don't think that's a good idea. Not on a weeknight.

Does that mean you'd say yes to spending time with me this weekend? Hayes, too.

Everleigh bit into her lower lip. She'd be lying if she didn't admit that she wanted to spend time with Wryn. That Hayes would also want to was a given. He was infatuated to the point he'd added "God bless Dr. Cooper and Brady" to his bedtime prayer.

What was he doing? He'd said he didn't date women with kids. She had a kid.

Plus, she was brand new at the clinic. Getting involved with a coworker wasn't smart when she didn't see the relationship going anywhere. If she got involved, when they ended, how would that affect her working environment?

What if it didn't end? a crazy voice whispered. What if she spent time with Wryn, he fell hopelessly in love with her, and they lived happily ever after with Hayes?

Everleigh snorted. She had no aspirations for someone to fall in love with her. She didn't even believe in happily-ever-after, so why would she ask herself such a silly question?

We need to talk, she typed. No Hayes.

That sounds ominous, he texted back.

That's me, Miss Ominous.

Her phone dinged before she'd even put it down. That's not what I'd call you, he wrote. I'd say more of a Miss Sunshine.

Everleigh smiled then caught Eva watching. She smiled at Wryn's nurse as if her smile had nothing to do with anything then spoke to Liz. "Is there anything else you need from me this evening before I head out?"

Liz shook her head. Everleigh went to her shared office space and dialed her mother's number. "Mom, would it be okay if I ran late getting home?"

"This wouldn't have anything to do with the man you spent the weekend with, would it? The one Hayes kept talking about?" her mother asked.

Everleigh's gaze shifted to another nurse practitioner in the room. The woman had acknowledged Everleigh's arrival with a friendly smile but had gone back to clearing out her task box. Everleigh didn't fool herself that the woman wasn't aware of anything Everleigh said, though. Even if Shelby tried not to eavesdrop, there was no way to not overhear the conversation. "If it's okay, I have an errand."

Her mother chuckled, letting Everleigh know she knew exactly what Everleigh's errand was. "You know it's fine."

Everleigh did but never wanted to take overt advantage of her mother.

"Thanks, Mom. Tell Hayes that I won't be too late." She

wouldn't. She'd talk with Wryn, stress that she didn't want to risk their friendship affecting her job and that, whatever, if anything, happened between them needed to stay just between them. She needed her job, her benefits. Even if she did feel a little extra pep in her step when he was around, jeopardizing her job would just be craziness.

And then there was Hayes. She would not risk his heart being broken by Wryn.

"Being a working mom is tough business," Shelby said when Everleigh hung up the call, confirming that the woman had been listening. "You're lucky to have your mom to help. Both my family and my husband's live out of state."

"I'd be lost without Mom." So true. Having her mother's love and support had made it easier for Everleigh to go to school while working full-time. She'd never had to question if Hayes was being looked after. Her mother absolutely doted on him.

Shelby went back to working on her messages, and Everleigh texted Wryn.

Can we meet to talk? Some place where we wouldn't be seen?

Anywhere you'd like.

She wanted nowhere close to where they were but didn't want to risk being caught in traffic so getting home to Hayes would be delayed if they drove too far.

Suggestions?

My place?

Frowning, Everleigh stared at her phone. He was crazy if he thought that's what she'd meant when she'd said they needed to talk.

Not for any nefarious reasons, he clarified. It would be private, and I know Brady would be excited to see you again.

Had he read her mind? She'd definitely jumped to nefarious conclusions. They needed to talk without little ears listening in and without bumping into anyone they knew. Whatever was happening between them or might happen between them in the future, there needed to be ground rules set now.

Okay.

You remember the address?

It's in my GPS. Not that it was difficult to find. He lived in an upscale neighborhood that wasn't far from the clinic.

I'm leaving now. See you in a few.

Everleigh sighed. She'd lost her ever-loving mind. Was she seriously going to Wryn's? Alone? To talk, she reminded herself.

Everleigh was still questioning her sanity when she pulled into his drive. Just as it had on Saturday, her reliable but ten-year-old car felt out of place in his upper-middle-class neighborhood driveway. She felt out of place.

She reconsidered while waiting for him to come to his front door, but Brady's barking was just on the other side which meant Wryn wouldn't be far behind. Having him see her run back to her car was less appealing than the thought of facing him. After all, she had been the one to suggest they meet.

Brady at his side, Wryn opened the front door. He'd changed into a pair of gym shorts and a navy-and-gold Nashville Predators T-shirt. He'd not put on any shoes, and there was something so down-to-earth about him opening the door barefoot and smiling.

"Come in."

Forcing her gaze from his hairy legs, Everleigh followed him. Once again, the house's beauty and functionality impressed her.

"If you're okay with talking in the kitchen, I have dinner going." He grinned. "I didn't do my usual meal-prepping yesterday."

She followed him to the kitchen taking in the glass containers lined up on his countertop and the simmering sauce in the skillet on his stovetop. Whatever he was making, the spicy blend smelled delicious, and her mouth watered.

Going around the large kitchen island to stand in front of the stovetop, he gave the sauce a quick stir in the skillet then turned to grab a spice bottle from a neatly arranged upper cabinet.

"Can I help while we talk?" she offered, feeling out of place to just be watching someone work while she did nothing.

"Can you slice vegetables?"

"I can."

"Then, slice vegetables you shall." He pulled out a cutting board and a vegetable chopper and then placed several zucchinis next to the board. "I've already washed them."

"Any particular way you prefer your vegetables cut?"

He shook his head. "Get as creative as you'd like."

She sliced the vegetables into chunks while he poured

the mushroom sauce over a slab of meat that was in a baking dish, covered the mixture and then put it into the oven.

She finished chunking the zucchini. "Now what?"

He raked her wares into a bowl, then said, "Now we take a thirty-minute break to give the tenderloin a head start on cooking." He seasoned the vegetables, put them into his refrigerator then turned to her. "What did you want to talk about?"

Straight to the point. Part of her liked that. Another would have liked to procrastinate the conversation indefinitely. Hayes was waiting at home, though, so she wouldn't dally.

"Us."

He leaned back against the countertop. "Is there an us?"

Everleigh's heart sped up as anxiety hit. What did she know about men? She'd not even dated in over five years. Taking a deep breath, she drew from an inner confidence that somehow felt right.

"There is a something." Her tone dared him to deny it. Part of her couldn't believe she was the one initiating the conversation. "Something that is maybe just friendship." But she didn't think so. "Whatever it is, we need to discuss it before we go any further, to shed some light on our... friendship."

Arms crossed, he nodded. "Talking seems a sensible thing to do."

"I'm a sensible girl." Most of the time. "What do you see happening?"

He shrugged. "I'm attracted to you, but I've intentionally never dated anyone with a kid."

"Why? You were wonderful with Hayes and seemed to enjoy spending time with him."

"Too messy."

That she understood. Dating while having a kid felt pretty

messy to her, too. Her reasons for not dating up to that point had to do with Bryan and not having time for a man in her life. Making time would have meant taking time from Hayes or school, and she hadn't even considered doing that. Now the biggest messiness came from a need to protect Hayes.

"Everything is messy when a child is involved, because the child comes first." She looked Wryn straight in the eyes. "Hayes is my whole world and my top priority."

"He should be." Although his words agreed and she didn't doubt their sincerity, Wryn averted his gaze as he said them, looking uncomfortable. Pushing away from the countertop, he walked to the refrigerator. "You want something to drink? We can sit by the pool."

It wasn't out of line for him to offer a drink and suggest they sit outdoors rather than continue to stand in the kitchen, but his change of subject felt abrupt.

"Water would be great. Thanks."

He got two plastic tumblers from his cabinet and filled them from his refrigerator's water dispenser. "Come on, Brady," he told the dog then shot her a smile, "You, too, Everleigh."

She followed him outdoors. The covered, stamped concrete patio area was as gorgeous as the inside of the home. Cream- and navy-colored cushions covered sturdy wicker furniture. There was a built-in stone fireplace with a large television mounted above a roughly hewn oak mantel. Ferns and other greenery Everleigh couldn't name added a lushness around the pool.

Brady brought a tennis ball and dropped it at Wryn's feet then barked.

Wryn scratched the dog behind the ears. "Not now, bud. We have company."

Brady seemed to understand as, looking disappointed,

he took off into the yard to inspect something near the privacy fence that bordered the entire backyard.

"Hayes will be upset if he finds out I visited without him," Everleigh mused, watching the dog bury his nose into the grass.

"You could have brought him."

"That wouldn't have been smart, nor would it have given us the opportunity to talk freely about whatever this weekend was. Coworkers? Friends? That's what we said—coworkers and friends—but is that true or is this something else?"

"Does it have to be something else?"

She took a deep breath. "I'm not good at this and don't want to risk making things awkward at work. Maybe talking about it is just making everything more confusing, but I believe getting things in the open is best." She held his gaze. "Which is why you're going to have to explain what this weekend was and why you asked me to dinner this evening."

"It might have just been two coworkers bumping into each other at the park and a friendly gesture to a new coworker," he began. "But it's not that simple, is it?"

She shook her head. "Our working together complicates anything beyond our being just coworkers. Plus, there's the whole thing with you saying you don't date women with kids." She narrowed her gaze. "If that's true, why did you invite me to dinner tonight, Wryn?"

Wryn fought flinching. There was a hint of accusation in Everleigh's tone. In her eyes, too. Their brown depths had darkened to a depth which, if he fell into them, he'd not be able to see his way free from.

From where she sat on the heavy wicker sofa, she held his gaze, and his stomach tightened. "I distinctly recall you suggesting we get pizza on Saturday and our going to the hospital together on Sunday. You are also the one who invited me to dinner tonight. Me and Hayes," she clarified, emphasizing Hayes's name. "Were those invitations just one coworker inviting another to do something? Or just two friends hanging out after work?"

He sat quietly, knowing he should cling to one of the options she'd presented but knowing they weren't the truth. He took a deep breath. "It would seem you're the exception, Everleigh."

She blinked. "The exception?"

"I liked you prior to this past weekend and am even more attracted to you after it. That's why I invited you to dinner tonight."

Everleigh's cheeks pinkened.

"This is going to be awkward if you aren't attracted to me, too, but I don't think you'd be here if you weren't."

Her lashes lowered. "I imagine there aren't many women who aren't attracted to you."

He snorted. "I imagine there are quite a few who aren't, but I'm glad you're not one of them."

Looking uncomfortable, she pressed forward. "I am attracted to you, but Hayes's well-being is more important than that attraction. My job at the clinic is more important, too." Her chin lifted. "If you can't deal with that, then we need to end this now rather than later."

Rather than later. She was admitting that she didn't see them lasting. Just as well: he didn't see himself lasting with anyone, either. He didn't deserve a happily-ever-after.

"I can deal with those things." He didn't foresee either being a problem as his job was more important, too. "So what does this mean?"

Her expression didn't budge. "That we will go slow, very

slow, and continue to explore our mutual attraction with no expectation of a future together, but just an enjoyable relationship while it lasts and with both of us keeping Hayes's well-being as our top priority."

"Okay." Because what else could he say? "So we'll go out this Friday night?"

She hesitated a moment then nodded. "But no Hayes."

"I don't understand."

"I don't think it's a good idea for him to spend more time with you."

He couldn't really argue with that one, could he?

"Maybe on occasion, but he latched on to you this weekend, and I just think that if he continued to spend time with you that he would be hurt down the road."

"You don't have to explain. I understand. What about work?"

Everleigh's nose crinkled, and she shook her head. "No one can know."

He arched a brown. "We're going to sneak around at work?"

Her jaw dropped. "Most definitely not. There will be no sneaking around. We're going to be professional at work. That's it. No one can know we're seeing each other."

What she was suggesting made perfect sense, was ideal in so many ways, so why didn't it sit well? "Not ever?"

She shrugged. "Doubtful. It'll make things simpler when we decide to call it quits."

"You want me to be your dirty little secret?" Wryn wasn't sure if he was impressed at her foresight or insulted.

"I guess, because I don't want anyone to know."

Interesting. She was right. No one knowing would make things much simpler down the road. And, as much as he'd enjoyed being with Hayes, what Everleigh was offering was ideal because it meant less guilt over spending time with a kid when he'd never done that with his own son. "No being around Hayes, and no one at work can know. Got it. What about if someone sees us out together? Then what?"

Looking thoughtful, she shrugged. "Then we'll deal with that when it happens. Hopefully, it won't."

What she was offering was a sweet setup.

"Any other rules or stipulations I should know about?"

She didn't quite meet his eyes when she said, "No public displays of affection."

His brow arched. "Does that mean there will be private displays of affection?"

Her breath audibly catching, she stared at him like a deer caught in headlights. But there was more than just that stunned look. There was a darkening that had him gulping.

"We'll deal with that when it happens, too." Her voice broke a little, and her gaze lowered to his mouth. She was thinking about kissing him. Her breath quickened, and the pulse at her throat sped up. There would be private displays.

"Maybe it should happen right now." He wanted it to happen, wanted to kiss Everleigh, to know what it felt like to feel her lips against his.

His words seemed to snap her out of her thoughts, and she swatted at his hand. "No. I'm not ready to kiss you, Wryn." She winced. "It's not that I haven't thought about kissing you." His heart pounded at her admission. "But the truth is that I haven't kissed anyone since Bryan. When I said we would go slow, I meant it."

That had cold water splashing over him. Was Everleigh still hung up on Hayes's father? He hadn't gotten that impression, but they'd barely scraped the surface of getting to know each other. Just one more reason that he needed to be careful around Everleigh. She had a kid and an ex that she might still have feelings for. He had a kid he'd never spoken to and an ex he didn't have feelings for other than to appreciate that she was a good mother to their son.

"So no kissing until you're ready. I can wait. However, you can't fault me for wanting to kiss you." Taking her hand, Wryn marveled at the zings their skin-to-skin contact triggered.

Everleigh must have felt it, too, as she pulled her hand away, then rubbed her palm over her thigh. "Faulting you for wanting to kiss me would be silly when I've admitted that I'm attracted to you."

Wham! Her words sent a lightning bolt of energy through him. She stood from the lounge chair, picked up the ball Brady had brought to him earlier, then tossed it toward where the dog was still intrigued by something in the grass.

"Fetch, Brady."

Excited at the ball landing near him, Brady lost all interest in whatever he'd been investigating. The dog grabbed the ball and happily made his way to Everleigh.

"Good boy," she praised, giving him a thorough petting, then tossing the ball again.

Watching them play, Wryn let their conversation soak in. They'd essentially made a pact to secretly date, take things slow, and end before they even got started. As he didn't seem able to stay away from her, it was the perfect setup. When it was time to say goodbye to their personal relationship, no one would be hurt. What could be better?

"You're making me self-conscious," she advised, giving him a look that was a tumultuous mixture of excitement and warning. "Quit watching me."

"Sorry. That wasn't my intention. I like watching you."

Taking the ball and giving it another toss, she then turned back to him. "Okay, but you've met your quota for the day."

He laughed. "My quota? I may have to renegotiate for better terms. I've not nearly gotten my fill of looking at you."

Excitement filled her eyes. But hesitancy was still there, too. He understood. Even with their pact, he was nervous, too. He motioned for Brady to bring the ball to him, and standing, he tossed the ball to the far end of the yard.

"Show-off," Everleigh accused him with a smile.

"You haven't seen nothing yet, lady," he promised. Witnessing how color splotched her cheeks, he reminded himself that they were going slow. Slow was good, and at the same time, slow was bad. The timer on his watch beeped, and he glanced at it. "It's time to grill the veggies. Do you want to stay to eat?"

Glancing at her watch, Everleigh shook her head. "My mom and Hayes will be wondering where I am."

"What are you going to tell them?"

"The truth." Her gaze met his. "That I got hung up with a coworker."

"Will I see you prior to Friday?"

"You'll see me tomorrow at the clinic," she reminded him.

"Thank God for work, then." His comment earned a smile and a pleased light in her eyes. She was such an enigma. Beautiful yet humble, as if she had no clue how attractive she was. And smart, yet she often second-guessed herself. With time she'd get past that, though. She had a good head on her shoulders and health-care skills in her arsenal.

They'd just stepped back into the kitchen when Everleigh's phone rang. She glanced at the screen. "I've got to take this." She answered the phone.

"Is everything okay?…I guess so…Of course not. He'll enjoy the visit…Okay, Mom. I'll see you later, then."

"Everything okay?" Wryn asked when she'd disconnected the call.

She placed the phone in her scrub top pocket. "That was my mom letting me know that she and Hayes stopped by a coworker's home. They've decided to stay for dinner. Mom's coworker has a granddaughter close to Hayes's age, and they play well together."

Implications of what she was saying hit. "You don't have to rush off?"

She took a deep breath. "I guess not. If your dinner invitation still stands, I'll stay."

Thinking this evening just kept getting better, Wryn grinned. "It stands."

"Good. I'm starved, and whatever you have in the oven smells amazing."

CHAPTER SEVEN

"I TAKE BACK my feeling sorry for you for meal-prepping. That was delicious."

Wryn smiled at Everleigh's compliment. He'd been on his own a long time. He'd never been a bad cook but had enjoyed improving his skills, even going so far as to take a cooking class a few years back. "You thought it wouldn't be?"

Toying with her fork, she shrugged. "You seem to be great at everything."

He laughed. "Not hardly, but I'm glad you enjoyed dinner. I like to cook."

"That's a plus in your favor. It's not something I'm crazy about. Or maybe I've just never had time to do much cooking other than quick meals. Plus, with Mom being at the house, cooking is her domain, and I'm good with that." She stood, carried her plate to the sink and rinsed the empty dish. "Shall I put this in the dishwasher?"

He'd picked up his own plate and joined her. "There's no rush. I can do them after you've left."

She frowned. "I'm not leaving dirty dishes."

"The reality is that there's only an extra plate, fork and knife beyond what I would have done if you weren't here. I think I can handle that extra workload without too much of a strain."

"When you put it that way..." She smiled. "But I would like to help. With both of us working, it won't take but a couple of minutes."

Everleigh loaded the used dishes into the dishwasher while Wryn filled food storage containers with the leftovers. When they were done, they went outside and threw the tennis ball with Brady again. Everleigh's throws weren't that far, but Wryn's sent the dog racing across the yard to catch the ball and bring it back to him.

"Hayes would be so disappointed if he knew," she mused. As much as he enjoyed playing with his friend Carla, Brady would win hands down. "He wants a dog and was so impressed by Brady. Me, too, for that matter. He's a great dog."

"He's the best. You should get a dog. Every kid needs a dog."

"Our getting one hasn't been a realistic option, not with my being in school and working so much." She paused, then clarified. "I worked full-time out of necessity while getting my degree. A dog would have created extra expenses I couldn't afford. Not to mention adding to the household's workload as I don't imagine taking care of a dog is easy." She wouldn't know as she'd never had a pet. The truth was, if she got Hayes a dog, she'd have to do a ton of research.

"You mentioned earlier that you live with your mom?"

Everleigh nodded. "It's what made sense for us all, financially and with Hayes."

His eyebrows furrowed. "Does your ex not help financially with Hayes?"

She snorted. "I haven't seen or heard from Bryan since our divorce papers were signed."

"He wasn't ordered to pay child support?" Wryn looked shocked.

"He might have been if he'd had a job at the time. He

didn't and hadn't for months." Instead, he'd let her pay their mounting bills while he did Lord only knew what. "I got everything I wanted from my divorce."

"Hayes?" he guessed.

She nodded. "Bryan gave me full custody. Since then, I've not seen or heard from him. That he'd give up his son so easily—" Catching that Wryn was wincing, Everleigh took a calming breath. She rarely talked about Bryan for this reason. She tended to get riled up. Rarely? She never talked about Bryan. Yet, with Wryn, she'd been blurting out all kinds of details about her past. No wonder he was wincing. "Hayes's well-being is all that matters," she continued in an even tone. "Speaking of which, I should head home so I can give him his bath and get him to bed."

"I'm glad you stayed, Everleigh, that we had this time together outside of work." He didn't say just the two of them, but Everleigh supposed that was true, too. It had been nice to talk freely without Hayes overhearing their conversation.

"Me, too." She wasn't lying. Other than the occasional awkward moment because of their blunt but needed conversation about their relationship, she'd enjoyed the evening. But as nice a time as she'd had, she'd missed spending the evening with Hayes.

They went inside, Everleigh got her bag, and they walked to the living room foyer. "Thanks for tonight, Wryn. For dinner and the company," she said, her hand on the door handle.

"You're welcome. Thanks for helping and staying." He hesitated, then laughed, sounding a bit nervous, too. "Is this where we shake hands again?"

Smiling and with her belly doing cartwheels, she held out her hand as her answer.

Chuckling, he took her hand, but rather than shake and let

go, he pulled her just shy of her body touching his and stared down at her. His hand still held hers as their eyes locked.

Everleigh couldn't breathe, couldn't move, couldn't do anything but wait to see what he was going to do next. Was he going to kiss her? After years of not being kissed, of not caring about such niceties, she fought leaning in to him. Which meant what? That she hoped he would kiss her? That he'd take the initiative, so she didn't have to question herself too much? That maybe her saying she wasn't ready for them to kiss had to do with a fear of becoming physically involved with someone again? For Everleigh, that physicality implied things she wasn't ready to feel again and maybe never would be? Acknowledging that didn't lower her awareness of the man inches from her. She'd swear his body held a magnetic pull. But rather than close the gap between them, he gave her hand a gentle squeeze and let go.

"Good night, Everleigh."

Heart pounding, her gaze searched his. "Good night, Wryn."

Wryn put a lot of thought into where he wanted to take Everleigh for their first official outing. Nashville had lots of cool options, and he considered taking her downtown to catch a music performance off Broad Street. But the strip was guaranteed to be busy, and they'd have higher odds of running into someone they knew. Eating well in Nashville wasn't a problem, but he wanted more than to just take her to a restaurant.

He ended up enrolling for a cooking class where they cooked their meals along with eight others in the class. The venue was in an old industrial building that had been converted into an open area that had a cooking station and to the far end of the room an invitingly decorated dining area that was situated on a huge rug to give it a separate feel from the rest of the business. The ceiling had been left in its original state, giving it an eclectic look.

Joining the other couples at the cooking stations, Everleigh's gaze narrowed. "I recall mentioning that I wasn't much on cooking."

"You specified that you hadn't had much opportunity as the kitchen was your mother's domain."

"True, but that didn't mean I wanted to cook while on a date. Isn't the idea to impress me?"

Her tone was teasing, though, and he grinned. "Are you not impressed?"

Her expression dubious, she snorted.

Liking that, although there was always a physical tension between them, she otherwise seemed relaxed, Wryn laughed. "Just don't start a food fight and purposely get us kicked out."

Her lips twitched. "I'll have you know that I've never been thrown out of school."

He shrugged. "There's always a first time."

"Apparently so, since I'm here with you."

Her smile stole his breath. He couldn't exactly call it flirty, and yet, he couldn't not call it that, either. She was such an enigma. "Touché."

The fiftysomething half-Greek chef introduced herself and had each participant give a brief introduction. When each person had done so, she gave the itinerary of what their night entailed, then got them started on their dinner preparations.

"I've only been alone with you on two occasions, and on both I've had to chop vegetables," Everleigh mock-complained and tsked.

Oops. He'd been going for something outside the usual date night. "I didn't think about that."

Fortunately, she didn't seem to truly mind. He wanted her to do more than just not mind, though. He wanted her to have an amazing time. Maybe they would check out a few bars to listen to live music. For Everleigh, he'd even whip out his middle-school-honed line dancing skills if she wanted to dance.

"Have you done one of these classes before?"

"Cooking classes, yes, but a date-night cooking class where I sit down and eat the meal afterward?" He shook his head. "I haven't dated a lot. When I have, it's usually dinner or a sports event, maybe a concert."

"That sounds amazing."

Wondering if he truly had messed up, he asked, "You like sports?"

"I meant the concert and going to a restaurant where you don't have to cook for yourself." Her eyes twinkled as she continued to cut the vegetables as their instructor had demonstrated.

"I'll keep that in mind for our next date."

"About that, I can't be away from Hayes that often. I don't want to be away from him that often," she clarified. "He's with Mom tonight, but he'll ask questions if I suddenly have a social life."

Wryn thought a moment. "What time does he go to bed?"

"Eight."

"Why don't we plan our next date to start after eight?" he suggested, sliding the vegetables into the wok that the instructor had set up on a burner. "That way, you can be there when Hayes goes to bed and be back before he wakes in the morning."

She stopped what she was doing to turn toward him. "You'd do that?"

"The night's still young at eight." Surely she realized he'd do much more than that to spend time with her.

Smiling, Everleigh nodded. "You're right. I'll talk to Mom to see if she has plans."

"For tomorrow night?" He was pressing his luck, but it was the weekend and neither of them had to be at work the next day.

Her gaze met his. "As long as Mom can watch Hayes and we start after eight so I can tuck him into bed and read his bedtime stories to him."

"You're very close to him."

"He's the best part of my life. Which is why, as fun as this is, I have continued to talk about him and miss him. Being a parent is the best thing I've ever done," she said with enthusiasm. "Seeing the world through his eyes is such a blessing. I'm constantly in awe."

What would it feel like to see the world through your child's eyes? Wryn swallowed back a thick mixture of envy and guilt. What would it have been like to see the world through Seth's eyes? To have experienced his son's take on the world?

"It's difficult to imagine that you haven't dated a lot." Everleigh's going back to his earlier comment pulled Wryn from his thoughts.

"Why's that?"

"Let's see. You're kind, sometimes funny," she said and grinned at him. "Smart, a doctor, and not bad-looking."

"Not bad-looking?" He furrowed his brows, but warmth spread through him at her compliments. "Thanks. I think."

"You want me to say how gorgeous you are?"

"Beauty is in the eye of the beholder," he reminded. "As long as you find me attractive, I'm a happy man."

"You must be ecstatic, then."

His gaze met hers. This time, there was no doubting the flirtatiousness in her words or smile. Everleigh did make him happy. Even when the past pressed into the present, she calmed the storm.

"You really are sunshine."

She laughed. "I'm telling you, it's the hair."

He shook his head. The warmth she exuded had nothing to do with her outer appearance and everything to do with the woman. He'd never known anyone like Everleigh, never known anyone who affected him so powerfully. Never known anyone who could displace the mind games he played with himself.

She'd said it had been over five years since she'd dated. He got the impression that when she had dated, things hadn't gone well, that she hadn't been treated as well as she should have. She didn't vocalize much, but little things he did seemed to surprise her. Her reaction made him want to do more, to show Everleigh what dating should be like so she never settled for someone who didn't value what a wonderful woman she was.

The thought of her someday dating someone and falling in love with them, of that person being worthy of her and Hayes, put his chest in a vise grip, but it's what he wanted for them both. Someday.

Selfishly, since he could never be that guy, he hoped someday was a long time away.

Everleigh was unlikely to make the elaborate meal at home, but it was delicious. It was also fun to sit at the table with the other four couples and chat while they ate. No judgment or funny looks or anything that made her feel uncomfortable. Just strangers who were there to have a fun date night, as well.

Wryn had made her laugh repeatedly while they did their food prep and cooked their meal. He'd also been a perfect gentleman. Her entire life Everleigh couldn't recall a man opening her car door for her. Wryn did so as if it were no big deal. To him it probably wasn't, but the gestures made her feel special.

Silly how such a small thing could have such a big impact.

Then again, if it were anyone other than Wryn, would it not matter how big the gesture?

Of that she wasn't so sure. From the moment she'd first seen Wryn, there had been something different. Something so appealing that she'd stepped far outside her comfort zone to go to his house Monday evening and say the things she had. But she was glad she had, because now they were on the same page. Coworkers, friends and dating.

Her dating Wryn. Just wow. Never in her wildest dreams had she imagined she'd ever have someone like Wryn interested in her. For the time being, she reminded herself. Nothing about them was permanent. She'd do well to remember that and not get caught up in the fantasy of being the center of his attention.

They were nearing the end of the meal when Everleigh's phone dinged. Recognizing the preprogrammed sound as a notification from her mother's continuous glucose monitor, Everleigh immediately checked the message.

Seventy-nine. Not dangerously low and just outside the preprogrammed low range indicating a notification, but Everleigh knew how quickly her mother could drop. Plus, the red arrow next to the seventy-nine indicated that the reading was on its way further down. Sweat popped out on the back of Everleigh's neck.

"Excuse me a moment." She pushed back from the table, then as she was dialing her mother, she walked to the far side of the kitchen area, hopefully minimally disturbing the others. "Come on, Mom. Answer the phone," she whispered, hoping it would manifest her mother to do so.

"I know, I know," her mother answered, filling Everleigh with relief. "Sorry it took me a moment to answer. I was in the kitchen getting a glucose tablet and had left my phone in the other room."

"You've taken the glucose tablets now, though?" At her mother's confirmation, she reminded her, "Eat protein, too. We have peanut butter in the cabinet."

"Yes, *Mother*," her mom teased. They both knew how serious her low blood sugars could be, though. They'd been down that road many times. Frequently, her mother would overcompensate and shoot her sugar too far the other way. That was easier to deal with than when her numbers dropped dangerously low, so Everleigh tried not to fuss too much. The important thing was her not going into a hypoglycemic coma again. They'd almost lost her the last time that had happened.

"Do you have your glucagon pen? Just in case you need it?"

"It's in my bedroom. I'll get it." Her mother's voice sounded shaky, further raising Everleigh's alarm.

"Keep it on you. Are you feeling okay? Do I need to come home? Is Hayes still sleeping? You can wake him if you think you may need him." Because of how unstable her mother's diabetes was, Hayes knew to call for emergency services and how to administer the glucagon pen. He'd never had to do it, but Everleigh had shown him and let him practice with a demo pen to the point where, if he had to, she believed he could do it since it was essentially just removing the cap and jabbing the pen into her mother's thigh.

"Hayes is sound asleep. I'm fine," her mother assured her. "I got clammy and could tell it was dropping. It's nothing major that my glucose tablets shouldn't take care of. I don't need to wake Hayes, and you do not need to come home. Enjoy your evening."

Right. Everleigh wouldn't be able to do that until her mom's glucose level was okay.

"When did you last take your insulin?" she continued, asking question after question, and wondering if she should go home. Seventy-nine wasn't that low, and she'd taken the glucose tablets, she reminded herself. Hopefully, her levels would respond, and all would be fine. Everleigh would stay on the phone until she knew for sure.

"With my evening snack, using my sliding scale, just like always. I shouldn't be dropping."

Something in her mother's tone made Everleigh suspicious. "What did you have for your snack?"

Her mother's silence proved her instincts right. She'd eaten something she shouldn't have and had likely overcorrected in hope of keeping the numbers from going up. *Oh, Mom.*

"Everything okay with Hayes?" Wryn joined where Everleigh paced at the far side of the large room. Concern shone on his face.

"Hayes is in bed asleep and is fine. My mom's continuous glucose monitor is reading at seventy-nine. I know that's not crazy low. But she's been known to tank fast, has been hospitalized multiple times due to rapid lows, so I worry, right, Mom?" she emphasized the last directly into the phone, then sent an apologetic look to Wryn. "I'm staying on the line until her numbers are on the rise."

"You don't have to do that," her mother replied. "I'm already starting to feel better."

"Smart thinking," Wryn said at the same time. "Is there anything I can do?"

The sincerity in his voice impressed Everleigh, just as everything about the night, about the man, impressed her. She'd had fun. Noting that a few of the other couples were staring in their direction, Everleigh shook her head. "I'll just stay over here until her sugar is up, to keep from bothering the others."

She'd expected Wryn to return to the table; instead, he eyed her with an understanding that made her knees threaten to buckle. Especially when he asked, "Do you want to go check on her?"

"Don't you dare," her mother ordered, obviously able to hear everything Wryn was saying.

Heavens, she was in trouble. Because Wryn's blue gaze was sucking her in and making her want to lean on him. That was silly. She didn't lean on anyone. Ever. Besides, it wasn't even as if her mother was in real trouble. She wasn't. Seventy-nine was not that bad.

"She's eaten and has her glucagon pen. She should be fine." Which was true, but past hypoglycemic episodes that had ended with ambulances and hospital admissions tugged at Everleigh. "Actually, would you mind? I know we aren't finished, but I'd feel better." She'd planned to explain, but Wryn held up his hand.

"I'll let the chef know that we're going to head out a bit early."

While listening to her mother's complaints that she was cutting her date short, Everleigh watched Wryn go back to the table, say goodbyes to the other cooks, tip the chef then return, carrying her bag.

"Ready?" he asked. He didn't look mad or upset that they were leaving early. Instead, he looked concerned. No questions asked, he was ready to go because she was worried about her mother when they both knew that, although not good, seventy-nine in and of itself wasn't dangerously low. He'd taken her word on how quickly her mother could change.

Bryan would have pitched a fit if he'd spent the money for the class and she'd wanted to leave early. Not that her ex ever would have arranged such an evening. Their dates, if you could call them that, had consisted of fast food she'd paid for and whatever television program he preferred. Why had she ever settled for someone who'd never put any effort into her or their relationship? Even with sex, it had always been about him. Maybe it was that way with every man. Everleigh wouldn't know, as her ex-husband was the only man she'd been with. She'd been too busy for the past five years to consider such things, but looking at Wryn, she wondered and knew everything about him was and would be different than anything she'd ever experienced because he was different from anyone she'd ever known.

"Thank you, Wryn. Other than Mom's sugar, tonight was perfect." Unable to stop herself and not wanting to, she leaned to where she could press a kiss to his cheek.

CHAPTER EIGHT

LATER THAT NIGHT, Everleigh's words and soft cheek kiss haunted Wryn. She'd looked at him as if he'd done something above and beyond. Once they'd arrived at her apartment, she'd introduced him to her mother who, fortunately, had already improved to where her glucose level was just above one-hundred.

"I feel terrible that y'all came home early," Vivien said for the dozenth time. They were sitting at the four-person table in the kitchen/dining area. He and Everleigh had water glasses and she'd convinced her mother to drink a protein drink.

"I would have been too worried to have enjoyed the rest of the evening," Everleigh reassured her mother, patting her hand. "It's all good."

Wryn had never been close to his parents. They weren't bad parents, but he couldn't say they were good ones, either. Once they'd divorced, they'd been absent, neither really wanting him nor wanting the other to have him. As they'd started new families, he'd been the odd man out. Once he'd left for university, he'd gone home less and less. He saw them one to two times a year, and that worked for them all. Watching the love between Everleigh and her mom filled him with envy because they shared a bond he'd never experienced. It was the same as watching her with Hayes. Everleigh's family unit might be small, but it was strong.

"Regardless, I want to make up for ruining your evening."

"You didn't," he and Everleigh insisted at the same time.

"Good to know." Vivien smiled, then yawned. "It's probably the sugar, but I'm calling it an early night. You two enjoy yourselves. Nice to meet you, Wryn."

Wryn stood. "Same, Ms. Bennett. I'm glad you are feeling better."

"Night, Mom." Everleigh stood and kissed her mother's cheek. "Get some rest."

As Vivien whispered something to Everleigh that had her cheeks turning pink, Wryn glanced at his watch. It wasn't that late but was past the point to where he'd suggest they go elsewhere.

When her mother had left the room, Everleigh turned to him and sighed. "Could you hear what she said?"

"I couldn't, so you're safe."

"Nothing dramatic, just that you were a keeper." Pausing, she grimaced. "I'll remind her tomorrow that you and I aren't in that type of relationship."

That type of relationship. One where he would be a keeper. Yeah, that wasn't what they were doing, despite the fact that Everleigh Bennett was a keeper.

If life had been different, if it weren't for Seth and Wryn's failures regarding him, Everleigh was exactly the kind of woman he'd want to keep.

"Do you want to stay for a while or just call it a night?" she asked.

Trying to read her to see what she was hoping he'd say, Wryn eyed her. "Are you tired?"

She shook her head. "Not really, but if you're ready to go

home, then I completely understand, especially as I'd not want to leave, just in case."

"So what would you like to do?"

"We could play a game," she suggested.

"Strip poker?" he teased.

Her eyes widened. "Sure, with Mom and Hayes just in the next rooms, that should be fun."

He grinned. "Nothing like living dangerously."

"Here I was thinking along the lines of—" eyes twinkling, she named a popular children's board game that he'd probably played at some point in his life, but if so, it had been decades "—and your mind is in the gutter."

"I was never worried that you'd agree," he replied, laughing. "So sure, we'll play your game about a land full of sweets."

"Seriously?"

"Why not? You'll have to update me on the rules, though. Otherwise, you can't hold me responsible if I make up my own as we go."

She arched a brow. "If I refresh your memory, you won't make up your own?"

"I'm not making any promises."

She set the game up on the table and they sat catty-corner from each other. With her laughter and silly excitement over moving ahead of him, she was enjoying herself so much that he was a winner regardless of who reached the castle first.

"Woot, woot," she cheered, keeping her voice low enough as to not wake her family.

"I guess you really are a princess who can do it on her own."

Her gaze meeting his, she smiled. "You're right. I am, but tonight has been nice."

"Beating me at a kid's game makes you happy?"

"Apparently." She laughed. "Maybe I'll let you win next time, just to keep things interesting."

Next time. Because there would be more games played between them. Games that with time would evolve beyond a kid's make-believe world.

They packed the game up then chatted for a few minutes in the living room, standing close to each other at the shelf where she'd returned the game to.

"What time will Hayes wake in the morning?"

"He's usually awake and going by seven."

"Never a time for you to sleep in?"

"*Sleep in*, what's that?" Smiling, she shrugged. "But seriously, life is the best it's ever been."

He hoped he played a small role in that but suspected not as she truly was a princess who needed no rescuing.

"I'm enjoying having weekends off to spend with him." Everleigh's lashes lowered. "I also enjoyed tonight. Thank you for a great time."

Wryn's heart flip-flopped. "I had a great time, too. Well, except the getting my rear end handed to me at a kid's game."

"Quit your whining." Her eyes twinkled as she pressed her finger to his chest. "I've already said that I'll let you win next time."

Rather than step back, her finger lingered. Wryn gulped. She'd insinuated they weren't going to have a physical relationship any time soon. But she'd kissed his cheek earlier, and now she was looking up at him with those big, gorgeous eyes, and he'd have to be blind to not see what shone there. She wanted him to kiss her. Stunned by just how looking into her eyes stirred so much more than just physical desire, he hesitated.

Further stunning him, standing on her tiptoes, hands

going to his shoulders, Everleigh touched her lips to his. Soft, warm, electric. She'd closed her eyes and seemed to be cherishing the moment as her mouth explored his. Wryn fought pulling her to him and taking control of the kiss, instead giving her the lead and taking his cue from her. But oh, how he longed to do some exploring of his own.

If he thought she was ready to be kissed the way he wanted to kiss her, he would. She wasn't, though. She needed to be in the lead, and that she was kissing him was what mattered most. Everleigh was kissing him.

Unable to keep his hands off her, he slid them around her waist, not pulling her flush against him, but helping support her tiptoed stance. With one last, slow caress of his lips, she opened her eyes.

Wryn's insides shook from the impact of being suckerpunched by the light in Everleigh's eyes.

That light was like a beacon in a darkness he hadn't even realized he'd been in. A light he wanted to race toward.

He was in major trouble.

A month passed. A month in which Everleigh pretended Wryn was just another coworker at the clinic, while she spent more and more time with him outside of work, while they held hands and shared good-night kisses that kept growing in intensity and the desire for more.

To Wryn's credit, he never pushed, even when he wanted to deepen their caress. That she understood. More and more she couldn't look at him at the clinic because she was afraid of how he made her feel being obvious. Eva and Liz suspected something was going on between them, but other than knowing looks, the two hadn't murmured a word about what was happening in front of their eyes.

On the surface she and Wryn were friendly and professional. Beneath that surface, she was a bundle of energy every time he was near. Every time she thought of him. For the most part, she'd limited his time with Hayes, but that was getting more and more difficult because he was so good with her son. Between Everleigh no longer working weekends and the addition of Wryn to their lives, Hayes had truly had the best summer of his short life. Wryn was so good with him: kind, patient, fun. He was all that with Everleigh, too.

Which was why she'd agreed to a pool day at his house and later grilling. Hayes had had a blast swimming and playing with Brady. Everleigh had had a blast playing in the pool with Hayes and Wryn. Hayes had been so happy to see the dog and Wryn that Everleigh felt guilty for playing interference so often. Still, she didn't want Hayes to expect Wryn to be a part of their everyday life when he wouldn't always be there.

Fortunately, Wryn seemed okay with their seeing each other after Hayes was in bed, her son never knowing that Everleigh was spending so much time with Wryn. As smitten as the rest of the family, her mom offered to watch Hayes so they could have earlier date nights, but Everleigh had only agreed a couple of times. Hayes was her everything, and she'd been away from him so much, had missed out on so much while going to school and working. She wasn't going to miss more of her son's life because of dating. Not even when those dates were with someone as wonderful as Wryn. Was it selfish of her to so strictly limit how much time Wryn and Hayes spent together? Hayes adored Wryn and their adventures. He also adored Brady. At whatever point Wryn tired of their status quo and moved on to someone else, Hayes would be heartbroken over loss of man and dog. Everleigh suspected her son wouldn't be the only one, and for all the good times they were having she need to remember that none of this had an end goal of any permanency.

Wryn would move on. He'd been upfront with her that he wasn't looking for a future together and didn't see himself in a father role. Odd because on the occasions Hayes was with them, watching him with her son it was impossible for her not to envision Wryn in exactly that role.

"I ran an EKG in room five." Liz handed her the heart rhythm printout. "You'll want to go there prior to the room that's next on your schedule. His oxygen saturates are in the low nineties, but I put him on oxygen. He's breathy."

Everleigh glanced down at the EKG, scanning over the machine's reading and then looking at the inverted T-wave on the test. Possible acute myocardial infarction.

"Heading there now. Call for an ambulance and get a nitroglycerin," she told Liz as she rushed toward the room. "Let one of the docs know what's going on, too, please."

Having worked in the emergency room for years, Everleigh had no issue working a code, if needed. But during an acute emergency at the clinic, protocol dictated that one of the doctors be present when possible.

In room five was a seventy-two-year-old Caucasian male who was fifty pounds overweight and ruddy-faced and worked hard with each inhaled breath. He wore the oxygen tubing and a nasal cannula.

"Hello, Mr. Davenport. I'm Everleigh, the nurse practitioner examining you today. Your test showed abnormalities that need further workup." Everleigh moved to where he sat on the examination table. Sweat beaded on his forehead, dampening his surprisingly thick silvery-white hairline.

"Am I having a heart attack?" he asked as Everleigh pressed her stethoscope to his chest to listen to his heart sounds. He had a normal sounding S-one-S-two lub-dub but with a murmur that Everleigh would grade as a three of six. There was also rattling in the lower lobes of both lungs. Glancing at the pulse oximeter covering his fingertip, she was glad to see his saturation was still in the low nineties. She'd like it to have been higher, but at least he was holding steady.

"It's possible," she admitted. She didn't want to alarm him, but she wouldn't lie. "Your EKG shows concerning changes indicating you need further workup at the hospital to figure out exactly what the issue is. But honestly, you're in so much discomfort, that even if your EKG had been normal, I'd have sent you for more testing. Do you know if you have a heart murmur?"

He shook his head. "Not that anyone has ever told me."

"Hmm. You do have one, but I can't tell you if that's truly a new finding or not." She'd dig back through his chart to see if anyone had ever documented hearing the abnormal swooshing sound. "Tell me about your chest pain. When did it start, and where does it hurt?"

He rubbed his sternum and to the left of his chest. "It hurts here. Not unbearable, but a heavy pressure that hasn't let up since it started. But it might just be bad indigestion."

Everleigh didn't think so. "Are you having heartburn?"

"A little." He rubbed his sternum again. "More heartburn earlier today when I first noticed something wasn't right. Now, my chest just hurts, and I feel like I can't get enough air."

Liz came into the room, carrying a plastic cup with a pill and handed it to him.

"Mr. Davenport, this is nitroglycerin," Everleigh told him. "It's a medication to dilate your blood vessels to make oxygenated blood get to your vital organs easier, especially your heart. Just place it in your mouth. It will dissolve, and the medicine will quickly go to work."

The man put the tablet into his mouth.

"The blood vessels dilating may give you a headache," Everleigh explained. "That's a common side effect, so don't be alarmed if it happens."

A knock sounded on the door, then Wryn came into the room. Everleigh's heart did the funny quiver it did any time he was near. She'd seen him earlier, knew he was wearing his blue scrubs that made his eyes pop, knew he had on a pair of brightly patterned tennis shoes that made her want to smile at that hint at the fun side of him, knew that when he smiled birds chirped and flew happily around in her chest and made her heart do funny things. Yet having already seen him that morning didn't dull her reaction. If anything, knowing that if she put her cheek to his and breathed in, her senses would be filled with his spicy freshness, knowing how perfectly his mouth caressed hers, heightened her awareness, leaving her a bit dizzy.

Gulping, Everleigh handed the EKG to him and made introductions. "Mr. Davenport, this is Dr. Cooper."

Wryn glanced at the reading then gave the paper to Liz. "I'm going to listen to your chest." He did so, then draped his stethoscope into his scrub top pocket. "How long have you had your murmur?"

The man shook his head. "Since about two minutes ago... when she told me about it."

Wryn glanced toward Everleigh.

"He's had one nitroglycerin," she told him. "The ambulance is on its way."

"Let's get a line put in while we wait on the ambulance," Wryn told her.

Nodding, Everleigh was on her way out of the room to grab the needed supplies with Liz when Mr. Davenport groaned.

"I'm dizzy." With that, he lost consciousness.

Wryn and Everleigh caught his slumped body before he slid off the examination table.

"Mr. Davenport?" Everleigh shook his shoulder as they lay him back. "Can you hear me, Mr. Davenport?"

She propped his feet while Wryn placed his finger on the man's wrist.

"His pulse is jumping from too low to tachycardic."

"V-tach?" She guessed his abnormal rhythm.

"Maybe." He glanced to Liz. "Get the defibrillator, just in case."

The nurse left the room.

"Mr. Davenport," Everleigh continued, saying his name. "Can you hear me, Mr. Davenport? The ambulance is on its way."

Seconds felt like hours as they observed the barely perceptible rise and fall of his chest. Liz rushed back in with the defibrillator.

They opened the machine's case. Everleigh undid Mr. Davenport's shirt buttons while Wryn tore open the lead patches. She spread the material apart just as he was ready to put the leads on the man's chest.

"Wryn." Everleigh noted the extended time it had been since their patient had last inhaled. Everleigh did a sternal rub, trying to stimulate him to take a breath. Nothing happened.

"His oxygen saturation is dropping," Wryn noted. "Pulse is still every which way. Let's see what the defibrillator reads and recommends."

Ventricular tachycardia. The machine recommended shocking the patient.

Everleigh removed the pulse oximeter from his fingertip.

"All clear," Wryn ordered then pressed the button.

Mr. Davenport's body jerked. His rhythm did a crazy jolt. Everleigh slipped the pulse oximeter back onto his fingertip and they waited for the machine to give a new reading. Seventy-six, which was too low. But fortunately, the man sucked in a breath and was now slowly inhaling and exhaling.

"It worked. He's out of V-tach." Wryn looked relieved. "For the moment, anyway. We need that ambulance ASAP."

On cue, they heard voices and the gurney being pushed through the clinic's hallway. Liz opened the door to guide the paramedics into the room. Soon the responders were rolling Mr. Davenport out of the building and into the back of the ambulance. Standing on the clinic's sidewalk, Wryn and Everleigh watched as the door closed.

Everleigh sighed. "That wasn't on my afternoon's agenda."

"Mine, either." Wryn glanced toward her. "You did good."

"Ha. We didn't do much, not compared to what I'm used to in the emergency room when working a code."

They watched the ambulance drive away then turned back to the clinic. "This setting is different, but you handled it well."

"Thank you, Wr— Dr. Cooper."

He chuckled. "You know we're not fooling anyone, right? Maybe in the beginning, but not anymore."

Everleigh's face heated. "Has someone said something?"

"You have to have seen the knowing looks. They know. We'll keep playing this game as long as you like, but they know."

As long as she liked, meaning he didn't care who knew that they were an item?

"I—" She started to say how proud she would be for the whole world to know. Then she reminded herself how extra awkward things would be once they ended if she also had to face the humiliation of everyone knowing. It wasn't that they wouldn't know, but more that if they never acknowledged they had a relationship, then they never had to acknowledge the end of said relationship.

Everleigh really liked the idea of not having to acknowledge an end.

"Mom's gone on a women's retreat with some ladies from church," Everleigh reminded Wryn when he asked her about their going somewhere that evening. They'd arrived at the employee parking area at the same time, and he'd parked his car next to hers, waiting as she got out of her car to say good morning and to confirm plans for that evening. "She won't be home until Sunday evening, and I'm not going to want to ask her to babysit Hayes first thing after returning."

Although Wryn and Hayes did spend time together, for the most part, Everleigh tried to stick with not going out until after her son was in bed. That had become an almost nightly thing, even if they just went to his gym to work out or to stroll along Broad to listen to music. Whatever they did didn't seem to matter so long as they carved out a few hours of together time outside of work.

"Hayes will be asleep. If she's going to be home anyway, she won't mind if we go somewhere."

"Probably not, but I don't think it fair to ask that of her." Her mother wouldn't mind. She adored Wryn, something Everleigh couldn't say Vivien had ever done with Bryan. They probably shouldn't be walking into the clinic together, either. But Everleigh agreed with Wryn. They weren't fooling anyone. Everleigh had almost let it slip earlier in the week when Liz had mentioned Wryn. She'd stopped just in time, but not in time to keep Liz from smiling at her, then Eva.

"I'd like to see you this weekend, Everleigh."

She'd like to see him, too. Amazing how much she'd come to like seeing him in such a short amount of time. How much should scare her, but when she looked into Wryn's eyes, she didn't feel fear, she felt...wanted. For the first time in her life, a man made her feel special, desirable and important in his life. That, in and of itself, was a heady sensation. That it was someone as wonderful as Wryn who made her feel that way just gave everything the wow factor.

"Why don't you come over and eat with us? We could watch a movie or play games with Hayes," she offered, knowing she'd miss him if they went all weekend without contact.

Wryn smiled. "Better yet, why don't you and Hayes come to my place, and I'll grill for us. Brady would love some Hayes time."

"You didn't want takeout?" she teased as they neared the employee entrance. Fortunately, they'd not encountered anyone else on their parking lot trek and slowed to prolong entering the building.

"I like cooking, so why not cook for my two favorite people?"

Warm fuzzies hugged Everleigh. "When you put it that way... We'll have to leave early, though, so I can get Hayes to bed on time."

"Or you and Hayes could spend the weekend at my place."

Stunned at his suggestion, Everleigh just stared at him. "How did you go from my inviting you over for dinner and kids games to our staying the weekend with you?" She'd explained to him the reasons why sex wouldn't be happening between them, telling him about Bryan, getting pregnant, and that her ex-husband had been her only partner. Wryn said he understood and hadn't pushed, but that didn't keep him from kissing her as if he wanted to devour her. Nor did it keep Everleigh from wanting to let him.

"With Brady, it's easier at my place than yours. You and Hayes can sleep in one of the spare rooms. We can take Brady and Hayes to the park in the morning before the temperature reaches scorching, then swim and hang around the house tomorrow evening."

He made it sound so simple, but what he was asking felt huge. And tempting. Still, she shook her head. "We can't spend the weekend with you."

"Why not? Your mom won't be home. It'll be one last summer adventure prior to Hayes starting school. Plus, we'll get to spend the weekend together."

"That's what you want? To have me and Hayes spend the weekend with you and Brady?" Why wasn't she telling him no? She didn't spend weekends with men. Then again, she didn't do lots of things she'd done with Wryn that summer, like have fun and laugh and feel young and cherished because he prompted all those things.

"You know it is, Everleigh. I enjoy being with you."

"I can't believe I'm saying this, but..." she took a deep breath, glad they'd stopped just outside the building rather than going inside "...okay." When his eyes lit with excitement, she shook her head. "Just don't get any funny ideas because nothing physical is going to happen between you and me."

"You're safe. When something physical happens between us for the first time, I don't want it to be with Hayes in the next room and we might be interrupted, Everleigh. I want to be able to keep you in my bed all night, without having to keep quiet, and to wake with you beside me without worrying that Hayes might catch you in my bed."

Unable to keep erotic images from flashing through her mind, Everleigh gulped. "Safe. Right."

"He and Brady are about a match on energy," Wryn said when Everleigh came back into the living room where he was channel-surfing. Brady curled up next to him on the sofa.

"He fell asleep almost immediately after I finished that last story." She sat on the opposite side of where Brady lay and stroked the dog's fur. "You didn't have to leave."

Yeah, Wryn had. Hayes's sweet good-night hug and cheek kiss had already gutted him. Watching Everleigh tuck the kid in and animatedly read the books she'd brought with her had sealed his fate. He was a deadbeat dad, and she should be up for Mom of the Year.

"Now what?" she asked, glancing his way.

"You want to watch a movie?"

She shrugged.

"We could sit outside and enjoy the night air."

She nodded. "I'd like that."

But rather than go straight out, he went to a closet and got out a quilt.

"It's July," she reminded. "I don't think we'll need to cover up."

"It's to lie on." He opened his patio door and stepped back, allowing her and Brady, who'd followed them, to go out first. "There's a new moon, no clouds, and the stars are amazing."

"And you offered me a movie?"

"No one gets everything right the first time around." He sure hadn't. What if he'd met Everleigh first? What if he'd had no past to sully the present and future? Going out to the grass and checking to make sure Brady hadn't left any surprises in the area, Wryn spread the blanket.

Lying back on the quilt, she stared up at the sky. After a few minutes, she sighed. "This is perfect."

"Close," he agreed, then laced their hands.

"You're right. That is better." She clasped his tightly. "I thought you were crazy for suggesting this and me for agreeing to it, but at this moment, there's nowhere I'd rather be."

Wryn's heart pounded. "I feel the same."

Turning to look at him, she smiled then lifted his hand to her lips and pressed a kiss there. "Sometimes, when I'm with you, I feel as if I'm dreaming, that none of this can be real. That you can't be as wonderful as you seem."

"I'm not," he asserted. He could tell her a few of his imperfections that would have her cringing. He should tell her. But how could he do that when doing so would burst the happy bubble enveloping them?

She laughed. "I mean, I know you're not really perfect. No one is. I just mean this, us. It feels right, doesn't it?"

It did. And it didn't.

"Why did you want me to spend the weekend with you, Wryn?"

Because he couldn't imagine going the entire weekend without her in it. "I've already told you why."

They were close enough that, even in the dark, he could tell her eyes sparkled. "Why is it so easy for me to talk to you? I feel as if I've known you my entire life, and yet logically, I know it's only been a few months. I've never known anyone like you, Wryn."

Wryn's chest tightened at the emotion in Everleigh's voice. "I've never known anyone like you, either."

She rolled onto her side, then scooted next to him, their locked hands smushed between them. "Kiss me, Wryn."

So many emotions were bombarding him that kissing her might have him completely coming undone. But he didn't fool himself that he was strong enough to deny her sweet request. Wryn kissed Everleigh. Soft, slow, exploring and yet starved for more. He kissed her until he could barely breathe, until every breath he took was hers, and then he kissed her more, the stars blanketing them beneath their celestial twinkle.

She'd given up holding his hand to bury her fingers in his hair. Wryn couldn't say how long they kissed, couldn't identify the moment the tempo changed and he and Everleigh couldn't get close enough to each other no matter how tightly they pressed against each other.

Every heartbeat lured them with its seductive rhythm. He knew they had to stop, knew they would, but for the moment, he gave in to the moment and just marveled at the wonder of being with Everleigh. Every brush of his fingers over her skin, every taste of her body beneath his lips, pure magic.

If things were different, if he could give Everleigh a future, he'd tell her all the things in his heart. Instead, he should be telling her all the reasons why he shouldn't be kissing her, shouldn't be feeling the things he was feeling. For her and for Hayes.

It was why he hadn't been able to stay in the room while she read to her son. Because he craved what he saw just beyond his reach with Everleigh and Hayes. A family of his own.

"I'm falling for you, Wryn," Everleigh whispered against his lips, cradling his head to where she could look into his eyes and see into his soul. "I know that's not what was supposed to happen, but maybe we were just fooling ourselves that it wouldn't."

He couldn't deny what she said. He didn't even want to. He only wanted to hold onto Everleigh so tightly that nothing else mattered. In the moment, it didn't.

He brushed her hair back from her face. "What is it you want me to say, Everleigh?"

She searched his eyes a moment then said, "What you're feeling right now."

"You know what I'm feeling right now. What I've been feeling for weeks. Maybe from the beginning," he confessed, knowing he shouldn't, but powerless to the overwhelming emotions zapping between them.

"I do know." Happiness shone in Everleigh's eyes. Happiness and a hope that he couldn't convince himself was justified. Was it possible to bury the past so deeply within him that it wasn't a constant reminder of why he shouldn't have the things he wanted? With Everleigh, could he leave the past in the past and just move toward the future?

CHAPTER NINE

"You're going to love my classroom." Hayes tugged on Wryn's hand as they walked into the school's front entrance along with several other families. Having started kindergarten and it being the night of his fall festival, Hayes had invited Wryn to go with them. After the weekend they'd spent at his house the previous month, Everleigh had given up on the limited interaction between the males in her life. But having Wryn with her at Hayes's school, for the other parents and Hayes's teacher to see her with Wryn, felt different.

"We have the best game. I hope I get a seven. Miss Georgia says there's only one number seven duck and a bunch of the other numbers."

Everleigh smiled at her excited son. He looked cute in his jeans and school-spirit long sleeved T-shirt. She'd bought a parent shirt for herself and, as he'd been at the house when Hayes had shown her the order form and Hayes had insisted he needed one, too, Wryn had ordered one. With them twinning, they looked like a family. More and more, Everleigh questioned if maybe, that was where they were headed. How could she not when Wryn was so good to her and to Hayes? Her son adored him, and Everleigh adored him, too.

"Do you know which duck is the seven?" Wryn held the heavy glass door open for them and a mom with two kids and a stroller.

Waiting just inside the doorway, Hayes's face squished. "She didn't tell us 'cause that would be cheating. Miss Georgia says it's better to lose than to cheat."

"Good point." Wryn gave Hayes a proud look that melted Everleigh's heart. "Maybe we'll get lucky and choose number seven."

Hayes nodded. "I hope so. I want to win the big prize."

"You said it's a megaphone?"

Eyes big, Hayes's head bobbed up and down. "Yeah, I need one."

Chuckling, Wryn's gaze shifted to hers. "Yeah, Mom. He needs a megaphone."

"He does." She slyly smiled. "For when we're at your house."

Wryn snorted. "You had me there for a second."

"Mama, there's Jimmy." Hayes bounced with excitement at spotting one of his friends. "Can we say hi?"

They did and ended up going directly to the school cafeteria to eat chili with Jimmy, his parents and infant sister, then walking with them so the two boys could play games together.

Everleigh enjoyed the couple, the boys' chatter and the light atmosphere of the night.

This, she thought. As admittedly scary as she found how happy she was, this was how life should be, full of smiles and happiness. *And Wryn.*

"So what about you two?" Jimmy's mother shifted the baby in her lap. "How long have you been together?"

"A few months," Everleigh answered.

"Really?" The woman put the baby's pacifier in its mouth. "Y'all seem so close. I assumed it had been years. I guess when you know, you know."

Glad Hayes had Wryn's attention, Everleigh blinked. "Know?"

"Falling in love at first sight."

Knowing Wryn could hear their conversation but not knowing how he'd take it, Everleigh shook her head. "That's not what happened."

But even as she denied it, she had to wonder. He had fascinated her immediately, evoking strong emotions even before she knew him. She glanced at him. Hayes and Jimmy were animatedly telling him about a cartoon character they both adored. Hayes's face shone with how he felt about Wryn.

"Like mother, like son."

Everleigh's gaze cut back to Jimmy's mom.

"No wonder," the woman continued. "He seems a great guy and just as crazy about you and Hayes. Good for you."

Uncomfortable at having someone vocalize what was happening between her and Wryn, Everleigh changed the subject by asking if the woman had signed up to help with their sons' Halloween party. But even as they finished their meal and had begun to make their way from one classroom to the next, letting the boys play games, Everleigh couldn't shake their conversation. She'd never let herself label her feelings for Wryn as *love*, just that she had fallen for him. But wasn't that what she'd meant? That she'd fallen in love with him?

Heat flooded through her. She'd not thought of herself as being in love with Wryn, but Jimmy's mom had defined Everleigh's feelings for her.

Glancing toward Wryn, their gazes met, and he smiled. Everleigh swallowed back the emotions choking her. She loved him. That both terrified and thrilled her. She'd once believed she'd never love again, and yet, looking at him, her heart felt so full.

He gave her a questioning look. Feeling shaky inside, she reached for his hand and clasped their fingers. Appearing confused, he squeezed her hand. "Everything okay?"

She held his hand tight. "Unbelievably, I think it is."

Her answer confused him further, but Hayes asked him something, saving Everleigh from making a fool of herself in an elementary school hallway. They made it about halfway through the classroom booths, stopping to let the boys play at each one that caught their eye. Unfortunately, Jimmy's little sister got upset and couldn't be consoled so his parents opted to leave. Wryn took over as Hayes's game partner, saving the day.

They finished with a ringtoss game then made their way to the gymnasium where a bouncy house was set up. They'd let Hayes play until time for her volunteer shift helping with his classroom's duck pickup game. Hayes had his tennis shoes off and was soon laughing and bouncing with friends.

Everleigh's heart smiled. That's all she could call it because seeing Hayes so happy made her insides joyous mush. She turned to thank Wryn, again, for coming with them and adding such joy to their lives when she'd never believed it possible. As she did so, her gaze went just beyond him to a stunning blonde who was staring at Wryn as if he was a ghost.

Pale, raising her hand to touch her face almost nervously, the woman said, "Wryn?"

The world spun around Wryn. Or maybe it was Wryn who was spinning. Although he'd not heard it in years, he knew that voice.

He'd known someone behind him had caught Everleigh's

attention because her gaze had snagged on whomever it was. Never in a million lifetimes would he have guessed that she'd been staring at Kara. Was it wrong that he wanted to fall through the floor? To do anything other than face his past with his present standing next to him?

Deep down, he'd always recognized that Everleigh and Hayes deserved so much more than he'd ever been or would be. But he'd let himself be deceived that maybe they could have a future so he hadn't had to give up their present. Their present was the happiest he'd ever been, filling him with hope. Kara's presence had just delivered a fatal blow, and all that hope bled from him and would ultimately leave an empty shell.

"Kara," he managed when he finally turned. His voice had cranked up a few octaves, but that was nothing compared to what his pulse was doing. Kara looked much the same as the last time he'd seen her. Long blond hair, green eyes and high cheekbones, just older. Kara looked shocked to see him. No wonder. He had no business being at a kids' festival.

Kara's gaze went back and forth between him and Everleigh, taking in their matching shirts. Everleigh's gaze shifted from Kara to him. Both women looked at him with confusion, clearly waiting for him to shed clarity on who the other was. The irony of the situation wasn't lost on him. No one could escape their past. He'd been a fool to think he might.

Kara swallowed then glanced around nervously. "It's been a long time. Why are you here?"

He could ask her the same. She lived just outside Atlanta. She shouldn't be at Hayes's school. *Where was Seth?* Every gut instinct said his son was near. Acid gurgled in Wryn's stomach. He'd never looked directly into his son's eyes. Was he about to? Dizziness hit.

How could he face the kid that he'd given up his rights to, especially while wearing matching shirts with Everleigh and Hayes? If he came face-to-face with Seth, how would he explain that? How did he explain where his mind had been when he'd made decisions he wasn't convinced he should have made? Now wasn't the time to analyze the past. His brain needed to focus on basics such as breathing, not letting his knees buckle and not succumbing to blacking out.

Blacking out might not be such a bad thing, but he didn't deserve an easy way out of this unexpected conundrum. He'd been playing with fire, fooling himself he could have happiness with Everleigh and Hayes. Fate was reminding him he couldn't.

"I lived here for four years and still have friends and family here," Kara reminded. "This is my cousin's children's school."

Another example of his brain not working. He knew Kara had a cousin in Nashville. He'd not thought of Sherry in years so hadn't known the woman had stayed rather than returned to Georgia as Kara had.

Next to him, Everleigh shifted, eyeing him more curiously, then glancing away to visually check on where Hayes jumped in the bouncy house. Before the night was over, he was going to lose them, he realized, further dread filling his belly. How dull his life was going to seem after the vibrancy Everleigh and Hayes had painted his days with.

Kara's gaze followed his, and she sucked in a breath. "You didn't want kids."

He tried not to flinch at the accusation in her verbal slap and failed.

"I never said that to you, Kara." He'd made that decision

after he'd fathered a child and signed away his rights. At one time, he'd wanted kids, a family in his future. Lately, he'd gotten a taste of that once-desired future with Everleigh and Hayes.

"Aren't you going to ask if Seth is here? Don't you want to know?"

Wryn knew he was. He sucked in another deep breath, this time because he needed the oxygen.

Everleigh had been quietly observing them, but her body had grown tense, and now her facial features were pale. "Who is Seth?"

But he held Kara's gaze, unable to look toward Everleigh as she'd see the guilt pouring from him. He probably didn't have to look directly at her for her to see what must be obvious.

"His… Never mind." Kara shook her head. "Seeing you caught me off guard. Seeing you at a school function wearing matching shirts with someone and…" Kara looked as desperate not to be there as Wryn felt. "I—I wouldn't have come here tonight if I'd known you'd be here."

"Same. I'm sorry."

Kara stared at him a moment, pain shining in her eyes, then she sighed. "Me, too, Wryn. I shouldn't have come over here, I just—as I said, seeing you caught me off guard. Have a good evening and life." With that, she walked off to rejoin another woman who was several yards away.

Spotting him, her cousin's jaw dropped then her gaze narrowed. Some things were better left in the past, things that one could do nothing about since the past couldn't be rewritten. And exactly what would he rewrite if he could? Kara was a good mother to their son. Every so often Wryn checked to be sure. At the time he'd made the decisions he'd made, he'd been broke, little more than a kid himself and overwhelmed with debt. He could have quit school, got a job, married her and had a different life. He'd been willing to do that. She'd laughed at him and reminded him that she was only there because the person she was already married to wanted to legally be Seth's father. She'd urged Wryn to do what she called *the right thing* by Seth and let the man he already adored and considered a father to be his father. Wryn had.

Next to him, Everleigh repositioned. "I don't understand much about what just happened."

No, Wryn imagined she didn't. What had he been thinking to get involved with her and Hayes? A fresh wave of guilt hit. He'd been fooling himself for months, telling himself that it was okay to spend so much time with Everleigh and Hayes, deceiving himself that the past was in the past and he should just move forward. Now, Everleigh and Hayes would pay the price.

"I'm trying to deduce what all that meant," Everleigh continued, studying him. He could tell she wanted him to reassure her, to tell him that the conclusions she was jumping to were wrong. "I'm not connecting the dots in any way that makes sense other than that she is an ex-girlfriend and has a son, and they are why you avoided dating women with kids until me. Am I anywhere close?"

"You're close." Everleigh would never look at him the same once she knew. She was already not looking at him the same because defensive walls were sliding into place. He glanced around the busy gymnasium. This wasn't the place for their conversation.

"She sounds hurt about your relationship ending." Everleigh's eyes pleaded with him to correct her. If only Wryn could. His stomach pitched, shooting more acid up his throat.

"Kara has a right to be hurt." Their relationship ending wasn't what caused hurt, though. He needed to get out of the school, to go somewhere he and Everleigh could talk without the noise and audience. Somewhere he could pour his heart out to her and beg her not to judge too harshly, to find it in her heart to forgive him. Somewhere he could find a few minutes alone to give in to the devastation hitting him at knowing he'd been in the same building with his son and wanting nothing more than to avoid the kid setting eyes on his sorry excuse for a parent. "Would you mind if we left?"

"We can't leave." Everleigh looked completely taken aback that he'd suggest they go. She gave him an accusatory look. "You offered to keep an eye on him while I'm volunteering in Hayes's classroom, remember?"

No, he hadn't remembered. He'd known. He'd offered. It's what he'd planned to do. But he'd momentarily forgotten.

"I—you're right." But he wasn't prepared for the emotions assailing him. Seeing Kara had blindsided him. If Seth was there, seeing his son, a stranger, would decimate him. He wanted to see him, to hear his voice, to hug him, to hold him tight and pour out his heart, but he'd given up that right, which was the hardest life pill to swallow.

His gaze met Everleigh's, and panic further filled him to the point where he thought he might be ill. He'd never felt so unable to breathe. Sweat popped out on his forehead.

"I'm sorry, Everleigh, but I can't watch Hayes or stay."

Jaw dropping, Everleigh blinked. "You're leaving? But Hayes and I rode here with you."

Wryn cursed beneath his breath. He couldn't abandon Everleigh and Hayes at the school. But that didn't make keeping his feet still easy. Sweat dampened the back of his nape.

Everleigh's expression crumbled. "You're in love with

her, aren't you? It's why you said what you did about not telling her you didn't want children. Because you did want them—with her."

Was that what Everleigh thought? What a mess of things he'd made. How much could he get into when they were standing next to a bouncy house inside an elementary school gymnasium?

"I was never in love with Kara. We had a good relationship in the beginning, but we stayed together longer than we should have because we were too busy to realize how much we'd grown apart."

"Wryn, what is going on? I'm so confused. I've never seen you like this."

She never should have. He should have told her. If he had, she would not have wanted him around Hayes and would have shut Wryn out, just as he deserved.

"Mama, did you see me jumping?" Hayes called, running over to them. Excitement shone in his brown eyes. "I jumped so high."

Everleigh gave Wryn one last look, letting him know that they weren't through with their conversation, then knelt to Hayes's level. "I did see you. You were so good. The best jumper in the bouncy house. Your timing is perfect as we need to go to your classroom for my volunteer stint. Are you ready to go show me the game y'all are doing?"

"It's called Lucky Duck," Hayes reminded her, sitting down to put on his tennis shoes. "You pick a duck and get a prize."

"I like ducks, especially lucky ones." With shaky hands, Everleigh helped him secure the Velcro straps on his shoes then smiled at her son as if nothing was wrong behind the mask she was presenting him. "Do you think Miss Georgia will be there to show me what to do?"

"I think she will," Hayes assured, jumping to his feet.

Everleigh stood. As she did so, someone beyond Wryn caught her attention, and she gasped. Gasped, stared in disbelief, then lifted shocked eyes to him.

"Wryn?" Her voice broke.

No need to turn to know what put that disillusioned look in her eyes. Not what, but who.

Seth was behind him.

He turned and soaked in the teen talking to his mother. All that he'd given up stood before him, and no matter his reasons, Wryn fought not to sob at just how great a sacrifice that had been.

Everleigh shook. Every single cell inside her body jolted as if it were being jackhammered with the intent of complete destruction. But on the outside, she smiled at each child and parent who stepped into Hayes's kindergarten class to play Lucky Duck. She was so rattled she'd had to force herself to focus on what Hayes was showing her when they'd first entered the room. *They* as in her and Hayes, no Wryn.

"Your duck has the number six written on the bottom" she told the preschool girl who held onto the yellow duck she'd picked from the water tub. Blond curls framed the butterflies painted onto her face. "Choose a prize from the number six prize bin."

She showed the cutie to the appropriate prizes which was just to the other side of where Everleigh stood. "Pick any one you want."

Taking a calming breath, Everleigh held her smile in place while the girl considered which of the cheap plastic school-spirit wristbands in bin six that she wanted. Smiling at the child should be easy, but all Everleigh wanted was to go home and decompress.

Wryn had a kid. A son. Seth.

He'd not had to say the words out loud. There was no doubting the strong facial features, the body build of the teenaged boy who'd joined Kara. His silky black hair and blue eyes were impossible not to recognize. The teen had been oblivious to them, talking with his mother, another woman and three other boys who were several years younger than him.

Even if the teen hadn't been Wryn's mini-me, there was no doubting the absolute devastation on Wryn's face when his gaze touched on the kid. His kid. Because Wryn had a son. He'd said he didn't want kids. To Everleigh. Because he'd already had one with a woman that he'd reminded that he'd never said to her he didn't want kids.

"This one." The girl slipped the band onto her wrist then held out her arm toward Everleigh.

"Nice," Everleigh managed then turned back toward where Hayes was helping a classmate pick a duck. Everleigh recognized the dark-haired girl as someone Hayes talked about frequently. Someone she suspected her son had a mini-crush on. *Run*, she wanted to warn. Run from anything that even remotely resembles interest in the opposite sex so you don't get your heart broken.

"Mama, Stacey got a seven." Hayes held up the girl's duck so Everleigh could see the number on the bottom. Excitement shone in his big brown eyes. "She picked the best one and gets a megaphone."

"You're right," she told her helper, fighting back the tears she wanted to give in to. "Seven is a lucky number. Good job."

Abandoning his post at the floating duck tub, Hayes showed the girl the labeled prize bin where the megaphones were. Stacey said something to him, and covering his mouth,

Hayes giggled. The exchange was cute, but all Everleigh could think about was that Wryn had a son and hadn't told her. How could he have failed to mention something so monumental? How? Everleigh forced her smile back into place. She had to pull it together. For Hayes. This was his first big school event. She couldn't lose her cool. Over a man.

From the moment she'd seen Wryn's mini-me, Everleigh had wanted to lose her cool. To scream. To pound on Wryn's broad chest and demand to know why he hadn't told her about his son. What kind of boyfriend kept the fact he had a son a secret? One who wasn't playing for keeps. One who didn't see her as important enough to share that part of his life. Looking into Wryn's eyes, seeing the guilt there, she wanted to curl into the fetal position and cry. Instead, she'd shaken her head in disbelief, taken Hayes's hand and walked away, trying not to let her little boy know she was falling apart inside, trying not to grab him and run home.

Run home. Now there was an ironic thought. She might have to do just that. She could call her mother to give them a ride home. But she would ask questions that Everleigh didn't have answers to.

Maybe Everleigh should have stuck around to find out. But she'd panicked and gone into self-preservation mode. She'd let Wryn inside the wall she'd kept securely erected since Bryan. She'd thought there was something special happening between them. Something that she could trust enough to let her guard down. That maybe she could have it all. Hayes, her dream job and Wryn.

She should have known better. *She did know better.* Why had she let him get close when it could only ever have ended in heartache?

The volunteer hour finally ended, and another parent relieved her. She wanted to go home, be alone and tear apart everything that had happened. But just because her life felt ruined, she couldn't let that ruin Hayes's fall festival. They'd visit each classroom, then she'd call for a hired car. Maybe the novelty of it would slow Hayes's questioning of Wryn not being with them. Hayes would question her, though. On the way home. After they were home. For days to come, maybe weeks, he'd want to know. Everleigh suspected her heart was going to be asking the same thing.

Her phone dinged and, hands shaking, she looked at the text message.

My car keys are in the console. Drive yourself and Hayes home whenever you are ready. I'll retrieve my car later.

Everleigh's fingernails dug into her palms. Seriously? He'd left his car? She should be grateful. Instead, she wanted to know where he was. How was he getting home? Who was he with that was driving him home? What were they doing? Saying? Was he with Kara?

Everleigh was jealous. Jealous of a woman Wryn said he'd never been in love with but that he obviously had strong feelings for. Jealous of a woman who had given birth to his son. Jealous of a woman he might be with at that very moment. She didn't want to be jealous. She didn't want to care where he was or what he was doing. But she did.

"Where is Wryn?" Hayes asked again as they left the school and walked toward where Wryn had parked his car.

"Something came up." She gave him the same answer she'd given when they'd left Wryn in the gymnasium. How was it possible to be so angry and so devastated at the same time?

"Is he sick?"

"No." Everleigh was the one who felt ill. "He's a doctor, and sometimes doctors have things come up."

Which was the best non-lie she could think of without trying to explain things to her five-year-old that adult Everleigh didn't understand. She managed to keep up with Hayes's chatter as she drove them home, hopefully smiling at all the right times. He'd seemed relieved with her answer and that they were in Wryn's car. Oh, Hayes. How could I have put you in this position? To have let you get close to someone who is going to leave you hurt?

She was hurt. Hurt that he'd not shared something so important when she'd thought they'd grown close. Hurt that she'd let him in to her and Hayes's life, behind the ever-protective wall she had, embracing their relationship, and he'd obviously not done the same. She'd told him about Bryan, about what it was like raising Hayes on her own, taking care of her mother while studying, working and being a single mom. She'd shared so many of her life's ups and downs. Why had he never mentioned Kara? Or Seth?

If he'd not told her about them, what else had he not told her?

Everleigh was still asking herself those same questions that night as she lay in bed. Part of her wanted to give in to the urge to cry. Crying would be so easy but would help nothing. So she clung to her anger at his betrayal of her trust instead.

At least anger shielded a bleeding heart.

CHAPTER TEN

Hayes's fall festival had been on Friday evening. Everleigh didn't hear from Wryn Saturday, but he had come by at some point as his car was gone from her driveway when she'd awakened that morning. Rather than knocking to get his keys from her purse, he'd used his spare set which meant he hadn't wanted to see her. Fine. She didn't want to see him, either.

Getting more difficult to appease, Hayes asked about Wryn, wanting to know when they'd see him next. She told him that Dr. Cooper was busy that day with other things he needed to do. She assumed that was the truth. She'd escaped questions from her mom due to her mother pulling a double shift at the diner. She rarely did that, but one of the other waitresses had called in ill, and her mother covered for her.

On Sunday, Everleigh refused to sit around the house and dwell on her torturous thoughts. After church, she and Hayes visited the children's science museum off I-65. Everleigh had driven past it numerous times during her mother's various hospitalizations, but neither she nor Hayes had been inside.

"I wish Wryn was here." Hayes looked a little pouty, which was saying something, since they were at a dinosaur exhibit.

Everleigh fought rubbing her temple. "Dr. Cooper has things he has to do besides hang out with us."

Hayes's expression said he wasn't buying her answer. "He normally hangs out with us."

Which was a good lesson for Everleigh to take to heart. In the future, she'd keep dates separate from Hayes. She needed to protect him from the disappointment he was currently experiencing. In the future? Wrong. There would be no dates in her future. Wryn had been a great reminder of lessons she should have learned from Bryan. She would not make that mistake again.

"Sometimes things happen in an adult's life so he can't hang out with someone as much as he'd like to," she told her son, trying to prepare him for what was to come.

Hayes frowned. "Did he break up with us?"

Everleigh's throat threatened to close. What did she say? Wryn hadn't broken up with them. He'd never been committed to them to need to break up. He'd just been pretending while she'd fallen head over heels.

"Wryn adores you." At least he'd seemed to, and either way she wouldn't have Hayes thinking otherwise. She never wanted him to question his lovability. "But he's not going to spend as much time with us." Because even if Wryn magically appeared on her doorstep, how could she ignore the fact that he'd not told her about Kara and Seth? She couldn't. He'd destroyed the very foundation of her trust in him, in what she was feeling for him, by not telling her about his son.

"What about Brady?" Hayes's eyes watered, and Everleigh filled with regret. All this was her fault. "Will he spend as much time with us?"

"I don't think so." That truth hurt, too. She'd grown attached to the dog. Maybe now would be a good time to consider adopting a dog, to give Hayes something to focus his precious heart on.

"Is Wryn mad at us?"

"No, honey, Wryn's not mad at us." Kneeling beside him, she looked him straight in the eyes. "It's going to be okay, I promise."

Wasn't that the same thing she kept telling herself?

After a moment Hayes nodded, and unable not to, Everleigh hugged him. He was such a great kid. She blamed herself for allowing this to happen. He didn't deserve to be hurt.

"I've been thinking that maybe this week we could visit the animal shelter and see if there are any dogs for adoption that would work for us?"

Although the look in his eyes said he knew what she was doing, Hayes perked up. "Really?"

She nodded. "Watching you with Brady makes me think any dog we chose to adopt would be very lucky to be loved by you."

As she'd hoped, Hayes's sadness lifted. They talked about what type of dog they hoped to find, ate mediocre food at a restaurant geared to kids then headed home to spend some time with her mother. Later, Hayes had his bath, three bedtime stories, a few more questions about adopting a dog and was tucked in for the night.

"Mama?" he asked as she turned on his night-light then flipped his light switch off.

"Yes, baby?"

"I miss Wryn."

Everleigh swallowed, sat down on the edge of his car bed then bent to kiss his forehead. "I know, Hayes. I do, too, but you and I are going to be just fine."

They would. She'd make sure of it.

"I thought he was going to be my new daddy."

Everleigh's heart shattered. "Oh, Hayes. I'm sorry you thought that."

Not that she could fault him for doing so. Hadn't she been blinded by how wonderful Wryn was with Hayes, too?

She stayed with him, gently rubbing his arm and talking about the dog they'd rescue to put happy thoughts into his head prior to his going to sleep. She wanted all his dreams to be good ones.

Quietly leaving his room, Everleigh returned to the living room and sat on the sofa where her mother was crocheting a blanket.

"Do you want to talk about it?" Her mother had gone with friends to lunch after church and had arrived home after Everleigh and Hayes. Fortunately, by the time he'd bathed and gotten ready for bed, Hayes had been too tired to do much more than tell his grandmother they were getting a dog and kiss her good-night. That's what Everleigh should have done herself, but her mother was the one person who had always been there for her.

"I think Hayes is responsible enough for us to adopt a dog, don't you?" Maybe her mother would take a hint and not push.

Instead, she frowned in that motherly don't-give-me-that way. "Not the dog, although I vote yes on that. I meant whatever happened between you and Wryn."

"Nothing happened." Everleigh hugged a throw pillow to her stomach, giving it a tight squeeze. Yeah, she didn't buy her pitiful answer, either. No wonder. Lots had happened. Her mother's brow lifted, and Everleigh sucked in a deep breath. "Except his ex-girlfriend was at Hayes's fall festival."

Her mother shrugged as if she didn't understand why that was a big deal. "Surely you didn't think a man like Wryn hadn't had previous relationships?"

"No. I didn't think that. I was just a bit shocked that his ex-girlfriend's son was with her." Everleigh paused then forced out, "The son she shares with Wryn."

Surprise lit in her mother's eyes, and she set down her crochet needles. "Wryn has a son?" Her forehead scrunched. "How did I miss knowing that?"

"For the same reason I missed knowing." Everleigh squeezed the pillow tighter. "Not once has he mentioned that he had a son. Not once."

She thought back to all the times they'd talked, to how she'd shared so much of herself with him. She'd thought he'd done the same when he'd talked about his childhood, his divorced parents, how he'd always wanted to be a doctor. She'd been wrong.

"I mean, when does he even see this kid? And not even a little kid, but more of a young man, probably fourteen or fifteen. I get that he must live with his mother, but Wryn has been with me and Hayes most of his off-work time." But not all of it. She didn't question where he went or what he did when they weren't together. She knew he went to a gym even on the days she didn't go with him, that he played pickleball and a few other sports. Usually, he'd mention whatever he'd been up to, just as she did. She'd just assumed he was doing things with friends when he'd mention whatever he'd been up to. Maybe he'd been with Seth.

"With as long as you've been…" her mother seemed to be choosing her words carefully "…friends, I can see how his not mentioning he had a son would be a problem. I admit to being surprised he didn't."

That her mother agreed validated how Everleigh was feeling, making her feel a smidge better at the anger coursing through her.

"What was his reason for not telling you?"

Everleigh shrugged. "He didn't give one."

Her expression thoughtful, her mother stared at Everleigh. "Did you give him the opportunity to give you one?"

"He's had opportunity for the past four months." Realizing she'd raised her voice, and not wanting to wake Hayes or talk loudly to her mother, Everleigh lowered her volume and added, "What kind of question is that, anyway?"

"When I saw you tonight, I knew something wasn't right and was just waiting until Hayes was asleep to ask. I see how upset you are, Everleigh." Her mother leaned forward and looked her straight in the eyes. Everleigh got the same feeling she'd gotten as a child when her mother caught her doing something she shouldn't have been doing. "I know how you shut out everyone when Bryan left. Then Wryn came along, and you blossomed, Everleigh."

Everleigh frowned. "I'm not a flower, Mother. I didn't blossom."

"Deny it all you want, but deep down you know I'm right. My question about you giving Wryn opportunity to explain was my way of wanting to make sure you aren't doing the same thing now."

"Mom, I've been in a relationship with Wryn for four months. He has had opportunity." Lots of opportunity. "He chose not to tell me. This isn't me shutting him out. It's him having never been invested in our relationship." Admitting that out loud hurt. "Besides, if anything, it would be him shutting me out. I drove his car home Friday night. He picked it up without letting me know he was here. If he'd wanted to explain why he'd never mentioned his fatherhood, he wouldn't have done that, don't you think?"

Her mother sat quietly then picked up her crochet hook and yarn. "I'd think that depends on what you said to him before you drove his car home."

Why was her mother defending Wryn? After how his deceit had devastated her and Hayes?

"If Wryn had wanted to talk, he would have knocked." As she said the words, she realized just how convinced she'd been that he would knock, that he'd explain that she'd misunderstood and give some wild story about how she'd gotten everything wrong. Instead, he'd come and gone with nothing. Why did that feel like a twisting of the knife in her heart?

"I didn't know you'd driven his car home. It was gone before I left for the diner. Maybe he didn't knock because he came by early and didn't want to wake you."

Reasonable assumption, but Everleigh didn't feel reasonable. Besides, if that were the case, what had prevented him from reaching out later in the day?

"He came early on purpose so he could get the car without seeing me." She knew it was the case.

"Perhaps, but I think you need to talk."

Everleigh bit into her lower lip. "What is there to say at this point?"

Her mother gave a stern look. "Everleigh, you work with the man. Do you really want to come face-to-face with him at the clinic tomorrow without having had a conversation about this beforehand?"

"There's nothing to discuss."

Her mother made a pfft sound. "You discuss that he has a son he didn't tell you about and how not knowing made you feel."

Moms. Always so reasonable.

Everleigh crossed her arms. "I'd rather not discuss those things."

"Because you're afraid of what he might say?"

"No." Everleigh shook her head. That wasn't it, because

what could he say that she hadn't already thought? "Because it's four months too late to be having that particular conversation."

"Agreed, but four months ago is no longer an option." Her mother pushed her hook through a yarn loop, catching it, then sat the blanket down in her lap. "Call Wryn. Better yet, go talk to him. Regardless of the outcome, talking tonight will be easier than dealing with this at the clinic."

"Come on, Brady," Wryn urged the dog, climbing out of the heated pool. He'd swum to the point of exhaustion and where common sense said to get out of the water. Okay, so he'd swum beyond that point, but common sense had been missing for some time.

Since he'd first seen Everleigh at the clinic and been hooked. Everleigh, who he never should have gotten involved with. Everleigh, who he'd hurt. Everleigh, who had looked at him with such disappointment. He knew how she felt. He was disappointed in himself. He'd let her down. Had let Hayes down.

They'd not been the first people he'd let down. Just the latest.

Exhaustion was his only chance of sleep. With only short bouts of dozing the past two nights, drifting off shouldn't be a problem, but short of resorting to self-medicating, slumber wouldn't find him yet again.

His life was in shambles. He'd thought he'd found a semblance of peace with his life choices, but he'd been wrong.

After towel-drying his hair, he took off his swim trunks, draped them over the back of a chair and rubbed his body dry. Wrapping the towel at his waist, he made his way into the house.

Brady knew the routine, had shimmied and shaken water

from his fur and waited in the utility area where he'd hang out until he dried further.

Brady gave a loud bark just before the doorbell rang and started to take off toward the front door.

"Stay," Wryn commanded, pointing at the dog. He was too tired to mop water from the floors, so maybe his intense swim had accomplished something.

Whimpering, Brady lay down in his utility room bed, placing his head on his front paws.

Not expecting anyone and not sure he wanted to answer the door, Wryn pulled out his phone, checking his security camera app to see who was there.

Everleigh. Pacing, chewing on her fingernail and looking as if she was debating whether to wage war or disappear prior to his letting her into the house.

Seemed he wasn't finished facing past mistakes yet that weekend.

Perhaps it was better this way. For them to talk in private. He didn't expect her understanding or her forgiveness, but since she was there, maybe she'd let him explain.

When he opened the front door, a gush of air escaped her lips and her jaw dropped.

"You're wearing a towel. Seriously? That's how you open the door?"

He'd forgotten about that.

"I can take it off if you want me to." Not what he should be saying to her, but he blamed his fatigue.

Swallowing hard, she lowered her gaze, letting it linger at his waist. "Is there anything under the towel?"

"Just me." How could he be exhausted, gutted and still react to her looking at him that way?

Not able to hide her reaction to him, she gulped. "Don't take it off."

Knowing that the chemistry between them really didn't matter at this point, he raked his fingers through his hair. "Why are you here, Everleigh?"

That seemed to deflate her. "Is someone here? Is that why you're only wearing a towel?" Her cheeks flushed to a bright red. "I never considered that you might have company. I feel so foolish. I—"

"Stop," he ordered before she completely went down the wrong rabbit hole. "There's no one here except Brady. And you. So I repeat, why are you here?"

She swallowed again then obviously chose to battle because her chin lifted. "Am I not welcome anymore?"

Temples starting to throb, he put his hands on his hips to keep from rubbing them. "As I recall, you are the one who walked away from me."

He shouldn't be confronting her. He should just let her say her piece and let her leave. It would be the kind thing to do.

"I did." She stood taller, but her gaze lowered to his bare chest again. Closing her eyes, she shook her head as if to shake the image. "Can you put on some clothes? I can't think with you standing there half-naked."

Under different circumstances he'd have pointed out that he was all naked and that they were alone. That she was still affected by him had useless hope soaring within him. He couldn't see her and shut off the physical part of him that wanted her, so he understood her reaction. That physical awareness of each other had been there from the beginning. He suspected that would never change on his part.

He stepped back and motioned for her to enter the foyer, and when she had, he closed the front door. "Make yourself comfortable. Fix a drink, whatever. I'll get dressed."

When Wryn returned to the open living area that connected with his kitchen, Everleigh was sitting at the island, running her fingers over the edge of a water glass. She was so absorbed in her thoughts that she seemed oblivious that he'd returned. Perhaps even to Brady's whining from where Wryn had shut him inside the utility room. Wryn ached at what he'd lost. But it had all been a delusion, his having gotten caught up in what they'd shared that summer. With each day that had passed, he'd known the window to tell her about Seth had disappeared and there was no going back. Everleigh was such a lovingly fierce, protective mother, she wouldn't understand a parent who'd given away rights to his child. Nor did he expect her to forgive him for purposely not telling her because he'd selfishly wanted to hold on to the solace he'd found in her arms.

Not wanting to startle her, he cleared his throat, and she turned toward him. Her eyes held such turmoil that his ache increased tenfold. *Oh, Everleigh, how can I fix this?*

"I'm sorry." True, but insufficient for the way things had gone on Friday night.

Her chin lifted. "For which part?"

"All of it." Also true. Despite her bravado, she failed to hide her pain. Pain he'd caused. He'd been selfish to get involved with her as anything more than a coworker. Selfish to want what they had to go on, to the point where he'd kept his secrets from her rather than risk losing her.

"Why didn't you tell me that you had a son?" Her tone was full of accusation. Pain. Anger. Frustration.

He had a thousand reasons, and yet he had none.

When he said nothing, she let out a frustrated huff. "Talk to me, Wryn. Maybe I'm completely wrong, but I feel as if you owe me answers."

She was right. He did.

"If I had told you about Seth, you'd have asked questions I didn't want to answer. You'd ask about Kara, about our relationship, about where Seth was and why he wasn't a part of my life."

"Which are all valid questions given the circumstances, don't you think?" She stood from the barstool and moved closer. Accusation burned in her eyes. "I told you about Bryan. I shared things with you I'd never shared with anyone." She paused, flinching at her own words. "Do you have any idea how it made me feel that I discovered you had a child the way I did Friday night?"

Wryn did some flinching of his own. "I didn't know Kara or Seth were going to be there."

She gawked at him. "Are you kidding me? Them being there is not the issue," she rightly pointed out, jabbing at his T-shirt. "The issue is that I should have already known they existed. I should have known that the man that I've been spending every spare moment with for the past four months had a child. That's kind of a big deal, don't you think?"

He did. "You should have known."

"Thank you." She sucked in a deep breath and then didn't seem to know what to do or say next, as if he'd surprised her by agreeing and she'd been more prepared to defend her accusation than deal with his surrender. "I—I shouldn't have come here. Mom said we needed to talk before work tomorrow and that seemed logical, but now that I'm here, I'm not sure my being here makes sense."

Everleigh's shoulders dropped. She closed her eyes, but not before he caught the unshed tears in them. He'd done that, caused that. He fought wrapping his arms around her, holding her until every tear had been shed and she'd somehow forgive him for the terrible mistakes he'd made. But even if that fantasy was possible in reality, he didn't deserve the happiness he'd found with Everleigh and Hayes. Deep down he'd always known that, and maybe that's why he'd clung to the illusion they'd created that summer while it had lasted. But this wasn't about him. It was about Everleigh and Hayes and him doing the right thing by them.

"Your mother is right. It is better for us to have this conversation tonight," he began, wondering if he could really do what he had to do. He had no choice. No matter the fallout, Everleigh deserved the truth. "I dated Kara when I was a freshman in college, and she was a senior. It was fun until it wasn't. We both knew our relationship wasn't going anywhere once she graduated, but we were together for most of my freshman year."

Everleigh's expression was thoughtful. "You were how old? Eighteen?"

He nodded, then motioned for Everleigh to sit back down. He walked around to the opposite side of the bar to put some physical distance between them to reflect the emotional distance he was sealing. "I was old enough to know better. She planned to move back to her hometown after graduation, and we ended things at semester's end so we could both focus on our future. With school and work, I didn't have much time for a social life, never as much as she'd wanted from me. I didn't think of our relationship demise as a big deal. School was my priority. I knew what I wanted most and that was to be a doctor." He paused again. "We ended amicably, so there wasn't a big emotional moment, just our saying goodbye and her leaving. I honestly didn't think much about Kara after our split until she showed back up in my life during my senior year to tell me about Seth."

"She hadn't told you she was pregnant? You didn't know you had a son until he was a toddler?"

Her words punched him in the gut. She sounded incredulous, but how could he have known? Kara had disappeared from his life. He'd had no reason to search her out.

"Kara didn't know until after she'd moved back to Georgia. Our relationship was over, and she'd met someone. She didn't want me in the picture complicating that relationship." He raked his hand through his still slightly damp hair. "She wouldn't have told me about Seth except she'd listed me as the father on his birth certificate."

"She should have told you. How could she have kept that from you? You had a right to know." The wheels in Everleigh's head were turning. Wryn rushed on before she came up with wrong conclusions. He was not the victim and didn't want Everleigh thinking he was. He'd made his bed and had to lie in it.

"Like I said, after moving away from Nashville and not knowing that she was pregnant, Kara had gotten into a relationship immediately with someone she fell head over heels for, and she married the guy right before Seth was born. A couple of years later, Henry wanted to make being Seth's father official by adopting him."

"But he couldn't adopt Seth without your permission because your name was listed on the birth certificate," Everleigh guessed.

"Correct. I've no doubt that Kara regretted that many times. My guess is that she wasn't thinking clearly when they gave her the form to fill out, or she never would have."

"In which case you would never have known about your son," Everleigh mused, looking stunned at what he was saying.

"Under the circumstances, my not knowing might have been better." Did he really believe that?

"How could not knowing that you fathered a child be better?" Everleigh was clearly confused. No wonder. She would never have made the same choices he had.

"Knowing about Seth didn't change anything in my life,

Everleigh." Not entirely true. He'd lived with guilt every single day, had avoided serious relationships and had planned to never have another child. How could he when he'd failed his first one so completely?

Realization dawned on Everleigh's face. "You let Henry adopt your son?" Complete horror shone in her eyes. "Why would you do that?"

Because he'd been a scared college kid trying to figure out what kind of future he could give the kid when he'd felt like little more than a kid himself. Because Kara had implored him to do the right thing for Seth by signing the papers rather than putting their son into a life of a divided family.

"It was the right thing to do." If only he could completely convince himself of that. "Henry was the only father Seth had known. He was there at his birth, changed his diapers, sat up with him when he was sick, witnessed his first steps. He loved Seth." Wryn believed that. "Kara was right. My coming into the picture would have confused Seth and put him into a tug-of-war between Kara, Henry and myself."

"You were his father." Everleigh's tone was accusatory. "You coming into the picture is what should have happened from the moment Kara realized she was pregnant."

"Not everything is so black-and-white." He understood Kara's reasons. Having him in the picture would have created strain between her and Henry, which might have bled over into their relationship with Seth. She loved Henry and had felt desperate. That he understood. "Biologically, yes, but Henry was Seth's father in every other way. Seth called him Daddy." That one had hurt. "He believed Henry was his dad. My not signing Kara's papers wouldn't have suddenly made me his father." At Everleigh's look of disbelief, Wryn added, "I was twenty-one years old, barely paying my rent and expenses each month and had nothing to offer a toddler. Henry was a dentist with a thriving practice, and he was a good man, a good husband, and a good father. My coming into the picture would only sully everything."

"How can you say that? Seth deserved your fatherly love."

"Seth already had fatherly love." Once he'd met Henry, he'd never questioned that. If he had, Wryn never would have signed the forms no matter how much it complicated things. Henry loved Seth as if the boy had been his own.

"Seth didn't have your love."

"No, he didn't have that," Wryn admitted but wondered how true it was. From the moment the shock of what Kara had told him eased, he'd sure felt something for the kid. Something protective, as if he'd had to do what was best for Seth no matter the cost to himself.

Or had that just been him justifying taking the easy way out?

Only, nothing had been easy about knowing about Seth and not being a part of the boy's life. Nothing.

CHAPTER ELEVEN

EVERLEIGH'S HEAD SPUN. Wryn hadn't known about Seth. When he'd found out, he'd let another man adopt his son. He'd given away his rights. Just as Bryan had given away his rights to Hayes.

Every motherly instinct within her burst to the surface. She couldn't imagine the circumstances that would have her willing give up Hayes. She'd die fighting to keep him.

But she could imagine the type of man who would be glad to walk away.

"I can't believe you'd just walk away and let another man raise your son." Having watched him with Hayes, she couldn't wrap her brain around his being that type of man. She'd thought he was nothing like Bryan. Nothing. How could she have been so wrong?

"Believe, because that's exactly what I did." His tone was so dry, so accepting, that she could only stare at him in horror.

"Friday night. What was that?"

"A bad coincidence that put Kara, Seth and me in the same place at the same time. Maybe it was karma and bound to happen someday."

Had he seriously just called seeing his son *a bad coincidence*? Her heart hurt so intently it might explode. How could he feel that way?

"He looks just like you."

Wryn didn't say anything.

"Do you ever see him?"

Expression tight, he shook his head. Maybe she'd misunderstood. Maybe it did bother him.

"Have you talked to a lawyer? Maybe there would be a way for you to get your rights back?"

"I don't want my rights back, Everleigh." His tone brooked no doubt. "Seth is a happy, well-adjusted teenager. Why would I want to turn his whole world upside down now?"

"Because he's your son and deserves to know the truth."

"What truth? That even though Henry is his father, I was his sperm donor?" Wryn shrugged. "All the paperwork is there, public record. I'm on his birth certificate. If Seth wants to know more, he'll have no problem."

Everleigh's shock continued to multiply. "You're okay with no role in your son's life?"

"He's not my son, Everleigh. Not legally."

It was all Everleigh could do to keep her jaw from hitting the floor. How could she have been so wrong about Wryn?

"Lucky you, eh?" Oh, yeah, she sounded condemning. "Fathered a kid and don't have to take any responsibility."

He didn't even flinch, just shrugged. "Seth has a good life with a good family."

Bile rose up Everleigh's throat, making her wonder if she was going to be physically ill. "You're no different from Bryan."

He met her gaze, and for the briefest moment she thought he was going to deny her accusation, was going to tell her how wrong she was. Instead, he shrugged. "I guess not."

Pain shot across Everleigh's chest. "Just another deadbeat dad who didn't even try." She got down from the barstool and squinted her eyes at him. "Work is not going to be easy with having to see you there. Make it a bit more tolerable by avoiding breathing the same air as me as much as possible, please."

With that, she gave him one last disillusioned and disgusted look then left.

Everleigh had been correct. Work wasn't easy. Not when Wryn looked the same and sounded the same, but nothing was the same. How could she miss him so much when he'd only been a part of her life for a few months and was so different from the man she'd thought he was?

And poor Hayes. It had only been a few weeks, but Hayes was not dealing well with Wryn's exit from their lives. His nightly prayers for Wryn were almost enough to have Everleigh lose it. Not that she didn't lose it in the privacy of her own room where no one could know or hear. Ugh, the number of tears she'd shed over a man she'd let deceive her...

She couldn't blame Wryn for hurting her and Hayes. For that she needed to look in the mirror. She'd let herself be duped because she'd wanted to believe he was different.

Part of her still didn't buy that he wasn't, but she acknowledged that that was the part of her that longed to believe.

Not that it mattered what she believed. Wryn hadn't reached out to her in any way. At work, he was a polite, indifferent coworker. Away from work, he was nonexistent outside of her and Hayes's heads.

Never ever again would she let a man steal her son's heart then crush it. Never.

"You okay?" Liz pulled Everleigh back to finishing up her morning's last patient chart so she could join the lunch meeting where they'd be having a guest endocrinologist speak about a new diabetes medication. She'd not been in a rush to get to the conference room because she'd wanted to make sure Wryn was seated where she'd be able to choose a seat away from him. She did not want to look at him or smell his spicy scent. Just feeling his presence in the building was enough to make her consider changing jobs. Working at the clinic was her dream, and she wouldn't allow him to take that from her the way he'd robbed her of her heart.

Realizing she still hadn't answered Liz, Everleigh nodded. "I'm fine. Just trying to get this last chart done."

"That's what I thought at first, but then you hadn't hit a key in several minutes so I wasn't sure." Liz gave her a pointed look.

"Sorry. I spaced out."

"You've been doing that a lot lately." Yeah, her nurse knew exactly what had happened. She and Eva might not have said a word, but they knew. Their empathetic looks said as much.

"Sorry. Lots going on at home." True enough, with poor Hayes's broken heart that rescuing a dog hadn't mended.

"Hope everything is okay."

They were interrupted by the receptionist. "Hey," she said to Everleigh. "I know it's your lunchtime, but I have a young lady who fell. She's bleeding in a couple of spots. You want me to send her to the emergency room?"

"No." Treating the woman would give the perfect excuse not to attend the meeting with Wryn. "I'll see her during my lunch."

Liz jumped up to call the woman back. Everleigh hit Save on the chart then went to the procedure room, disinfected her hands and began setting up a basic laceration tray. She'd let Liz add any needed items to it while Everleigh examined the patient, assessing the extent of the woman's injuries. Hopefully it wouldn't be anything too complicated.

Unfortunately, she had multiple lacerations and some bruising. She'd come in with a bloody dish towel pressed to her knee and tied there by a man's sock. She'd made a similar makeshift bandage for her arm.

"I'm Nurse Practitioner Everleigh Bennett. What happened?"

"I was rushing and fell down my front porch steps. I hit the steps and rolled to the sidewalk."

Ouch. "Did you hit your head?"

"I don't think so. Honestly, it happened so fast that I don't know what all I hit other than where I'm bleeding."

"Was anyone with you?"

The patient shook her head. "No. My boyfriend works day shift, and I work nights. I wish he had been there as he'd have been helping me carry the groceries."

Everleigh pulled the rag away from where it was secured against her arm. She didn't wince at the deeper of the cuts, but she easily could have. Double ouch.

The woman tugged her skirt up to midthigh, further revealing where she had rags bound around her knees. "Tying those there seemed the best way to try to stop the bleeding. One cut on the left knee looked deep."

Untying the sock, Everleigh lifted the towel. The wound was deep and actively bleeding. It would need internal stitches as well as external. The main one on her forearm seemed straightforward.

"The cut on your arm appears to just need cleaning and some sutures. The one on your knee needs internal sutures as there's a small arterial bleed that needs to be closed. Fortunately, everything else should be able to be Steri-Stripped and dressed. Any allergies?" The woman shook her head, and Everleigh turned to her nurse. "While I clean the wounds, will you draw me up an anesthetic?" She named her preferred one and how many milliliters she wanted.

"With or without epinephrine?" Liz asked.

"Let's do with." Everleigh rinsed the wounds with normal saline, making sure there were no foreign materials in either site. "There were tiny bits of gravel, but the wound appears clean now." She rinsed the forearm laceration and was just finishing when there was a knock on the procedure room door. "Come in."

Wryn stepped in, and Everleigh's heart squeezed. It had been three weeks since they'd gone their separate ways. Three weeks since she'd looked into those eyes and seen... what? Not what she'd thought she'd been seeing. That had just been foolishness.

"Eva sent me in here to help," he said by way of explanation. Was he making sure she knew that he wasn't there because he wanted to be? However, he wasn't looking at her but rather at their patient. "I'm Dr. Cooper. What happened?"

"I've got this, if you want to go to the lunch meeting," Everleigh assured him, but he shook his head.

"I don't mind helping or even letting you go to lunch."

Of course he didn't. For the briefest moment Everleigh considered taking him up on that and walking out of the room. However, she couldn't bring herself to just walk out on a patient.

"Well, if you want to help, her right knee and left forearm both need sutures. The knee also needs internal sutures as there's a small arterial bleed. The forearm is longer but not as deep, so I was planning to put simple sutures there."

"Why don't I take the knee and you do the forearm? That way we should both finish before our afternoon patients start back?"

Everleigh nodded because what he said made sense. Because she didn't want to get behind with her afternoon patients, and the reality was that, although she had sutured several times, she wasn't super fast.

Eva entered the room, exchanging looks with Liz. Had Liz said something to her when she'd gone to grab the new vial of anesthetic? Wryn's nurse quickly set up a tray for him to work from, while he washed his hands and gloved up.

Taking the syringe of anesthetic from Liz, Everleigh chatted with the woman, hoping to ease the woman's anxiety. Too bad there wasn't someone there to help Everleigh with hers.

"This should be the worst part of what I'm going to do," she reassured the woman. Everleigh injected the anesthetic within the open wound.

The woman flinched. "That burns."

"That should ease any second."

"You'd think it was already hurting enough that I wouldn't have even noticed the pain." She sighed. "I still can't believe I tripped. I was in a rush and just missed the step. I should have slowed down."

"Hindsight is twenty-twenty."

Everleigh glanced up, meeting Wryn's gaze. Had that comment been for her? Meaning what? That he'd have done things differently regarding her?

"Most of us have done things we wish we hadn't," Everleigh told her patient. "That if we'd just known the outcome, we'd have avoided the situation from the beginning."

"Sorry to do this, but it's my turn to numb you," Wryn warned as he finished disinfecting her knee.

The woman nodded then visibly braced herself.

Hoping to distract her, Everleigh called her attention to what she was doing. "I'm going to check the boundaries of your numbness. Without looking, I need you to tell me when I touch you."

Squeezing her eyes closed, she nodded.

Everleigh pressed the needle bevel against various areas around the wound. "Anything?"

"Only at my knee, and what Dr. Cooper is doing hurts."

He had a habit of hurting people. Heat flooded Everleigh's face as for a moment she thought she had muttered the words out loud. She needed to focus on what she was doing and not on the man sitting on the opposite side of the reclined examination chair.

"Did you drive yourself here?" she asked, taking the suturing needle between the tip of the needle driver.

"I did," their patient confessed. "My car is a wreck from where I was bleeding. I've called my boyfriend, and he's coming as soon as he can. He works on the opposite side of Nashville, so it's going to take him awhile to get here, though."

With Liz helping to approximate the wound edges, Everleigh pushed the needle through one side of the wound and out on the other, pleased with her spacing. She wrapped the Ethilon around the tip, tied a knot, wrapped from the opposite direction, tied a knot and repeated the process. When the knot was secure, she had Liz clip the thread. "One down."

Quite a few to go. As nerve-wrecking as it was to have Wryn in the room, she did appreciate that he was. As slow as she was at suturing, she would have been behind the rest of the day.

But if it weren't for making her patients wait, she'd have chosen that over having to be closed in the room with him, hearing him talk to all of them. Being so close to him drove home the emotional distance in ways that just being in the office hadn't. Everleigh bit the inside of her lower lip.

Just get finished. That's all she had to do. Just finish suturing the woman, let Liz dress the more superficial places and go breathe before starting back with her afternoon schedule. Breathe, because doing that with him so close was difficult.

Finally, she tied off the last suture, let Liz clip the thread and surveyed her work.

"Looks good," Wryn offered from where he was finishing the top layer of sutures.

His gaze met hers, but his hands kept working, wrapping the suture material around the needle driver's tip. Averting her gaze because she couldn't look into those eyes, she realized he was on his last suture and that maybe he was talking about his own work rather than praising hers as she'd originally thought.

"Liz, I'm going to let you dress the places on her arms, review her wound care at home and get her set up for a recheck in a few days and a suture removal in around ten days." She forced a smile at her patient and her nurse. "I'll be in my office if you need me."

Not her best patient encounter, but she'd forgive herself since she'd given up the majority of her lunch break to keep the woman from having to go to the emergency room.

Fortunately, the nurse practitioners she shared her office with were at still at the lunch meeting when Everleigh got there. She closed the door behind her, sat down at her desk and laid her forehead on her desk.

The clinic was her dream job. Working near Wryn would get better with time. If not, she'd get a new dream.

Wryn finished with their patient, gave Eva a few further instructions on helping Liz finish with her then left to grab something to eat. When he snuck into the meeting, he realized Everleigh hadn't come. Which meant she hadn't eaten.

He grabbed a boxed lunch, then loaded up three extras for him, Liz and Eva. He dropped off the nurses' food at their desks, earning smiles from both. He doubted he'd earn a smile with his next delivery, but he knocked on her closed office door anyway.

"Come in," she said without checking to see who was there.

Yep, no smile. Just a wince as he entered the room, closing the door back behind him.

"You should have left that open."

Probably. He wasn't even sure why he'd shut it other than that it had been shut prior to his entering.

"I brought lunch."

Eyes still as wide as a deer's in headlights, she sighed. "I'm not hungry."

"Then, I'll set it here in case you get hungry later."

"I— Thank you."

"You're welcome." He should go. She obviously wanted him to go. So why weren't his feet moving? "I'm sorry, Everleigh."

She squeezed her eyes shut for a few seconds then rubbed her temple. "Can we not do this? Because everything has been said that needs to be said, and we're at work, and beyond that I don't want to have this conversation."

Everything that needed to be said by her might have been said, but not everything by Wryn. There were a lot of things he'd like to tell her. Things about Kara, about Seth, about her and Hayes. But Everleigh didn't want to hear any of them.

He'd made so many mistakes. He'd lost her trust. He should have told her everything. But that she'd shut him out completely rather than being willing to try to work through things said that she'd have eventually shut him out, regardless.

She was probably right. Everything that needed to be said had been, and he just needed to let her go.

Let her go? Who was he kidding? She was already gone, and although she'd been the one to walk away, he'd been the one to push her out the door.

CHAPTER TWELVE

"Your next patient has the cutest little girl who kept chatting about what she was dressing up as for Halloween," Liz told Everleigh as she sat down at her workstation. "Has Hayes decided what he wants to be for Halloween yet?"

Everleigh shook her head. "Not yet. He's wavering between a dinosaur and his favorite superhero. We're costume-shopping this weekend. I've told him he's running out of time and must choose one way or the other or he'll be going as a costumeless little boy."

"Bless him." Liz smiled then indicated that the patient was ready. Once in the room, Everleigh agreed that the woman's daughter was adorable and talkative. The visit was a simple one as the patient was only there for medication refills on her gastroesophageal reflux disease medication. Everleigh did a quick medical history review, making sure the woman's health maintenance was up-to-date. When she'd finished, she gave the girl a couple of stickers, finished the chart and moved on to her next patient.

"Hello, Rita," she said to the woman she'd gotten to know well since seeing her the first week she'd worked at the clinic. Although still mildly jaundiced, Rita looked so much better than she had during that first office visit. "How are you feeling?"

The woman's smile answered before she even said anything. "I recently saw my liver specialist and am seeing my hematologist, and both say I'm doing great."

Everleigh nodded her approval. "How's the drinking?"

Liz shrugged. "I haven't completely quit, but I'm just having a drink or two when out with friends. That's it. Nothing like I was just a few months ago."

"I'm glad you're cutting back." With the woman's liver disease, she'd advised her not to drink at all. "Keep working on it, as alcohol is hard on your liver."

She glanced down at the Rita's most recent lab results. "Your ALT and AST levels are still elevated but are so much better."

They reviewed the rest of her labs and her specialist appointments. Everleigh examined her then answered her questions before advising the woman to return to the clinic in three months since she'd have had multiple follow-up appointments with her specialists in between.

They were just finishing when Liz poked her head into the room. "Hey, sorry to bother you, but Hayes's school is on the line, saying they've been trying to reach you."

Everleigh pulled her phone out of her pocket and glanced at the screen. She had multiple missed calls. "Ugh. I must have accidentally silenced my ringer." Turning to Rita, she apologized. "Sorry to rush out, but overall you're doing great. I'll see you in a few months."

She went to the nurses' station, took the phone receiver that Liz handed her and said hello when her nurse connected the call.

"This is Everleigh." She listened to the school staff member. "Mom never picked up Hayes?" A bad feeling crept up Everleigh's neck. Something bad would have to happen for her mother not to be there. She never would have no-showed

Hayes, knowing he'd be waiting to be picked up from school. "I'll be there in just a few minutes."

"Everything okay?" Liz asked as Everleigh hung up the phone then glanced at her missed messages.

"Mom didn't pick up Hayes." Scrolling through the missed messages, she clicked onto her mother's continuous glucose monitor app to check her reading. Sweat beaded on the back of her neck. She wasn't getting a reading. Nothing. Why didn't her mother have a sensor in place? Or was her sensor defective?

She dialed her mother's cell number and didn't get an answer. "Oh God," she mumbled. Please, please, please let Mom be okay, she prayed as she turned to go to her office to grab her purse.

"Everleigh?"

She'd been so caught up in trying to check her mom's glucose reading she hadn't seen Wryn come to the counter and almost collided into him. "Mom's sugar may be bottomed-out." She hit Redial, hoping her mom responded. Still nothing. "She's not answering, and I'm not getting a reading on the app." In her gut she knew something wasn't right. "I've got to go to the house to see if she's there. I'm going to call nine-one-one, but I'm not sure where to tell them to go." Had her mother taken off to get Hayes, bottomed-out and been in a car accident? She did so well with her continuous glucose monitor and the app notifications when her numbers started dropping so she could prevent the hypoglycemia. *Why wasn't she getting a reading?*

"Where is she?" he asked, walking with her as she headed down the hallway to grab her purse.

"Home, I think. Maybe. She was supposed to pick up Hayes from school but never showed." Panic hit. She needed to go to her mother, but no one had picked up Hayes. Her heart squeezed. "I've got to get Hayes from school. His teacher is waiting with him, but he'll be worried no one is there. It's way past time for him to have been picked up, but I have to find Mom. It's been years since she's had a bad low, but she had a few dangerous ones where she's ended up in the hospital."

"Go. I'll get Hayes."

Stunned, she cut her gaze to his. "You?"

"Unless you've taken me off the approved pickup person form you filled out at the beginning of the school year."

He'd been at the house as she'd filled out Hayes's school forms. He'd never actually picked up Hayes, but he was on the list.

"I haven't, but you—" She didn't have time to argue. She needed to find her mom. Time might be of the essence, depending upon what her mother's glucose level was. "Fine. Get him and meet me at our apartment. If I'm not there, he knows where the key is hidden. Just wait there with him until I call."

"I know where the key is hidden," he reminded her.

Yeah, she supposed he did.

"Wryn!"

"Hey, bud," Wryn greeted the boy he'd missed unbelievably over the past few weeks. "Your mom needed me to pick you up today." He smiled at Hayes's teacher. "Hello. We met the night of the fall festival. I'm Wryn Cooper. Everleigh asked me to pick up Hayes. I'm on the pickup list."

He wasn't going to go into the reasons why, not in front of Hayes. The teacher double-checked the list by calling the office then told Hayes that she'd see him on Monday morning.

"You have my car seat," Hayes pointed out when they got to Wryn's car.

"Yeah, your mom wanted to make sure I kept you safe." She might have been in a rush to get to her mom, but she'd been thinking clearly enough to insist he get Hayes's car seat.

"Are you my mom's boyfriend again?"

Wryn winced. "Your mom and I are friends, and we work together." Friends and coworkers. They were back where they had started.

"You don't come to our house anymore. I miss you."

"I miss you, too, Hayes." So much that he ached with it.

"Does Brady miss me?"

Hayes nodded. The dog really did.

"Why didn't my mom pick me up?"

"She needed to check on your grandmother."

"Is her sugar bad?"

"Your mom is worried that it might be."

"She gets really sick when her sugar is bad." Hayes continued to chat, jumping from one subject to the next. Wryn loved chatting with him, but his brain had gone ahead to where Everleigh was. Had she found her mother? Was she okay?

Relief hit when he pulled his car into her driveway, and he saw hers parked there. Now hopefully she'd found her mother and Vivien was fine.

But when they went into the house, he found Everleigh bent over her mother.

"Mama is Grammy's sugar bad?" Hayes asked, taking in the scene.

"Yes, but I gave her one of her sugar shots, so she should be feeling better soon." Her voice was calm as she spoke with Hayes, but Wryn heard the fear in her voice.

He knelt next to where she was on the floor and put his hand to Vivien's neck to get a pulse. Her skin was clammy.

"She didn't have her sensor on. I'm not sure why, just that she didn't have one on. I gave her shot to her then checked her sugar. It was fifty."

Fifty. Dangerously low.

"I've called for an ambulance."

"Good." His gaze met hers, and for a moment the world stood still. Not more than a second passed, but the connection he felt to her was stronger than a thousand lifetimes. "Everleigh," he said then stopped. Now was not the time. It might never be.

Everleigh ignored his saying her name and shook her mom. "Mom, can you hear me? Mom?"

"Is Grammy going to be okay?" Hayes stood next to them, eyeing his grandmother. Concern shone in his eyes.

"She is." Wryn hoped so.

"How about you put your backpack in your room, check on Razzle since he's barking like crazy and get a snack?"

Wryn was sure Everleigh made the suggestion to try to de-escalate the seriousness of what Hayes was seeing.

Hayes gave a considering look at his grandmother then went to put his backpack in his room.

"Do you have glucose tablets?"

"I have sugar." Everleigh pointed to the container on the countertop. "I gave her glucagon then put some sugar on her tongue right before you and Hayes walked in." Panic heightened her voice. "Why isn't she waking up?"

Good question, and one he didn't have the answer to. With the glucagon injection and the sugar, she should be coming around. Hopefully any minute she would regain consciousness.

"I'm checking her sugar again." Everleigh had the glucometer next to her from where she'd previously checked her mother's glucose reading. She took the lancet and jabbed the tip of her finger, then used the strip to collect a small blood sample. The machine counted down to the reading.

"Fifty-two."

Which wasn't much of a change for someone who had an injection and sugar on their tongue.

"She must have been plummeting when you gave her the shot for her to just be up a little. Give her more sugar."

Everleigh put small amounts of sugar into her mother's mouth, letting it dissolve, then added more. "She used to crash so hard, but it's been months. She's done so well for so long that I—" Hayes came back into the room, and Everleigh stopped whatever she was going to say to tell him, "Baby, get a snack from the snack drawer. Grammy's sugar is still too low, and we've got to get her levels up."

"I'm not hungry, but Razzle is." He went to the drawer and studied its contents, looking their way every few moments. Poor kid. Wryn wanted to hug him and tell him everything was going to be okay, but he was worried that Everleigh's mother hadn't come to.

"Mom." Everleigh shook her mother again. She glanced at her watch. "It's been about ten minutes since I gave her the injection. She should be coming around."

"Do you have another pen?" They might end up pushing her too high and likely would, but for the moment getting her out of the danger zone as quickly as possible was top priority.

"It's in the kit on the countertop. If she's not come around within fifteen minutes, I'm supposed to give another. She's never not come around, though, and not that you don't already know," Everleigh babbled as she checked her mom's pulse. "She's tachycardic."

"Not unusual during a low blood sugar."

Her mother's eyelids fluttered, giving a quick glimpse of her eyes.

"Oh, I think she's waking. Thank God."

But in that moment, her body convulsed, shaking all over.

"She's seizing. She's never seized. Oh God, what do I do?"

"Mama, is Grammy dying?"

"We keep her from hurting herself," Wryn told Everleigh. "Let's turn her onto her side." Then to Hayes, "Buddy, I need you to grab me a pillow off a bed, fast."

Hayes ran and brought back a pillow. Wryn put it under Everleigh's mother's head.

"Okay, bud, I have another job for you. I heard the ambulance a moment ago which means they're going to knock on the door any minute. With your dog's barking, we might not hear them. I need you to go listen and let them in so they can help your grandmother, okay? It's an important job, but I know you can do it."

Hayes glanced toward his still-seizing grandmother then met Wryn's gaze and nodded.

Wryn and Everleigh stayed on the floor with Vivien, making sure the pillow stayed beneath her head and that she didn't choke. They were still there when Hayes led the paramedics into the room.

Knowing Everleigh wasn't going to leave her mother's side, Wryn moved back, making way for the paramedics to do their thing. He immediately went to Hayes, lifted the boy into his arms.

"Great job, Hayes. You did perfect."

Hayes, who had been calm throughout the whole episode, wrapped his arms around Wryn's neck and began to cry.

Feeling helpless, Wryn hugged him tighter, kissed his head and made assurances that he hoped were true.

* * *

Exhausted, Everleigh drove to Wryn's. Not what she'd thought she would be doing on a Friday night ever again, but then, life was unpredictable.

And precious as she'd been reminded of earlier that day.

Thank God her mother was going to be okay. She'd been admitted to the ICU, had regained consciousness and was stable. Everleigh had stayed until ICU visiting hours ended. She'd not wanted to leave and might have asked to stay since she'd known one of the nurses from their days of working in the ER together, but she needed to get Hayes.

Bless him. He'd been so good, so brave and so upset after the paramedics had arrived. When she'd looked up and seen him in Wryn's arms, taking in Wryn comforting Hayes, something had cracked inside her. She was pretty sure it was the protective casing around her heart. Not good. Especially since Hayes was with him, but she'd needed to follow the ambulance to the hospital, and he'd offered to take Hayes and Razzle to his house to spend time with Brady. Having no doubt that playing with Brady would be therapeutic for the evening's trauma, she'd agreed, kissed Hayes bye and promised she'd be there to get him as quickly as she could.

Wryn opened his front door before she knocked and made a shushing gesture. "Hayes is out. I'm not sure if the doorbell would have awakened him or not, but whenever it rings Brady goes crazy, and that definitely would have awakened him. Both dogs are in bed with Hayes."

Feeling awkward walking into his house when the last time she'd been there she'd told him not to breathe the same air as her, she followed him into his living area.

"Can I get you something to drink? Or something to eat? Did you get dinner?"

Everleigh shook her head. She'd not even thought of food. "I'll grab something when I get home."

"There's leftovers from the dinner Hayes and I made," he offered.

"You and Hayes cooked?" As exhausted as she felt, she was intrigued.

He nodded. "I asked him what he wanted, and then we made it."

"You made macaroni and cheese?"

He grinned. "Okay, so maybe I used the power of suggestion, and he went along with it." He walked to the refrigerator and pulled out a dish. "Just as I'm going to use the power of suggestion and say you need to eat something."

Everleigh's stomach growled. What would it hurt to stay long enough to eat? She'd eat and then get Hayes so they could go home.

"This is delicious," she admitted a few minutes later after taking a bite. "What spices did you use?"

"You'd have to ask Hayes that question because he was in charge of adding spices to the chicken, and he came up with his own mixture."

She paused, her fork midway to her mouth. "Thank you, Wryn. I hated to leave him, but they wouldn't have let him in the ICU room with Mom, and I wouldn't have left him in the waiting area which would have meant me sitting in the waiting area rather than being back with Mom and—"

"You're welcome," he said, cutting off her rambling. "I'm glad I could help."

She took the bite then said, "You did more than that. I know you turned a bad day into a good one for him. I bet he was excited to see Brady."

"Not nearly as excited as Brady was to see him. He about licked Hayes to death. Razzle wasn't so sure about Brady doing so, but Hayes and I took them out back to throw ball with them, and they soon made friends."

Everleigh smiled. "I don't know how I can repay you."

His brows knit together. "Like I said, I'm glad I could help. Hayes is a great kid."

"The best."

"Speaking of great kids, I've spent time with Seth."

Looking up from her almost empty plate and wondering if she'd inhaled her food, she exclaimed, "What?"

"I met with Kara and Henry, told them I didn't want to interfere with their family and wasn't out to try to take Seth from them but that, if he was interested, I wanted to meet him and get to know him and for him to know me."

"They agreed?"

He nodded. "They were hesitant to begin with, but they've no reason to be. They've done an amazing job raising him. He's happy and has a good home life. I'd never try to disrupt that. He's old enough that I explained why I made the choices I did, not claiming that they were necessarily the right choices, but they were the ones I made and I've had to live with them. It was awkward at first, but it's already getting better."

"Oh, Wryn. That's wonderful."

He nodded. "It is much more than I ever expected."

Everleigh took the last bite and walked to the sink to rinse her plate. She placed it in his dishwasher then put her hands into her pockets. "It's been a long day. I should get Hayes and Razzle so we can go."

"I— Okay. He's in my room."

She followed Wryn there. He had the lights dimmed but not off in case Hayes woke. Lying in Wryn's big king bed was a tiny sleeping boy with two dogs spread out beside him. Brady had one paw lying protectively at Hayes's waist.

At their entrance, Brady lifted his head, looked at them then laid his head back down against Hayes. Razzle had opened his eyes but didn't budge otherwise.

"They look so peaceful that I hate to bother them," she mused.

"Then, don't. Let him sleep."

"I'm exhausted, Wryn, and ready to crash, myself."

"He can stay here."

She shook her head. "I'm not leaving him here all night."

"I meant for you to stay, too, Everleigh. You can take my room with him, and I'll sleep in the guest room."

Sleep in Wryn's bed? Nope. Not happening. "I don't think so."

"Why not? It makes sense for you to stay. In the morning you're going to want to go straight to the hospital to check on your mom. I don't have anything going on that I can't do with Hayes."

Was it just that she was so tired that made what he was saying sound sensible?

She was exhausted. Not that she was sure she could sleep at his place, but…she glanced at how peaceful Hayes looked. She hated to wake him.

"I don't have any clothes to change into. I'd have to go home anyway."

"You can borrow a T-shirt and some drawstring joggers to sleep in and swing by your place tomorrow to grab clean clothes when you're fresh. It's not worth risking driving when you're so tired. If not for your sake, then Hayes's."

He was right. She knew he was right. Still, she hesitated because how could she spend the night at Wryn's home? Sleep in his bed? But she truly was exhausted and not fit to drive herself and Hayes home. "I… Okay. We'll stay."

"I'll grab some things for you to choose from for sleep."

He quietly got a T-shirt and sweatpants from his closet. "Help yourself to anything you need in the bathroom. Mrs. Callahan was just here yesterday, so I haven't demolished it too badly yet."

It was immaculate as she suspected it usually was, as Wryn was a neat person by nature. Everleigh showered then put on the cotton pants, pulling the drawstring tightly at her waist. She pulled on the shirt but felt exposed so opened his closet to grab something thicker. The closet was as big as her bedroom and neatly arranged. Spotting a sweatshirt, she swapped out the T-shirt for its thicker material.

She started to crawl into the bed with Hayes and Brady but realized she'd left her purse and phone in the living area on the bar. She definitely wanted her phone close in case the hospital called.

Tiptoeing in case Wryn had gone to bed, she made her way to the living area and was not entirely surprised to see him sitting on the sofa with a sports game on the large screen.

"Feel better?"

She nodded. "I hope it's okay that I swapped the T-shirt for this."

"I told you to help yourself to anything you needed."

Fine. She needed him. No, she did not need him. Only, standing there in his living area, wearing his clothes, him having taken care of Hayes, having taken care of her and her being exhausted, she admitted she did need him.

Acknowledging that she'd lost her mind, Everleigh forgot about her purse and phone and walked over to the sofa and curled up next to him. Swallowing to tamp down her nerves, she lifted his arm and wrapped it around her shoulders.

"Everleigh?"

"You said I could help myself to anything I needed."

He stared at her. "You need me to hold you?"

"I do."

"Then, I can do better than this." He pulled her closer, cradling her into his lap, and wrapped his arms around her.

"You're right." She nuzzled her face against his chest, breathed in the scent of him. "This is better."

He held her. For how long Everleigh wasn't sure. What she knew was how good it felt to be held, to just lean against him and for the moment feel it was okay to not carry her load by herself, to let him shield her from the world in the comfort of his arms. And that's what he did, not pushing to make their embrace sexual, although she was certainly aware of his body next to hers, but rather his touch was gentle, comforting, foreign because she'd never had this. Not with anyone except Wryn.

With that thought a tear ran down her cheek then another.

"Everleigh?"

But she didn't want to talk, to have to put words to what she was feeling, so she turned her face into his chest.

"Everleigh, are you okay?"

"Just hold me, Wryn. Let me cry, hold me and don't let me go."

Not ever.

Wryn's arm had fallen asleep a good hour ago, but he didn't care. Repositioning himself might wake Everleigh, and he wouldn't risk that when she was sleeping so peacefully. Not yet. When she'd first fallen asleep, she'd made a whimpering sound a few times, one that was filled with pain, and he'd done as she'd requested, holding her and not letting her go.

Which was what he was still doing. What he wanted to continue doing.

He must have dozed off, because when he had his next

conscious thought, he was still holding Everleigh but they'd lain down on the sofa, their bodies spooning.

It took him a moment to register why they were there, the events of the evening tumbling back.

Everleigh. He breathed in her scent, picking up traces of his shampoo mingled with her unique scent. He liked that. Her smelling of his things, wearing his clothes, asleep in his arms. *Oh, Everleigh.*

Her breathing changed, and he realized he'd said her name. Wondering if she'd scoot away and go to his room where Hayes was, he was surprised when she laced her hand with his and gave it a light squeeze.

"Thank you, Wryn."

But he didn't want her gratitude. Not when he was the one who owed her so much.

"I am the one who should be thanking you."

She twisted, turning to face him, the glow from the television giving off enough light that he could see her face. "What have I done worthy of you needing to thank me?"

"Brought me to life."

Her face twitched. "What do you mean?"

Thinking she might have thought he meant sexually, he rushed to explain. "I didn't know I was dead inside, Everleigh, but I was. Then I met you. And Hayes. And I felt alive in ways I didn't know I could." He swallowed. "I've been miserable this past month without you. I know I messed up, that I should have told you. I just didn't know how without disappointing you, and that's something I never want to do."

She searched his eyes for what felt like an eternity then placed her hand on his cheek. "I've missed you, too. So much I ache with it."

"Everleigh."

"I felt so betrayed that you hadn't told me about Seth."

"I'm sorry."

"Let me finish," she told him, placing her fingers over his lips. "The truth of the matter is, deep down, there was a part of me that expected you to hurt me, Wryn. That part of me latched on to you not telling me about Seth, and I just completely shut you out because you scare me."

"I don't want you scared of me."

"Love is scary, though, isn't it?"

"Love?"

Her fingers trembled against his cheek. "I love you, Wryn. Whether I'm supposed to or not, I do. Seeing you holding Hayes at the house while he cried, it hit me how much he and I love you."

"I love you, too, Everleigh."

"Does that scare you?"

"Terrifies me, but as odd as this sounds, it also gives me the greatest sense of peace I've ever known."

She smiled. "Ah, so you're feeling the same thing I'm feeling."

"God, I hope so, because I need you to love me, even if it's just a smidge of what I'm feeling, then that's enough."

Rather than say anything, she pressed her lips to his and kissed him. The sweetest kiss that was full of reassurances of what she was feeling, filling him with elation and a growing desire to deepen the kiss.

They kissed until Wryn was completely breathless because every breath he took was Everleigh's and vice versa. Thankfully he had just enough awareness of their surroundings to catch the sound of Brady's paws coming down the hallway.

"Hayes is awake," he whispered just before Brady, Razzle and the boy came into the room.

He'd thought Everleigh would pull away from him, but instead she just turned toward her son's approach.

"I woke up," he said, rubbing his eyes and looking uncertain.

"Come here, baby," she told him, sitting up and giving him a hug. "Grammy sends her love. She was doing great when I left the hospital. They're keeping her overnight to keep a good check on her."

"I'm glad Grammy is okay." Hayes eyes shifted from Everleigh to Wryn and back again. "Is Wryn our boyfriend again?"

"Would you like that?"

He nodded.

"What about you?" Her gaze shifted to Wryn's. "Would you like it if you were our boyfriend again?"

He'd like it if he was a lot more than just their boyfriend, but one step at a time. They had the rest of their lives to forge their happily-ever-after and would.

Because looking into Everleigh's eyes, he saw forever and knew that was what was shining back at her from his.

Forever. That had a nice ring to it.

"Wryn?" Everleigh prompted when he'd not answered.

"I don't think Brady would forgive me if I said no."

"He wouldn't," Hayes agreed, climbing up beside them on the sofa. "Neither would Razzle. He and Brady are friends now."

"I wouldn't forgive myself, either, Hayes, because I love you and your mom. Being with you makes me happy."

Hayes smiled. "You make me and Mama happy, too."

"Good because I plan to spend the rest of my life continuing to do just that."

And he did.

EPILOGUE

Liz held up her cell phone for a selfie with Everleigh. "You look absolutely stunning. The most beautiful bride ever."

"Here, I want one, too." Eva moved closer, and Liz snapped another photo then, being careful not to muss Everleigh's dress, they hugged her.

"Thank y'all for everything." Trying not to get overly emotional but knowing she was fighting a losing battle, Everleigh hugged them back. "My bridal shower and all the help at work while I've been so distracted with wedding things."

"Girl, you've been great. We'd barely have known you were getting married if not for the gigantic smile on your face and that gorgeous ring on your finger."

Everleigh glanced down at the beautiful classical diamond solitaire on her finger with a smaller-stoned band. "Wryn did good, didn't he?"

"With the ring and the woman," Eva asserted. "We're so happy for you both and the happiness you've found together."

Everleigh's eyes watered, and noticing, her mother shooed the two bridesmaids back.

"Okay, you two stop making my beautiful daughter cry. You'll ruin her makeup."

"Thank you, Mama." Everleigh kissed her mother's cheek,

then posed with her for a photo when the wedding photographer told them to smile. "I hope Hayes is being good."

"He's being the angel he always is." Her mother beamed then chuckled. "It's those dogs that have me concerned."

"Oh no. Are Brady and Razzle misbehaving?"

"Let's just say I'm questioning your decision to have them as your ring bearer and flower dog."

"If they act up, it'll be okay. Aren't the things that don't go quite perfectly always the best wedding memories?"

"I'd say the best memory about today is going to be Wryn officially becoming my son-in-law and Hayes's father." Vivien's smile was proud.

"He's already Hayes's father in every way that counts."

"It's wonderful that the adoption went through yesterday morning."

They'd sat in the courtroom the previous morning and cheered when the judge signed the paperwork. Once upon a time Everleigh couldn't imagine giving another person legal rights to her son; now she couldn't imagine not. Wryn was going to be the best daddy.

He already was. To Hayes and to Seth.

The teen had been a frequent visitor over the past year. Not surprisingly, once they'd got past a short-lived awkwardness, they'd become two peas in a pod. Make that three peas in a pod, because Hayes was usually right there with them.

Who would have thought Everleigh would become such good friends with Kara when her appearance in Everleigh's life had wreaked such havoc? She and Henry were honored guests and had been seated near the front of the church.

"Ladies, it's time," the photographer told them.

Everleigh hugged her mom. The next few minutes passed in a blur, and then with her mother at her side, Everleigh moved to where she could see Wryn waiting at the front of the church. His immediate smile and hand to his heart had her eyes threatening to leak again.

"He loves you so much," her mother whispered.

Too choked up to talk, Everleigh nodded and tried to be careful not to trip walking toward Wryn. Seth and Hayes stood at his side. Both dogs had been sitting at the boys' feet, but when the guests stood, they had, too. Razzle gave a single loud woof when Everleigh neared, but otherwise, they were picture-perfect.

Everleigh only had eyes for Wryn but was aware of her handsome six-year-old moving to beside his grammy when the preacher asked who was giving away the bride.

"We are," they said in unison. Hayes grinned then moved back to his spot as a groomsman.

"Be this happy always," her mother whispered then was seated.

"You're beautiful," Wryn told her as he took her hands into his, lifting them to press kisses to her fingertips. His hands shook, but everything else about his demeanor was pure confidence.

"So are you," she found the voice to say. "I love you, Wryn."

"I love you, too." He said the words aloud, and they wrapped around Everleigh, enveloping her in their sincerity and their power.

They exchanged the vows they'd written to each other, did a ribbon knot-tying where Seth and Hayes participated and were pronounced husband and wife.

Wryn kissed her, thoroughly and completely claiming her as his. As they made their way down the aisle hand in hand, he stopped, dipped her back and kissed her again.

"Wryn," she said, laughing as he straightened her then

lifted her off her feet. "I don't think this is how this is supposed to be done."

He grinned. "Just wanted to set the tone from the very beginning, Everleigh, that I'm going to be here to lighten your load, to carry you through the rough times and celebrate the good. You are my life. You, Hayes and Seth."

Oblivious to the fact that they were halfway down the aisle to exiting the church, Everleigh placed her hands on his cheeks, stared into his eyes and let his love flow through her.

"Good, because you're mine now, and I'm keeping you forever."

"*Forever* sounds perfect, Mrs. Cooper."

And it was.

* * * * *

If you enjoyed this story, check out these other great reads from Janice Lynn

Flirting with the Florida Heart Doctor
Breaking the Nurse's No-Dating Rule
Heart Doctor's Summer Reunion
The Single Mom He Can't Resist

All available now!

MILLS & BOON®

Coming next month

RISKING HIS HEART FOR THE ER DOC
Traci Douglass

'Remember, team. Secure knots mean the difference between a successful rescue and... Well, let's just say we all prefer happy endings here,' he said, earning chuckles from the group. 'All right. Everyone ready to start?'

Andy avoided Jules's gaze as he moved among the team, double-checking their equipment himself to ensure they were all fastened properly. 'Good. Let's start the simulation.'

'Excuse me, Dr MacDonald?' Jules asked from behind him, and Andy closed his eyes, taking a deep breath for fortitude. 'Could you double-check my alpine butterfly loop again, please? It's been a while since I've done one and I want to make sure I have it correct.'

Andy took another breath then stepped back in front of her, his gaze fixed on the knot as his fingers brushed hers and that odd spark that always seemed to happen whenever she was close flared to life inside him again. He snuffed it out fast. He'd put all that behind him a long time ago. He didn't want to bring it into the present now. Especially since she was on the team and also starting in the ER at Teton Memorial, which meant they'd be seeing more of each other there, too. And he knew personally what a bad idea it was to get involved with a colleague in any way beyond strictly professional.

Continue reading

RISKING HIS HEART FOR THE ER DOC
Traci Douglass

Available next month
millsandboon.co.uk

Copyright © 2025 Traci Douglass

COMING SOON!

We really hope you enjoyed reading this book. If you're looking for more romance be sure to head to the shops when new books are available on

Thursday 25th September

To see which titles are coming soon, please visit
millsandboon.co.uk/nextmonth

MILLS & BOON

MILLS & BOON TRUE LOVE IS HAVING A MAKEOVER!

Introducing

Love Always

Marrying a Royal
Nina Milne
Suzanne Merchant

Summer with the Billionaire
Rachael Stewart
Justine Lewis

Swoon-worthy romances, where love takes center stage. Same heartwarming stories, stylish new look!

Look out for our brand new look
COMING SEPTEMBER 2025
MILLS & BOON

FOUR BRAND NEW BOOKS FROM
MILLS & BOON MODERN

Indulge in desire, drama, and breathtaking romance – where passion knows no bounds!

BILLION-DOLLAR TEMPTATIONS
Melanie Milburne & Kali Anthony

GREEK Scandals
Abby Green & Caitlin Crews

SEXY RICH BOSSES
Maya Blake & Tara Pammi

One Night, Nine Months
Heidi Rice & Emmy Grayson

OUT NOW

Eight Modern stories published every month, find them all at:
millsandboon.co.uk

afterglow BOOKS

Afterglow Books is a trend-led, trope-filled list of books with diverse, authentic and relatable characters, a wide array of voices and representations, plus real world trials and tribulations. Featuring all the tropes you could possibly want (think small-town settings, fake relationships, grumpy vs sunshine, enemies to lovers) and all with a generous dose of spice in every story.

@millsandboonuk
@millsandboonuk
afterglowbooks.co.uk

#AfterglowBooks

For all the latest book news, exclusive content and giveaways scan the QR code below to sign up to the Afterglow newsletter:

SCAN ME

afterglow BOOKS

Let's Give 'Em PUMPKIN to Talk About
ISABELLE POPP

The Secret Crush Book Club
KARMEN LEE

- Grumpy/sunshine
- Small-town romance
- Spicy

- LGBTQ+
- Small-town romance
- Spicy

OUT NOW

Two stories published every month. Discover more at:
Afterglowbooks.co.uk

OUT NOW!

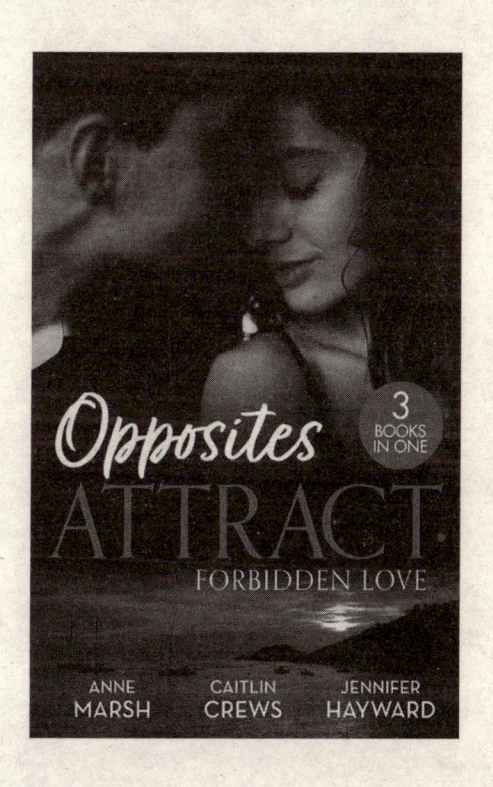

Opposites Attract: Forbidden Love

3 BOOKS IN ONE

ANNE MARSH · CAITLIN CREWS · JENNIFER HAYWARD

Available at
millsandboon.co.uk

MILLS & BOON

OUT NOW!

SECOND Chance
— A COWBOY'S RETURN —

3 BOOKS IN ONE

MAISEY YATES CHARLENE SANDS KAT CANTRELL

Available at
millsandboon.co.uk

MILLS & BOON

OUT NOW!

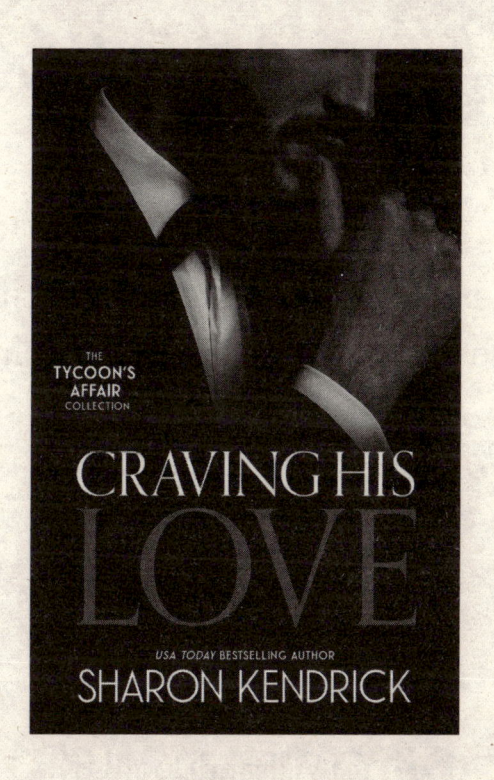

THE TYCOON'S AFFAIR COLLECTION

CRAVING HIS LOVE

USA TODAY BESTSELLING AUTHOR
SHARON KENDRICK

Available at
millsandboon.co.uk

MILLS & BOON

LET'S TALK
Romance

For exclusive extracts, competitions and special offers, find us online:

- **f** MillsandBoon
- **X** @MillsandBoon
- **◉** @MillsandBoonUK
- **♪** @MillsandBoonUK

Get in touch on 01413 063 232

For all the latest titles coming soon, visit
millsandboon.co.uk/nextmonth